INSURRECTION

Book One in the Legends of Ralladin

Gunner Long

<u>*Note from the author:*</u>

You are currently holding a book written by a thirteen-year-old boy who sacrificed so much of his time and energy to write a book. This book took him many sleepless nights to write. It demanded his attention constantly. It gave him a ride of emotions, from the thrill of creating the world, to the pain of rewriting and editing, to the feeling of relief upon finishing.

He hopes you enjoy reading it as much as he did writing it.

Dedicated to my family, who encouraged me the entire way through the writing process. I probably wouldn't have finished if it weren't for your support. Thank you.

IT IS THE YEAR 315. The continent of Ralladin, originally unified as the Empire of Ralladin, has long since divided into three kingdoms, and the tempest of war consumes the land.

To the east, viciously fighting to control Ralladin, lies the dark kingdom of Elara. Since their secession from the United Empire, they have been at war with the other kingdoms for over two hundred years. In that time, it has conquered many lands, and as time wears on, more cities and regions continue to fall into the kingdom of shadow's dominion.

Controlling the west of Faldon is the kingdom of Kallary. Although considered a unified kingdom, it is divided into dozens of alliances and territories, all at war with each other. Since their separation, they have made little progress in conquering the lands, and infighting tears the entire country, with no central ruler or monarch to control the kingdom.

And in the center of Ralladin, the kingdom that never separated from the Empire of Ralladin, is the domain of Faldon. Since the division of the empire, they have fought tirelessly to preserve the remnant of the broken world and fight back against the dark forces of Elara. Although they have long been considered the strongest kingdom in Ralladin, their constant fighting has weakened them, and their enemies are gaining considerable ground as they falter and lose.

These three kingdoms dominate the continent of Ralladin, each one at war with the other. Only time will tell which kingdoms will rise and conquer, and which will be destroyed.

PROLOGUE

*E*LARA, *FAR TO THE east.*

The land was vast and empty, void of any signs of life or vegetation. Vast, that you could look for miles in any direction, and empty, that in those miles you would see almost nothing. Rocks were the only things worth telling of, scattered across the ground in sizes ranging from pebbles to boulders. The ground was hard, made up of gray sediment that was almost like clay.

Overhead, the sky was a bleak gray. Even though it was in the afternoon, the sun failed to show even a glimpse of itself through the oppressive clouds. The air, thick and heavy, hung over the region without a breeze, mixed with the suffocating smoke that infested the air. The smoke made the air hazy and unclear.

Nothing lived here.

Far in the distance, forming what looked like a spiked wall, stood a tall line of black, foreboding mountains. They stretched as far as the eye could see and rose sharply out of the coarse earth. The mountains stood like sentries, silently watching the empty land below. Coming sharply to a point at the top, their black peaks stood out sharply against the gray sky above. From there, a sweeping view of the area could be seen. Not that there was anything worth seeing.

On one peak stood two knights. They wore heavy armor that was black and plated. Both were at least seven feet tall, they made no movement, standing as tall and silent as the mountain they were on, silently looking down on the empty plain as if there was something worth looking at. Large barbute helms covered their heads. Two metal spikes ran down from the sides and met in the helmet's front, twisting together as they came down the black helmet. The T-shaped hole in the fronts would have allowed anyone to see the wearer's face, but no face was visible through the slits. Only darkness.

"Do you know of your mission?" The larger one spoke, his voice deep and guttural.

The other knight grunted. "Of course not. That is why you called me here, is it not?"

"Indeed. The kingdom shall not conquer itself!" The tall warrior swept his gauntleted hand over the land below.

The smaller but still huge warrior looked over the land. Bleak and empty. Since the Great Darkness, the land surrounding the Mountain of Power became barren and lifeless. The power that came from the mountain had shrived the vegetation and killed most of the animals in Elara. Only some species survived. These creatures became savage and corrupt, killing anything in their path without hesitation.

It wasn't always like this. The land around the Mountain of Power used to be the most fertile and green land in Ralladin. Fruit trees grew wild in large clusters, colorful birds flew around their boughs, blue rivers gently flowed through the forests and plains... it was paradise. The weather was always perfect, and nothing ever seemed to go wrong.

Until the massive doors at the foot of the great Mountain of Power were opened.

Almost instantly, the dark power that came from it killed every living thing. The plants withered and disintegrated. The animals dropped dead where they stood, and the rivers turned black and reeked with foul odors. Everything in the wake of the scourge was immediately corrupted.

The same happened to the people as well. Fortunately for them, the power radiating out of the mountain diminished as the distance increased, and most of the towns and cities were far enough away that many people survived the power. They instead were driven mad or lost their minds, either turning savage and brutal or mindless and depressed. Slaves to the darkness, without free will.

"How nice that would be." The taller knight continued. "But I did not summon you here to talk about such trivial matters, Gornar. I summoned you to inform you of your next mission."

He turned his broad build towards Gornar, preparing to brief him of his mission. Gornar made no move, still looking out at the land below as if nothing he said was important. It was part of a mental game, clearly saying that, though the larger knight was superior in rank, Gornar did not recognize him as such.

Irritated but ignoring this, the towering knight began. "I have no doubt that you know of the... insurrection, we have planned?"

Gornar grunted indifferently, "Of course I have, Thrall." He ignored the warrior's title. He had exceptionally low tolerance for people that were over him, even though he regarded Thrall as under him. He added sarcastically, "Are we here to have tea and chat? Pity, then, it seems I forgot to the bring the cakes."

Infuriated at Gornar's disregard for his superior, Thrall put a warning hand on his sword hilt, located in a back scabbard. His voice was like smooth ice. "Do not test me. There is a reason that I am above you, a good reason. If you have a death wish, then I could swiftly make it a reality." He took a step towards the black knight, who was still ignoring him. "Well?"

Gornar grunted. "Get on with it."

Thrall hesitated. Were he in charge, Gornar would be dead, added to the list of other knights under his command who fell into his "unneeded" category. He was warned, though, that if he continued this habit, he would meet the same fate. Although he cared little about what his captains thought, he knew they meant what they said.

Putting his pride aside, he removed the hand from the sword and crossed his arms. "It seems there was a rat in the wall."

Gornar offered no reaction. "That boy who knows of our plans? Of course I know." He wanted to include, *do you take me for a fool?* But he knew better than to push the massive captain too far.

Thrall nodded. "Well, it seems that instead of cowering like a good boy, he decided to do something about it. He is within three weeks' travel from Loronis and is intent on alerting those ignorant fools about our plans."

"And this is a concern to us?"

"It will become your concern if he succeeds!" Thrall yelled, angry at Gornar's lack of interest. More than ever, he wished to knock

Gornar's smug head clean off his shoulders, but he managed to control himself. "Our plan will take effect in three weeks. There's a chance, however unlikely, that he will arrive in time to tell them what we will do." He paused to let what he said sink in.

Gornar finally turned to face Thrall, who was glaring spitefully at him. He paid no mind. "I see." He replied apathetically. He was enjoying how much anger he was causing his commander. "So, you wish for me to remove this boy myself?"

The superior knight nodded. "Indeed, go to the Idonia mountains and wait for the boy to come to you. Depart at once. And do not fail."

Gornar turned and glared at Thrall. "Don't you think that such a demeaning task is under me?" There was anger evident in his voice.

Thrall, seeing an opportunity to get back at his inferior, replied smugly. "Oh yes. Which is why I thought this mission was perfect for you."

Gornar whipped around and placed his hand on one of the two sword scabbards on his back. Seething rage emitted from his movements. The empty eye slits seemed to spew fury at his captain.

Thrall merely returned the scowl with crossed arms. He knew there was nothing Gornar could do. If the warrior were to draw his sword on his commander, it would be a crime punishable by death. Thrall knew this, and he knew Gornar knew it as well. If the warrior valued his life, then he wouldn't dare draw his sword.

Gornar knew that he had lost. In a fuming tone, he said, "I would like nothing more than to kill you right now!"

Thrall calmly retorted, "And that would earn you death, Gornar. You know that." Not waiting for a response, he continued with forced patience. "If you value your life, then you will go to the Idonia mountains and wait there for the boy to come to you. And when he does, you will get rid of him, then and there. You understand what's at stake." Then he added darkly, "And don't fail."

Gornar grunted and removed his hand from the hilt. He knew he had no choice but to obey the commander's orders. "What makes you think I will?" Gornar commented with disdain.

Before Thrall could respond, Gornar took a few steps forward, towards the edge of the mountain ledge they were standing on. He looked out over the plain for a few seconds, then bowed his head downward and clenched his fists.

It started at his feet. Black wisps came slowly from the ground around Gornar's feet, circling around him as it traveled up his greaves and body. He made no movement, silently waiting for the process to end. The wisps seemed like black snakes, creeping around the dark knight in long, thick threads. It rose slowly, creating a ring around Gornar. The wisps grew thicker and thicker, until before long, the warrior was no longer visible as the last of his helmet was surrounded by the pitch-black darkness that churned around him.

Then it began to rise. It became less thick, disentangling itself as it reached upward, spreading out and becoming fainter. It became like smoke, rising steadily higher. Gornar was gone; he dissipated into the black wisps that swirled around him. The now hazy darkness finally vaporized into the air, blowing away toward the west.

Left alone on the pinnacle of the great black mountain peak, one of the many that made up the mountain range, Thrall stood in silence, watching the west, looking over the desolate landscape.

Then he uncrossed his arms and, as if Gornar were still there, he spoke before turning away.

"If you fail and return, then you will die with the boy."

I

TIME WAS RUNNING OUT.

Despite the furious storm that thrashed him in wind and rain, Trenson attempted to quicken his pace. Keeping his head down, he let the cowl of his cloak drape over most of his face, staring down at the muddy ground to keep the water out of his eyes. He breathed in the cold, damp air. The endlessly falling water drenched his clothes, sapping his warmth and energy.

He had been walking like this for weeks now. His legs had long since going numb from fatigue and cold. It felt like he was walking while asleep, the constant rain and cold putting him into a dazed state of mind.

Trenson continued to trudge forward, trying to keep his balance against the onslaught of wind. He looked up from under the hood to see what was ahead.

It had been a few minutes since he entered the small town. With a brilliant boom, a streak of lightning flashed across the sky, illuminating the small houses on the sides of the street. Small and huddled together, they crouched along the roadside, occasionally broken by an alleyway or street. The wind whistled as it beat on the houses, causing windowpanes to shudder. Water poured from the slanted roofs, creating a small gulley along the ground, while more flew off edges in large sheets.

With each step, Trenson's worn boots sunk deep into the mud, squishing as water seeped through the threadbare leather. His pack hung on to his shoulder. It had been waterlogged for so long that he wondered to wonder how heavy it was when it *wasn't* soaked in water. The quarterstaff strapped to his back reminded him that he was armed, although he doubted that he would run into any trouble in the rural town.

To keep his mind off his dismal condition, Trenson looked up at the sky to guess what time of day it was. The sky was almost black in color, so it was impossible to tell. He could only determine whether it was day—dark—or night—pitch black dark. It was only dark now, but it was slightly darker than it had been earlier, and judging from how long it seemed since he woke up, Trenson guessed it was evening.

Evening. A thought occurred to him: why not seek out an inn to spend the night? He could have food and water, warmth, shelter, a good night's rest...

Then another part of him quickly disagreed. He still had to get to Loronis, and soon. Time was short. If he were to fail, then the kingdom could be lost. He didn't have time to waste, especially in some tavern. The fate of the kingdom comes first.

Sighing, Trenson was about to agree when suddenly his foot caught on a large rock partly submerged in the road. Stumbling forward, he tried to regain his balance, but his weary knees gave way. He splatted into the wet mud. He attempted to stop himself by putting his hands down on the ground, but they slipped on the waterlogged road and his entire body laid flat in the wet, uncomfortable mud. Cold mud immediately coated his face. Cold water seeped through his clothes. And the stiff wind blew around him.

In short, he was now even more miserable than before.

And that's when it snapped. *That's it! I'm finding a tavern to spend the night. Drat the kingdom! What good is it if I'm not alive?* Trenson had felt hypothermia overcoming him in the past few hours, and now he felt it stronger than ever, his eyes bloodshot, eyes heavy and his senses shutting down, his body crying out for sleep.

Painfully, he rose to his feet, steeling himself to press on. Muscles screaming in fatigue and mud covering his face and clothes, he began searching for a tavern to spend the night. He glanced around at the buildings along the road, searching for the hanging sign that heralded inns and taverns alike. It was hard to see anything through the increasing darkness and wind and rain. He hoped he wouldn't miss it, or that he had already passed it. The thought made him even more miserable.

KRACK KOOM!! Another whip of lightning cracked through the sky, shining brilliantly before instantly disappearing. It rumbled across the ground, making the houses creak and moan. Rain and wind continued to pound Trenson mercilessly. He glanced up often to look for the familiar sign, but frequently pulled his head down. He was walking into the rain, only allowing him to look up for a few seconds before the elements forced his head down again.

After some time without seeing any tavern, Trenson began to worry that he had passed it. The idea lowered his spirits even more.

He wasn't about to turn around and lose ground just for a good night's sleep. He would just have to sleep in the rain, again.

It's not so bad. It could be worse.

A tremendous gust of wind suddenly slammed into Trenson's face, throwing his cowl backwards and hurling water into his eyes. He fumbled with the hood and draped it once again over his face, not before his hair and face were even more soaked.

Not by much.

Then he heard a creaking noise. Unlike the windowpanes of the houses, this one was continual, like... the swinging of a tavern sign.

Hopes instantly raised, Trenson strode to the sound's source. As he got closer, he could make out a large, two-story building with a hanging sign, creaking loudly as it swung back and forth in the wind. *Looks like I'll get a good night's sleep after all.* Orange light streamed out of the windows of the tavern, occasionally flashing from those inside walking in front of the candles. Laughter and music came from inside. Trenson walked up to the door and paused, looking up at the sign swinging wildly in the wind. "The Warm Hearth," it read.

Perfect.

***

"Here you are, sir." the serving girl cheerfully set the bowl of steaming hot soup in front of Trenson.

He regarded it with hungry eyes. It had been weeks since he had a hot meal. *A decent hot meal*, he corrected himself. The meals he cooked while on the road were hot, but far from decent.

After setting a spoon and tankard of water on the table, the girl briskly turned and went to work serving other customers. With the unfavorable weather outside, all the townspeople flocked to the inn like moths to a flame. Almost every bench in the room was jammed with people, talking and laughing loudly, spilling food and drink everywhere, not paying their tab... the entire inn was in an uproar of yelling and laughing. Several men were seated playing winded and stringed instruments, barely audible above the other sounds filling the air.

Trenson looked back down at the soup. His stomach rumbled greedily, and the aroma rising from the bowl was almost too much to bear. He hesitated, looking keenly at the wooden spoon next to the bowl, then shrugged, quickly caught hold of the bowl and leaned back, tipping the contents of the warm broth into his mouth. Never had soup tasted so good. It trickled down his throat and his stomach, its warmth radiating from the inside out. The cold that plagued him only minutes ago began to diminish, and he set the bowl down, now furiously grabbing the large pieces of carrots and potatoes that formerly floated in the soup and shoving them into his mouth. He paid no attention to the spoon he had been given.

The bowl was now empty. Trenson turned his attention to the large jug of water. It took him only seconds, gulping the water continuously, to finish the mug. By the time the serving girl returned, there was not a single trace that she had filled the bowl or the jug. She barely had time to recover from the surprise — she had served the food and drink to him minutes ago — that the dripping, muddy man held out the bowl and tankard expectantly. "More?" he asked plainly.

The girl gingerly took the items and walked towards the kitchen. Another wandering vagabond, she thought. There had been many of those lately, many of them not very honest or moral. Or rich, she added, remembering the many times one of them slipped in the tavern unnoticed and acted as though he paid for the food and stay. This man, however, had paid his share when he walked in, so she doubted that he would be of any trouble. At least, she hoped.

Meanwhile, Trenson turned around in his chair, leaning back against the table. He let out a long sigh. This was the first time he could relax in weeks since starting his journey. Mentally, he counted the weeks he had been on the road, finally concluding that it had been three weeks and two days. Which would mean... he reached for his waterlogged pack and pulled out the small map that detailed the area around Faldon. Frowning as the crinkled map dripped water, Trenson smoothed out the map on the wooden table and scanned the map until he found the town he was looking for: Tarsen.

At that moment, the serving girl returned with a full jug of water and a bowl of soup. Eager for the food, Trenson pushed the map to the side and took both items from the girl's hand. He asked, "This town is Tarsen, right?"

She replied, "Yes," before turning away to continued serving people. After downing the soup the same way he had the first bowl,

Trenson looked at the map again. Tarsen was about three weeks' travel from Loronis, where he intended to go.

He still had a rough road ahead of him, though. The Idonia mountains were about four days away, and after that it should be easy going. *Should be*, he mused. Rarely did things go as he wished they would.

Realizing it was getting late, Trenson slowly rose from his chair, stretching his stiff calves and thighs and stuffing the map back into the satchel. He would have to dry out everything once he got to his room. At the prospect of a warm, cozy room ahead of him, he put a coin on the table and walked towards the stairs where the rooms were. He let out a sign of contentment. *Finally, a warm bed at last. What could go wrong now?*

The innkeeper, a large burly man with no hair, threw a large black cloak around him. Pulling the hood over his head, he looked over at the smaller man beside him, who was doing his best to change the innkeeper's mind.

"Are you sure about this?" the smaller man asked.

"Of course I am! Who else could it be?" The innkeeper was starting to become annoyed at his assistant's stubbornness.

The two men were standing behind the counter in the tavern, whispering loudly and glancing around the room, afraid of some-one hearing them.

"Trust me," the innkeeper continued. "I've been the landlord of this inn for over ten years, and I know a troublemaker when I see one. Look at him!" He gestured over at Trenson, who had finished his second bowl of soup and was gazing at his map. The innkeeper scowled at him. "Tall, dark hair, under 20, has a *quarterstaff*." He put emphasis on the last word. "I tell you, he matches that report exactly. Tall, dark hair –"

"Yes, I see that." The assistant cut him off. Looking over, he assessed the man at the table and frowned. Truth be told, he did look a lot like the criminal leader that was said to be prowling the area. The reports didn't give too many details, but from what they did say, this man could more than likely be him.

Lately, there had been reports of towns being raided and burned to the ground in the area. Such happenings were common, but this band had earned a reputation for its brutality and ruthlessness. The local peacekeepers, who acted as the protection and were the knights who protected each town, had issued a reward some time ago for the capture of the brigand's leader.

Maybe they would become a report to some other town, the assistant reminisced. He could hear it in his head already: *Tarsen was a wonderful town, had a great inn, in fact, but there's not much left now...*

Still, it wouldn't be wise to be hasty. "But if it is the criminal, then why is he alone at our tavern?"

This brought the innkeeper, who was fussing over his cloak, to a complete stop. The burly man's brows knitted together. He hadn't thought of that. Why *would* he be at the inn by himself? Glancing over, he saw the "criminal" had risen and was going up the stairs to the rooms.

The innkeeper shrugged. "I don't know. Maybe he's checking out the town to see if it's worth raidin'. But that doesn't matter." He looked around the room and noticed that one candle on the large wooden candleholder suspended above the room was out. He would have to make sure they were all lit next time. But no time for that now.

"Listen, I'm going out right now to tell the peacekeepers about the criminal, so watch the place while I'm gone. They'll handle him, I know it." Stepping over to the door, he took one last look at the uncertain assistant. "And keep an eye on our friend, make sure he does nothing... unsociable." He pushed the door open, pulling the hood down as the wind and rain came in through the doorway. "Don't worry, I'll be sure he hangs at dawn."

II

PRINCE JAYFOR, THIRD SON of king Hailar, eased more comfortably into the wooden seat in his study and continued to read the book on castle development and structure in his hands.

At last, he thought, *some time alone.* There had been precious little of that lately. During the past few days, the flurry of activity in the palace had kept him on his feet all day. He was busy helping his father, the king, to manage the many affairs of the palace, which left him little to no time for himself.

It was only normal that the palace was more hectic than usual. In about three weeks, Jayfor's father, king Hailar, would step down from his throne and pass the crown to his firstborn son, Annor. The grand coronation ceremony that would follow invited everyone in the kingdom. Music and food and games would all be welcome at the celebration. Jayfor could hardly wait.

After the coronation and the feast that would follow, Hailar would retire from his kingly duties and live in peace in the castle, without the burden or stress of maintaining the empire. Unlike in some kingdoms, the king could pass the crown down to his successor whenever he pleased. It was tradition for the king to resign from his duties before his death to guide the new ruler in his early years as king. It was a prudent decision, and Hailar knew it well.

Jayfor yawned heavily. The only downside to his brother becoming king was that it made him lose his quality sleep time, which was something he valued highly. There was always some servant pounding on his door calling for him, no matter what time it was, asking his preference on food or decorations or whatnot. Like he cared.

Although he knew he would enjoy himself at the ceremony — the best musicians and food in the land would be there, he couldn't wait for all the hassle to be over. It was ruining his sleep.

All the more reason to enjoy this time, he thought. He yawned again. He almost dislocated his jaw with how heavy his yawn was, but he couldn't help it.

Then a thought occurred to him: Why not make up for all the lost sleep right here? He could take a nap now, wake up in a few hours completely energized, and continue about his day without the risk of falling asleep in public.

If it weren't for the years of instruction in acting "royal," he would have dozed off then and there. It wasn't that he cared about what people thought about him; in fact, he couldn't have cared less. Still, he knew his father would reprimand him, and if a servant found out about it, there would be snickering and whispering about it.

Like he cared! He shrugged inwardly. What did it matter? It would be worse if he dozed off in a public meeting. *Then* he would be chastised. It was better to sleep here than there, right?

It was settled, then. He would take a nap here, no matter what the consequences may be.

Jayfor set the book on the table beside him. After stretching his arms and back, he turned his chair to the side and propped his legs on the table, leaning back comfortably. His eyelids heavy, he let out a sigh of contentment and closed his eyes. He let drowsiness overcome him as he drifted off to a peaceful sleep...

Until there was a loud knocking noise on the door.

Jayfor's eyes shot open. Startled by the unexpected interruption, he realized that he was falling backwards. His arms flailed to steady himself, but it was too late. With a cry of surprise, he fell backwards.

The chair clattered to the ground with a crash. Jayfor tumbled backwards and out of the chair, rolling backwards before landing face down on the ground.

A voice came from the other side of the door. "Prince Jayfor? Is something the matter?" The voice was brimming with concern and a hint of suspicion.

Jayfor, his breathing heavy and his head throbbing from the sudden adrenaline rush, quickly rolled over into a sitting position. "No! Just... one minute!" He hurriedly rose to his feet and returned the chair to its original position.

"I can return later, if you wish, my prince." The voice from the other side of the door said.

After fixing the chair, Jayfor smoothed his ruffled hair and tried to assume an innocent tone. "No, it's alright!" He wished he were somewhere else. *Annor better hire fewer annoying servants,* he thought grimly. After feeling confident that everything seemed normal in the room, he called back in a forced casual tone, "Come in."

The door cracked open, and an aged servant with gray and white hair peered around the door. Jayfor immediately recognized it as Gransis, the oldest and most trusted servant of the house. The servant swept his gaze across the room before his light brown eyes rested on Jayfor.

"I am sorry to have disturbed you, my prince. I did not know that you were so... unprepared for my arrival." He smiled, but there was also an underlying question in his words.

Jayfor returned the smile knowingly "Ah, yes, well, we can't be ready for everything, can we?" Eager to move on to another topic, he quickly added, "You wanted to see me?" He figured he might as well get this over with. Then he could resume his nap that had been so rudely interrupted.

Gransis pushed the door completely open. "Indeed, my prince." Jayfor saw that the elderly servant was carrying a plain rectangular box under one arm. The servant entered the room in a slow stride and placed the box gingerly on the table in the room. "We finished your order today," the servant said. "As soon as word reached me that it was done, I brought it to you as quick as I could. I know you have been waiting a long time for this." He began untying the cords that fastened the box's lid shut. He was having considerable trouble at the task, though, as his fingers lost their dexterity long ago.

As soon as Jayfor saw the box, he immediately knew what it was. His excitement quickly overcame his desire to be alone. He helped the aged servant with one knot that was tightly bound. Jayfor had trouble with the knot as well, though, as he was so excited that he fumbled as he worked.

At the recommendation of his father, Jayfor had placed a special order at the regal blacksmith. The smith had made countless weapons for the king and his family, but even he admitted that this would be a massive undertaking. Nonetheless, he agreed to fulfill the order. The smith warned, though, that it would likely take several months to complete the project.

Since that time, Jayfor had waited patiently for the order to be fulfilled. He knew that great things took time, and that the longer he waited, the better it would be. Jayfor found waiting to be painstaking, and as time passed, his anxiety for his order to be finished only increased.

Now, after all that waiting, it was finally finished.

Eventually, the last cord was undone. Gransis stepped back from the table, knowing how long the prince had waited for his order. Jayfor pushed back the lid and looked down at the item within.

Inside, on top of a satin red cloth, lay a sword.

But not just any sword. The hilt, inlaid with gold and ridged for better grip, glistened in the light streaming from the glass window. At the bottom of the pommel, it formed a downward triangle, sharp on the end where the two points met. At the center of the hilt guard was the brilliant star symbol that was the emblem of Faldon. The gem in the star's center was transparent, and it blazoned the light that fell on it in a thousand directions.

But it was the silver blade that caught Jayfor's eye.

"The blade is a mixture of a steel alloy and tronkelli, my prince." Gransis said, bringing Jayfor out of his trance. He couldn't stop staring at the blade. He had never seen anything like it. It had a similar appearance to steel, but there was something... Different about it. It had a white gleam to it, and the edges were sharp to a fine, almost invisible point, all the way to its tip.

Tronkelli meant "Unbreakable" in the old Ralladin language. And it earned its name rightly. It was first discovered in the mountains in the south, hundreds of years ago. At first, no one could forge anything from it. It was so incredibly strong that the veins of the metal had to be removed all at once, with huge sections of rock that were attached to the metal unable to be taken off.

It took years of engineering and study for the people to achieve a way to use and manipulate the virtually indestructible metal. Using a complicated combination of heating, smelting and engineering, a way was finally discovered to craft the metal in weapons and usable items.

Because of its extremely durable structure, anything that had an even minuscule amount of tronkelli was worth hundreds of pounds of gold. It was the most precious thing in all Ralladin. Commonly, an exceedingly small amount of the metal was added and distributed among the metal of a weapon when it was being forged. This allowed the finished product to be considerably stronger than before, but even the small tronkelli added was worth more than most people earned in a year. It was because of this that only the royal family could afford the costs of forging the metal into their weapons.

"It's... well, it's perfect." Jayfor couldn't think of much more to say.

Gransis, on the other hand, wasn't so tongue-tied. "At your command, the blade was folded sixteen times."

Slowly, as if the blade would shatter at his touch, Jayfor reached into the box and grasped the hilt firmly. He raised it out of the box.

Instantly, he felt the weight of the sword equally distributed across the whole of the weapon. The weight of the weapon was not overly heavy, but enough to deliver strong and deadly blows. He held it before him and marveled again at the craftsmanship.

Gransis, feeling as though he was virtually oblivious to the prince, cleared his throat. "Is there anything else that I may assist with?"

Jayfor said nothing. It was clear that he did not hear the servant. He was lost in his own world.

Gransis felt like he should say something before walking out. After all, it wouldn't be very polite to walk out on the prince without saying something. He could need something.

Then he realized that even if Jayfor did want something, he wouldn't get anything out of him while he was staring at the blade. And so, shrugging inwardly, the aged servant made it to the door and silently walked out.

His departure was not noticed by Jayfor, who was mesmerized by the intricate patterns and craftsmanship of his new weapon. He ached to use it immediately, but knew it was late and that he would be better off trying it tomorrow. He couldn't wait to practice with it in the training yard.

I can't wait to try this. Hopefully, sometime soon, I shall be able to use it in an actual battle!

Little did he know that day would come soon.

III

THE BLINDING MORNING LIGHT streaming from the room's window fell on Trenson's closed eyes. Shifting slightly on the cot, Trenson's mind was dragged out of unconsciousness and into reality. His mind fuzzy, he slowly opened his eyes, and was immediately blinded by the blazing light. The world was blurry and unclear. He slowly sat up on his elbows.

And then instantly wished he hadn't. His muscles screamed with aches and pains; one of the many side-effects of traveling non-stop for weeks. His legs felt like they were on fire from exhausting days and nights on the road. It felt as though he had been molded by a blacksmith, stuck in a blazing forge and beaten over and over again.

For a few seconds, Trenson wondered where he was. His mind wasn't fully awake yet, and he glanced around the room, trying to remember.

Then it hit him like a hammer: His mission. He had to reach Loronis, the capital city of Faldon. He had to warn the king of the insurrection.

Time is running out.

Ignoring the dominating urge to lie back down and sleep, Trenson swung his legs over the cot's edge. He groaned at the pain that radiated throughout his body. He stood on the cold wooden boards of the room.

He glanced around the room and frowned. Last night, he had laid out all his gear on the floor in hopes that it would help to purge some of the water from it. Instead of becoming dry, though, the equipment had created puddles of water around themselves and soaked in them all night. In the end, nothing was much drier than it had been to begin with.

Trenson stretched his tense muscles, extending his arms above his head and pulling his knees to his chest, and felt a little better. After donning the same clothes he had worn for weeks now, he gathered all his still-wet equipment and shoved it into his pack. The loaf of bread that he had bought a week ago could hardly be recognized from all the mold growing on it. It was gross, but he figured that he could take all the mold off and eat the inside of the bread, which was hopefully still half-decent.

While he was packing his things, Trenson suddenly felt as though something was different. Like there was something he should notice. He couldn't quite place it, but he innately knew it was there. His eyes drifted to the open window when he realized what it was: it wasn't raining. The sun was out.

Walking over to the small window, he saw that most of the clouds that had relentlessly oppressed the sky for over a week were mostly gone, save the occasional white cloud floating in the blue sky. The mold on his week-old loaf of bread made it almost unrecognizable. A blazing sun reflected off the many puddles and ditches in the road. A few townsfolk sauntered through the village, dressed in the usual brown clothing that was easy to afford.

Judging by the position of the sun in the sky, it was clear that he had slept longer than he had intended. Shoving the rest of his gear into his pack, he grabbed his quarterstaff, which was leaning against the wall, and made his way to the door. He stopped at the doorway and looked around at the room one last time. He mused that he would probably not stop at any more inns along the way, for the sake of keeping a steady pace.

After all, he had to keep moving. If he was too late, then hundreds, maybe thousands, of people would die, and nothing would stop the dark forces of Elara from conquering the world.

But he could not save the kingdom on an empty stomach, could he?

***

The boards creaked loudly under Trenson's feet as he walked down the stairs. The stairway had apparently been built a long time ago and did not appear to be getting in any better condition as time went on. Trenson was a little worried the boards may break under his feet and that he would be sued by the landlord. Which would be wonderful, he thought to himself. The last thing he needed was more problems.

When he was almost to the bottom of the stairs, Trenson looked up just in time to see the door of the tavern swing open and a figure rush out the open door. The man ran out too quickly to see any details, but it was clear that he was in a great hurry. Trenson wondered who the man was, but shrugged it off. He wasn't really interested in other people's business.

The food looked delicious. The plate placed in front of Trenson was loaded with hot bacon, steaming eggs, and toasted biscuits slathered with jam. His mouth watered at the sight. It had been so long since he had seen a meal so good. Well, he had dinner last night, but besides that, it had been ages since he had a good home cooked meal.

At least, it was probably good. He scarfed the food down so fast, he did not really know how it tasted.

Bright morning light streamed through the windows, making the excessive dust that hovered around the room visible. The innkeeper stood behind the counter and looked to be wiping down the counter. He wasn't very focused on his work, though. He kept looking up at Trenson and then back at the door, with a worried countenance on his face. When he caught Trenson looking back at him, he always looked away quickly and bent over his work with sudden vigor.

Trenson felt something wasn't right. First the runaway man at the door, now the suspicious attitude of the innkeeper. And the fact that nobody was in the inn was even more evidence that this wasn't normal. Just yesterday, the tavern had been packed. Now, besides the innkeeper and the serving girl, there was not a soul to be seen.

Trenson shoved the last piece of bacon into his mouth and waited for the serving girl to return so he could ask for more. He assessed his progress on the road so far. He remembered that Tarsen was about three weeks from Loronis, if the road ahead was easy and clear. The only thing left was the Idonia mountains. After that, it would be easy going to Loronis and he would be done. Only three more weeks.

Twenty-one more days.

Five hundred and four more hours.

And way too many minutes.

So much for being positive.

At that moment, the serving girl returned and, when he had requested more food, left promptly with his plate. He searched her face for a hint of what was going on. Nothing could be discerned from her, he found out. She was in the same cheerful mode as yesterday.

Maybe nothing was off. He was probably just being paranoid.

As he was devouring the second plate, Trenson heard a creaking noise above him. When he looked up, he was amazed to see what looked like a large wagon wheel suspended in midair from the ceiling. The wheel was turned sideways, and candles were attached to the top, giving light to the entire room.

He had seen nothing like it. The entire structure was made of wood, and the candles in the lightholder were still all lit. Trenson saw that the entire thing was held up by a thick rope that was attached to the roof. The rope came down along one of the walls, and it followed the wall down until it ended tied in a knot to a post to the wall at about waist level. He guessed that this was to lower it when the candles needed relighting or changing. The innkeeper was probably immensely proud of it.

But he didn't need to waste time gawking at some innkeeper's fancy lightholder. Shrugging inwardly, he shouldered his pack, heavy with equipment, and grabbed his staff. *Well,* he thought dully, *another long day of nothing happening.*

That's when the door crashed open.

IV

THE DEADLY STEEL BLADE shot forward, straight for Jayfor's chest. The thrust was well timed and executed with skill, designed to end the conflict at once. It caught Jayfor off guard, and he barely managed to anticipate it in time to counter it.

Jayfor instinctively stepped to the side and let the thrust expire. Now it was his opponent who was off balance and open. Jayfor shifted his momentum forward and swung his sword in a wide arc towards his adversary's midsection.

But the opponent was no less skilled. He saw the blade arcing towards him and dropped low on the ground. The blade passed over his head. He disengaged from the fight and stepped back a few paces.

They had been at it for almost half an hour now. Sweat dripped down both warrior's faces. Jayfor's limbs ached, and his breathing came in ragged gasps. He hoped his opponent felt as worn out as he did.

He was determined not to lose this duel. His new sword, gleaming brightly in the afternoon sun, pointed at his foe indigently. He would keep fighting until he dropped from exhaustion, which didn't seem too far away. He held his stance and glared at his foe, waiting for him to make the first move.

He didn't have to wait for long. Throwing caution to the wind, the warrior charged at Jayfor and let loose a fury of hacks and slashes, grunting with every swing.

Jayfor resisted the onslaught with skill, his blade stopping each blow before they could land, but he felt himself faltering. Forced backwards, he knew he would need to change tactics soon or the fight would be over. His foe knew that Jayfor was falling back and continued to barrage him relentlessly.

This is getting nowhere, Jayfor thought. He decided to try something that he had been working on for weeks.

Attempting to end the battle subtly, the adversary brought his large broadsword halfway up and around his head, leaving a large portion of his body temporarily vulnerable. The speed that he accomplished this, however, guaranteed that Jayfor, in his weak state, would not be able to take advantage of it. Jayfor knew it was now or never.

He gritted his teeth. Everything would have to be perfect. If he gripped his sword too tightly or didn't perform it correctly, then he could break his arm. Then the fight would definitely be over. On top of that, it may dent his new sword. Then again, he told himself, his blade was forged with Tronkelli. That probably would prevent it from being dented. Hopefully.

Still, if he planned on winning the fight, it was the last hope.

The opponent's blade began its descent vertically towards Jayfor. The warrior expected the prince to try to dodge it, or at least parry.

But instead, Jayfor hurled his sword with all his might directly in the path of the oncoming blade, keeping it moving up even as it slammed into the opposite weapon.

The blade collided with a resounding *clang!* Sparks flew from the collision. Jayfor's arm rattled like teeth on a cold day. Ignoring the uncomfortable feeling, he saw that it had worked: his foe was now completely off balance. Before the warrior could regain his focus, Jayfor had placed the razor-tip of the blade at the man's throat.

The beaten man looked at him with fury in his eyes. He gripped his sword tightly in his hand, as if he still planned on continuing the duel.

"Yield." Jayfor's voice was firm and absolute.

Reluctantly, the defeated man let his sword fall to the hard dirt of the training yard.

Jayfor grinned at the other man and sheathed his sword in his waist scabbard. The warrior still stared at the prince angrily.

Jayfor wiped the sweat from his brow. "You fought well, brother."

The man grunted and muttered something under his breath as he slid his sword forcefully into his sheath. "You got lucky."

Jayfor's smile widened. The times when he was able to beat his brother in combat were few and far between.

"Luck had nothing to do with it, Xavson." Gleefully, he walked with his brother to the wooden benches stationed at the training ground's edge.

They both sat down, exhausted. Jayfor reached for the waterskin on the ground beside the bench, and Xavson did the same. They drank heavily, appreciating the cool water and letting their breathing slow.

Satisfied, Jayfor put the skin down and looked over at his brother, who was running his fingers through his long black hair, trying to dry it out. Jayfor knew that Xavson couldn't stand it when sweat got into his hair. Jayfor made fun of his brother frequently for this.

He decided he would rub in his victory a little more. "It seems that my new sword came in handy."

That had been the whole reason for the fight. Earlier, Xavson had made a curt remark about Jayfor's sword, which he was wearing. Xavson had received his own special sword years ago. He was four years older than Jayfor and the second son of the king. He had always used his slightly elevated authority as much as possible on Jayfor, correcting him in everything and telling him what to do.

But lately, he had begun to be unkind and even cruel to Jayfor and his brother Annor, who was the first son of the king and heir to the throne. Particularly to Annor. Jayfor guessed that this was mainly out of envy for Annor's birthright. After all, the position of king was something that most people would give everything for. Xavson would make comments such as "If I were king, then I would..." and this confirmed Jayfor's suspicions.

Still, Jayfor mused, the position of second prince was something Xavson should be grateful for. It was a higher rank than he was.

Xavson huffed. "Trust me," he said in a cold voice. "It will not be so helpful soon."

"What do you mean?" Jayfor asked, puzzled.

"Nothing." Xavson took another long drink of water, clearly implying that he had no interest in Jayfor or his questions.

Jayfor frowned at his brother's disposition. When they were younger, Xavson was always playing with him or helping him. They were best friends. He couldn't count the number of times the older prince had helped him with his sword training.

Those days are over and gone now, Jayfor sadly thought. Now, the only comments on his training were harsh criticism. The older prince had become unobtrusive and secretive, always keeping to himself. Jayfor rarely even saw him around the palace anymore. He was always "in town" or somewhere, doing who knows what.

Which reminded Jayfor of something he wanted to ask Xavson while he was here. "Xavson, what do you do all day in town?"

Slightly startled at the lack of precedence, Xavson turned to Jayfor with anger. "What?" He demanded. There was confusion in his voice, but also a hint of fear.

"I said, what do you do all day in town? You are never at the palace, and it's the only other place I can think you would be. I was just wondering."

Jayfor intended to continue, but Xavson quickly cut him off. "What does it matter to you what I spend my days doing?" He rose from his seat and grabbed his sword and waterskin. "I do what I please, how I please, when I please! What I do is none of your business."

Apparently deciding that the young prince was not worth his time, Xavson began to walk to the large doors leading out of the training yard.

Jayfor sat confused, wondering what he had said wrong.

At that moment, the large door opened, and Annor peered out, wearing a garb similar to the one he would wear when he became king. He looked relieved when he saw Jayfor and Xavson, who was almost to the doorway where he was standing.

"There you two are! I have been wondering where you were." He saw the fuming look on Xavson's face. "What have you been doing?"

Xavson, who stood almost a full head above Annor, pushed the future king aside and jerked his thumb back at Jayfor.

"Answering his dim-witted questions," was the only answer he got.

Walking past the confused heir, Xavson disappeared down the hall that continued down to the main palace.

Annor looked at Jayfor questioningly. Jayfor shrugged and gathered his sword and waterskin. Slinging the strap of the scabbard over one shoulder and under the other, he walked over to where Annor stood.

"Well, that isn't exactly the full story."

Annor nodded. "I guessed as much." He held the door open for Jayfor as they both walked into the hall.

Jayfor looked over at Annor. Unlike their brother, Annor was calm and calculated, always looking for ways to improve and thinking things through. Surprisingly, instead of the prospect of becoming king making him arrogant, he instead seemed to become even wiser and intelligent.

I wish some of Annor's attitude would rub off on Xavson, Jayfor thought.

The two walked down the large hallway with a high ceiling that connected to the main palace where they lived.

"I presume you were training?" Annor said.

Jayfor nodded and wiped more sweat from his brow. "I was." He grinned broadly. "I'm afraid that Xavson's ego shall be bruised for a time."

Annor returned the grin. He knew as well as Jayfor that Xavson could be overbearing with his pride at times. "So, you defeated him, did you?"

Jayfor nodded and took another long swig from his waterskin. "I did." He said when he had finished. "He made a snarky comment on my sword while I was wearing it in the training yard. He said, 'You think you're so high and mighty with that new sharp stick of yours?' So I challenged him to a fight." Jayfor's grin grew even wider. "He won't be making any more comments about my sword again, that's for sure."

Annor nodded. "I'm glad about that. It's about time Xavson was humbled a little."

The light from the overhead stained glass displayed squares of blue and white on the red carpeted floor.

"Why were you looking for me?" Jayfor asked.

The future king shrugged. "Just curious where you were is all. I haven't seen you all day, and I know that once I become king, I will have even less free time."

Jayfor took another drink from his waterskin, draining the last of the contents. That was bound to happen, he knew.

"And how have preparations for that been going?"

Annor looked at his youngest brother. "Do you speak of the coronation ceremony?"

Jayfor nodded. There was no one else in the hallway except the two princes. Their footsteps echoed against the sturdy walls around them.

"In short, it is going very well. Yesterday, I was given a false crown that weighs as much as the crown I will wear when I become king." He shook his head, clearly grateful that the crown wasn't on top of it. "If only you knew how heavy it is! I understand that it is a symbol of a monarch's power and authority, but thirty pounds? It's absurd. And all this training to become a dignified king?" He shook his head again. "I daresay I shall ever grow accustomed to it.

"I'm sure you'll get used to it. After all, Father wears his crown all the time and is used to it, or at least seems to be, so you should as well."

"I hope you are right." Annor replied.

There was a brief pause, then Annor spoke again. "I still cannot believe that in less than three weeks, it will be me who sits on the throne!" He raised his arm to scratch fiercely at a nagging seam under his arm. "I still don't know how I will do it. All of Faldon will be counting on me to lead them. And now that Kallary and Elara are gaining ground, I may have to lead our kingdom in battle."

A pang of fear hit Jayfor as he realized the truth of these words. His brother was right. On the map of Ralladin and Surrounding Isles, it could clearly be seen that Ralladin was divided into three kingdoms: Kallary, Faldon, and Elara. Kallary dominated the west of Ralladin, while Elara controlled the east. Unfortunately, Faldon was in the middle, and both kingdoms were at war with it, particularly Elara.

"They have overrun our borders again?" Jayfor asked, although he thought he already knew the answer.

Annor sighed. "They have. And this time, it is no small raid. It is a full-scale invasion, and it is being done by both kingdoms."

Jayfor looked at Annor in surprise. "What?"

Annor simply held up his hand. "A special defense council has been called in response to the invasions. Besides what I have told you, I know nothing more myself. I will be there, and you and Xavson are more than welcome to join."

"I see," Jayfor replied. They were almost at the end of the long hallway, where a large wooden door stood.

"Speaking of Xavson," Jayfor said. "Have you seen him much lately?"

"No, I haven't. Why do you ask?"

"Because I haven't seen him much at all either. I don't know where he goes all day. Do you know what he spends his days doing?"

Annor thought about this before replying. "I don't—"

Just then, the large door in front of them opened slightly, and a small servant poked his head out. He looked at Annor expectantly. "Your highness, I beg your pardon, but there is something the requires your attention."

Annor sighed and looked at Jayfor, not even trying to hide his impatience. "I have to go." They both walked through the door, held open by the servant, and began to go in opposite directions, another servant leading Annor to what he needed to see.

Before he got too far, Annor looked over his shoulder. "I guess I shall see you at the defense council, then."

Jayfor nodded. "I will be there."

V

ONCE THE DOOR CRASHED open, six men barraged into the tavern. They pushed each other aside and made a considerable racket. The door lay splintered in pieces on the floor. The men piled into the room with swords in hand.

Trenson stopped, bewildered at the sudden intrusion at the inn. He had all his gear in hand and was only a few yards from the door. He didn't know what was going on. So, there *was* something off. He quickly assessed them and came to the bitter conclusion: peacekeepers.

A contingent of knights appointed to guard a specific town and its inhabitants, peacekeepers were supported by the taxes of the town they protected and, in return, were supposed to offer that protection to everyone. Their purpose was only to settle small problems and alert the nearest fort if a raid or invasion was in play. Even though they were politically below the prefect of the specific town, they were usually obeyed more readily than any of the leaders.

Most of them were lazy and arrogant, though. They usually left the people to fend for themselves in times of need, while they drank and had feasts in their barracks. They were obeyed but far from respected.

This probably had something to do with the man that ran out the door earlier. Which made Trenson wonder, *what are they doing here? Are they here for me?* There was nobody else at the inn.

He quickly dismissed the thought. *No, I haven't done anything wrong. They must be after someone else. They are probably in the wrong place.*

The leader of the peacekeepers, a tall and alarmingly skinny man with a pale complexion and faded hair, stepped forward from the back of the group. He stood erect, visibly proud of his position, and scanned the room. His eyes landed on the only person in the room, who brandished a quarterstaff and had a suspiciously bulging pack.

"There he is, men!" The captain pointed an accusing finger at Trenson. "Surround him!"

So much for that idea.

There was no time for him to consider what he may or may not have done. He needed to figure a way out. Being arrested would end his quest immediately.

His mind immediately began thinking of ways to escape. He had his fair share of tough scrapes, although being accused as a criminal wasn't something he had ever experienced before. Still, he had seen enough to know that there was always some way out, some way of escape.

Except in this case, the only way out was through the front door, and at the moment, that idea was less than ideal.

The peacekeepers began to disperse across the room to circle Trenson.

This wasn't good. He needed to get out *now*. He could run back upstairs to where the rooms were. No, that would only leave him more trapped. What about the kitchen? That wouldn't work either. He doubted there was a way out there.

The only way out was through the door. But how would that work? Then he realized: as the peacekeepers spread out to circle him, the door was less guarded. He could make a dash for it.

But they probably had horses outside waiting. If he ran for it, they could easily catch him.

He had to figure out a way to slow them down.

"Criminal of the land!" The loud voice of the captain broke Trenson out of his trance. Now he was surrounded by peacekeepers in a tight circle. He reprimanded himself for wasting all his time. The fancy swords of the peacekeepers, never used by the looks of it, pointing inches away from his chest.

The captain cleared his throat. "By the jurisdiction of the regal peacekeepers of Faldon and the town of Tarsen, you are hereby pronounced guilty of the following crimes: theft of possessions; breaking and entering; excessive plundering of many establishme nts..."

As the leader continued, Trenson continued trying to devise ways to slow the peacekeepers down, but he couldn't think of anything. He was just about to give up when he heard a familiar creak overhead.

That's when inspiration struck him like a hammer.

He searched the lightholder with his eyes until he spotted the rope that attached it to the roof. He followed the somewhat thin rope from the lightholder and traced it down the wall until it was tied to a hitch at waist level, on the wall opposite the door. Perfect.

"... armed assault; resisting and escaping arrest; and murder." Out of breath from the long oration, the captain took a few seconds to catch his breath. The circle of peacekeepers around Trenson didn't move.

The leader was surprised at the young man. He expected to see fear in his eyes, but all he saw was confidence. The young criminal seemed to be daring him to continue.

He was slightly unsettled by this, but he shook it off. "Because you have been deemed too dangerous to arrest and sentence formally, we have the right to execute you now." He paused to see if this brought any reaction. Surely the prospect of death would shake the resolve of this criminal. But there was no reaction. In fact, there seemed to be amusement in the young man's eyes.

Realizing that he wasn't going to get any fun from this man, the captain briskly asked, "Before you die, do you have anything to say?"

Without missing a beat, Trenson casually replied, "Just one thing: why is your mother at the door?"

Instantly, the tension in the room snapped. The heads of all the peacekeepers all spun towards the door. The leader didn't recognize the ploy, and with a face filled with fear, swept his eyes to the door, fearing the worst.

And that gave Trenson the opportunity he needed.

In seconds, he crouched down and performed a backwards roll out of the tight circle. He regained his footing and stood up. Then, without hesitation, he gripped the quarterstaff from his shoulder and brought it down hard on the nearest peacekeeper's head.

The peacekeeper's eyes rolled backwards, and he sank to his knees. The last thing he could recall from that time was the sensation that his sword was being yanked from his grip.

The Peacekeepers, after seeing no "mother" at the door, recognized that it was a trick. They returned their gaze to the criminal — only he wasn't in the circle. He was standing on the other side of the room now, and with a sword. The leader saw the unconscious man on the floor and realized that he had let the vagabond outsmart him. He silently cursed his foolishness.

"Get him!"

As the peacekeepers sauntered hurriedly towards him, Trenson didn't move. It was almost too easy, what he was about to do. He checked the position of the peacekeepers to the lightholder. *Just a little more... almost...*

Perfect.

Keeping his eyes on the peacekeepers, he gripped his new sword in his hand and swung it around and across his body. He let the weight and momentum of the weapon carry the blade onward through the air. It hit the rope just above the hitch where it was tied. The rope severed cleanly. The force of the blow caused the edge of the blade to embed itself into the wall.

At that moment, the captain, seeing the criminal cut the rope, suddenly had a feeling that something bad was about to happen.

A low creak came from above. The large wooden lightholder swayed uncertainly. The peacekeepers heard the noise but looked up all too late.

Trenson watched with satisfaction as the huge lightholder dropped from the roof and, with a massive crash, crushed the entire group under a wreckage of wood. The structure immediately went from elegant and polished to ruins and a chaotic shamble of wooden beams.

As the dust settled, Trenson saw that his plan had worked. Most of the peacekeepers were knocked senseless, while others moaned painfully under the wreckage. Not a single peacekeeper had escaped from being buried under the lightholder. In fact, Trenson could hardly see any sign that there was anyone under the wooden mass, other than a boot sticking out from one side.

Suffice to say, Trenson was quite pleased with himself.

Trenson heard a strained gasp. He turned and saw that the innkeeper had watched the entire event unfold silently from behind the counter. His eyes were wide and his face was deathly pale. He gawked at what had happened to his tavern. Trenson thought the man would pass out.

It didn't take the innkeeper long to recover. He turned his seething gaze on Trenson. His face slowly turned from white to red. He shook with anger.

"YOU!" the innkeeper bellowed. "I'll fix you, you little... " He let out a string of curses that made Trenson, who was used to strong language, wince.

Trenson made a helpless gesture. "I am what I am, sir."

It was more than the innkeeper could handle. With a cry of fury, the innkeeper ran around the counter and charged at Trenson, deciding he would tackle the young man himself.

It was a mistake. The innkeeper wasn't as spry as he imagined himself. As soon as the man got near, Trenson dodged to the side and stuck his leg out in the path of the innkeeper. The man stumbled over the foot and slammed into the wall with tremendous force. The windowpanes rattled.

Although the innkeeper was still conscious, he was dazed by the impact, and this gave Trenson the time he needed to make his escape. He yanked the sword from the wall. The peacekeepers from under the wreckage had begun to stir, coupled with increased groans of pain. Before long, they would emerge from the destroyed lightholder. And now there was smoke.

Smoke? That's when he noticed that some of the candles in the lightholder were still lit. They had rolled onto the floor after the structure had fallen and had already ignited some of the wooden tables and chairs. Already, some of the legs were popping and crackling, and the flames were only spreading.

Ignoring the increased hardship in breathing, Trenson dashed for the door and, going around the pile of wreckage on the floor, burst through the door.

A wall of chilly midmorning air instantly crashed into him. He looked around and saw that the streets were almost entirely deserted as well. That would make it easier to get away. He checked to make sure he had everything.

He glanced around and saw the peacekeeper's horses bolting away, frightened by the loud noises and him bursting out the door. Of course, they didn't tether them, he thought grimly.

He heard more noises behind him at the inn and saw that the smoke was billowing out the doorway. He needed to leave *now*. Adrenaline pumping and heart racing, he broke into a full sprint.

He didn't see, but behind him, the exasperated innkeeper barged out of the door of the tavern. He leaned over and put his hands on his knees, gasping for air and red in the face. A peacekeeper came out behind him, dragging an unconscious peacekeeper behind him.

The inn was really on fire now. Smoke curled from around the doorway, and the flames roared as they consumed the building. The rest of the six peacekeepers, either walking or carried, eventually made their way out of the blazing inn. They sank to their knees, also red in the face and panting for air.

A window shattered from the immense heat inside. More smoke and flames poured from its opening. The entire building, both inside and out, was now engulfed in raging flames. A crowd began to gather, watching the massive fire burn and seeing the smoke rise into the air.

Finally catching his breath, the innkeeper looked up to the see the retreating figure slowly fade into the distance. Seething rage overcame him. There was nothing he could do. Half of the peacekeepers were knocked out, and the other half wouldn't risk going after him. And on top of that, his establishment, which he had run for many years and had been in his family for generations, was being burned to a crisp.

He pointed a quivering finger at the man who had cost him so much. "YOU! You will pay for your crimes! *I SWEAR IT!*"

<u>VI</u>

“T HE SITUATION IS MORE dire than we like to believe.”

Sir Agrond, supreme battle commander under the king of Faldon, indicated the extremely large map on the table. The rest of the men in the room, which was composed of all the generals, Jayfor, Annor, and king Hailar, looked down at the map with concern in their eyes. Xavson was not in attendance.

The captain was right. Displayed on the map was the continent of Ralladin, its borders marked in red. The map shaded Faldon's dominion in gold, Kallary in green, and Elara in black. Jayfor had seen the map many times at strategy meetings and defense councils.

An uneasy feeling gripped Jayfor. He remembered the map having a larger area of gold the last time he saw it.

“And this map isn't completely up to date. From what I've last heard, their forces have probably moved to here.” Agrond took several small black and green cubes, made of wood, and placed them several inches within Faldon's border, with colors matching the respective kingdoms.

Jayfor's spirits dropped even farther. He knew they were losing, but he didn't know it was this bad. He glanced over at his brother.

Annor, cool and collected most of the times, was visibly uneasy, and this meant it really *was* bad.

King Hailar regarded the map thoughtfully. Having ruled the kingdom of Faldon for over fifty years, he was wise enough to know that no matter how you put it; they were at a significant disadvantage. He had gone to great lengths to ensure victories and had ridden out to battle numerous times. He, even more than Agrond, understood the concepts of war. He knew a losing battle when he saw one.

And this was a losing battle.

In the days of old, no kingdom would dare challenge the mighty kingdom of Faldon. It was considered by everyone to be impregnable, and with good reason. After The Darkness was unleashed on Ralladin, Elara lost vast amounts of troops trying to break through their borders, but the Faldon army had held their ground firmly.

Faldon's troops were far superior to those of Elara. Because the Mountain of Power was in Elara, it radiated its oppressive power throughout Elara. The people of Elara were slaves to the power that came from the mountain. They had no free will. They simply gathered in groups and relentlessly assailed Faldon's border, using no tactics or strategy. It had been rumored that the commanders of Elara were dark beings, black knights that could use The Darkness to manipulate and control the Elarians at will.

The kingdoms had been at war for over two-hundred years. And unless Faldon managed to counter the enemies' advances, that war could end soon.

"I see Elara has managed to seize most of the Splitting Waters." Hailar referred to the large group of rivers to the north. "I didn't think that they were skilled in naval warfare."

"They aren't, your majesty, but neither are we. With their fire arrows, they simply barrage our small vessels until they sink. Besides, we had little troops there to begin with, both on ground and naval." The commander pointed at the river group. "I suggest that we send reinforcements to the area immediately. It is a critical region to control."

Jayfor raised his voice for the first time since the council began. "Critical, you say?"

The rest of the council, absorbed in discussing their next move and thinking hard on the best way to do it, was slightly startled by the prince's voice. They had forgotten he was there. Hailar glanced at Agrond, who answered Jayfor's comment.

"Yes. See, the Splitting Waters lie just east of the Endless Mountains." He gestured to the mountain group. "So if Elara took control of the river group, then we would be cut off from the northern regions, which are already basically defenseless. They then will have surrounded us in a tight circle, and we would be even harder pressed."

Jayfor nodded. He was glad to have people like Agrond in the service of Faldon. The general's skill with tactics was impressive, and he knew it was often due to men like him that determined the fate in war.

As the council proceeded, Jayfor watched with interest. He always admired men like his father and Agrond, able to develop plans and maneuvers effortlessly. Most of these gambits were what turned the tides of battle and resulted in great victories.

Jayfor always enjoyed going to war councils. Jayfor had never actually fought in a real battle — a life-or-death battle against a real opponent — but he had watched enough battles and spoke with commanders enough to know that there were many factors that influenced the outcome of battles. Morale, stamina, skill, terrain, weapons, even what the soldiers had for lunch. It was complicated, but he had heard of small groups beating off armies twice their size just by good leadership and insurmountable willpower.

Sometimes, Jayfor would offer suggestions to the council that were approved by the council and set forward and carried out by the army. Many times out of not, his inventive and unique strategies were large difference-makers in the war. Jayfor always felt a surge of pride whenever he heard that his plans had secured a victory, and even more pleased that his knowledge in warfare earned him respect in the council.

"What about moving the forces north of the Endless Mountains south?" Hailar suggested. "We could use them to reinforce the garrison at the splitting water without using our other deployed regiments."

"It's a good idea in theory, your majesty," Agrond replied. "But that would leave the northern regions even more vulnerable. It's not that we especially need the territory; the only thing that it gives us is trouble. But the important thing is that Elara and Kallary don't seem interested in it either. If we took all the troops from it, Elara would jump at the opportunity to gain territory without bloodshed, regardless of whether it was good or bad. Then we would be surrounded from the north too, and the fact that we took back the Splitting Waters wouldn't be of any help."

Seeing the logic behind what Agrond said, Hailar agreed with the commander. They were already hard pressed, and more problems from the north certainly wouldn't help.

Jayfor spoke to voice something that had caught his eye. "What about the area around of the Great Desert?" He gestured to the location, which was now shaded gray. "What happened to our forces there?"

Everyone in the council shifted uneasily. No one answered for a minute. Jayfor looked around the room and caught the uncomfortable expression on everyone's face, and he could already guess what the answer was.

Agrond was the one to respond. He cleared his throat. "That has been a grievous loss for us. Not too long ago, the armies of Elara and Kallary destroyed our line of defenses below and in the desert."

Even though Jayfor had been expecting this turn of events, it still caused a sting of pain in his heart. Faldon's biggest disadvantage was the fact that it was pinned between two rival empires. This forced Faldon to divide its forces on two fronts, while the other two kingdoms only had to fight on one. No matter its strength, Faldon could not hold back the two kingdoms forever.

"I see," Jayfor replied bluntly. He couldn't think of anything else to say. Looking over, he saw that Annor had the same forlorn mood as he did.

Agrond saw the despair in the two prince's eyes. "Both kingdoms are working together to employ a military strategy that at any other time I would have thought was brilliant. They started at the southernmost tip of our kingdom." He indicated the spot where Faldon's border formerly lay, below the Great Desert at the edge of the sea. "Once they took that over, they were able to attack on three fronts, and easily pushed north." He let out an exhausted sigh. "Now we are trapped in a V-shape. They simply need to push up from the south and we're done. It's as simple as that."

A murmur traveled across the room. Every face was downcast. Everyone knew they were hopelessly outmatched.

"Are Kallary and Elara allies?" Annor spoke for the first time since the council was brought to order.

Hailar answered, "As we know of, no. But even though they border each other in the south, not once do they attack each other. My guess is they follow the phrase, 'the enemy of my enemy is my friend.' More likely than not, they each want to focus on one thing at a time. If they overthrow us, then they will doubtless fight tooth and claw with each other as well."

Jayfor huffed. "With all in the rebellions in Kallary, they wouldn't stand a chance."

A murmur of agreement traveled across the room. Even though Kallary was considered unified, it was really made up of hundreds of regions and city-states, each one vying for more power and switching sides constantly. In truth, the only reason Kallary was even fighting Faldon was because all the barons and counts on the border wanted more land, in turn attacking Faldon to get it. The kingdom had not even officially declared war.

Hailar knew this and nodded. "Indeed. Kallary is definitely less of a problem than Elara. Which is why I believe we should reposition—" He suddenly stopped. His eyes grew wide. His face turned ashen white. He gasped for air, then slumped forward in his chair, face twisted in pain. He let out a low moan and whispered, "Help... me..." His eyes rolled back, and he slumped unconscious on the table, on top of the map that lay there.

For a few seconds, nobody moved, as if waiting to see if this was some kind of cruel joke.

"Father!" Jayfor and Annor both cried at once.

Then, all at once, in a fury of activity, knocking over chairs and raising a loud clatter, all the council members rushed over to the king's side. Jayfor's mind went blank, and he could think of only one thing: making sure his father was all right.

As fast as they could, Jayfor and Annor pushed their way through the crowd. "Get the healer!" Annor screamed at a nearby servant. The servant, already startled at this turn of events, ran to the door and fumbled with the latch before running down the hall.

Jayfor and Annor stood by their father's side. "His pulse is weak," said Agrond, who knew something about matters like these. "This isn't good. It's bad, really bad. Where is that healer?"

A few seconds later, the healer strode into the room, a bulging satchel of supplies hanging at his side. An older man with a long nose, he pushed his way through the throng that surrounded the king. Before long, he stood before the king.

"For the love of all that's good, stand back! Give him some air!" The healer shouted to the crowd. The crowd quickly obeyed his orders. If anyone can help him, Jayfor thought, it was this healer. The young prince couldn't stop shaking from adrenaline, and his head wouldn't stop spinning.

In seconds, the healer checked the king's pulse and performed other things on him. By the look on the healer's face, everyone guessed that Hailar's condition was dire.

"I need him moved to the infirmary." He said subtly to the guards by the king's chair. They nodded and lifted the pale king by his shoulders with relatively little effort. The look on his father's face almost brought tears to Jayfor's eyes. It was a look of suffering and terror.

The council watched silently as attendants carried the king from the room. Every heart was downcast. The king was noble and just, and everyone loved him dearly. To lose him would be a devastating blow to the kingdom.

Jayfor felt a hand on his shoulder. He saw that it was Annor. The future king nodded silently through the tears that streamed down his face, at a loss for words. Jayfor suddenly became conscious of the tears that ran down his face as well, and he wiped them away furiously. His father, his mentor and his dearest friend could be on the verge of death. And there was nothing he could do about it.

And for the first time in Jayfor's life, he felt lost.

VII

I T WAS BLACK AND silent on the streets of Loronis. The capital of Faldon had long since fallen asleep in the dark of night. The air was chilly, and it blew gently around the houses of town, which sat like silent watchers over the cobblestone streets. Nobody was out on the streets at this time, save the occasional stray cat in search of a rat.

A few houses still had lamps lit, visible through the windows. They created a glowing square on the sidewalk, the only sign that anyone was still awake.

But other than that, it was pitch-black. It was even darker in the alleyways of the deserted streets, where the cold air drifted through and chilled the walls of the houses on its sides, silent as a grave.

In one of these alleyways stood a lone figure, tall and discreet, leaning casually against the hard, cold wall of the adjacent house. Other than his outline, nothing else could be made out of the figure. He blended in with the darkness so well that he seemed to be made of it himself. He was waiting for someone.

Thick clouds blotted out the moon and stars, which usually shone brilliantly through the night sky, overhead. The wind seemed to mutter faintly to itself as it traveled around the houses and streets. Eerie silence hung over the town.

The man in the alleyway felt the hairs on the back of his neck rise as he sensed a presence nearby. Without moving his head, he scanned the streets, but saw nothing. Then he felt something coming from deeper in the alleyway, where nothing could be seen.

The man suddenly felt the impulse to run. He didn't know why. He was expecting the visitor, and they had met several times. Still, every time they met, there was always a part of him that wanted to flee. Pushing away the feeling, he stood straight and whispered firmly into the darkness. "Are you there?"

There was no answer. Then the man could faintly see the outline of someone else in the corridor. Someone massive.

The newcomer didn't answer his question. "You put the arcane poison into the king's wine, I see." The voice was raspy and deep, seeming to reverberate through the air even though the voice was kept low.

The man nodded, though it couldn't be seen through the darkness. "Just as you said. It worked. He's been bedridden for days." He huffed indifferently.

"Good, good..." The voice was filled with eerie pleasure. "You have done well."

The man didn't reply immediately. He glanced down the streets to make sure they weren't being watched. "Yes." He said at last. "Will he... die?" There was hesitation in the question. He didn't know why he asked it. He already knew the answer.

Even though the shadows concealed the massive figure's face, the man could feel the icy gaze on him. Nothing was said for a time.

The man didn't like this. All this sneaking around and hiding. He preferred things out in the open, where you could see your enemy better. He forced himself to oblige, though. It seemed to be how the massive figure and those with him did things. And if they preferred hiding in the shadows, then he would have to get used to it. After all, he needed their help to finalize his plan.

"Did you put the bottle of poison in Annor's room?" The newcomer ignored the man's question. He spoke the future king's name with disdain.

"Yes, it is all in order. I have done everything you have told me to."

"It is well that you have." Then the newcomer added, "for your sake."

The last three words made the man stop. The cold hand of fear gripped at his heart. *They* were helping *him.* Why should he fear for his own sake?

Knowing that a rebuttal was soon to happen, the large figure continued. "You have done well. Because of our work, a new era will dawn on the world." His voice rose in volume. "No more will Va'ar continue to plague the land. The true lord shall rule!" He emitted a guttural laugh. The man glanced down the street again to make sure nobody had heard them.

The newcomer continued. "When this coronation happens in three weeks, it will be you, my friend, who sits upon the throne, not Annor. A new line will be born, and soon, this war will be over." He put emphasis on the last words.

With each passing second, the man grew more anxious that someone would hear them or notice them. He had heard enough of these rants. He wanted to leave now, before they were spotted.

He spoke to voice his last question. "I know. But what will we do about the king's sons?"

If he could see the figure's face, he was sure it would be smiling cruelly.

"That I leave to you."

VIII

THE MOUNTAINS WERE COLDER than Trenson expected. The warm spring weather may have spread on lower ground, but the higher he walked the colder it became. It would take a while for the mountains to grow warmer. Although judging by the mounds of ice piled at their tops, not all the snow melted in summer.

Thankfully, he didn't have to climb all the way to the mountaintop. A narrow path winded up the mountain group and offered a somewhat reliable road to travel on.

Snow crunched under Trenson's feet with every step. His feet were freezing. He had not come prepared to walk through snow and cold to this level, wearing simple boots, and the pain in his feet testified of this. At least it wasn't windy, he told himself. *That* would be miserable.

The sky was clear overhead. Trenson saw no signs of life as he traveled through the winding road, not even a deer or a mountain goat. He had heard of mountain goats before, although he had never seen one, much less a regular goat. He was hoping he would see one. That would brighten his mood a little at least.

The snow should have been white, but it wasn't. It was just barely above the temperature that ice stays frozen, so the snow had mixed with the rocks and dirt to make a dull, gray-colored snow. At least the snow wasn't very deep. He had no trouble walking up the slowly inclining ground.

He passed by many large boulders on the roadside. Some of them were small, about waist high. Others were almost twice as big as Trenson, even blocking out the sun. Thankfully, he didn't encounter many of these giants on the road, save one or two, and he was able to walk around them.

Sometimes, he would hear large boulders tumbling down the mountainside, eventually either stopping or dropping down the steep ravine that lay on the other side of the road. It made Trenson constantly check the tops of the mountains to make sure no massive rocks came down on him. The last thing he needed was to be hurled down the mountains with a boulder on top of him, sending him falling down the ravine.

It was beside the ravine that he was walking now. The sheer drop of the canyon took his breath. There seemed to be no bottom to it; it was too dark to see to the bottom. His journey would quickly be over if he fell down that. He traveled on, taking great care not to get too close to the ravine. Ahead, the path curved out of sight around a bend in the road.

Suddenly, Trenson felt something was off. He felt a chill run up his back as the hairs on his neck stood up straight. He looked around, expecting to see something bad that made him feel this way. But there was nothing. For no reason, he felt colder than he had just seconds ago. He also felt...

Fear?

Puzzled by the abrupt change in the air, he tried to shake the feeling off, but it clung to him. He knew something wasn't right. Why did he feel an evil premonition all of a sudden? He saw nothing that should make him feel this way. *I must be imagining things.* Perplexed, Trenson turned the bend in the road.

And caught sight of a massive black warrior standing in front of him.

The feeling of dread instantly returned. Trenson froze, the cold hand of fear gripping his heart. Now he understood where the foreboding aura was coming from.

His hand instinctively went to his staff. Rapidly, he slung it off his shoulder and gripped it in his hands. His fear made him clench it so tightly it hurt.

The dark knight, dressed in black armor and standing over seven feet tall, showed no signs of knowing Trenson was there. His back was all that Trenson could see, covered extensively in black armor. Trenson couldn't see his face, but he guessed it was as malicious as the rest of his figure.

"So, this is the rat I was sent to kill."

The voice was deep and raspy. It dripped with dark intent. It echoed in Trenson's mind. More than ever, he wanted to run away, to escape the terror of this warrior of darkness. The warrior could easily end his life, and showed an intention to do so.

But he couldn't abandon his mission now. He had come too far.

"Normally, I would not be sent on such an undermining task." The knight paused, letting the tension wreak havoc on Trenson's nerves. Trenson set his jaw and tried not to shake in fear. He didn't know what it was, what was causing him to fear this warrior so much. He felt as though a dark aura was radiating from the knight, and the very presence of evil was too much to bear.

Then, slowly, the warrior turned to face him. "But from what I've heard, you're more of a pest than you look, Trenson."

What Trenson saw made his blood turn to ice. It wasn't the metal horns that came out of the sides of the black helmet and twisted together at the front. Nor was it the crooked emblem on the breastplate with the mountain symbol on it. It was what he saw, or rather what he didn't see, in the T-shaped opening in the helmets front that made Trenson realize that he was dealing with something beyond anything that he could ever imagine.

There was no face. Trenson could clearly see into the helmet through the eyeholes, but where the head should have been there was nothing.

Only darkness.

Adrenaline racing, Trenson mustered the courage to speak. He gripped his staff so tightly that it was beginning to creak under the pressure. "You know my name?"

The reply was an integration of a laugh and a grunt. "I know more about you than you could ever realize." Crossing his thick arms, he seemed to survey Trenson to see how long to toy with him, as a cat toys with its prey.

With each passing moment, Trenson was regaining his courage. "And who, may I ask, are you?"

"Bold words from someone who is about to die." The dark knight waited to see if this caused any reaction. The young man was holding his ground with more resolve than he expected. This was unusual. Maybe this mission wouldn't be so boring after all.

"But since you will not live to tell another soul, I shall tell you. I am Gornar, warrior of Tar-Ra and knight of the Great Power. I am among the many who will reforge the world." Trenson had the strange feeling that Gornar was smiled crookedly. "Not that you'll be there to see it."

Gornar was enjoying himself. Few were the times when he was able to mock the lowlifes that he was sent to deal with.

Trenson planted his feet in a ready stance, one foot slightly in front of the other. He adjusted his grip on his staff, which paled in comparison to the double swords strapped to Gornar's back. He still had the peacekeeper sword, but his skill with a staff far exceeded that of a sword, and he felt more confident with the weapon.

"Not if I have anything to say about it."

Gornar let out a single laugh. This knave was more amusing than he had thought. "*You* won't have *anything* to say about it." His hands began moving to the swords strapped to his back. "Your 'quest' is over. You have failed. You have come all this way, chasing after the aspiration that you could save your pathetic kingdom, only to fall to ruin in the end."

Gripping both ridged hilts, Gornar slowly pulled the blades out of their black scabbards, which were engraved with snake symbols that ran down their lengths. He held the two weapons before him.

Trenson stared at the two swords. They were pitch black. The emblem of a snake twisted around the hilt, traveling up the blade and ending with its mouth open, as if the metal blade was coming out of its mouth.

If indeed it was metal. It was a serrated black blade. It seemed to pulse with darkness and power. Black and purple wisps swirled around the weapons, circling around it slowly and curling itself around the edge. Trenson grimly knew that he stood no chance against this adversary of evil.

"But I have said enough." Gornar flipped both swords around in his hands, anticipating what was to come. "Enjoy your last breaths while you can, Trenson, and prepare to die."

With that, he strode towards Trenson with murderous intent.

Evaluating his situation, it didn't take long for Trenson to find his predicament was hopeless. He had a staff, which in truth was nothing more than a big stick, a sword he didn't know how to use, and no armor. Gornar, as the warrior called himself, had two swords, full body armor, a massive frame, and from the looks of it, skill well beyond Trenson's. He would have to find some way to escape.

The problem was there was *no* way of escape, at least not that Trenson could see. The black knight blocked his way forward, and not only would he have to get around him, but he would need to find a way to outdistance him. And by the look of it, this personification of nightmares would have some way of catching up with him.

He had no time to devise a plan. The first stroke came, strong and lethal, in a broad downward cut. It was meant to end Trenson's life there and then. He barely managed to predict the move and jump back.

Whooshing through the air, the blade came down. It skimmed past Trenson's face and scarcely missed his chest.

Phew! That was close.

Gornar didn't stop, though. Trenson had not even regained his footing when the next swing came. Gornar swung his left sword to the left and the right sword to the right, the black, ominous edge splitting the air. There was no time for Trenson to even think about using his quarterstaff.

Trenson crouched down low as quick as he could. He felt the rush of air overhead as the two blades passed above. Chills ran through his body from the action and intensity of the moment. His senses sharpened and ready, he rose to his feet.

And saw the next blow coming all too late.

It was a low, rising uppercut from below, and an unlikely choice. For any regular swordsman, the move would likely never be chosen. There just wasn't enough time to bring the sword down and then back up. It was even harder to put enough force into the awkward slice for it to be lethal.

But this was no regular swordsman. This was a monster.

The tip of one of the blades caught the bottom of the right side of Trenson's jaw. It sliced up his face and scarcely missed his eye, continuing up his face to just above his eyebrow. The cut burned like fire. Trenson stumbled backwards, and before he could do anything, Gornar smashed his gauntleted fist hard into Trenson's unprotected stomach.

The air instantly whooshed out of Trenson's lungs. Pain exploded across his chest, making the gash on his face feel like nothing. He flew backwards through the air, his head throbbing, and landed hard, face-up on the rocky ground. He lost his grip on his staff, and watched out of the corner of his eye as it bounced across the ground, right over the edge of the ravine and down.

He closed his eyes for a few seconds, unable to focus and see clearly. His entire body ached, and he felt the warm blood trickling down his face from his gash. The wound continued to burn much more than it should have.

When he opened his eyes, he saw Gornar standing above him, one sword pointing inches away from Trenson's throat. The black knight blocked out the sun, casting a shadow over Trenson.

"You proved better than anticipated." Gornar let out a series of low, deep laughs. "But all things must come to an end." He looked down at Trenson through his empty eyehole. "Now you die."

With that, Gornar raised both of his black swords over his head, in preparation for the final deathblow.

So this is how it ends. Trenson wanted to move, but couldn't. Every part of his body screamed with pain, and even if he could, it would be hopeless. There was no escape. *I came so far… only to fail.*

He closed his eyes in defeat, waiting for the black blades to pierce him and for him to be swallowed by darkness.

Only they never did.

There was a loud crashing noise. The ground trembled. A rumbling noise reverberated through the air. Trenson opened his eyes, and what he saw took his breath away.

A huge boulder, similar to the ones Trenson had seen before on the mountain path, was rolling down the mountainside above him. It tumbled down the mountain at breakneck speed, making the ground shake in its wake. It was only a few yards away. And it headed straight for Gornar.

Before the black knight could react, the unstoppable boulder was on him. With a crash, the rock smashed into Gornar. He cried out in fury, but there was nothing he could do. The boulder tumbled off the edge of the mountain, taking the black warrior with it. Hurdling down into the chasm at the side of the road, Gornar screamed in contempt and hatred.

The cry echoed throughout the mountainside before there was a loud crash of the boulder hitting the ground. Then everything went silent.

Trenson lay on the ground, motionless. It had missed him, and now he was alone. He was dazed. What just happened?

Out of the corner of his eye, he saw movement higher up on the mountain. Turning his head, he looked up to see a hooded figure high on the mountainside. It looked quietly down on Trenson from above. Before Trenson could call out, it turned and quickly ran into the mountainside, disappearing from sight.

IX

A T LAST, THE LARGE wooden door that Jayfor was waiting in front of opened. The diminutive figure of the healer stepped out. Hardly had he walked past the doorframe when Jayfor barraged him with questions.

"How is he? Is he getting better? Can I see him?"

The healer simply held up his hand in a silencing gesture before quietly closing the polished door behind him. He turned to the prince with a forlorn countenance. "One question at a time." He adjusted the satchel of herbs that he always carried with him to the king's chambers over his shoulder and took a deep breath.

"He is sleeping." The healer said in a hushed tone. "I gave him some treatments to help with the healing and pain, but only time will tell if it works. As for your questions, I shall answer them one at a time. The king has not improved at all in the past few days. In fact, it is clear that he has gotten worse."

The words hit Jayfor like a hammer. He swallowed and nodded, waiting for the healer to continue.

"He can barely stay awake for more than a few hours at a time, during which he complains of nausea and a swimming head. He is too weak to sit up or eat, sometimes even to talk. And occasionally, he falls into fits of pain, sometimes so severe that he begins screaming and foaming at the mouth. It's... horrible."

The healer ran his fingers through the few wisps of hair he still had. He was exhausted. In all his life, he had not lost anyone of royalty in his care. Not one. Now, he was in danger of losing his first patient, and worse, it was the king of Faldon.

"That answers your first two questions. Can you see him? No. He is asleep, and I believe it is best to let him rest." The healer had the authority to preside over those under the king when a health crisis happened.

Jayfor nodded, the hope that his father would recover sinking even lower. It had been almost a week since Hailar had suffered from the effects of whatever had happened to him. The symptoms, the healer had said, were similar to poison, but there were other possibilities. Some illnesses were known to strike down the victims almost immediately, without any precedence. Everyone suspected this was the case. After all, the king didn't have any enemies in court or in Loronis. He was well received by the people. So who would poison him?

Investigators had been assigned, however, to search for any clues that would indicate that the king had indeed been poisoned. Everyone that had been near the king or worked in the palace was searched and thoroughly questioned. So far, no leads had been found.

"I don't understand it!" The healer continued. "For forty years, I have been the healer of this palace, and I have studied and memorized every cause of sickness known to man. I have never lost anyone that was a member of this family to any sickness. Not one.

And yet the one person who is struck by a mysterious illness that nothing seems to work on is the king!"

He stopped suddenly. It hadn't occurred to him that he was ranting on to the king's son that he couldn't cure his father right to his face. He glanced at Jayfor sheepishly and bowed his head in apology. "I... I am sorry, my prince. I did not mean to be disrespectful."

Jayfor smiled as best he could. "It's all right. We appreciate your efforts."

"Thank you, my prince." The healer bowed again, then began walking away. He made a mental note to be a little more proper when around those of high authority.

Looking at the closed door before him, Jayfor wished more than ever that they would be able to find a cure. The coronation was fast approaching, and everyone was busier than ever. Annor was occupied preparing for the big day, and Xavson was off doing who knows what. Jayfor was often alone every day, bored to an extreme extent, anxious for his father. He tried to ignore the feeling by sword training and horseback riding, but his mind could not forget that fateful night at the defense council, the image of his father's face struck in pain and terror.

Before turning and leaving, Jayfor looked one last time at the wooden doors. *Father... don't leave us now. We need you more than ever.*

X

THE SECOND TRENSON GOT to the end of the mountain range, he started looking for a way to get a horse.

Not that he could afford one. He barely had enough money to buy a loaf of bread. He just hoped he would be able to find one and be able to... borrow it for a while. If he ever had the chance, he might give it back —– if the chance ever arose.

All that mattered was getting to Loronis. Soon. An insurrection was soon approaching, one that would cause a massive shift in power and allegiances in Faldon. If Trenson didn't reach Loronis in time to warn the king, then the only kingdom in Ralladin that stood against the darkness would fall.

After his near-death encounter with the massive black warrior, Trenson had only one objective: Deliver the message to the king. It was clear that some dark force knew about his mission, and even more clear was the fact that they were out to stop him. There was no doubt that Gornar was just one of many who were obsessed with Faldon's destruction. If he knew about Trenson's mission, then inevitably others would too, and Gornar may not have been the only one sent to destroy Trenson.

Which was a big reason why Trenson slept little and traveled day and night, always peering over his shoulder and jumping at every sound. It was nerve-racking.

Trenson was still trying to wrap his mind around his encounter with Gornar. He had no idea that there were such beings in the land. What were they? He knew that Elara was sometimes called the land of shadow. Maybe that's where he came from. But was Gornar the only one? Were there more?

If beings like that existed, then the world was in danger. Trenson had been lucky to escape alive. And only because he had help.

And what about that figure standing on the mountain? He had to be the one that pushed the boulder down. But why? How was he there at that exact moment and place?

All the questions made his head spin. He hoped soon that he would find the answers. But for now, he set his focus on the road ahead.

The gash on his face bled for a very long time. He kept dabbing it with the inside of his cloak, hoping it would just heal itself, but it continued to the point where it looked like he had just skinned a deer, being dabs of blood here and there on his garment from wiping it off his face. Those would fade with time. He wasn't concerned about that. But his face, he was.

He checked his reflection in a puddle that was on the road. An ugly gash, but the strange part was that the wound wasn't closed. It looked fresh, even though it had been days since his encounter. Weird. He splashed some water from the puddle over it. He regretted it the moment he did, as it felt like he was throwing hot coals into the wound.

It must have been something about Gornar's blade, he thought. At least it wasn't too serious. He tried to forget about it. Thankfully, the pain diminished over time, and the wound did close, but it was very, very slow, and the scar was noticeable.

It took him a couple of days to reach the nearest village. It was small, with farms dotting the surrounding area around it; big, empty fields ready to be planted. Here, Trenson found an opportunity.

He was walking through the rural settlement in the middle of the day. The sun shone brightly through the cloudless sky, and the streets were more or less empty. With winter coming to its end, there was work to do to cultivate the fields and prepare them for planting. As a result, there were few people on the road.

The noise of people inside the local inn caught Trenson's attention. Not for the first time, he remembered the incident at the last inn and, also not for the first time, felt a pang of guilt for burning it down.

A sudden whinny from the stables adjoining the inn, however, caught his attention.

Walking along inconspicuously —– or so he hoped — he strode to the door leading to the stable and casually pushed it open. Acting like he was just leisurely letting his horse out for a ride would attract much less attention than sneaking around.

The smell of hay and sweaty horse immediately filled his nostrils, and he wrinkled his nose slightly. He saw that in small, closed pens lined across the edge of both walls were no more than ten horses. They turned their heads in his direction as he walked down the small barn. He assessed each animal. Besides himself and the horses, there was no one else in the building.

He didn't see any that caught his eye. Most of them were small or fat or hairy or a bad color or too skinny or smelled bad or something like that. Many of them weren't built to travel long distances at a time, either. They were simply used for gentle strolls around the countryside, the opposite of what Trenson planned to do.

He had almost given up hope of finding one when, at the end of the stable, at the last stall, he spotted one that caught his attention. Tall, well-built, and muscled, a chestnut with a look of persevera nce... it was just what he was looking for. Deciding this was a good horse to take, he walked over to the animal and held his hand out to its nose. It sniffed it gingerly, searching for treats, and Trenson slowly stroked its face and neck. It made no motion to back away, and even turned its head to the side as Trenson was scratching it, and bobbed it up and down, apparently enjoying itself. Trenson knew this would make a fine horse.

To his delight, he found the horse already saddled and harnessed, completely ready to go. The owner must think that he won't be in the inn long. Remembering that he needed to hurry, he quickly undid the knot that secured the horse to the post and walked to the animal's side. Then he hesitated.

He had never ridden a horse before. Well, to be fair, he *had* ridden one while someone else sat forward and controlled it while he held on for dear life. The thought hadn't occurred to him before, but the more he thought about it, the more he began to worry. Could he just get on the horse and ride it? It looked easy enough. He had seen many people ride horses. You pull the reins where you want it to go, right?

The horse looked at Trenson patiently, knowing what was coming next. His ear twitched as a fly buzzed around his head.

You're wasting time, Trenson told himself. Get on now and figure out how to ride later. He put one foot into the stirrup and waited, seeing if the animal would let him ride it. His head pulled up and his ears turned Trenson's direction, but he did nothing else. Trenson took this to be a good sign.

Quickly, Trenson swung his other leg over the horse's back and sat erect in the saddle. It felt odd. He never realized how much higher up he was on horseback.

Ah, well. He'd get used to it. Now he just needed to figure out how to get it to go.

"Go." He said.

The horse did nothing.

"Go!"

The horse did nothing.

"GO!"

The horse did nothing.

Trenson sighed. "Come on!" Why wouldn't this horse go? Maybe he was wrong about how good a horse this would be. What's the point in taking a horse that won't even go forward?

Maybe he was just doing it wrong. He decided to try something different. He had seen people ride horses with small metal prods at the heel of the shoe, and they seemed to be pushing the prods into the horse's side while they were riding. Maybe he should do that.

So, he lifted both heels up and out of the stirrups and then slammed them back down on the horse's side as hard as he could.

Before Trenson even realized what was happening, the animal took off at full speed. One second, he was just standing there, the next minute he shot off like an arrow from a bow. Trenson jerked backwards from the force and barely managed to grip the pommel of the saddle in fear. They flew out of the stable and through the open door into bright sunlight.

The wind whistled through his face and ears and Trenson held on for dear life. The horse continued to gallop at full speed down the road, and Trenson dug his heels in harder to stay on. They raced down the street.

At that moment, a man came out of the inn. He was poorly dressed and had a gruff look about him. He caught sight of the horse racing away from the stables. "Hey! That's mine!" He started to run after them, as if hoped that he would be able to run faster than the horse. He shouted angrily while pointing. "Horse thief! Get him! Stop him!"

Startled, heads turned in the direction of both the man running and Trenson, but nobody tried to stop the horse. The man owning it had a less-than-honorable reputation, so they were content to let it run away.

Trenson didn't hear the man yelling behind him. Nor did he notice the startled faces of the people that he shot past. The feeling of speeding through the town on horseback, wind tossing his hair wildly, was exhilarating. He was having too much fun to notice.

XI

T HE END WAS FINALLY in sight.

From the vantage on his horse on top of a tall green hill, still dowsed in the early morning dew, Trenson saw in the distance, looking as if it were the size of a coin, the grandest city in all of Ralladin: Loronis.

Even from far away, he could tell that this city was beyond anything he had ever imagined it to be. He could make out the tall walls and watchtowers, the moat that guarded the perimeter, passible by the large drawbridge that lay across it.

Most of all, though, he gazed with wonder at what stood like a beacon at the center of Loronis, the architectural wonder that had earned the capital its name. The immaculate palace of Loronis. Loronis itself was named after the palace. The name literally translated as "Grand Palace." Trenson was too far away to make out any details, but from what he saw, he could tell that it was big. Really big.

He was so close now. Less than a day's ride, and he would be there. He felt relief that he had made it this far. After bearing hunger, thirst, cold, weariness, callous terrain, black warriors, and ornery innkeepers, he was finally in reach of what he had strived for. Soon it would be over. He would have saved Faldon from destruction, single-handedly at that.

In the past days, since he had taken the horse, he had learned how to control it better and how to get it to stop, something that Trenson found a hard time doing. He was still getting used to the side-to-side movement of riding a horse, and his backside was sore from riding all day. It was better than walking, though.

There was nothing in his way now. Driving his heels into the horse's side, he sped off towards the capital. The task was nearly complete.

***

Today was the coronation ceremony. In the next few hours, Jayfor mused, his father would relinquish the throne to Annor, and his brother would rule over Faldon.

No matter how many times he told himself this, he could not seem to accept it. His whole life he had known Annor, and even though Annor was technically much higher in rank than Jayfor, they always saw each other as equals. Together they laughed, studied, explored, had fun... now, his brother would be made king, and Jayfor feared that a rift may grow between them.

Of course, he was happy for Annor and his future role in the kingdom. He just hoped this change wouldn't influence their friendship.

Once again, Jayfor was sitting in his study, this time reading an absorbing book on different techniques and methods of sword fighting. He had become adept with his new weapon, and even the generals at the palace thought twice about challenging the young prince. As much as his skill was praised, however, he knew there were always ways to improve.

The reading also helped take his mind off his father, who was growing worse every day. Because the king was barely able to move, Annor's coronation would have to be performed by someone else. The chief secretary would act in his place.

Although Jayfor still desperately hoped that a cure would be found, he couldn't ignore the possibility that his father would not live much longer. The pain of the prospect was crushing, and his thoughts seldom wandered from it.

Which was one reason that he was glad to find something to take his mind off the painful subject.

He was interrupted by an abrupt knock on the door.

Probably another servant, he thought. "Come in." He did his best to not sound annoyed.

To his surprise, instead of a servant coming through the doorway, Xavson himself opened the door. This was different. Jayfor couldn't remember the last time Xavson wanted to see him, let alone come into his study. His face was set in worry as he strode into the room without making a sound. *Something must be wrong.*

"Jayfor." Never had Xavson spoken so kindly. "I have some... disturbing news." He gazed at Jayfor with great sadness.

Now Jayfor was more puzzled than ever. "What do you mean?"

Xavson sat down in the chair opposite to Jayfor and began rubbing his hands together. Jayfor set the book on the table and regarded Xavson with interest. Xavson took a deep breath. "I will start with the good news. Earlier today, they found the man that poisoned our father."

Relief swelled in Jayfor. They finally caught him. The feeling was quickly replaced by anger. "Well? What's so disturbing about that? We caught him at last! He should be executed at once."

For a second, there was a strange gleam in Xavson's eye. It quickly vanished, and he nodded before replying. "Yes, he should be. But there's bad news: that man is Annor."

***

The castle was closer now. Not by much, but just by a little. Trenson could make out the walls with greater clarity, and he saw that they were even more unbelievable than he originally thought. Standing above a hundred feet high, he guessed, the massive structures stood tall and strong, the watchtowers towering above the walls even higher.

A few hours at most from his long-awaited destination, Trenson urged his horse forward. The animal had plenty of stamina left in it, and continued to ride forward, bearing his rider to his quest's end.

***

It took some time to register the shock. "What?" Jayfor asked, barely audible.

Xavson nodded solemnly, but for some reason, he wasn't as sad as Jayfor thought he should be. "It is indeed true, my brother. I found this in Annor's room."

He pulled out a clear cylinder bottle from his sleeve. It was filled about halfway with fine white powder that Jayfor didn't recognize. The bottle fit easily in his palm, and the cork was buried deep into the top.

"I gave it to the healer earlier," Xavson continued, "and he confirmed my fear. It is a lethal poison, uncharted in medical history. Annor must have put some into Hailar's wine at the defense council. That is the only explanation."

Jayfor still could not believe what he was hearing. He stared at Xavson, aghast. "But... why? He will become king regardless!"

Xavson suddenly became analytical. "It all makes sense if you think about it. Although our father will have stepped down from the throne at Annor's coronation, he will still have some unspoken authority, mainly influential. If Annor took act on something that Hailar disagreed strongly about, then our father could use his public standing and turn the people against the king. By poisoning the former king of Faldon, Annor will not have to worry about any revolt."

Jayfor said nothing. He was still stunned at what he had heard. His brother, who had been so kind to him all these years, was now a cold-hearted murderer.

That is, if he decided to believe Xavson. In fact, he was already beginning to have doubts.

Xavson took another deep breath. "I fear this means our brother will try something extreme. We must act immediately."

With waiting for Jayfor to respond, he stood and began pacing the room. "It is clear what must be done. With this evidence, Annor will be exposed as a murderer and be executed." The lack of emotion behind Xavson's words shocked Jayfor. "When that happens, I must take his place as heir to the throne." He stopped walking and turned to Jayfor with an unemotional stare. "We must move quickly. Let's go." Walking briskly to the door, he opened it and looked at Jayfor expectantly.

Despite the whirlwind of emotions and thoughts that swirled through Jayfor's mind, something didn't line up in what Xavson was telling him. "When did you find the bottle?" He finally managed to ask.

"A few moments ago. I came straight to you. Listen, we need to—"

"I thought you said you gave it to the healer, and he told you what it was." Jayfor was starting to see more and more holes in Xavson's story.

Xavson seemed annoyed at his brother's questions. "That doesn't matter! Just come—"

"Xavson, I know Annor didn't do this." He spoke with resolve. He meant it; he knew Annor would never do anything like this. It was impossible.

Suddenly, Xavson stopped. His expression changed from urgency to something else, something Jayfor had never seen before. He stared at the young prince with cold eyes. "You... don't believe me?" His voice was dark. Why was he like this all of a sudden?

There was no turning back now. Normally, Jayfor would investigate situations before he made claims, especially something of this extent. He wasn't one to be hasty.

However, something told him that this couldn't be true, that what Xavson was telling his wasn't right. Annor would *never* do something like this.

And there was something about Xavson...

"No, Xavson. I don't believe you."

Silence. Xavson stared at Jayfor, jaw set and eyes dangerous. Jayfor wondered what on Ralladin was going on with his brother.

Then a crooked smile appeared slowly over Xavson's face, and he closed the door.

XII

"Not too much longer, boy," Trenson spoke softly to his horse. The faithful animal snorted as it continued to plod on. The horse, as strong as it was, had been galloping nonstop for a long time. Sweat ran down the sides of its brown coat and soaked it thoroughly. It didn't help that the man who expected so much was sitting on his back the entire time. Still, the horse carried on.

Trenson was right: it wouldn't be too much longer. The walls towered even higher above them, and judging by their pace now, he reckoned he would be there in less than an hour.

And that hour couldn't pass soon enough.

***

"You're smarter than I took you for, Jayfor." Xavson's voice was dangerously smooth.

Jayfor was at a total loss now. What was going on?

Xavson closed the door behind him and glowered at Jayfor. "Well, no matter. Your cooperation means little to me. It may have made things a little easier at best, but it seems that will not be the case."

Jayfor had never heard or seen Xavson like this in his life. Xavson continued. "This will be unfortunate. For you, anyway."

"What are you talking about?" Jayfor demanded.

Xavson scowled at his brother with never-before-seen hatred. "You really are a fool, Jayfor. Even after everything that has happened, you still don't see the truth." He was clearly toying with Jayfor, making Jayfor even more confused. "Lies seem to do no good against you now, even though they have worked so well in the past. But since you still die before the day is over, I don't see any harm in telling you.

"For years now," Xavson began, "I have been plotting to take over the throne. No one in the past had the power or strength to lead Faldon into a new age as I will, or to crush those standing in our way, which I will accomplish. I realized a long time ago that I am the only one who can reforge the world and rule Faldon with supremacy, and only I have the might to do so." Xavson glanced at Jayfor. "You have to understand, Faldon is a pitiful resemblance to what it once was. What happened to the kingdom that no one dared attack, or even curse under their breath? That kingdom is gone, and do you know why? Because our kings are *weak!* Father is weak, his father was weak, and most importantly, Annor is weak. Every generation gets softer. This cycle of insanity has to end for Faldon to become what it once was, or it will be too late. I saw this and resolved that the only way to break the cycle was to do it myself."

Another series of chuckles followed. "So, as you can see, it was necessary to remove those who stood in my way. But first, I needed an asset that would solidify my plan of conquering the throne. And so, conveniently, I found the Dark Order. Or rather, they found me."

The Dark Order. Chills ran up Jayfor's spine. The Dark Order was the masterminds behind the kingdom of Elara, and it was them who were leading Elara to destroy Faldon. They were a hidden group that no one had seen for years. Evil, menacing figures with swords of shadows. They were the stuff of nightmares. And now his brother was in league with them.

Xavson continued to speak with a twisted smile. "If only you knew of the power that they hold. It is beyond anything you could possibly imagine. With us working together, a new era will dawn, and the world will be made anew.

"Seeing that we both had the same motive, we joined forces and soon made a plan. I spent many days in town and in the barracks, slowly currying favor and turning the people against Hailar and the lies that he has tried to ingrain in us. With a little money, it is easy to make people believe what you want. Traveling to inns and buying them trinkets and drinks and whatever they wanted, it didn't take long to convince them who should be the true king.

"After that, it was simple. I put the poison into his water, then placed the bottle in Annor's room. I have already swayed the peo-ple into thinking Annor is a dim-witted fool, and so this evidence will be the final step. Hailar will not last much longer, and Annor will die, either by an executioner's hand or my own, and I will rule the people myself!" There was a gleam in Xavson's eyes that Jayfor had never seen before. It was the look of an obsession with power.

Jayfor felt beads of sweat appearing on his forehead. What was happening? This couldn't be happening. It had to be a dream. But his senses told him otherwise. This was all too real.

"I hoped you would believe me, brother. That you could live here in ignorance and maintain my subjects for me. But you saw through it." There was no regret in Xavson's tone. "So that means you die, and then nothing will stand in my way."

He pulled back part of his long cloak, and a sword scabbard was revealed at his side. It was a sword and a scabbard that Jayfor had never seen before. A twisted snake symbol was on the pommel, and the scabbard itself was gray.

"Now you shall fall, knowing that any hope you have for Faldon is lost. It's over, Jayfor. I am king."

***

Now the capital was even closer. Trenson's palms began to sweat. He couldn't believe he had actually made it this far, and now his goal was close.

Not much longer now. Just a little farther.

***

This was not how it would end, Jayfor resolved. Now that he had discovered the truth behind it all, he had to stop his brother. He couldn't let Annor die.

The only problem was that he would have to escape the room. That would be difficult, providing that he was unarmed and that his power-hungry brother was on his way, stalking towards him with sword drawn. He would have to delay Xavson enough so that he could run out and warn Annor.

He jumped quickly to his feet and, in one swift motion, grabbed the chair he was formerly sitting on and held it before him as a shield. No sooner had he done so that Xavson's blade began to descend on Jayfor from above with tremendous force. Instinctively, Jayfor held the chair up as a last resort.

Had the blade hit the flat part of the chair, it would have easily sliced through it and into Jayfor. However, instead of landing on the sitting part of the chair, it miraculously struck the foot of one of the legs. Xavson's sword must have been no ordinary steel, for it sliced down the leg like butter, the force behind the blow pushing it down through the wood. Fortunately, the blade stopped its descent through the wood a few inches from the flat board and stuck firmly.

Jayfor saw an opportunity and took advantage of it. He threw the chair to the side, sword still embedded in its leg, while simultaneously pushing Xavson back with all his strength. Xavson wasn't expecting it, and he fell backwards and lost his grip on the sword. The chair fell to the side, sword sticking awkwardly out of its leg.

Jayfor lost no time. He rushed to the door and threw it open, leaving Xavson to recover and regain his sword. He stopped and looked out from the high balcony where he was standing. His study was situated at a higher level, and a wide terrace circled around the level he was on to the open area below. The only way to the bottom was the stairs. Jayfor sprinted towards them.

He heard the creak of the door behind him. Jayfor knew that Xavson wasn't far behind. When he reached the edge of the stairs, he raced down them as fast as he could, stumbling often, his head pounding and heart racing.

"Annor!" Jayfor yelled as he ran down. He heard Xavson behind him, "Stop!", but he paid no attention. All he could think about was saving his brother.

Just then, Annor came around the corner from downstairs, already wearing his robes for the coronation. He looked up and was puzzled at the clamor his brothers were making. Were they racing each other down the stairs? It seemed like it. Jayfor was stumbling down the stairs at full speed, and Xavson was right behind him, carrying a strange sword he had never seen before. What was going on?

"Annor!" both Jayfor and Xavson cried at the same time. They were almost at the bottom of the stairs, nearby where Annor was standing.

"Annor!" Jayfor yelled. "R —– ahh!" It felt as though it were in slow motion. Jayfor's feet got caught in the red rug that lay along the stairs. He fell face first on the ground, hitting his ribs hard and knocking the breath out of him. Uncontrollably sliding down the steps until stopping only a few steps from the end, he saw Annor staring at him, confused. Xavson immediately passed by Jayfor and towards Annor.

"Run..." Jayfor tried to yell, but he had no breath in him, and it came out as a whisper. Desperately he tried to get up, to stop Xavson, to do *something*, but he couldn't. All he could do was watch.

Xavson ran up to Annor, sword still in hand. He seemed to smile warmly, but it was a smile that didn't reach his eyes.

"What in the world are you two doing? I was —– Xavson, what are you—-."

He got no farther. They were the last words he ever spoke. In one swift motion, Xavson, now close to Annor, without hesitation, pulled the sword back and, without any expression, thrust the dark blade deep into Annor's midsection and out the other side.

"NO!" Jayfor screamed. He could only watch helplessly as Annor's eyes widened and his face turned white. He looked down at the blade that had pierced him through, then slowly looked up at Xavson.

The murderer smiled and pulled his sword out of his brother, stepping back a few paces. Annor clutched his midsection and looked at Jayfor one last time. Surprisingly, he showed no fear, and instead of pain or anger, the expression was different: peace.

"Brother." Annor looked at Xavson, his life quickly fading away. "I..." He sank to his knees and gave one last effort, "forgive you."

Falling to the ground, he breathed his last and died. Jayfor never forgot that moment.

XIII

It was when Trenson was less than an hour away from the capital that he realized something was wrong.

Great trumpets bugled in the distance, coming from within the castle walls. They made low, mournful tones that broke the silence that Trenson was used to hearing. Trenson didn't exactly know what this meant, but he guessed it wasn't good. People don't usually blast horns for fun.

There was also a feeling in the air, an atmosphere, that made Trenson uneasy. A feeling of anxiety, or dread, or both. He had no idea why he felt this way, but his instincts told him he needed to hurry.

***

Run.

That was all Jayfor could think about. Run from his brother, who had destroyed everything he loved. Run from Annor, who lay dead on the floor. Run from the palace, from his past, from everything. He had already been running for a long time down the halls, not caring where he was going.

Xavson didn't even try to pursue Jayfor as he ran away down the palace halls. He just stared after him with a crooked smile.

Which led Jayfor to one conclusion: If Xavson was not willing to pursue the one person who knew all his plans, then he must not think that Jayfor would leave the palace alive. He probably had the soldiers that he had turned looking for him right now. After all, it would be hard to incite a riot if the army was against you.

Just then, the sound of a company of knights came from around the corner ahead. Jayfor quickly ran to a pillar near the wall and flattened himself against it. He felt certain that they could hear his heart beating.

He heard the sound of armor clanging stop and knew that they must have halted. The voice of who he guessed to be the captain barked out, "You six, down that hallway! Search every corner and room. King Xavson has ordered that Jayfor is to be caught and brought to the prison. He is not to leave the palace!"

Jayfor couldn't believe that Xavson had been able to order his arrest so quickly. He must have had a company waiting nearby from his study, ready to receive orders if anything went wrong.

Jayfor felt a stab of fear as he realized that some of the knights were coming down the hallway he was in. The pillar he was hiding behind was fairly small, and he felt positive that he wasn't fully concealed. The sound of guards marching down the hallway reached Jayfor's ears, and he flattened himself against the pillar, holding his breath and standing as still as he could. He didn't dare turn his head to watch them, as he was too afraid of them seeing him.

Eventually, the sound of the guards' footsteps faded into the distance. The hallway was once again silent. After a sigh of relief, Jayfor continued to run down the hallway, this time quieter and more careful.

He was right: the soldiers *were* on Xavson's side. His brother had done some work to ensure his success. He would need to escape quickly, or else the entire palace would be looking for him.

He decided to make his way to the stables. Once there, he reasoned, he could retrieve his horse and make a swift getaway. Besides, it was closer than the front gate and probably less guarded. All he had to do was to avoid being caught.

Ironically, he rounded the corner of the hall and came face to face with a huge group of knights who were gathered in a circle.

"Prince Jayfor!" The captain of the group called out.

Jayfor started to turn and run, but recognition hit him before he could. "Agrond!"

"Thank goodness you're here! I feared that Xavson and his traitors had found you first." Agrond looked relieved to see Jayfor. The other soldiers caught sight of the prince, and a chorus of gladness rose from the group.

Relief washed over Jayfor. He knew that he could still trust at least someone. "So you know about Xavson?"

"Ha!" Agrond snorted. "I know plenty about that murderous usurper. Should have known from the beginning that he was no good. But we're wasting time."

Walking to Jayfor, Agrond held out the prince's sword, still in its sheath. "I think you will need this."

Jayfor took the scabbard readily and ran it through his belt, feeling security knowing that he was armed. "Thank you, Agrond. You're a good man." He wondered how Agrond was able to assemble a force of men that were loyal so quickly, as well as know that he would need his sword. He decided now was not the time, however. "I was on the way to the stables so I could escape from this wasp's nest."

Agrond shook his head gravely. "I wouldn't do that. The stables are crawling with Xavson's pawns. Already there are battles going on between soldiers that are with Xavson and those that are against him." He smiled. "I managed to gather this group together to search for you. Since we all wear the same armor, they won't be able to tell friend from foe, making it easier for us to escape."

At that moment, the silence of the palace was pierced by the bugle of a trumpet sounding. All the knights glanced at each other nervously. The ringing continued for a few seconds, then died away. A brief pause followed, then another trumpet sounded.

"We need to hurry." Agrond's worried countenance matched his tone. "There is another way out: the front gate. Don't look so surprised; it's actually the smartest choice. They expect us to escape through the smallest and least conspicuous route. They will never think that you'll be escaping using the main entrance of the city on the east side."

He turned to the knights that were listening intently to their conversation. "One of you, give me your helmet!"

About ten knights simultaneously began to remove their helmets to offer Agrond. One of the knights closest to the commander was able to give him it first, though, and the rest awkwardly replaced their helmets to their heads.

Agrond took the helmet and offered it the Jayfor. "Here's what I had in mind: Take a small group of some of my best men towards the eastern exit. You're smaller than most of the knights, no offense, and so wearing this helmet and keeping in the center of the group, you'll blend in easily. Meanwhile, I'll loudly take a group of men to the north exit and distract them. It should be fairly easy for you to escape using the eastern exit, and after you are out, leave Loronis through the eastern gate."

Not for the first time, Jayfor was grateful for the commander's wisdom. He took the helmet from Agrond and held it in his hands. "I see your reasoning, and I agree. Very well, then. With any luck, we will meet together again after we escape."

Agrond nodded, but while there was resolve in his eyes, there was also sadness. "It would have to be great luck at that. As I said, the north gate is heavily guarded. I don't expect to survive."

Jayfor's spirit instantly dropped. He could not bear to lose any more people in his life. "Surely there's another way."

Already, the sound of armor clanging against itself seemed to come from every hallway. The small group of knights looked around nervously, gripping their weapons tighter.

"There's no time!" Agrond said defiantly. "You need to go now, or you'll never escape!" He turned to face the group of knights. "You four and you six, get Jayfor out of the city! The rest, come with me!"

As the knights began to group in their positions, Agrond looked one last time at Jayfor. "I'll be fine, my prince. Do not worry about me." He held out his forearm.

Jayfor gripped it tightly, although the captain's grip on his arm was something else entirely. "Thank you."

With that, they stepped back. Jayfor sadly thought that he might never see the burly commander again.

"All right, those of you with me, follow me! And be loud!" Agrond held his axe high in the air to emphasize his point.

A roar of resolve rose from Agrond's group, and with that, they began to run down the opposite corridor of the hallway. Jayfor listened to the group continue down the hallway, making sufficient noise to wake the dead, until their clatter grew quieter.

He turned to his own men. They were gazing at him intently, ready to receive their orders. Inwardly, Jayfor was glad that some of the men had not betrayed him.

He put the helmet on his head. "Let's go."

***

Trenson didn't know much about big cities, but he was pretty sure that huge columns of smoke weren't supposed to be rising from them.

He was almost to the city now. The last hour had seemed to pass by like an eternity, but finally he was within reach of his goal. That is, if he could even still complete his goal. He had seen the smoke a little while ago, a gray, billowing smoke. It rose in small clusters from many points above the city and continued upward into the blue sky above.

Am I too late? The horror of the thought clung to him. To travel all this way, through thick and thin, only to be there to watch the city of Faldon fall to ruin...

No. *I can't be. Maybe they're just having a party.* Although he immediately began to see flaws in his theory, he forced himself to believe it. He would not be too late. He would not fail.

The faithful animal that he was riding on seemed to also feel anxiety. It continued to race forward. Even though it gladly would have stopped miles ago, it kept going none the less. Not for the first time, Trenson was glad to have the horse, even if it wasn't technically his.

The horse let out a loud whinny while running, prompting Trenson to look up and see what had captured its attention. It didn't take long to see.

The good news was: the drawbridge to the city was only about a hundred yards away, and it was down over the moat.

The bad news was: a large battle was happening on top of it between two groups of knights. And the group closest to Trenson was losing, led by a smaller, strange soldier that had no armor but a helmet.

***

It was all over, Jayfor knew as he desperately fought back his skilled opponent on the drawbridge. There would be no escape this time.

It had been easy enough getting out of the palace. As Agrond predicted, the main exit of the palace wasn't as heavily guarded, and because of his smaller stature and helmet, he was able to walk out the exit, surrounded by his fellow knights, easily. Every knight they encountered assumed that the group was on their side, so they were able to avoid any skirmishes.

It was after they made it out of the palace and into the streets of Loronis that Jayfor began to understand just how horrible this revolt was. The townspeople were split into two factions: those who sided with Xavson, and those who stood against him. The people who decided to stand against Xavson gathered in groups to protest. They stood before the palace gates and began to beat on them, calling out Xavson as a traitor. Jayfor could only watch as guards were issued from the palace and began slaughtering the people, one by one, until they disbanded and fled.

The revolutionaries had taken things into their own hands. They went to the houses of those who refused to join them, raiding the property and burning the houses to the ground. They didn't care if those inside made it out. Many of the houses were already up in flames, and the marketplace was a turmoil of rioters and thieves, razing everything that wasn't nailed down.

So, this is what my brother spent so long trying to accomplish, Jayfor thought. Was this the empire that he said he was trying to build, that everyone else had fallen short of? It saddened him that someone so close to him could be so evil.

"Please, no!" a man cried out from a street corner. "This house is all I have left! Everything I own is in it! My family will starve!" His wife and two young girls clung to him and each other with faces filled with tears and fear.

The man who was leading the revolutionaries at the man's house spat on the ground. "Do you think we care? You have made your choice. Now you will suffer." He turned to his comrades, already holding blazing torches. He spoke with twisted glee. "Burn it! Burn it all!"

"No! Please!" The family broke down, sobbing as everything they ever owned went up in flames.

One of the knights near Jayfor saw the prince staring at the scene and could tell that Jayfor was on the verge of running to the aid of the family. "I wish we could help them, too. But we can only do that if you escape." He looked around the capital, overrun with chaos. "We will help them when we return. Right now, all that matters is your safety."

Although Jayfor strongly disagreed, he was forced to comply. In that moment, gazing around at the destruction and death as he ran through the city, he made a promise. He swore to return, to never give up until he returned, and set the people free. *I will not abandon you. I swear by Annor's death, I will return.*

On the bright side, no one paid any attention to them as they ran through the streets. With the massive size of the capital, it would take a while to make it to the exit. Weariness began to catch up with Jayfor, but he pushed it aside.

At last, the tall, arched gateway was before them and, to Jayfor's delight, the drawbridge was down. As they approached the massive walls, Jayfor felt relief, seeing that soon they would be out of the chaos. *Maybe I'll live after all.*

"You there! Stop right there!"

Maybe not. A group of about twenty soldiers were standing before the lowered drawbridge, apparently keeping guard. One of the soldiers had noticed them, and the rest all turned to look.

Jayfor and his group stopped. He didn't know how this would go down. Jayfor's comrades gathered around their prince.

The guards hastily formed a line in front of the opened gate, barring the group from passing through. They drew their swords and held them ready.

"No one is to leave the city by order of..." The man in the middle of the defensive line, who seemed to be the leader and was addressing Jayfor and the group, stopped when he caught a glimpse of the soldier in the center of the group, who had no armor but a helmet. "Who are..." Then realization struck him. "That outfit! It's him! Prince Jayfor! Get him!"

And that was why they were currently engaged in a hopeless struggle on the drawbridge.

Jayfor's group had since been reduced from eleven to four, including himself. They were facing skilled opponents, intent on preventing them from leaving the city at any cost. The guards, on the other hand, had only lost a few men. They were quickly overpowering the small group.

Jayfor was still fighting the same man that he had when the battle began, and the situation hadn't changed much since when they first engaged. His helmet, which was the only armor that he was wearing, was hot and heavy. He knew it could save his life, which is why he kept it on, but it was still strange fighting with no other armor on. Jayfor had only ever engaged in mock battles in his training; never had he engaged in a life-and-death duel. Jayfor was trained to pull up every time he was about to strike at an opening to not kill his adversary. That instinct was now a disadvantage, though, as when he did get an opening, he was hesitant to take it.

His opponent, conversely, seemed to have no trouble landing debilitating blows on the prince. He was trained to dispatch his targets as quickly as possible, then move on. This young man, the soldier thought, annoyed, was more of a challenge than he should have been.

"Go, Jayfor!" One of Jayfor's soldiers cried out. "Run! Don't worry about—" He never finished. The sword of the soldier's adversary suddenly pierced through his midsection. He screamed in pain and dropped his sword. The guard pulled his sword out of the man with satisfaction, and the soldier fell lifeless to the ground.

Now it was three against fifteen. The odds were against them, Jayfor admitted. The chances that they would survive growing smaller and smaller.

Another brutal swing came down on Jayfor from above. Jayfor, seeing the move coming, decided to take a risk. As the blade began to come down on him, he timed it and swung his sword up and around his head in an overhead arc.

The blade of his opponent was knocked to the side. The guard was off balance, just as Jayfor had planned. He wouldn't hesitate this time. Pulling his sword back, he thrust with all his might into the midsection of the guard.

The blade pierced through the armor easily and sliced deep into the flesh. The guard screamed in pain and fury and grew limp. When Jayfor removed his sword, the guard slumped on the ground, never to rise again.

"Jayfor! Leave, now!" Another one of Jayfor's comrades yelled. The soldier was locked in a perilous duel against two men on the edge of the drawbridge. His sword flew back and forth as he desperately tried to defend himself. The guard to his left sudden kicked him backwards. The knight flailed his arms, but it was no use. He fell backwards off the drawbridge with a cry, and landed with a splash. There was no chance he would be able to swim in the heavy armor he was wearing.

All is lost, Jayfor grimly thought. He and his last comrade stood no chance against these knights. They were surrounded. There was no escape.

Suddenly, Jayfor heard a voice behind him yelled, "Get on!" Jayfor turned to see... a man on a horse? The stranger atop the horse, who didn't look much older than Jayfor, was holding out a hand to him.

Although there was really no reason why he should trust this man, the look in the stranger's eyes was enough. Grasping the hand, he was pulled up into the saddle behind the man. The horse shifted with the extra weight.

"Come on!" Jayfor shouted to his only comrade left. He was valiantly deflecting blows from three guards at a time. He turned and looked to see what Jayfor was shouting about.

And it proved to be his downfall. Two blades instantly pierced him at once, running through his chest and out the other side. He screamed and reached out to Jayfor, hoping by some miracle to reach to prince. Then he fell to the ground.

"No!" Jayfor cried. Then he yelled at the man in front of him on the horse, "Go, go, go!" He didn't need any prompting. The horse shot off at a full gallop, and Jayfor gripped the edges of the saddle tightly. The angry yells of the guards behind him, mingled with the screams and chaos of Loronis, faded into the distance as the wind blew through his hair and his head throbbed from adrenaline.

All is lost, Jayfor thought. He didn't know it, but the figure riding in front of him was thinking the same thing.

XIV

"Not that way!" The soldier riding behind Trenson panted. They were not even a mile from the capital, and Trenson turned to look at the knight, a questioning look on his face. The soldier was even younger than he thought, hardly old enough to be a soldier. It didn't seem like he was too much older than Trenson. He didn't seem like much of a knight, either, wearing a blue, loose-fitting outfit that was definitely not armor. He did have a helmet, though, which Trenson had to give credit for.

"Which way, then?" Trenson had no idea why the soldier had a preference on which way they fled.

"North. Agrond... he's at the northern gate. He's on our side. We must help him!" The soldier had removed his visor and tossed it off the horse to breathe better, Trenson guessed. The soldier's hair was sand colored and soaked in sweat.

Our side? A troubling thought occurred to Trenson. Whose side was this knight on? What if this knight was on the usurper's side?

Despite his premonition, Trenson shrugged inwardly. The soldier looked like he could be trusted, and that was good enough for him. *Still be cautious, though.* "Okay." He replied blankly. It sounded dumb, he realized, but he couldn't think of anything else to say.

The soldier looked relieved. "Thank you. Now, hurry!"

"Which way did you say to go?"

"North."

Trenson had no idea where north or any other direction was. He made a guess and made his horse to the right. The horse, though it was covered in sweat and obviously tired, obediently turned and continued to gallop swiftly.

"That's south. North is that way." There was a hint of annoyance in the soldier's voice, and he pointed a finger behind them to indicate where they should be going.

Corrected and slightly embarrassed, Trenson turned his horse around and towards what was north. *Come on, horse. Just a little longer.*

The walls of Loronis ran beside them about a hundred yards away as they plodded on to the northern side of Loronis. The noises of turmoil and havoc from within the capital echoed out into the air. The incredible height of the walls prevented Trenson from seeing within the city, but he guessed that it was pretty bad.

As Trenson looked at the walls of the city that he had striven to reach for so long, he felt a stab of pain, knowing that he had failed. For once, he had the chance to do something right, to do something that would have made his father and mother proud. And he had failed.

Instead of wallowing in the self-pity and regret that filled him, he instead focused on the task ahead. The past was gone, finished.

Feeling sorry for himself would get nowhere. All that mattered was doing everything possible to shape a better future.

"There!" the soldier behind him yelled. It didn't take Trenson much looking to find what the soldier was talking about. Another drawbridge and archway in the city, smaller than the one they had just left, was a little way before them. A huge group of knights were fighting across the lowered drawbridge. They all wore the same armor, but it was clear they were divided into two sides. The continuous clang of metal dimmed screams of pain and battle cries as spears crashed into armor, swords parred off swords, and axes slammed into both weapons and people.

Amid the fray, surrounded by soldiers all fighting for their lives, stood a taller knight, clearly the leader of the side that was closer to the end of the drawbridge. He brandished a gleaming axe in his hand, stained red. "Come on! Is that all you've got?" he cried enthusiastically. With each crushing swing of the axe, another knight fell, until the bridge was littered with the bodies of his foes.

"Agrond!" the knight behind Trenson shouted. Not knowing exactly what to do, Trenson reigned in his horse to a stop about a stone's throw from the battle. Thankfully, no one in the battle seemed to notice them.

"I'm going to help them!" The knight behind Trenson declared as he slid off the horse's back. He drew his sword. "For Annor!" he cried as he charged forward towards the group.

Trenson didn't know what to do. He had no weapon, or rather, no useable weapon, and he didn't know how to fight. Running into that whirlwind of swords and axes would be about as safe as jumping off a cliff.

He didn't have to think about it for long. Suddenly, before the knight that he helped reached the drawbridge, there was a loud clang and a creaking noise. All the soldiers fighting on the drawbridge immediately stopped fighting.

At first, Trenson thought that the drawbridge was breaking. Then slowly, it began, with the clanging of the chains that held it, to rise from the ground. The metal chains started to retract back into the holes in the walls, taking the bridge up with it.

Panic ensued on the drawbridge. As the bridge slowly rose, soldiers broke into sprints. The knight Trenson had helped stopped a few feet from the moat's edge. He called out to them, "Hurry!"

The knights needed no prompting. Some soldiers, presumably the ones "on our side," Trenson guessed, ran to the edge of the bridge and jumped on the dirt ground outside the city. But as the bridge rose higher from the ground, they were forced to jump the distance across. Others ran back into the city, not trusting their ability to jump the gap, instead choosing to fight the men in the capital. And still the bridge rose higher.

With a thud, the large warrior who the soldier had called out to jumped off the bridge and onto the ground, a wild look in his eyes. "That's our men!" He shouted enthusiastically. "They got control of the drawbridge, just as I had told them to!"

The knights who made it off the bridge were breathless, some sitting down while others lay sprawled on the ground, panting heavily.

A few of the enemy warriors made it off the bridge to the other side as well, but most of them simply ran back to the town. The few that did make it over were quickly dispatched by Agrond, who seemed to be enjoying himself much more than everyone else was.

The bridge was much higher now. Trenson watched as a few more knights jumped the gap, barely making it to the other side. Then, with a hopeless cry, the remaining knights trying to reach the other side lost their footing on the almost vertical drawbridge. They slid back down the way they came, flailing wildly for something to grab onto, but there was nothing. Except for axes and spears waiting for them at the bottom.

Then, with a slam, the drawbridge shut.

"Agrond!" Jayfor cried, running towards the group of knights who managed to make it off the drawbridge and were catching their breath.

With the top of his battleaxe on the ground, his hands resting on the pommel and a feel-foolish grin visible through the upturned visor, Agrond turned around and smiled even wider when he caught sight of the prince. "Jayfor!" he cried. "I never thought I would see you again!"

Jayfor couldn't help grinning as well. Something about Agrond's smile was contagious. Not to say that he wasn't already filled with relief that his trusted friend had managed to escape alive. He had many things to be thankful for.

Agrond continued. "I'm glad to see you made it out safely! I was worried our plan would fail, and you'd be caught. It seems I had nothing to worry about!" He chuckled. Even during an insurrection, Agrond always managed to lighten the mood.

Jayfor wiped another streak of sweat from his forehead. "I am as well. It's good to see you, my friend! I cannot be more grateful for you escaping that hornet's nest. I would not have been able to escape on my own, however. I had help."

He motioned for the rider who had helped him to come towards them. At the moment, he was sitting awkwardly on his horse at a distance, clearly unsure of what to do. He urged his horse forward on seeing the prince motioning him to join the group.

"Without this man," Jayfor said when the man stopped his horse alongside them, "I most likely would not be here. Or alive, for that matter."

Agrond directed his smile towards the rider and lifted his eyebrows in surprise. This was a figure that he had never seen the likes of before. Shabby clothing, so worn and beaten by the elements that it was impossible to tell what it had originally been intended to look like, dark hair that matched the rider's eyes, and a mysterious look and countenance both seemed to be innate traits of this man. And was that blood on the man's outfit? And a recent scar on his face?

Agrond wasn't about to discredit this man based on his sketchy appearance, though. He held his hand forward for the rider to shake. The rider just stared at the outstretched hand and made no motion to shake it. He looked over at Jayfor, then back at Agrond with a confused look in his eyes.

His good humor only slightly dampened, Agrond retracted his hand and rested it casually on the pommel of his axe. "I cannot thank you enough for what you have done! I am forever in your debt, mister..." He waited for the man to finish the sentence.

"Trenson." The stranger had a trill in his accent that Agrond had never heard before.

"Trenson. I like it! I can't thank you enough, Trenson!"

Trenson simply nodded. "Are you his father?"

Agrond burst into laughter. The knights who heard the remark chuckled, and even Jayfor smiled. *He is old enough to be my father,* Jayfor thought. Trenson looked bewildered. He didn't see what was so funny.

"No, no, you've got it all wrong!" Agrond said, trying to contain his mirth. "If I was his father, then I would be the king!"

"King?" Trenson's annoyance and lack of understanding was clear in his tone.

Agrond started laughing again. "You do know who this is, don't you?" He slapped Jayfor heartily on the back. When he was happy, Agrond seemed to forget who was in charge. "This is prince Jayfor, son of king Hailar! Have you been living under a rock?"

Trenson looked awestruck at the soldier he had rescued from the bridge. He never would have guessed that it was the son of the king that he had saved from the bridge.

"It's true." Jayfor said, but there was no pride in his voice. Instead, there was longing, even sadness. "But we are running out of time. It's only a matter of time before they get that drawbridge back open, and I wouldn't want to be around when they do. We need to move. The woods nearby should give us the cover we need."

Even though he still had many questions, Trenson nodded, and Agrond did the same. The commander shouted to the men. "Alright men, let's get moving! The farther we are from Loronis, the better. We can rest later. Or would you rather wait for them to open the gate? Didn't think so. Now move it!"

XV

"MY LORD, THE INSURRECTION has begun." The messenger bowed on one knee, head down, in front of the large black throne.

"Excellent." The iron-clad figure seated on the throne looked down on his inferior as he spoke. "Inform Lord Tar-Raw of this immediately. He will be pleased to know of our progress."

Rising to his feet, the messenger bowed his head once more. "At once, my lord." He turned and walked towards the two massive doors at the end of the hall. Two guards, standing watch over the doors, stepped forward and opened them for the messenger. The messenger walked through the open doorway, and the guards returned the doors to their closed positions, the doors creaking until they came together with a thud.

The black knight seated on the throne turned to his side, his helmet turning as he faced the warrior standing beside his throne. "To think, after all these years of war, Faldon shall soon be ours!"

The other knight nodded once. "Indeed. For centuries, they have been slipping through our fingers, always whimpering for accursed Va'ar to save them." He chuckled darkly. "But where is He now? The Greater Power is now in control of the land. In time, the hope these people have will be crushed."

Thrall, who was on the throne, emitted a twisted chuckle that reverberated against the shadowy pillars that stood in the hall. Finally, those who stood for Va'ar would be no more.

The room was dimly lit, the small traces of sunlight coming through the tall windows creating long shadows. It was the throne room of Thrall, in his castle in Elara. Here, the sun rarely showed its face through the oppressive smog and smoke that polluted the sky.

"We must take action at once," Thrall said. "Has Gornar returned from his mission?"

The warrior beside the throne shook his head. "No, my lord. At least, we do not know. We have neither seen nor heard any word since he left."

Thrall leaned back on his throne. Gornar, although conceited at times, wasn't one to spend a long time on missions, or to be slow to return from them. "Alert me at once when he returns."

The other warrior nodded. "I shall, my lord."

There was a pause. Thrall seemed to be thinking intently about something. The standing knight waited for more to come.

At length, Thrall spoke. "The sooner those vermin in Faldon are killed, the better. The new king of Faldon, due to our help in acquiring the throne for him, will join our side. So he says." Thrall added in a dangerous tone. "If he betrays us, then you what to do."

The standing knight nodded and waited for Thrall to continue.

"Once he has solidified his authority in Faldon, he will send word to us, inviting us to come into their city and meet with Xavson. When this opportunity comes, we will march our troops into the city and kill everyone."

"Everyone, my lord?"

"Yes, everyone! The Hope must not survive. The One must not be able to come. If He does, then everything we have worked for will be in vain. Everyone in the city, no, in all of Faldon will need to die. Do you understand?" There was an edge of suspicion in Thrall's voice.

The other warrior was quick to reply. "Yes, my lord. Give me the word when the time comes, and your bidding is my command."

"Good. When the time is right and I give the word, do not hesitate."

"My lord!" Another messenger, who had entered the room un-noticed by the two warriors, ran before the throne and bowed low before it. It was clear that what he had to say was urgent. "A large army of Senver has formed a defensive line at Faldon's border, barring our progress!"

Thrall was taken aback and swore under his breath. The other warrior was no less surprised. Senver were the chosen knights of Va'ar. They weld powers of light and were the sworn enemies of Thrall and the Dark Order. Battles were fought frequently be-tween the two. Almost always, the Senver and the Krenors, as the dark warriors were called, were never seen by mortal eyes. They stayed hidden, clashing in secret within the shadows, the fate of Ralladin in the hands of two forces no one had ever seen.

Well, almost no one.

"Your orders, my lord?" The silence was finally broken by the messenger, who seemed to be in a great hurry.

Thrall's voice seethed with hatred as he replied. "Kill them... Kill them all!"

XVI

"**E**ASIER SAID THAN DONE." Trenson said.

Jayfor shrugged and talked on as if it were nothing. "I know. Still, what do we have to lose?"

"Everything. Including our lives," Trenson countered. Jayfor threw him a harsh look.

"Trenson does have a point." Agrond said. Jayfor gave an equally harsh glare to the battle commander.

The small band was gathered in a clearing in the nearby forest they had retreated to. It was the day after the insurrection. Agrond, Trenson and Jayfor were discussing their next plan of action separate from the group of knights that made it off the drawbridge. Currently, the knights were sprawled under the shade of the trees, gathered in small groups. A gusty breeze made the boughs above quiver, and everyone enjoyed the moment of respite.

They wouldn't stay for long, though. The woods where they had stopped were still close to the capital, too close for comfort. They had traveled through the forest for the remaining of the day yesterday, and for most of the morning today. Everyone needed a break, Jayfor was forced to admit, so he had called the group to a stop. He set up lookouts throughout the forest in case any of Xavson's patrols decided to come looking for them.

"We only have about thirty men. That includes us," Agrond continued. "Against the armies of Faldon, that's as good as nothing. Not even with a hundred men would our chances be much better. We simply don't have the power to retake Faldon right now."

Jayfor crossed his arms. "You're right. *Right now,* we don't have the power to retake Faldon. I never said I wanted to retake it right now. I also never said that I didn't have a plan." He paused and let his words sink in.

Agrond nodded. "Go on." He prompted.

"The way I figure it," Jayfor began, "Xavson has no real idea where we are, or even if we are alive. Oh, sure, he could ask the soldiers for information. But in the middle of a battle, no one pays attention to details, and it's likely that, after a lot of digging, he will end up figuring out that I managed to escape the city. With some help." He cast a grateful glance at Trenson, who was intently listening to the prince's words, expressionless.

"He might also figure out that Faldon's most trusted and revered battle commander also managed to escape the capital with a certain number of men. Well, so be it. And it might also enter his thick and rather small head that a chance may exist that the two groups have met up. I doubt he will get that far, though. He will probably assume that we scattered in all directions, and never hope to take back the kingdom from him. Unfortunately for him, he's wrong.

"Anyway, right now he is probably doing all he can to cement his authority. Rebellions are likely still going on within the city, and it will take a while to purge the city of those who oppose him. On top of that, after word gets out that he is the new king and he announces the radical things he plans to do, he will have even more trouble keeping the rebellions at bay from other cities.

"In short, we are, or will be, the last of his worries. If we keep under cover, we can organize a rescue mission on the capital when he least expects it."

A silence followed. Agrond and Jayfor mused over the prince's words, knowing they were true and contemplating what to say next.

Surprisingly, it was Trenson, who had kept quiet the entire day, who spoke first. "Xavson plans to ally Faldon with Elara. To end the war with union," he said to no one in particular. "He has worked with Elara to get where he is now. His first order will be to tell his soldiers on the borders to stop fighting; to let Elara pass through." He met eyes with Jayfor. "The army will resist. Without the army on his side, Xavson will be defenseless."

Jayfor nodded in affirmation, but he felt a pang of suspicion. How did this stranger know what his brother had planned? They had not discussed what had happened very much. They didn't have time to. Jayfor had not told Agrond or Trenson anything about what had gone down in the palace. Yet this man seemed to know.

Jayfor was a little skeptical about Trenson. Sure, the man helped him get off the bridge, but that wasn't enough to earn his trust. A lot was at stake. He had already been betrayed once by someone he thought he trusted.

He glanced at Agrond, but the battle commander seemed to have no skepticism towards Trenson, and was as chipper as always. Jayfor frowned. He wished the battle commander wasn't so gullible. It was diverting, but not very helpful.

"You're right, Trenson," Agrond said. "We are the least of Xavson's worries." He turned and looked back into the woods in the direction of the palace, as if worried that someone might come bursting through the underbrush at any minute. "Unless we are discovered, of course. If we are found, then we will probably make it to the top of Xavson's priority list."

Trenson nodded. "Probably." He turned his piercing gaze on Jayfor. "What do you propose we do?"

Jayfor decided that there was no risk in letting Trenson in on their plan. "It's possible that other contingents of knights have escaped from the palace. Our first step should be to see if there are any others that made it out, and that should increase our numbers, even a little. There are fiefs and forts in the area as well. It's likely that word hasn't reached them about the insurrection yet either, and many of them will probably oppose when Xavson starts announcing his plans."

"What plans?" Agrond interrupted. He didn't know Xavson's motives for usurping the throne. He assumed it was greed for power, but both Trenson and Jayfor talked as if there were something else. "You mean allying Faldon and Elara?"

Jayfor nodded sadly. "Yes. He has abandoned all hope in Faldon and believes that the Shadow is the true power in Ralladin. As a result, he has thrown his lot in with Elara and believes that the only hope for the world is to join the Shadow. He has worked with the

Dark Order to take the throne, and he will continue to work with them until Elara and Faldon are completely unified."

There was a spark in Jayfor's eyes, a look that told of a resolve that would never give up. "I will never let that happen. We will stop it. When I was in Loronis, I swore to return and liberate the people there. I don't make promises in vain."

There was another pause as the two men let the prince's words sink in. Then Agrond broke the silence. "You won't have to do it alone. I am with you, my prince."

"As am I," Trenson said, with determination.

Jayfor looked at the two men. He was walking a dangerous road, standing in between Faldon and Elara. But these men were willing to follow him despite the odds stacked against them. Their support meant more to Jayfor than they knew.

"Thank you. Now, let's get started."

They set out shortly after. As they had all agreed, they were too close to Loronis for comfort. Thankfully, the forest they were in was rather large from what Jayfor said. "Ashdin Woods also borders a few fiefs. If any of these fiefs decide to ally with us, then they will be able to send supplies through the cover of the woods. We'll form a camp farther into the woods."

It was a good plan. Besides, no one was overly eager to leave the woods, anyway. So, they plodded deeper into the wood, not using any roads in fear that they would be discovered. It was safer, but the tangled underbrush, not to mention they were still in armor, made it difficult. Their pace was slow.

Trenson didn't mind, as he followed the group on top of his horse, slightly detached from the others. It gave him a chance to think over everything that had happened, and to think about where he was going now.

It was clear that he had failed. His mission was over. The insurrection had taken place. He traveled all this way for nothing. So many... His jaw tightened in anger. So many people had died. Not just soldiers, but people, innocent people that had nothing to do with what was going on. He could have stopped it. He was so close, arriving just in time to witness it, and help a few people, but that was it. If he had traveled through one more night, urged his horse on just a little faster, then he would have made it. Then Faldon would have been saved. Then his mission would have been completed. Then he would be a hero, someone people would actually look up to.

He failed.

In his anger, Trenson had squeezed the sides of his horse harder with his heels, and the animal had sped up a little ahead of the group. He let off the pressure and returned the animal to its normal gait.

But what could he do about it now? It was in the past. Finished. No amount of wishing or pitying would ever change what had happened. The insurrection had been successful. So? What would he do about it? Return home to nothing but servitude and loneliness?

Trenson looked around him at the group that surrounded him. He had a chance to make things right. All hope was not lost. He had saved the prince of Faldon, and along with a battle commander and a few men, they were going to wage war on the one who had taken the throne. He would not abandon hope now, Trenson resolved. He had come too far to give up now. It was a fool's errand, but if he died trying to reclaim what had been lost because of him, then he would gladly be called a fool.

So it was settled, then. He would stay and help Jayfor and Agrond, no matter the cost. He had nothing to lose, after all.

He would just need to be careful about revealing his past, though. Who knows what they might do if they found out about his former life.

***

They rode through the underbrush in silence. Jayfor and Agrond walked on foot, while Trenson rode on his horse in between them. Behind them followed the rest of their group, knights on foot.

There was nothing really to say. Their next plan of action had been decided, they had discussed all the details of their plan, and all that remained was to ride deeper into the wood until they felt safe enough to set up a more permanent camp.

For the most part of the journey, they kept quiet, listening to the sound of feet landing on grass and Trenson's horse's feet clopping in rhythm. A gentle wind wafted among the trees, and the sun shone briefly in irregular patterns on the ground. It was early in the afternoon. Earlier, the men had found a few berry clusters among the bushes, and they readily ate what they could and grabbed handfuls of what they didn't, eating them as they traveled.

Jayfor frowned as the memory brought up a concern: they would need to find a reliable food source. Berries couldn't nourish a man forever. They could probably set some snares and maybe catch wild game. Still, feeding thirty men would be a challenge with the little resources they had.

That was another reason to join with one of the local fiefs, he thought. They could provide the resources and men. Seeking their help would be the first thing they should do. Jayfor held on to hope that at least one of the fiefs would agree to help them. If they didn't, or if they were sided with Xavson, then their entire mission was over. They would be imprisoned and handed over to Xavson, no doubt.

He told himself, there was no point in thinking about what bad might happen. He needed to say focused on the task ahead. Worrying about all the bad that could happen would only slow them down.

He continued to walk forward, watching his step over old fallen logs and tangled grass. They walked on in silence.

"So, tell me about yourself, Trenson." Agrond's loud voice shattered the silence like a trumpet. Both Jayfor and Trenson jumped with surprise, and Trenson, half asleep in the saddle, almost toppled off his horse. The animal spooked and nickered nervously.

"What?" Trenson said, a little bad tempered. He had been on the verge of sleep, and like a crack of lightning Agrond's voice had ended that hope. He calmed his horse with a reassuring hand.

Agrond, with a ridiculous grin on his face, replied with an ever-present optimism, "I said, tell me about yourself! I know nothing about you other than your name."

Jayfor cringed at the volume at which the battle commander spoke. Apparently, Agrond didn't know when to not speak at the same volume as he did when he was giving orders in battle.

Trenson cleared his throat and didn't seem to know exactly how to answer the question. "I...," he fumbled for words. "I don't know." He eventually replied.

"Oh come on! How can you know nothing about yourself? Where are you from?"

Trenson looked like he would rather be anywhere but here now. "East. I'm from east of here."

"East?" Agrond said, one eyebrow raised. "There isn't much to the east."

"I know," Trenson replied briefly. He didn't follow it up with anything, so it was clear that Trenson had no interest in continuing the conversation.

There was a pause, then Agrond's voice exploded through the air once more. "What town are you from?"

Jayfor grinned at Trenson's discomfort. He felt a little bad for Trenson. In fact, he was thinking about telling the battle commander to leave Trenson alone. But he was bored, and this was interesting, so he decided just to let it happen.

"Marindale. That's what it was called. Marindale." Trenson reluctantly replied.

"Marindale? I've never heard of it! Where is it?"

"East." Trenson made his answer abrupt and somewhat curt in hopes that Agrond would just stop talking.

But his hopes were in vain. "Well, of course it's to the east!"

"Yep." Trenson mumbled, but Agrond wasn't finished.

"Is it far away?"

"What?"

"Marindale!"

"Oh. Yes."

"How far away?

"Five or six weeks."

"Five or six weeks! That's a long time."

"It is."

It was here that Jayfor decided to commented before they got too far off the subject. "You must have had a good reason to come here, seeing as it's so far away."

Almost instantly, Trenson, who had been growing more relaxed as the conversation went on, sat erect and on guard as he whipped his head around to face Jayfor. "Maybe." He said coldly.

Jayfor was surprised at this sudden change in demeanor, and decided it best not to pursue the matter any further. Trenson obviously had no intention of talking, setting his eyes forward as the scowl on his face wore away. Even Agrond was wise enough to keep quiet, and the silence resumed.

What is he hiding? Jayfor wondered.

XVII

"I HAVE NEVER SLEPT better in my life." Jayfor commented as he met with Agrond and Trenson a few mornings later, who were huddled around a tree stump that served as their meeting table. Agrond jokingly referred to it as the "grand hall."

Agrond grinned. "You said the same thing yesterday morning."

Jayfor stretched his arms above his head and yawned heavily. "I barely got any sleep the night before last. I was too worried about Xavson and what might happen if they found us. Now that we've set up a camp farther away, I'm finally able to get some quality sleep."

Agrond nodded knowingly. He had trouble sleeping the other night as well, but used most of the time he was awake, taking watches, letting the other knights get some sleep.

Trenson looked around the camp, although "camp" was a rather generous term. There was nothing here that would signify a camp, no tents or wagons filled with provisions. It was just a group of knights, huddled together in individual small groups, talking and fidgeting with blades of grass or whatever else they had.

Trenson hoped that Jayfor's plan worked, and that they would get some provisions soon. His stomach growled continually. He had picked some berries the other day and, although they were somewhat bitter, he was so hungry he didn't really taste them. But that had hardly been enough. He had already used all the provisions in his pack a few days before he reached the palace, even though he had been rationing them.

"How do the men seem to be doing?" Jayfor asked Agrond, looking in the direction of the twenty or so knights.

"Alright, they say. I spoke to most of them earlier this morning. We have to try to keep their morale up, or else they may become pushy and abandon us. I asked them how they were holding up, and they said fine. I could tell by their looks that they were putting on a brave face, though. They said they were hungry. Water's no problem. There's a clean stream just north of here. It's the food, though." Agrond's voice was serious.

Trenson nodded. "I agree. Unless we find a way to secure reliable rations, we will not last long."

"I know," Jayfor agreed. "Hopefully, that problem will be solved today." He turned to Trenson. "Do you have a map in your satchel?"

Trenson nodded and reached for his satchel, which lay at his side. Extracting the old, weather-worn map, he unraveled it and smoothed it out the best he could on the wooden stump.

Jayfor nodded his thanks and began. "From what I can guess, we are about here." He leaned on his hands on the stump and pointed at the woods that lay beside the capital, close to one of the fiefs that bordered the wood. "I moved us here for a reason. Fort Ronar is just on the opposite side of the woods. It should be no more than half a day's travel to reach it."

"I'm guessing that's where we will try to get help from first?" Trenson said.

"Exactly."

Trenson looked down at the map and frowned. "I thought you said there were more fiefs near the woods."

Jayfor looked puzzled. "I said that there were a few."

"Well, you made it sound like there were more than two, and that's all that I see that border the woods." Trenson was a little crestfallen. He had envisioned having the help of four or five forts to retake the capital. Two seemed like not enough.

"Two will be enough to provide provisions and shelter. Ronar will be our first try in securing help, but if that doesn't work, then there's still Fort Lyson." He pointed to the other castle on the map. "That one is farther away, but still worth a shot. If we can get both castles to ally with us, that would be ideal."

"But is that enough?" Trenson asked, a little doubtful. "We're talking about besieging the one of the largest capitals in the world. Two fiefs, or forts..." he met eyes with Jayfor. "What's the difference?"

"They're basically the same thing," Jayfor explained. "Technically, both castles are fiefs. A fief is a large estate governed by a baron or some other leading noble, and they rule this estate within their castle. It isn't really a city, since it all belongs to the baron and he mostly sets up farms within his dominion, although people are allowed to live on it if they swear service to the baron. It's more complicated than that, but that's a brief idea of what it is. Fort is a vague military term used to describe anywhere castle-like, although there are some actual forts, giant defensive castles, near the borders."

Trenson only understood about half of what Jayfor said, but decided not to question further in the matter. "Two fiefs, then. Anyway, it doesn't seem like enough to me."

"I don't plan to besiege the castle," Jayfor replied. "There are other ways to take over capitals. But just leave that to me. Each fief should have anywhere from one- to three-hundred men-at-arms, give or take. They could also call up men from the countryside to fight as levies."

Agrond cut in. "Calling up men at arms would be risky, though. Like you said, our entire plan revolves around staying secret. If Xavson catches wind of fiefs calling up every man able to fight, then he will probably get suspicious."

"True," Jayfor replied. "If we get to a fief before Xavson's messengers get there, and persuade that barons there."

Trenson pointed at the map and added, "And I'm guessing we will start with Fort Ronar?"

Jayfor yawned massively once again. "That's the plan," he said while yawning, making it almost indiscernible.

Agrond, for once, had a look of doubt. "*Norman* is the baron at Ronar fief," he said, as if it explained it all.

Jayfor blinked. "And?"

"Well..." Agrond pursed his lips. "You know Norman. He is not the bravest or most respected baron, if you know what I mean."

"What's so bad about him?" Trenson asked.

"Well, let's just say he's stingy, weak, and a little timid. More than a little, from what I've heard." Jayfor shrugged. "I've never seen him before in my life. But I have heard talk of him before, and he doesn't seem to be too bad of a fellow. Of course, people say what they want. He may be better than what I've heard."

"I've seen once or twice," Agrond commented. "Mainly when we host a celebration. He doesn't come to many of those, though, and he doesn't really talk to people. Just secludes himself from the others and waits for the last course to be served. Then he leaves."

Jayfor furrowed his brow. "I've been to every one of those harvest festivals before. I've never seen him at any of those."

"I know. That's how long it's been since he came to one." Agrond swatted at a fly that was intent on landing on his forehead.

"In any case," Jayfor continued. "We shouldn't hold a bad opinion of him yet. We'll need to see him for ourselves. We just need to get to him first. If one of Xavson's messengers gets to him first and there is any threating, Norman probably wouldn't think twice about complying."

Trenson nodded. "That makes sense. So, when are we leaving?"

Jayfor smiled. "Why not now?"

***

It was decided that the knights should follow the three, but once they got near the castle, the knights would stay behind. "If we don't return by sunset, then something bad has happened." Jayfor told the knights. "If that happens, *do not* try to come rescue us. You will accomplish nothing and will probably get captured. Stay in the woods and continue the resistance."

Although the knights were a little reluctant, in the end, Jayfor forced them to agree. Secretly, Jayfor was glad they had objected. It showed that they cared about their commanders, and that they were willing to risk capture to save them.

He was surprised at Trenson. Jayfor would have expected the somewhat reclusive man to be met with suspicion by the group. However, Trenson was surprisingly well received by the knights. He even talked to the knights, something Jayfor had a hard time believing. He didn't know what they talked about, which was a little disappointing since Jayfor wondered what Trenson's interests were. If he had any interests.

On the other hand, Agrond was always talking with the men. He seemed to be friends with each and every individual and to remembered everything they ever told him. His loud, sometimes overbearing voice didn't bother them any, and most of the day Agrond was found chatting. Jayfor grinned once when he saw this and thought *he would have made a great nobleman.*

Jayfor's trust in Trenson was growing more each day. It wasn't that the prince suspected him of treachery or anything like that. But he had thought the same about someone else, and it cost him dearly.

They all went on foot. Trenson led his horse by the reins. When Jayfor asked why, Trenson replied that he thought his animal might be tired, since he had been riding him a lot the last few days. Jayfor thought about telling Trenson that the horse looked fine and it would take a lot more riding to wear out a horse like he had, but he figured it was best to keep silent. Trenson probably wouldn't care what he said and would go on walking.

Agrond had fallen behind to talk with the knights as they walked, so it was just Trenson and Jayfor walking together in front of the group.

It was while they were walking that Jayfor noticed that Trenson had a sword on his hip. "You any good with that?" He asked casually, pointing at the sword at Trenson's side.

Trenson looked down and was a little surprised. He had forgotten all about his weapon. "Not really."

"Oh. Is there another weapon that you prefer?"

Trenson nodded. "I'm decent with a quarterstaff."

Jayfor frowned. The quarterstaff was a weapon of brigands and vagabonds, hardly a lethal weapon anyway.

Trenson continued. "I used to have one, but it broke before I got here. So now I'm stuck with this." He motioned to the sword strapped to his belt.

"I see." Jayfor concluded the conversation.

There was a period of silence. The air was warm and breezy, and Jayfor was content enjoying the pleasant atmosphere.

Then, offhandedly, Trenson asked, "Will you teach me to use a sword?"

Jayfor considered the question. He was no teacher, and only a modest swordsman himself. Teaching such a complex skill was a daunting task, not to mention the time and energy it would take. "What makes you think I'm good with one?" He asked.

Trenson didn't know how this wasn't already obvious. "Well, you're a prince, right? Princes use swords and are the best with them. At least that's what I thought."

"Not exactly..." Jayfor let the sentence hang in the air, like he intended to say more, then didn't. He hoped that Trenson would forget about asking about the sword. He wasn't in the mood to teach anyone, especially with all that was at stake. He glanced at Trenson, and saw that he was staring at him expectantly, waiting for an answer. Jayfor sighed. "It's not something that can be taught in one day," he tried to explain. "It will take a lot of time and energy."

"I know." Trenson replied doggedly.

Jayfor sighed again. When Trenson had his mind set on something, there was little use in trying to persuade him otherwise. "Well..." Then he stopped when he looked harder at Trenson's sword. "Where did you get that?" Jayfor's tone was questioned.

Trenson realized that he would need to think up a story, fast. He couldn't just tell the prince of Faldon he burned an inn down. He planned to keep the event a secret from everyone, anyway. How else could he have gotten a sword? "I found it." He finally said.

"Found it?" Jayfor repeated.

Trenson, although nodding convincingly, was inwardly kicking himself. *'Found it'? When does anyone just 'find' a sword?*

"Where did you find it?" Jayfor continued his interrogation. There was still an edge of suspicion in his voice. Trenson guessed that he recognized the sword as belonging to the peacekeeper order.

"On the road." Once again, as soon as the excuse left his mouth, Trenson cringed at how terrible it really was.

"On the road?"

"Yes, on the road." Trenson hoped he looked convincing.

"You saw a sword just lying in the middle of the road?"

Trenson nodded. He knew that if he didn't say anything, no more terrible excuses could come out.

"In broad daylight?" Jayfor obviously wasn't convinced.

"Yes, in broad daylight." Trenson kept his eyes locked ahead and didn't risk a glance at the prince.

"So you are walking down the road, in broad daylight, and see a sword lying right in the middle of it, and you pick it up and leave? You just took it?"

"Yep."

"You didn't try to find out who it belonged to?"

"I didn't know where to start!"

"Huh."

At last, Jayfor stopped his questioning and shrugged, deciding that it would be of no use to ask anything else, much to Trenson's delight. They kept walking. A bird called in the distance, chorusing a series of high notes before descending into a series of low notes. It was answered in the distance by another bird, who made a similar call.

"The thing is, that sword looks a lot like a peacekeeper's sword."

Trenson didn't know it, but Jayfor was messing with him. The prince was bored, and decided to see how much the broody man could endure. He didn't mean any harm. He had done it with his brothers at the palace. It was simply friendly badgering.

What Jayfor didn't know, however, is that Trenson didn't see it that way. "It does." Trenson replied. It was easy to say through clenched teeth.

"Maybe it is one."

"Perhaps."

There was another period of silence. Trenson finally thought that he might be able to enjoy the day without Jayfor's infuriating badgering.

"So, where were you when you found it?"

It was too much. "I don't care!" He exploded. "Why do you care so much about it?! *It's a sword! It cuts things!* What more do you want to know?"

Trenson nearly lost control of his horse, as the animal was spooked by his master's sudden outburst. Jayfor reeled back in surprise, and even some of the knights behind them snapped their heads in their direction to see what the loud noise was coming from.

His face red from rage, Trenson glared at Jayfor as if daring him to keep at it. Jayfor put both his hands up in a defenseless gesture. "OK, OK! You win! I'll stop now." *Now I know not to push Mister dark and broody too far.* He couldn't help but smiling. It was certainly entertaining, he had to admit, to see Trenson go berserk.

Trenson took a deep breath, either from relief or to calm himself, or both. "Thank you," he said. There was another period of silence, then Trenson asked, "So, will you?"

Jayfor turned towards him with an innocent expression. "Will I what?"

Trenson's anger started to resurface. "Will you train me to use this sword?!"

Jayfor chuckled. "Alright." What harm could it do? Sure, it would take time and energy, but it would be an effective way to train and spend time at once. Plus, after what he put Trenson through to get his answer, he earned it. "I'll try. Just a warning, I'm not the best, but when we have time, I'll show you what I know." Then he grinned and decided to try one last jest. "Why didn't you just say so?"

Trenson didn't think it was very funny.

XVIII

"SO THAT'S THE CASTLE," Trenson said, a hint of awe in his voice.

Jayfor nodded, gazing in the same direction as Trenson. "Yes, it is. Is it smaller than you thought?"

Jayfor was used to massive castles and lavish exteriors. He had grown up in one of the largest and richest capitals of the world and was used to the fanciful and majestic structures of the city. This particular one didn't bring out any feelings of awe or majesty. In fact, Jayfor was a little disappointed. This castle seemed small to him. He was hoping for something bigger, more like what he had at home.

For Trenson, however, the castle was enormous. Tall gray walls, made of stone mortared together, towered over the landscape. It was situated on a hill, making it seem even taller and more impenetrable. The afternoon sun streamed down on the fortification, causing large shadows to stream down from its sides. Trenson had only ever seen Loronis from the outside, and yes, the walls of the capital were much more formidable than these. But Trenson was still amazed by the sheer height and structure of the defensives.

Trenson shook his head but didn't say anything. He was too busy admiring the mighty castle.

"It's a standard castle, not much more." Agrond commented.

"It's technically not a castle," Jayfor put in with his dignified tone. "It's a manor, strictly speaking. It doesn't look like a manor, but that's what it's called, along with fief. In fact, "fief" is technically a term used to describe land. It is common speech, however, even among the nobles to call the castle or manor that the baron lives in a fief. The baron is also sometimes called the lord of the manor. It started out that barons and the leaders of the area lived in real manors. But with raids from brigands somewhat common, they kept fortifying their residence until now a fief is really no different from a castle. There are a few differences, though, as a fief usually doesn't have a moat. In fact—"

"Well, that's very interesting, but I really think we should get going," Trenson interrupted. He was becoming tired of Jayfor's going into great depths into subjects, so much that it was annoying, at least for him. He wondered if all nobles were like this, extremely talkative and informative. He hoped not.

Jayfor was a little taken aback from the interruption, and opened his mouth to say something, but then thought better of it and closed it.

"Yes!" Agrond chorused. "Food soon!"

***

"I'll do most of the talking," Jayfor said quietly to Agrond and Trenson as they neared the castle. Fief, Trenson corrected in his mind. Or manor.

Trenson and Agrond nodded, knowing that the prince was much more skilled at handling diplomatic matters than they were. If anyone was to convince the baron of their cause, it would be Jayfor.

They were near the front gate of the fief now. Two guards stood on each side of the lowered cross-barred gate. They had been reclining against the stone walls, with their spears propped on the ramparts, until they caught sight of the three figures coming towards them, at which they hastily grabbed their weapons and stood erect and ready at their posts. They left their visors up to take a better look at these newcomers.

"State your business, sirs," the one on the right of the gate said.

All three of the men were dirty and ragged. One was tall and in full armor. Another was grim faced and had a look of trouble about him. The one in the middle of the two was shorter but carried himself with confidence and somehow seemed to have an air of authority. The guard frowned. None of these characters looked to be law-abiding citizens.

"We are here to speak with baron Norman. Urgent business." The shorter one said.

The guard on the right pursed his lips thoughtfully. He felt like he had seen the shorter one somewhere before. "The baron is busy. He cannot receive you."

It was the usual response to said, even if they had no idea what the baron was doing, such as right now. They were instructed to give this response to anyone they didn't recognize, or that looked suspicious. And all three of these men fit the criteria well.

The shorter one, who seemed to be the leader, looked surprised, as if the guards should not have thought twice about letting them in. "He cannot receive me?" he said.

"No," the guard replied, unflinching. "The baron has many matters on his hands at present. Leave, now."

"The baron is always 'busy.' Busy doing what? Fingering his coins and hiding from everyone that scares him?"

Both guards were startled by this response. Everyone else they warned to go away usually left quickly, but not this rough-looking man, who instead insulted the baron in reply. The guards stepped forward. "Watch your tongue! Brazen language towards the baron is punishable!"

"Leave, now!" The other soldier pointed his spear steadily at the one who had spoken.

The other two men took a few steps back, confused looks on their faces. They glanced at their leader, who gazed defiantly at the soldiers. In fact, much to the soldier's frustration, he seemed amused. "I have no intention of leaving. I will see Norman now, whether you like it or not."

The soldier on the left raised the backside of his spear to strike down on the young scoundrel. "I'll teach you!"

"You would dare attack a prince?" the young rogue said loudly.

Both knights froze, the spear suspended in midair. They stared at Jayfor, squinting and furrowing their brows. A second went by. Then another.

Suddenly, the soldier who was about to strike the young man gasped. He dropped his spear and stumbled backwards. "Prince Jayfor!"

The other knight quickly realized who it was as well. His eyes widened in fear. He had just insulted and almost hurt the prince of Faldon! Both knights fell to their knees, their heads bowed so low that they almost touched the ground.

"Forgive us!" One guard said, in a voice so filled with fear it sounded like a squeak.

Jayfor chuckled, clearly amused at the soldier's sudden change in behavior. "I will, on one condition."

"Yes, anything!" the soldiers both said in unison.

"May I please see the baron now?"

***

The large wooden doors made no sound as they opened, revealing Norman's office as Trenson, Jayfor and Agrond were ushered into the room. Trenson took note of the interior. On the left wall were a few large glass panes that stretched from the floor to the roof, allowing ample sunlight to shine in.

At the other end of the room, sitting behind a desk and looking intently at some papers in his hands with hand-held glasses, was the man who Trenson guessed was Norman. As Trenson, Jayfor and Agrond came towards him, their footsteps echoing on the hardwood floor, Norman looked up. Seeing the three visitors, he quickly shoved the glasses and the papers he was looking at into a drawer in the desk. He stood up to receive his guests, wringing his hands nervously.

In truth, Trenson was shocked. When he had heard earlier Jayfor and Agrond talk about some traits of the baron, Trenson could picture the baron perfectly: small, slightly hunched-over, elderly, bald except for a few wisps of white hair, wrinkled and with a crooked nose...

What Norman actually looked like, however, was completely the opposite. Norman was tall and broad, sitting straight, middle-aged, square chinned, and had the appearance of a warrior.

This man could be a great fighter, Trenson thought. It was obvious, though, that Norman rarely went outside. His height and build were right to be a knight, but his skin was a little pale, and his slightly rounded belly testified to lack of exercise.

Norman's eyes darted to each one of his visitors as they approached his desk, his hands still rubbing together.

"Welcome, welcome... it is an honor to have you here, your highness. Although, I must say, your arrival is unexpected." Norman's voice was slightly deeper than Trenson guessed it would be and held a note of nervousness. He motioned for them to sit down in the chairs before the desk, which they all did. Jayfor sat directly in front of the baron.

"Yes, I apologize for the lack of precedence," Jayfor replied, trying to sound as diplomatic as he could. "Had I the means, I would have warned you ahead of time."

Norman nodded quickly. "Well, you're here now. Please tell me, to what do I own of the honor of your presence here?" Having never truly met the prince in person, Norman was a little unsure of how he was expected to act. And the fact that Jayfor had arrived so abruptly and so dirty, with only two rough-looking men as company, made him even more sure that something was off.

Jayfor's eyes stared steadily into Norman's, his face showing no emotion, which was how he was taught to look when negotiating. "Have you not heard of what transpired at Loronis?" It was the moment of truth, to see if Norman had heard of the news and had aligned himself with Xavson.

To everyone's relief, Norman shook his head. "I have not heard anything. Has something happened?" Norman's nervousness was getting worse, and his hands started rubbing together again.

Jayfor took a deep breath. Trenson knew it going to be painful to retell all that had happened. "Well…" and Jayfor told him everything. Every event that had led up to the insurrection. His father poisoned at the defense council, his confrontation with Xavson and learning about what his brother had done and what he planned to do, Xavson's murder of Annor, the revolt and chaos they had left Loronis in, and his escape with help from Agrond and Trenson.

Trenson listened intently as Jayfor told his story. He knew most of the details, but some small points were unknown to him. Trenson couldn't imagine how much it must have hurt to recount such events again. Jayfor choked up a little at some parts, and his eyes were misty when he told of how Xavson had killed Annor, but he held himself up as best he could.

Trenson watched as the baron gasped at each detail, his face turning ashen as the story went on. Norman remained silent while Jayfor related of what had happened, but Trenson could tell that the baron was greatly disturbed. Inwardly, and a little surprisingly,

Trenson was relieved. If the baron thought what had happened was terrible, he reasoned, then he was more likely to join their cause.

Jayfor finished his retelling and leaned back in his chair, sweat building on his forehead. It had taken some time to tell Norman everything. He waited for a response from the baron.

At first, Norman did nothing. His features remained the same as when Jayfor was telling the story, his face as white and his eyes staring into the distance. After a few seconds he seemed to regain himself and, methodically, he opened a drawer in his desk and pulled out a small wooden box and set it on the desktop. He hastily closed the drawer and opened the lid, revealing a pile of small, pink sugar-coated candies. Norman grabbed a handful and shoved it into his mouth, chewing loudly. He didn't offer them any.

Jayfor glanced skeptically at Agrond, one eyebrow raised. Agrond shrugged in return.

Thankfully, Norman seemed to calm down from the candies. He swallowed slowly. "You shouldn't scare a man like that, your highness. With all those awful details, and you didn't slow down one bit for me to take it in! It's not good for my health."

Just like those candies, thought Trenson. Norman popped another handful into his mouth. This was apparently what the baron did when he was nervous. It explained the belly.

Annoyed by Norman's weak heart, Jayfor's voice held a hint of impatience. "I didn't come here to lament over the past, Norman. I came here to organize an army to oppose Xavson." He stopped to let his words sink in.

The candies seemed to give Norman extra strength, and he nodded. "I supposed that was why you were here." After shoveling another handful into his mouth, Norman talked around the sweets. "What would you have me do?" Spit flew across the table as he spoke.

Not exactly an ideal baron, Trenson thought, *but better than nothing.*

Jayfor was doing his best to put aside Norman's irritating habits. "We don't ask much. As I told you, we have about thirty men strong with us. We need food and shelter for now, but we need you to keep your men at the ready as well. When the time is right, we will send word to you to call upon all men at arms that you have. With the support of others, we will march our troops into Loronis and, with a plan that I have in mind, we'll retake the capital, and Faldon will be free." Jayfor gave a somewhat pleading look at Norman. "That is, if you'll join us."

It seemed like a long time before Norman responded, when in reality, Trenson thought, it had to have been only a few seconds. Norman nodded. "Yes, I will join you."

Trenson, Agrond and Jayfor couldn't help but feel relieved.

"Xavson will only continue to grow stronger," Norman continued. "If he indeed unites Faldon and Elara, then the world will face more turmoil and evil than ever before. That is not a world I want to live in."

Jayfor couldn't hide the smile that crept over his face at the baron's decision to join them. "Thank you. It is good to know that there are at least some good men we can trust."

Norman absently reached his hand into the box of candies, then frowned as he realized that the box was empty. Inwardly, Jayfor was glad. Finally, maybe Norman would stop with the nervous habits and start talking like a man. It was vain hope, however. Norman reached into his desk drawers and pulled out yet another identical box, with identical candies, and set it out on the table, removing the old one and placing it in a different drawer. He popped another handful of sweets into his mouth. Once again, Norman didn't offer them any.

"So, what will we do next?" Norman asked, his courage seeming to build as the conversation continued.

"Well, that depends. How many men do you have?" Jayfor asked.

Norman reached into a drawer in his desk and pulled out a thick parchment, rolled into a tight cylinder. He hastily unrolled it, and his eyes scanned the page. "Ronar has about seventy soldiers at the ready here in this fief, and among the villages and towns under its jurisdiction, about two hundred and fifty men fit for service and ready to be called up."

Jayfor did the math in his head. Three hundred and twenty men were an able force. If the other fort that he planned to try next had around the same amount, then they should have six hundred and forty. That was a good number. He searched his mind for anything he could remember about military strategy from the capital. He had never thought then that he would be using it against his own brother. "That's more than I expected. That will be a great help."

Norman placed the scroll back in the drawer and slid it shut, and reached for another handful of sweets. Halfway through reaching his hand in, he seemed to remember his guests, and tilted the box towards them in an offering gesture. Jayfor and Agrond both declined, but Trenson nodded eagerly, and grabbed one of the square candies. He popped it into his mouth, then immediately wished he hadn't. The sweetness and explosion of sour was beyond anything that he had ever imagined, and he couldn't help his lips from puckering. Thankfully, Norman didn't seem to notice, and mindlessly shoveled more into his mouth.

"We will need to procure more men before we attempt our attack. I have a feeling that baron Randolph will be as equally sympathetic to our cause." Jayfor was juggling numbers and resources and other probabilities in his head. "If we take that into account, then we should have an ample force to assail Faldon."

Norman raised one eyebrow doubtfully. "One of the greatest capitals of the world, and you plan to take it over with merely six hundred men? It seems a little... too little, in my opinion."

"It's actually not, if you think about it," Jayfor explained. Trenson rolled his eyes, knowing that Jayfor was about to go on another one of his tangents. "Everyone thinks that Faldon always has a massive standing army, whether in war or peace. But to pay and maintain all those thousands of troops, for so long a time? It is better to simply call upon men in the area as levies when the time comes than to hold them for months. So Loronis doesn't have a very large guard force because there is no war nearby at the moment. We also sent most of our troops to the front lines against Elara, reducing their number even more. On top of that, many soldiers deserted or fought back when they heard that Xavson had usurped the throne. This all means that Loronis is weak, and the sooner we strike while it is that way, the better."

"That makes sense," Norman said.

Jayfor shrugged. "I prefer to be that way when I can." He shifted uncomfortably in his seat. The chairs really needed to be more comfortable.

Norman seemed to grasp what Jayfor was getting at. "So you want me to call upon all the levies, and send them to you in the woods, along with a weekly round of supplies?"

"No! Well, yes to the supplies part," Jayfor corrected. "But not to the men part. Keep your levies on hand and be ready to call them up when the time is ready. I will let you know when that is."

Norman's brows knitted together, clearly not understanding.

Jayfor inwardly sighed. *Must I explain everything?* "Xavson is going to be watching for me and for any signs of rebellion like a hawk. If most of the levies and soldiers in your area suddenly vanish, what do you think he will do? He will ask you what has happened to them all, and will begin investigating. After that, it's only a matter of time before they find us. Keep your men here, but call upon them when I give the word."

"I see," Norman responded. "But what am I to do if Xavson or one of his men come here and ask questions?"

"Then you lie to them."

"Me?!" The baron's timidness and frightened state was beginning to return. "I can't lie!"

Jayfor shrugged. "Unless you wish to be killed as a traitor in Xavson's eyes, then you better learn."

Norman gulped.

"Anyway, we are camped in the Ashdin woods, and shouldn't be too hard to find. We need shelters and provisions as soon as possible and will need provisions weekly. I will send word when the time is right for you to call up your levies. Until then, everything we do must be kept secret." Jayfor stared hard at Norman. "Can you do that?"

Norman gave a weak nod, which Jayfor had no choice but to be content with.

Suddenly, there was an anxious rapping on the door. Norman frowned. "Yes?"

The same servant who had led Trenson, Agrond and Jayfor into Norman's office now pushed the door barely open, and poked his head through the crack, a worried expression on his face. "My lord, a messenger from Loronis has arrived. He says he is sent by 'king Xavson.' "

XIX

Norman's face turned white once again. "No! It can't be! I mean, send him away. Tell him I'm gone!"

"He is right behind me, my lord," the servant replied.

Aghast, Norman opened his mouth to say something, then shut it. His face contorted with fear, he looked at Jayfor for an answer.

Jayfor was no calmer than Norman. "Well?" he whispered urgently. "Tell him you are not ready to receive him, or something!"

Norman looked back at the servant. "You are not ready to receive me, or something! Wait, no! I mean, I am not ready to receive him. Tell him to wait!"

The servant was even more confused now, but he knew better than to ask questions and closed the door.

"We need to get out of here!" Agrond whispered frantically, although Agrond didn't whisper very quietly. "Now!"

Trenson glanced around the room to see if there was any visible escape route, but nothing that he saw offered any hiding place or way out. *This is bad. Really bad.*

"Is there a way out?" Agrond asked.

Norman, lips pursed together in fear, nodded and pointed at the front door behind them.

"Not that way!" Agrond yelled, evidently angry. "I meant is there another way out?"

Unfortunately, he was a little too loud. "Norman!" A new voice said from the other side of the door. "Who are you talking to?"

The baron's face was shaky. "N-No one! Nobody's here! Please wait!" He grabbed another handful of candies and shoved them into his mouth.

All four of the men had risen to their feet. "Do the windows open?" Trenson asked frantically.

Norman shook his head. Sweat poured profoundly down his face.

"Where else can we go?" Jayfor whispered desperately, "There's nowhere!"

An idea suddenly struck Trenson. It was a terrible one, but those were the only types of ideas left. "What about behind the desk?" He gestured to the desk Norman was sitting behind. Under the desktop, there was the open area where your legs went. But on either side was a column of drawers. They might be enough room to hide behind.

Jayfor looked at him sideways and was about to say something when a different voice cut him off. "Norman! Open this door!"

Jayfor realized it was there only option. He nodded to Trenson and ran around the desk, crouching down behind the drawers, hopefully out of view from in front. Trenson followed beside him. Agrond hid behind the other column, since he was too big to be on the same side as them.

Trenson looked up and saw Norman, exasperated, staring down at him. "What do I do?"

"Anything!" Trenson responded quickly. "Just don't tell him we're here!"

Norman gave a weak nod, cleared his throat, and tried to appear as normal as he could. He yelled in the direction of the door, with a none too confident voice, "You may come in now."

Almost instantly, the doors of office opened, then quickly shut. Then Trenson heard footsteps, hard, arrogant steps that clacked each time they hit the ground. He must be wearing riding boots, Trenson thought. He wanted to chance a glance at the messenger, but he didn't dare.

"Took you long enough." The tone clearly showed the speaker's annoyance and arrogance.

Trenson looked up and saw Norman's face, panic-stricken and white, simply nodding very quickly up and down. The ambassador must be intimidating, Trenson thought. Of course, he reminded himself, it took very little to intimidate Norman. Unconsciously, Norman reached his hand into the box of candies and piled more into his mouth, smacking loudly as he chewed. Jayfor muttered something under his breath.

"I-I apologize," Norman said, a mouth full of sweets, but his voice still quivering with fear. "I——my office was too messy to receive you. Yes, that's why."

He really is *bad at lying.*

"Too messy, eh?" The messenger's tone was smooth and cold. It sounded as though he knew exactly what he was hiding.

Norman swallowed and nodded. "Yes. Well, it's clean now, so all's well." Jayfor frowned when he realized that the baron's desk *wasn't* clean. Papers and inkwells were scattered broadly across the table's surface. Jayfor desperately hoped that the messenger was gullible.

The next words shattered his hopes. "I don't give a beggar's scraps what your office looks like."

Norman swallowed again. "Yes, o-of course."

Trenson stole a look at Agrond and was somewhat encouraged by the fact that the burly battle commander appeared as uncomfortable as he was. Cold sweat built on Trenson's forehead.

"Who were you talking to?" The messenger's voice demanded.

Jayfor analyzed the voice. He knew many of the couriers at the palace, and could immediately tell that whoever had just come into Norman's office was not one of them. It must be someone new, he concluded. We wouldn't hire ambassadors like that. Xavson must already be replacing the men with his own cronies.

Norman did his best to feign surprise. "Me? I wasn't talking to anyone! No, not me. I don't enjoy talking to anyone, especially not fugitives. No, even if prince Jayfor himself came in here, I wouldn't say a word."

The three fugitives behind the desk unanimously cringed.

"Prince Jayfor?" The messenger repeated. "So, you know of Jayfor and Annor's plot to kill Xavson?"

Jayfor's jaw tightened. So, this was the lie Xavson had cooked up to hide the truth. Not a very good one, he had to say.

"Y-yes, I have heard."

"Good. It will make my work here shorter."

Trenson heard the heavy clanking of footsteps again. For a second, he thought that maybe the messenger was finally leaving.

Then a shadow suddenly fell on his him, and when he turned to see what caused it, he froze.

As he had noted earlier, large windows stood at intervals along the walls, stretching from the floor to the roof. One of these windows was right behind where Jayfor, Trenson and Agrond were hiding, perpendicular to the back of the desk.

And, for some unexplainable reason, the messenger decided to walk and stand right in front of that window.

Please don't turn around. Please, please don't turn around. Trenson, Agrond and Norman shot a look at Jayfor that said, "What now?" but Jayfor motioned for them to be quiet.

The courier continued looking out the roof-to-floor window, totally oblivious that the prince of Faldon was crouching right behind him. "King Xavson is a wise king. He has already proved that in the past few days, and hopes for the cooperation of all the barons to make his visions of restoring peace come to fruition..."

As the messenger rambled on about politics and "Xavson's visions," the four men behind him all looked at each other desperately. They were trapped. When the courier stopped looking out the window and turned around, they would be caught, and execution was imminent.

Jayfor held one finger to his lips and, to Trenson's amazement, silently, never taking his gaze off the messenger, slowly stood up. Trenson shot him a crazed look and mouthed, "What are you doing?" Jayfor merely motioned for him to be quiet and follow him.

Trenson shot a glance at Agrond that said, "He's crazy." Agrond shrugged and started to stand up as well, watching Jayfor to see what he did next. Trenson had no choice but to follow his comrades, so he sighed and stood up as well.

Very quietly, Jayfor made his way around the edge of the desk and towards the door. Trenson and Agrond did the same, testing each step and shooting fearful glances at the messenger, who seemed quite occupied.

"... Because king Xavson is wiser than any previous king, he takes steps to ensure that the alliances with Elara will benefit everyone. You have no reason to fear in putting your hopes in with his..."

Norman looked like he wanted to get up and follow the three men out of the room as well, but knew better. Instead, he motioned for them to hurry.

They were halfway to the door now. Trenson knew that they were still in danger. All it would take was the courier turning around, and that was it.

Closer...

"... Of course, no matter what the barons, yourself included, think of the king's ambitions, he will achieve his goal, nonetheless. Although, I must add, not agreeing with king Xavson is the mark of treason and shall be met with appropriate measures..."

Closer...

"But with everyone's support, it shall be far easier."

Finally! They were at the door. Jayfor grasped the handle and pulled the door open slowly. Thankfully, it made no sound. It seemed like they would make it after all. He held the door open just enough for them to get through and motioned for them to go ahead.

"In short, I came here to determine one thing: will you support the king in his quest for unity, or will you refuse and be delt with?"

The messenger looked like he was about to turn around. Norman looked at Jayfor out of the corner of his eye, and the prince gesture for him to respond. "Y-yes, of course," Norman stammered. "I support the king."

Trenson and Agrond made it through the door and breathed a huge sigh of relief. Jayfor slipped through the opening and turned around to shut the door, hearing the messenger reply, "Good."

He shut the door. A little too loudly.

"What was that?" The muffled voice of the courier came through the closed doors.

They never heard what Norman's reply was, for they took off, hearts pounding in their ears down the stairs. Almost tumbling down as they went; they brushed past confused servants but didn't stop. They couldn't get away fast enough.

XX

"That was close," Agrond gasped when they stopped at the border of the Ashdin Woods.

Jayfor, his hands on his knees and red in the face, looked up at Agrond. "Yes," he panted. For once, he didn't launch into a long analysis of the events. "Yes, it was."

Trenson looked at each of the men with an eyebrow raised. He didn't feel tired at all. It wasn't a long distance they had run. If fact, it felt good to run a little. They had simply dashed out of the castle, out of the gate, and a short distance into the woods. Trenson would prefer to keep running but had stopped when he saw the other two stop. They both looked like they were about to throw up.

"It wasn't that far," Trenson commented, a note of judgment in his voice.

Jayfor, wheezing, shot Trenson a dubious look. "Easy for you to say."

Agrond sank to the ground and sprawled out, his breathing sounding like a bear.

Trenson crossed his arms impatiently. A battle commander and a prince ought to be a little more fit. It wasn't even that far. He looked back over at the castle and noticed that it was a little speck in the distance. OK, maybe a little far. Still.

Seeing Trenson's impatience, Jayfor said, "We'll move again. Right after a short break."

***

The "short break" turned out to not be so short, but eventually they made it back to the group of knights, who were eagerly awaiting their return. When they caught sight of the three figures, they quickly gathered in front of Jayfor and waited to hear the news.

"Well, what is the baron's decision?" asked one of the knights. The soldiers all fixed their gaze on Jayfor, knowing that the baron's decision would alter their situation dramatically.

Jayfor cleared his throat. "He said," he spoke loudly so everyone could hear, "that he will aid us."

A joyful cheer erupted from the group. Jayfor smiled as he watched the newfound spirit in his men. Of course, the men's main reason for being so merry was because of the guaranteed food, but that wasn't any reason not to be happy. The men would need light hearts for the days ahead.

Eventually, the cheering subsided, and Jayfor rose his voice once again. "Yes, this is great news. With Norman's aid, our forces will improve and become stronger; a force to reckon with!"

Another cheer of approval rose from the knights. Agrond leaned over to Trenson and whispered, "He's giving the troops some morale. It's important to keep our spirits up. Many battles are fought and won not by the biggest army, but by the one with the most morale."

Trenson nodded, then returned his attention to Jayfor, waiting to see what he would say next.

"With the supplies and information Norman provides, no longer will we be just an insignificant pest to Xavson. We will join with others who oppose Xavson's made quest for uniting Faldon and Elara. If he succeeds, all of Ralladin will be plagued into an age of darkness, one that will be unparallel to anything the world has seen.

But I know that, if we band together and never give up, we can stop him. Together, we can make sure that the kingdom we have protected for so long will not fall.

"So, I ask you: join with me in my fight against the forces of evil! Together, nothing will stop us! We will not lose!"

The roar of approval that resounded around the woods was deafening. It sounded as though there were a hundred men rather than thirty. High did they raise their weapons. "For freedom!" they cried.

Trenson watched the newfound courage in the men with amazement, and for the first time, he started to see how respectable of a leader Jayfor really was.

"That was quite a speech, Jayfor." Agrond commented a little while later.

Jayfor shrugged. "It was nothing. I simply used the moment to encourage the men. I don't want them to feel like we care nothing about them except their ability to fight."

Trenson asked, "Do you really think that we can we win?"

Both Agrond and Jayfor's heads swiveled in his direction. Trenson felt like he may have asked the wrong question. "I mean," he continued, "we don't have many men or resources, and we're up against the largest capital in the world…" His words drifted off, but it was clear what his point was.

"It's true. We may not have as many men and resources as Xavson. But that doesn't mean we can't win." Jayfor smiled encouragingly.

"For sure," Agrond agreed. "With Va'ar on our side, we have nothing to fear."

Va'ar? Trenson thought. Was this some ally they had that he didn't know about? "Va'ar?" he voiced his question out loud.

Agrond's eyes widened in surprise. "You mean you don't know who Va'ar is?" Jayfor looked just as shocked. Trenson shook his head, a blank expression on his face. Agrond and Jayfor looked at each other hesitantly. "You really don't know?" Jayfor asked.

A second time, Trenson shook his head. "Who is he?" he asked.

Jayfor inhaled and exhaled forcefully and glanced over at Agrond. The battle commander's expression said, "go ahead." Jayfor looked back at Trenson.

"Va'ar is… He made… Well, He's not a person, but…" for once, Jayfor didn't know what to say. Trenson was surprised. There must be something different about this Va'ar character for Jayfor to get so tongue tied. He glanced at Agrond, but he simply held up his hand in a gesture of patience.

After a short pause, Jayfor finally seemed to find a way to explain. "Va'ar is not really a person, at least not like you and me." He paused again; his lips pursed with the effort of thinking how to explain.

"What is he, then?" Trenson asked to push Jayfor on. "Is he an animal?"

"What?! No, no! Of course not!" Jayfor said hastily. "He is... well, he just *is*. He is an all-powerful, all-existing being. He cannot be seen or heard, but he is everywhere and knows everything." He looked at Trenson and shrugged. "I don't know how to explain it. Do you understand what I'm saying?"

Trenson shook his head. "Not really."

Agrond grinned. "I don't think anyone fully understands who and what Va'ar is. He prefers to be that way, I think."

Trenson thought hard about what Jayfor had told him. "So Va'ar is someone who has lots of power and knows everything?"

"Not really a 'someone', like you're thinking of it." The more Jayfor talked about it, the more confidence he had. "He is a being. What's the difference between a being and a person? Well, for one, a person is three-dimensional. I can tell you don't know what that means. It basically means that you are present here and now. You are nowhere else at this moment –— you will always be right where you are. Va'ar isn't limited by a physical body, though I suppose he could have one if he wanted, and so is everywhere at the same time. He is also in the future and in the past." He slowly trailed off when he saw that Trenson had no grasp of what he was saying.

Trenson felt bad. Jayfor was trying so hard to explain, but he didn't get any of it. "I still don't get it," he stated bluntly. Jayfor hadn't been wrong about anything yet, but this idea of a 'being' that was everywhere and could do anything seemed a little far-fetched.

Jayfor sighed. Agrond chuckled a little. "Hey, don't feel bad, Jayfor. You've been taught what Va'ar is your entire life. It makes sense that Trenson has apprehensions." He returned his eyes to Trenson. "It's hard to explain, but it's true. Leastways, I believe it. Many don't, but I don't care what they think. What most people believe does not make what they believe true. I think that's one reason we are losing this war, because we have lost our trust in the King who founded us."

Trenson's head was almost spinning from everything he was trying to take in. "Wait, wait," he held his hands up in a halting gesture. "I still don't really understand."

Agrond, and ever-present grin on his face, glanced at Jayfor. "I think we should start at the beginning."

Jayfor nodded. "That's probably a good idea." Trenson waited eagerly for what they were going to say. Maybe it would make sense and not be just some crazy belief.

"It's a long story," Jayfor began, slowly, "but I'll try to make it quick. In the beginning, before anything was made, there was only Va'ar. There was no land, no sea, no trees or animals, no wars or kingdoms. It was just blackness. Or I think that's how it was. Anyway, the only thing in this blackness is Va'ar, who, as I tried to explain earlier, is an all-powerful 'being' who is everywhere and knows everything. He didn't plan to leave the emptiness be empty.

"So he made the world. He made everything that you see now, all the life, all the flowers and plants, all the oceans and water, all the animals, he made it all. And he made people as the last and best part of his creation, but he made them differently. He gave them The Breath, which, from what I understand it to be, is free will and a spirit. So, he made everything that you see. It was all perfect.

"But Va'ar also made another place. Far, far away to the west, so far that if traveled for hundreds of years you would never reach it, across the sea, is Va'ar's kingdom where he lives. He made similar things there as he did on Ralladin, but this was His kingdom, and so he made a grand palace for Himself to reside in, even though he is already everywhere, and he also made a group of elite warriors that have His power in them, called the Senver. They have extra-ordinary abilities and swords of light and fight for Va'ar.

"And everyone that dies on Ralladin that believed and served Va'ar will go to this place, and live on the land eternally, because unlike our world, His kingdom is still perfect, and those who die and go there will live there in Va'ar's glory and be happy forever. Of course, in those days, the world was perfect, so they didn't need to worry about death. They didn't even know what it was.

"But anyway, so Va'ar made Ralladin and His kingdom. Back then, Ralladin had one big kingdom, divided into three regions: Kallary, Faldon, and Elara." Jayfor saw a faint glow of understand-ing in Trenson's eyes. "You see how this is going, don't you?"

Trenson nodded, but remained silent.

"Well, everything was fine, until one of the Senver got thirsty for power. There was a mountain to the east in Elara, called the Mountain of Power. There were two large doors that stood in front of the mountain. Va'ar warned everyone that if they opened the gates to the mountain, then they would know good and evil, but would also die. This Senver convinced the king of the Empire of

Ralladin to open the gates, telling him the Va'ar was trying to keep them from becoming too powerful. In the end, the king opened the gate.

"And that's when the perfect world ended. The rest of the story you can probably guess: Each of the three regions split off and waged war with the other. The Senver who convinced the king to open the gate became the Lord of the Land of Shadow, and his dark knights, who are other Senver who joined him, obey him and rule of Elara.

"And since then, we have been at war for almost three-hundred years, and we're losing." He shot Trenson a fake smile. "Not really a good 'happily ever after' story, is it?"

"Aye," Agrond said. "But this is no fairy tale." Jayfor crossed his arms and shrugged.

Trenson pondered over what he had just heard. It was... well, it was a little bizarre and fanciful. It sounded like a children's tale. "Do you know for sure if this story is true?" he asked both Agrond and Jayfor.

Agrond replied first. "I know it is. After all, it explains everything about the world perfectly."

Jayfor was silent for a few moments, and when he noticed that both Agrond and Trenson were waiting for him to reply, he shrugged again nonchalantly. "It's a story. Who's to say whether it's true or not?" Noticing Agrond's face clouding, he continued in a matter-of-factly tone. "It happened hundreds of years ago. No one can be certain about anything that happened that long ago. It may be true, but I guess we'll never know."

After he finished, an uncomfortable silence blanketed itself over the three men. None of them said anything. Trenson was going over the story in his head, then inwardly shrugged. It didn't matter too much whether he thought the story was true or not. How would it affect anything about life? Nothing would change. He sided with Jayfor in that it wasn't really that important. He would decide whether or not it was true later.

Jayfor broke the silence, his pleasant demeanor returning. "Well, I guess there's no use talking about it further." He rubbed his hands together. "Grab your sword, Trenson. Let's see how good you really are with that thing."

***

After grabbing their swords, Jayfor and Trenson found a small open area, free of trees, a little way from the camp. It was large enough for them to practice with ample room, but still close enough to the other trees to provide them with shade. And with the weather becoming warmer and warmer every day, shade was always appreciated.

Trenson was looking forward to finally learning how to use a sword. Now, it was an extra weight to carry around. He hoped it would soon become a tool of defense. Without his quarterstaff that he was so familiar with, he was vulnerable. A weapon with an edge would be more effective than a blunt weapon, he assumed.

In addition, becoming proficient with a new weapon would hopefully help him to put his past behind him. The quarterstaff was a deadly weapon in Trenson's hands, but it brought back painful memories of what he had done before.

Plus, the sword was the weapon of choice with all the kings and knights, right? All the heroes in the stories had swords. If all the important people had them, why not he?

Once they reached the area, Jayfor turned to Trenson. The prince wasn't quite sure how to teach Trenson. He assumed earlier that teaching would be easy. After all, all he had to do was show him what to do and what not to do. However, seeing Trenson staring expectantly at him, his sword held awkwardly in his right hand, made him consider that this may be more than he bargained for.

He decided to start by seeing how much Trenson knew. "OK, so to start off your training, I'm going to first determine how much you know. I want you to hold your sword in a battle-ready position."

Trenson didn't have the foggiest idea of what a battle-ready position should look like, but he decided to guess. His feet close together and facing squarely forward, he held his arms forward and held his sword, tip straight in the air, out far in front of him.

It was then Jayfor realized that he had a lot of work to do.

"OK." Jayfor said slowly. "Well, first of all, are you right-handed?" Trenson nodded in reply. "Then you need to put that hand below your left one. No, not that far down. There, that's better. The more skilled you become, the lower you will be able to grip your sword. And also, you should, as a rule of thumb, always keep your sword pointed at your opponent when you're not engaged in combat." Jayfor pulled his sword clear of its scabbard with a quick *shing* of steel. "Like this." He demonstrated by showing Trenson the ready stance that he had been taught for years.

Trenson couldn't help but focus his attention on Jayfor's sword rather than his stance. He silently marveled at the blade, the edges that seemed to disappear into the air, the shining steel that gleamed in the sun, the polished handle and the intricate engraving on the hilt guard — he felt a pang of jealousy as looked down at his pathetic peacekeeper sword. It wasn't even his! Maybe that's why he wasn't good at this. His sword was holding him back.

None the less, Trenson tried to copy the stance. It felt odd, but strangely right. His version of the ready stance was much different from Jayfor's, but he had an innate feeling that he was one step closer to doing it correctly.

"Your weight should always be at the front of your feet as well, so you can move around easily. Like this," Jayfor pointed down to his feet and Trenson noticed that Jayfor's heels weren't even touching the ground. Instead, his heels were slightly up and off the ground, and the front of the foot was the only part touching on the ground.

Trenson realized that this might not be so different from using a quarterstaff than he thought. He had been taught to remain on the balls of his feet when using a quarterstaff as well. To see if his theory was correct, he changed his position and held the sword similarly to how he would with a staff. It was a little different in terms of holding the sword, which he did as Jayfor told him and pointed it at his opponent, but he knew that it was probably more correct than the say he had stood before.

Jayfor noticed the change in position and regarded it with a little surprise. It was different than what he was using, to be sure, but it was still pretty good. In fact, Trenson was applying some finer points in his stance than Jayfor thought he was ready for. *At least he has some skill. This will make it a little easier.*

The thought caused Jayfor to remember something that his instructor had told him a long time ago. "Very good. It's a little different, but it's still a big step from what you were doing. Also, keep in mind that everyone uses a sword differently. Although you can always get better and use better form, there is no right or wrong way to do it. There are hundreds of different stances, styles, techniques, and strategies. You will just have to experiment with different things and see what works. Whenever I'm teaching you something, you can choose to apply it or not, or to modify it to your liking. You're going to fight a little differently than me. The important thing is to find out what works best for you."

Trenson nodded, understanding what Jayfor was getting at. He was eager to move on to the actual fighting side of the training, so he kept silent. After a few more pointers, Jayfor soon got on the topic.

"Now let's start the actual combat training. When you are in combat, whether it's with a skilled knight or someone who has never even held a weapon, you have one objective." He paused and eyed Trenson. "Do you know what it is?"

Trenson thought about it for a few moments. "Winning?" he said uncertainly.

Jayfor smiled. "Well, in a way. Your objective is to kill the enemy. When you fight, and you are fighting someone below your skill level, you will feel a strange desire to drop your performance down to what your enemy is. Innately, this is because you want more competition, and you feel a little sorry that your adversary is so weak." He shook his head sadly. "I've seen many knights die from this. The same goes for a singular strong opponent. You will be pushed to the limit, which your body likes, and so you will be tempted to keep the battle going."

Jayfor continued, trying hard to make sure Trenson understood. "But every second that your opponent is alive, the higher your chance of dying is. They are trying to kill you as well. If you get an opportunity, then you *must* take advantage of it. You can still be killed by a terrible swordsman if he takes advantage of an opportunity."

Trenson thought about the words for a few seconds. "That makes sense," he said. "Now," he raised his sword, pointing it at Jayfor, "can we please get to the actual fighting part?"

Jayfor smiled. He could relate to Trenson's readiness to begin. "Of course. The most basic move, although the most important at the same time, is the thrust. To pierce through armor, you're going to need to use a blow that has a massive amount of power and cutting potency. The thrust aims at a usually lightly guarded area, the midsection or the neck, and has the power to bring down almost any opponent. Most fights end with thrusts." He demonstrated by gracefully thrusting the way he had been taught in the palace, in one fluid motion. "Now you try it."

Trenson readied himself and attempted to thrust forward and backward in the same flowing motion that Jayfor had done. Even though it lacked the years of skill, training and muscle memory that Jayfor possessed, it was still surprisingly better than Jayfor guessed it would. *He's a fast learner.*

"Good job," Jayfor said. "If your opponent didn't parry, then they would probably be dead right now."

For hours they practiced the ready stance, the proper grip, and the parry, which Trenson had a little trouble with. They even fought a little, their swords clanging against each other and disturbing the quiet afternoon atmosphere. Jayfor refrained from teaching anything else. "It's better to learn a little at a time than to learn a lot at once," he told Trenson, seeing that he was hungry for more.

Considering that this was the first time Trenson had ever properly used a sword, Jayfor was surprised how well he caught on and rarely needed to be corrected twice. Already, Jayfor could see the markings of a skilled warrior. He was surprised how quickly the sun was moving when they were training. He decided that this was enough for today, and together they returned to camp.

It's just like the days at the palace...

XXI

XAVSON COULDN'T SLEEP.

It had nothing to do with the bed. The bed was perfectly fine. In fact, new sheets had recently been made by Loronis' finest craftsmen, designed to be even more comfortable, after he had given the order to make them. He thought that was what it was. But it wasn't.

Xavson turned over and tried to fall asleep, laying as still as he could, but every time he was about to drift off to sleep, he saw his brother's face, contorted with pain and fear and sadness. Not sadness for himself, but sadness for Xavson. And his final words, "I forgive you," echoed in his head over and over and over.

He cursed and rolled over to the other side of the bed. The craftsmen had done a terrible job. He would have them executed first thing in the morning.

The thought reminded him of something. He would need to erect more gallows near the prisons. In the last three days, he had imprisoned and executed more people than ever. And he had only been king for three days. The people were rebellious, rioting in outside the palace gates and causing trouble.

As much as he had tried, word had gotten out that Xavson had killed Annor and usurped the throne. No matter how much he tried to convince the people of his story of the truth, that both Annor and Jayfor tried to kill him, and he had only defended himself, they wouldn't believe him. All the sweet talking he had done in town before to sway the people to his cause was wasted.

Knowing that he wasn't going to sleep anytime soon, he sighed and rolled out of bed. The moon shone full outside, its light casting a square shaped glow on the center of Xavson's chamber. He walked to the doors on the opposite side of the room and pushed them open quietly, revealing a small balcony just outside.

He walked outside into the cool air and placed his hands on the rail that surrounded the balcony. The city had calmed down at night. A few lights dotted the town sparsely below, but that was it. He caught the reflection of armor in the moonlight in the streets below as soldiers moved silently through the streets.

As one of his first acts as king, and to extinguish some of the uprisings, Xavson had ordered that a curfew be set on the streets at night. No one was to leave their homes after dark. Anyone caught outside during the curfew was imprisoned for a week.

Xavson smiled to himself. Before the curfew was set, riots would go on well into the night. But now, not even one was to be seen. Of course, he had ordered his soldiers to imprison or kill any that were caught openly declaring their displeasure, but with this new law, now there were even less.

This was what the root of the problem was: Faldon's laws were not strong enough. He had seen it before. The people were lazy and did whatever they wanted. Crimes were punished, but, in his mind, the punishments were so lax that they would be let out from prison, only to be caught in the act again. They would cause problems for the crown and stir up trouble. And the nobles would do nothing, instead trying to "help" the people lead a better life and to win the people's favor.

Look how well it worked. Nothing had improved, and the cycle only continued. The people needed to know that they would support the throne or be punished, work and obey or be imprisoned, listen to what they were told or be killed. That was the only solution. That was what he would do. Faldon would be made stronger as a result, and crime would go away. What use did morals serve if they didn't contribute to the advancement of the world? He would show the people their error. They wouldn't listen, he knew. But he would make them obey.

And after the kingdom allied with Elara, there would be no threat of war, no reason for them needlessly to deplete their resources against something they couldn't beat. When they were united, all Faldon's problems would go away. It would be a slow process, but he was patient. He had waited this long to take the throne. He could wait a little longer.

Xavson frowned. Everything was going according to plan. He had set the wheels in motion, and time would solve the rest. So why couldn't he sleep?

Once again, the image of his brother appeared in his mind, a sword piercing his midsection, breathing his last words. "I forgive you."

Xavson cursed again. Why couldn't Annor have said something that showed his anger? Something like "Curse you!" or "Why?" Instead, he had said that he forgave Xavson.

Xavson pondered the words. How could Annor forgive him? He had just killed him. He had ended his life short and taken away his privilege as a king. There was no reason why he should forgive him. And yet he did.

Annor was probably just trying to look good, he decided. Annor was always doing that, showing off and doing his best to impress people. Then it occurred to Xavson: why would Annor try to look good in front of nobody? There was nobody else there except for Jayfor. As much as he tried to think about it, Xavson couldn't come up with a reasonable conclusion.

Jayfor. He hadn't thought about him much. He wondered where he was. It was unlikely that he had been killed, for he would probably have heard word of it by now. It was possible that he was hiding out in the city, in someone's house, or somewhere else. He probably didn't make it out of the capital, because he had stationed men at the city gates and doubted that Jayfor could have gotten that far. Or he might just be dead on the ground somewhere.

Either way, he didn't really care. Jayfor was giddy-headed and too compassionate. He probably would just run and hide, hoping that he wouldn't find him. And even if he did try to organize a force to oppose him—which Xavson doubted he would—then it would be small and without a plan. He would crush it quickly.

He didn't really consider Jayfor a threat. If he found him, however, he would have him killed. Jayfor had declared he wasn't going to join him. And so, he would need to be disposed of.

Xavson looked one last time over the quiet city, then turned and went back into his quarters.

XXII

I T DIDN'T TAKE LONG for the supplies to arrive that night, and everyone was glad about that. They had posted guards in a perimeter around the camp, and one of them caught sight of a horse-drawn cart being led through the woods, and he showed it the way to the camp. Everyone was tired, but once they heard that food had come, they were more than happy to wake up and help unload the supplies. Even Trenson, who was like a bear when it came to mornings, was out quickly unloading the supplies from the wagon.

Jayfor was soon talking to the carter, who was in a farmer's attire. "Thank you for bringing these supplies," Jayfor said gratefully. "We wouldn't have lasted much longer without them."

"Isn't no problem at all," the man had a drawn-out accent. "I appreciate what y'all are doin' now. Xavson isn't going to make anything better, I know that as a fact. Anything I can do to support your cause, I'm willin' to do. I'm coming back tomorrow with more tents and stuff, so let me know if there is anything more you need."

There was a sudden cheer from the knights. Jayfor looked and saw, in the torchlight, that the men had discovered a big block of cured meat. Already, some of the knights were gathering kindling to make a fire and roast some of it.

The wagon driver grinned knowingly at Jayfor. "And it looks like I may need to bring back some more of that meat there."

Jayfor returned the grin. After the last of the supplies were unloaded, the small cart turned and was about to leave, when Trenson, who was helping the men with lighting the fire, suddenly broke off from the group. Jayfor saw him run up to the carter and say a few words, to which the man nodded. Then he started his horse back into the woods, and Trenson returned to his position with the knights. Before long, the small cart had disappeared into the woods.

It was late before anyone went to sleep that night, but when they finally did, they slept feeling something that they hadn't felt in days: full.

The next day, while Agrond and the knights were cooking breakfast—surprisingly, the battle commander was an adept chef —– Jayfor asked Trenson what it was that he had said to the carter before he left.

"Bows, arrows, and throwing knives," he replied brusquely. It was still a little early in the morning for talking, in his opinion.

"Throwing knives?" Jayfor asked questioningly.

Trenson shot a curt glance at Jayfor. "The bow and arrows are for hunting. It's been a while since I've done it, and who knows when we'll make our move against Xavson, so I figured it was a good way to spend time."

"But we have enough food here." Jayfor gestured to the group of men that had gathered around the fire and, on the verge of drooling, were watching a large chunk of meat being turned over on a spit, which was included with the supplies they received last night.

"I know that," Trenson said impatiently, trying hard not to think about the meat. "What harm will extra meat do us?"

Jayfor decided it was probably best to drop the subject before Trenson was pushed too far. But there was one thing he wanted to ask. "And the throwing knives?"

Trenson grunted. "A weapon I know how to use."

Jayfor waited for more, but none came. He could tell that Trenson really wanted Jayfor to leave him alone, and so he obliged. *Throwing knives?* He thought to himself as he walked away.

The remainder of the day, they passed by training. After breakfast, which left everyone feeling energized, Jayfor gathered the soldiers together and soon had them sparring with each other. He knew it had been a while since the men had been in combat, and he didn't want the soldiers to become lazy or sloppy with their fighting. The forest rang with the sound of swords and spears clanging against each other. In friendly sport, Jayfor declared that they would host a "tournament," where every soldier fought another, single elimination. The soldiers had lots of fun with it, laughing and jesting in good friendship with their other knights. At the end of the "tournament", Jayfor awarded the last man undefeated with the crown of the realm—in reality a few vines twisted around in a loop — and all the knights bowed to their "new king." It didn't take long for everyone to burst into laughter, and even Trenson smiled at the comical sight.

True to his word, Jayfor trained Trenson in the art of the sword later that day after the tournament. This time, they worked on offense and defense, and the general techniques used in each. Jayfor noted with satisfaction that Trenson was often unwilling to change from offense to defense, instead preferring to use powerful strokes and slashes to expose an opening and then thrust at it. Most people tended to switch to defense as soon as they felt as though they were losing. In all, Jayfor was once again impressed with Trenson's aptitude and ability to learn quickly.

Everyone waited eagerly for the cart when night came. It wasn't that they were desperate for supplies as they had been earlier. In fact, Jayfor thought that maybe everyone had eaten *too* much of the previous rations. He did have to admit that they were a little chubby, notably Agrond. It was because the cart was delivering tents and other necessities that they didn't have. The carter was regarded as a sort of hero now, and everyone was willing to help with unloading it.

It seemed to take forever, but the cart finally arrived, along with the materials promised. The tents were quickly unloaded and set into place, and a few other items, namely a few lanterns and fire starters, were added as a courtesy by Norman. "He sends his regards." The carter informed Jayfor. "Says to tell you that I'll return in a few days with more provision and knickknacks and whatever else you think you'll need."

Trenson was accordingly handed a small bundle wrapped in cloth, which he received thankfully.

Before long, after much thank-you's were said, the carter left, and the men set to putting up their tents. Jayfor walked over to

Trenson, who had laid the cloth on the ground and opened it, revealing a neat row of ten throwing knives of curved shape and small size. There were also two small armbands in the cloth. "Are they good?" he asked. It was an odd question, he realized, but he couldn't think of anything else to say.

Trenson simply grunted and slid the armbands onto his left and right wrists. Jayfor saw now that there were many small notches in the bands, probably to hold the knives. Trenson carefully set fives knives into each of the armbands, filling in all the notches. He pulled one of the knives from its notch. Standing up, he zeroed in on a nearby tree about fifteen paces from where they were standing. In one swift, fluid motion, he pulled a knife from the band, held the hand up and beside his head and, holding the blade by three fingers, threw his arm forward, his wrist flicking down and then up as the knife left his hand.

All this happened is a few seconds. The knife whirl-winded around as it flew swiftly to the tree. A resounding thump emitted from the knife as it landed square in the center of the bark. The handle protruded out at a right angle to the tree.

Trenson nodded, pleased. "Good enough," he said.

The next few days were relatively quiet. With no clear direction on where to go next, Jayfor decided to wait a period before they tried going to Fort Lyson.

In the meantime, Trenson and Jayfor spent their time training. Trenson was rapidly improving in his speed and adept with the sword. There were several times while they were sparring that Trenson had Jayfor on the retreat, but Jayfor always managed to regain his footing with a quick combination of slashes.

Trenson loved every moment of it. He hadn't anticipated that he would enjoy sword fighting as much as he did, yet here he was. He could see now why the sword was such a popular weapon. While the day seemed far off, he still anticipated the day he would finally defeat Jayfor.

As a sort of trade, Jayfor attempted to learn how to throw knives from Trenson. The result was not as optimistic as Trenson's swordsmanship. For starters, Trenson was not the best teacher. He would tell Jayfor to "throw the knife at the tree," and when Jayfor missed, he would simply say "try again." He did offer a few somewhat helpful tips, though, such as "spin the knife when you throw it," and "try not to miss." Jayfor had no real motivation to learn knife throwing other than boredom, so he soon gave up on the ordeal.

Trenson, on the other hand, was a master of knife throwing. Jayfor didn't know how he did it, but he could effortlessly throw five knives at a tree from at least twenty yards and hit it every time. It was as if the knife was an extension of his body. A detaching extension of his body, that is.

Jayfor asked one day, as Trenson was pulling the knives out of the tree and sliding them into the wrist sheaths, how he did it so easily. Trenson looked up blankly as if he had no idea what Jayfor was talking about, then he realized he was talking about his knife throwing. "I did it a lot," he said. He resumed pulling the blades out. They were embedded deep in the dark bark.

"Before you came here?"

Trenson nodded and slid the last knife into the sheath.

While he was on the topic, Jayfor decided to ask, "What did you do before you came here?"

Trenson immediately tensed. His casual demeanor was replaced by caution and guard. He met eyes with Jayfor. "Some things I'm not very proud of." He said slowly. Then he walked off, leaving Jayfor to wonder at his words.

What is he hiding?

XXIII

"THAT'S A DEER AND three wolves that you've killed today!" Agrond exclaimed. Trenson unstrapped the quiver from his side and placed it on the ground, alongside his bow, then he sat on the ground beside them and shrugged.

"They gave me a shot, so I took it." He answered.

Earlier that day, in the morning, Trenson said he was going to go hunting as something to do. He took only his knives, bow, quiver, and a dozen arrows. He was only gone a few hours before he returned, dragging a female deer with an arrow in its side back into camp. The knights had congratulated Trenson, and before long they had skinned it. They didn't have any way to preserve the meat, so they decided that they would go ahead and eat what they could. Any that they couldn't eat, Trenson said, he would drag the carcass somewhere into the woods and put the leftover flesh with it. For wolves, he said. He wanted a wolf pelt, and a carcass was the best way to attract them.

Jayfor had doubted that there were wolves in the woods, but he decided he would let Trenson think what he would.

His doubts proved wrong, however. When Trenson returned later that day to the carcass, three wolves were already there. Trenson didn't give many details —— not surprisingly—but from Jayfor could gather, Trenson had shot one with his bow, and when the other two wolves came for him, he dispatched one with a throwing knife to the head, and the other one with his sword.

So in all, Trenson was increasingly revered by the soldiers. His skill with knives and his success in hunting had earned him respect among everyone, and even Agrond was impressed.

"I still can't believe it!" Agrond said. "A deer and three wolves! That is amazing! What do you plan on doing with the pelts?"

Trenson considered the questions. "Wolves are hard to hunt," he said. "I wanted to do it mainly for the challenge. Maybe sell the fur when I get a chance?"

Agrond nodded. "That's a good plan. You already skinned them, right?" Trenson replied in the affirmative. "That's good. Did you stretch the skin and dry it?"

Trenson furrowed his brow and shook his head. "I've never heard of doing that. I just clean it and use it right away."

"Well, it's easy! Here, where did you put the furs?"

Trenson nodded towards the camp, where the other soldiers were. "Over there," he said.

Agrond rose to his feet. "I'll show you how to do it if you'd like. It's easy, and they last longer in the end."

Trenson stood up as well. "I would appreciate it." They started walking towards the camp. "I didn't know you were into hunting."

"Oh, I did it a little in my former days, back before I was a commander..."

The voices faded off as the two men walked away from Jayfor, leaving him alone in the edge of the wood. Jayfor looked after the men as they approached the furs and saw Agrond pick out an unusually large fur and hold it up. Some of the knights came over and began marveling at it as well.

Jayfor felt a little jealous as he watched Trenson being congratulated once again on the hunt. Why should *he* become the hero of the men all of a sudden? He had killed three wolves and a deer. Big deal. Others had killed more, probably. And yet Trenson was even more revered in awe by the men than before. It didn't make sense.

Jayfor wasn't used to sharing attention with others. His whole life, everything was about him. It wasn't his fault; when you are royalty, that's just how life is, and no matter how humble he tried to be, it was impossible to not develop a mentality that it was about him. What *he* wanted, what *he* thought about something, how *he* wanted things to go. He certainly wasn't prideful or arrogant. But he had never *not* been paid attention to. He wasn't used to sharing fame. And now a man with a questionable past and no lineage whatsoever was suddenly more important than him.

It angered him slightly. He was the one holding the entire group together! They wouldn't be here without him. In fact, he should be receiving even more praise than he was already receiving.

Jayfor shifted his gaze to the bow and quiver, loaded with arrows, on the ground. A thought struck him.

He had never been hunting before. He realized that this could be a problem, but he dismissed the thought. Hunting seemed straightforward. You walked around until you saw an animal and then you shot it. Simple as that. He was OK with a bow. Well, in truth, he had never shot at a target that was farther than fifteen yards back at the palace, but hopefully any animal that came out would be closer than that.

Before he changed his mind, he stood up and briskly walked over to the hunting gear. Trenson and Agrond were busy with the hide and didn't notice the prince strapping on the quiver and taking up the bow in his hand. Jayfor wasn't surprised. Maybe after he brought down a few animals as well, he would gain the prestige he deserved.

He wouldn't do any harm. He would just go into the woods, hunt whatever he could before it got dark, and then come back, hopefully with a few skins to show for it. What could go wrong?

After checking to make sure he had everything, he slipped quietly into the woods without anyone noticing.

***

"Hey Jayfor! Come look at this! We managed to stretch all three skins across—" Agrond saw the empty area and stopped. "Oh." He swept his gaze across the small gathering of trees, but didn't see the prince. "He's gone."

Trenson, who was following beside Agrond, noticed something. "The bow and arrows are gone."

Agrond looked at Trenson as if waiting for more. "And?"

"Well," Trenson said patiently. "What do you think he would do with a bow and arrows?"

Agrond silently pondered the question. Before long, realization hit. "Ah, I see. He's gone hunting."

Trenson nodded. "Probably."

Agrond walked over to the ground where Jayfor had been sitting earlier. "I didn't know Jayfor like to hunt. It's kind of strange that he would go off without telling anyone." He shrugged. "Ah, well, he'll be back."

Trenson looked over his back at the sun, which was sinking low and orange over the horizon, as if it was struggling to keep its head above the ground. "Night is not far away," he said. "Jayfor needs to be back before long, or he will be lost in the dark."

"Aye, but I don't worry about it. He's smart. He'll be back, you'll see."

Trenson agreed and sat down beside a tree, leaning lazily against the trunk. Agrond did the same. Trenson didn't worry about Jayfor. The prince would know to return before it got too dark.

A faint smile touched his lips as Trenson thought about the reason for Jayfor's departure: jealousy. He was jealous of the fact that Trenson had received so much respect from his successful hunts. Truth be told, Trenson was a little surprised himself at the success he had. Three wolves and a deer in one day was no small feat.

He didn't take the praise from the men to his head, though. In a week, the entire thing would be forgotten, and Jayfor would once again become the head of attention.

"So, Trenson, where did you get that horse?" Agrond suddenly asked.

Trenson shifted his gaze to the horse he had stolen, tethered to a tree, but with lots of slack so it could roam about freely. It was contently munching on the underbrush grass, leaving a mowed-down patch in its wake.

Trenson scrambled for an excuse. He had not told Agrond or Jayfor, or anyone for that matter, why and how he got here. And because of that, they had no idea that the horse wasn't actually his. "It was... a gift from a friend." That sounded realistic.

It turned out to be realistic enough. "I see," Agrond said. "I was just curious. It's a fine-looking animal."

Trenson felt the familiar pang of guilt as he remembered his crime. "It is."

"What's its name?"

What's its name? Trenson didn't know how to reply. After a period of silence, he said, "It doesn't have a name."

"What? How can it not have a name?" Agrond wasn't convinced. "Everything has a name. What do you call it?"

"A horse," he said bluntly.

"I mean, what is its specific name?"

"It doesn't have one."

"Really?"

"Yep."

"That's strange."

"I guess it is."

"It didn't have a name when you got it?" Agrond asked.

"Nope." Trenson replied.

"Huh."

The discussion finally ended. Agrond was silent, much to Trenson's relief, and Trenson resumed relaxing against the tree. He was content doing nothing, just letting the light cool breeze sift through his hair. It was refreshing, as the days were becoming increasingly warmer, and shade and breeze were welcomed.

Before long, one of the soldiers walked over to the area where Trenson and Agrond were. "Sir Agrond!" he said lightheartedly and with a grin. "Peller says that he thinks that he could beat you in a sword fight."

Then, from a distance, came another voice. "I did not, Deloys! I simply said that I thought that I could give him a fair fight." The speaker was one of the knights from the group, a young, tall and broad-shouldered man with long hair, bearing a similarly large grin. The other knights watched eagerly to see how this would play out.

Agrond smiled. "Is that so?" He turned to Peller and spoke loudly. "I always knew that you thought you were better than me!" There was humor in his voice.

Peller walked over to Agrond, a sword shining in its sheath at his hip. The other knights followed him from a distance, casually observing the scene. "Maybe at planning and cooking, Agrond, but with a sword?" He patted his sheath and grinned even wider. "Let's face it, Agrond. You may be good with that big, heavy axe you got there, but where's the skill in that? A sword requires skill. Precision. And agility." Peller laid emphasis on the last word. A murmur of suspense rose from the group. Peller's tone was joking, but there was still a hint of a challenge.

Trenson glanced at Agrond. He had to agree. The commander didn't look to be very agile.

Agrond placed his hands behind his head, apparently unconcerned by the statements. "What is it that you propose, then?"

"It's simple. A one-on-one sword fight. The person who is disarmed, or wounded, or surrenders, loses. Of course, I have no need to worry about that." There was cockiness and a slight arrogance in his voice. Clearly, he had not the slightest apprehension that he would lose.

Everyone was silent as they waited for Agrond to respond. Even Trenson was in suspense to see what Agrond would say.

Agrond was silent for a moment, glancing at each of the faces staring at him. He seemed to relish and enjoy the tension that he was causing. Finally, he let out a deep breath. "Oh, I would like to, Peller. But you see, it's late, and I'm an old man compared to you, none too agile." This brought a chorus of laughter from the knights, save Peller. "And you must understand that I am a nice man. I don't like to destroy people in duels and make them cry, which I'm afraid might happen." Another chorus of laughter, save Peller. "But I think it would be unfair to leave you without a fight, seeing as how you asked so nicely."

The suspense in the air was electrifying. Everyone was on edge.

"So, how about I let Trenson be my representative and let him fight for me?"

Trenson was shocked. "What?" he said in disbelief. How did he get roped into this?

A whisper of surprise ran across the group of knights. Before Trenson could reply, Peller was already assessing Trenson. A faint smile spread across his face. Trenson would probably be even easier than Agrond to beat. "You mean to say that Trenson will represent you? His loss will be your loss?"

"Exactly!" Agrond smiled at Trenson. Trenson didn't return it. "Trenson will act in my place. He'll give you a fight to remember, you'll see. If he loses, then you can consider yourself a better swordsman than me. Of course, if... *when* he wins, you'll be put down in your rightful place. Is that good with you, Trenson?"

"Well—" Trenson began, and was about to said *I don't think so,* but Agrond cut him off.

"Excellent! Well then, it seems that's settled. Give us a few minutes to get ready, and you'll have yourself a fight."

Peller nodded. "Yes, prepare yourselves all that you need. It won't do much good." He shot a fearless glance at Trenson, then turned and walked away. The other knights followed him.

After they had left, Trenson turned a baleful eye on Agrond. "Thanks for that."

Agrond's expression was seemingly innocent. "What? So I pair you up for a sword fight. What's the harm in that?"

"The harm in that," Trenson's voice was cold, "is when you use *me* to solve your problems! I have no part in your rivalries, and never asked to be dragged into this." His voice grew louder. "Now I have to fight a knight, one who's probably been trained his entire life and is much better at fighting than me, to settle your competitions! I'm not even that good! You'll humiliate us both!"

Agrond seemed amused at Trenson's outburst. "Oh, come on, Trenson! Where's your sense of adventure? It's a *friendly sword fight.*" He pronounced each word distinctly. "The worst that can happen is you lose. I'm practically doing you a favor."

"A *favor?!*" Trenson roared. "How, may I ask, are you 'doing me a favor'?"

Agrond shrugged. "Well, for one, you'll get more practice with your sword. Second, you'll be fighting a different opponent than Jayfor —— each swordsman has his own technique, you know.

Lastly, you'll set Peller in his place. He has always been a bit arrogant. This will teach him to be a little humbler."

"That is, if I win," Trenson retorted.

"Oh, I have no doubt you will. You're a better swordsman than you think. Come on, let's get you ready. It's not polite to keep Peller waiting."

***

This was not as fun as Jayfor thought it would be.

Jayfor gripped his bow tighter in his right hand and tried to walk quietly, a task that he deemed impossible. The leaves underfoot exploded with every step that he took, despite every effort to keep them silent. He was sure that every animal in the forest could hear him.

He had been at it for an hour now, and so far, he had nothing to show for it. The certainty of bringing back some game and impressing everyone with his success was slowly vanishing. It had never occurred to him that he might not even kill anything. Now he was afraid that he would return to camp empty-handed, which would lead to him being even less respected than he was before.

He continued to walk forward in the slowly diminishing daylight. He had a few hours, no more, before it would be too dark to see anything. Then there would be no hope of finding any game. Jayfor could see shafts of lights shining through the foliage behind him from the slowly setting sun, reminding him that time was running out. Still, he had time; he told himself.

Up ahead, a rabbit bounded lazily from the shrubbery and then stopped and sniffed at the ground. It was unaware of Jayfor, who was within bowshot of it. It apparently decided that whatever it was sniffing was good, and set to munching on it, jerking the grass out of the ground and chewing it quickly.

This was the chance Jayfor had been waiting for. He stopped abruptly, keeping his eyes locked on the rabbit. Slowly, taking care to make the least amount of noise possible, he pulled an arrow out of his quiver and set it into the string. Then, he raised the bow and, with one eye, looked down at the rabbit from the metal arrowhead.

The rabbit perked its head up and swiveled it in Jayfor's direction. Its eyes stopped on Jayfor, and that's when the prince decided it was time to shoot. He let go of the string. There was a familiar *twang* of the string and the *hiss* of the arrow as it shot forward...

And over its target, flying clear over its head and sailing into the tangled flora behind it.

The rabbit instantly bounded away and into the woods, rustling the leaves as it went and disappearing in seconds. Jayfor gritted his teeth angrily. The first sight of game in an hour and what does he do? He misses by a long shot, literally. He sighed. He was going to have to do better than that if he wanted to get anything before dark.

Looking back over his shoulder, he saw that it *was* almost dark. The last rays of light were fading away, the sun blazing bright orange in a final crescendo before it faded away. The moon was starting to become visible in the opposite direction.

He fetched the arrow and resumed his pace. Crunch, crunch, crunch, went the leaves under his feet. He heard birds twittering their last song of the day above. Maybe he could shoot at one of them? He looked up and then quickly changed his mind. The birds looked like tiny specks in the trees above, and he knew it would be better if he didn't try to shoot anything that far away.

As he was thinking about this, he suddenly heard a hollow sound under his feet. Before he could think, the ground gave way beneath him. He was falling. He let go of the bow and flailed his arms for anything to grab onto, but his arms swished through the air. The last thing he remembered was hitting his head on something hard and losing conscious and being engulfed in darkness.

***

Even though it was dark, the knights had torches that Norman had sent them, and now they lit them and formed a circle for the fight to happen.

On one end of the ring was Peller, decked in full armor and a helmet, the visor up so that he could see better before the fight. He seemed not, in the slightest, concerned about his opponent.

Trenson, on the other side of the ring, was also decked in full armor and helmet that he had taken from Norman's supplies. He had the visor up and returned Peller's stare with one of his own. Unlike Peller, though, he was more than a little concerned about his opponent.

For the hundredth time, Trenson thought, *how did I get into this?* He saw Agrond's familiar grin from the onlookers, and the commander smiled encouragingly. Trenson didn't return it.

Deloys agreed to act as the judge of the fight and stood between Trenson and Jayfor. The circle of soldiers around the area was tight, leaving just enough room for two combatants to battle with ample space. The ring was split into two teams: one which was for Peller, and the other was for Trenson. The light of the torches threw wild shadows on the ground as the men cheered for either Trenson or Peller.

Deloys gestured for each opponent to come forward, which they did. Deloys spoke loudly to be heard above the crowd. "We're using the standard sword-duel code," he said, turning his head to look at each man to make sure they were listening. "Whoever is wounded, disarmed, or surrenders losses. Both of you are going to leave alive. Am I clear?" Deloys was reminding them that this was just a competition. They would not actually try to kill each other. Both men nodded.

"Good," Deloys said. Then he backed up. "Ready yourself!"

Each man drew his sword and held it ready in his hand, Trenson with his peacekeeper sword, Peller with his menacing broadsword. Their visors clanked as they fell into place. Each man stood in a ready position. Trenson ran through every tip and skill that Jayfor had taught him.

"Let the fight begin!" Deloys shouted.

XXIV

AND IT STARTED. THE cheering immediately grew louder, but Trenson barely heard it. He was locked on to his opponent. Both men pointed their swords at the other and circled each other, trying to spot a hole in the other's defense. Trenson stayed light on his feet as he assessed his opponent. He immediately noticed that Peller wasn't as light on his feet as he was, which Trenson noted as something he could use to his advantage.

It was Peller who made the first move. Moving in closer to his foe, he made a forehand swing at Trenson's left side. The blow was weak and meant to start the fight, in which many weak blows would be exchanged until one of them revealed an opening. Without even thinking about it, Trenson raised his sword to the side. The swords clanged together, sparks flying, and Trenson slid Peller's blade off the to the side. Now Peller was open, and Trenson took advantage of it, thrusting forward towards Peller's midsection.

But Peller was just as skilled, if not more, than Trenson. He easily dodged the thrust and returned with an overhead arc. Trenson barely recovered from the thrust and held his sword up before the blade came bearing down, and he felt his arm rattle as the force of the blade collided with his. Both swordsmen disengaged and backed away, once again circling the other and looking for an opening.

The duel continued in this fashion: The combatants would circle each other until one of them decided to make a move. A short skirmish followed and, if neither landed a blow on the other, they would once again disengage and circle each other, waiting for another opportunity.

Trenson's breath felt hot in the visor. The armor was heavy and seemed to trap his heat and sweat until he was starting to think that he would lose to exhaustion. His opponent was skilled, that much was clear, but they were closely matched. The outcome could go either way.

Once again, Trenson advanced, making a volley of forehands and backhands at Peller's defenses. The knight deflected them but was briefly pushed back from the onslaught. Trenson knew he needed to take advantage of this and released more slices and volleys. He could feel Peller's parry's growing weaker, and decided to knock away at his defenses a little more before attempting to end the fight.

But Peller knew what Trenson was trying to do. Suddenly, Peller ducked under one of Trenson's swings and dropped to his knees. Trenson wasn't expecting this, and the momentum of his swing pulled him forward and made him off balance. His gut instantly tightened as he realized in how dire a situation he was in.

From his knees, Peller swung his sword in a semicircle, aiming for Trenson's legs. Trenson anticipated the move, and with all his strength, jumped backwards to avoid the blow. He felt the blade slice through the thin chain covering on his shin, but ignored whether it was a lethal blow.

Trenson backed away to regain his balance and footing, and Peller used the time to scramble to his feet. Both men pointed their blades at the other, and once again, the fight continued.

From the sidelines, Deloys walked around the ring to see the damage on Trenson's legs. If Trenson had a large gash or any remnant of a sword stroke, then Peller would automatically win. However, he didn't see any gash. The chain link was severed, and a faint, almost invisible red line ran across where it opened, but nothing serious. He shrugged. Technically, he could call that out as an injury, but it was so small, and everyone was having fun, so he decided to let the fight resume.

Trenson was starting to get worried. He couldn't hear the surrounding crowd, nor did he even see them. He had entered a new state of mind. It was him and Peller. He didn't need to think about how to parry each shot. He just let it happen.

Peller thought that victory was in his grasp. He had Trenson on the back foot, and now was the time to end the fight. He landed another average forehand on Trenson, which was easily parried. But instead of pulling back his blade for another strike, Peller instead flipped his blade around Trenson's and pushed it away.

The double force of Trenson's parry with Peller's extra blow caught Trenson off guard. He was pulled to the side from the momentum. He instantly knew that he was in a dire situation and attempted to regain his footing and pull his sword back up and into a ready position.

But there was no time. Peller was right behind him. He turned his head to look just in time to see Peller preparing for a final thrust that would end the fight, his sword pulled back and eyes locked on his target through the eyeholes in the helmet.

Desperate times call for desperate measures. Trenson knew he needed to do *something*. At the last second, right before Peller's blade screamed through the air for the final blow, Trenson threw all his weight to the right side, jumping into the air and landing awkwardly. Peller's blade barely nicked Trenson's armor, but it didn't pierce through it.

Trenson stumbled and turned around to face his opponent. He saw that he was off balance and had his sword stretched out in the act of thrusting. An idea came suddenly to Trenson's mind, a move that Jayfor had taught him that could end this fight.

Of course, if he did it wrong, then the fight would end quickly anyway, only in the wrong direction. But if he didn't win the fight soon, then his chances of victory would slowly diminish. Trenson was weary; his arms ached, and he felt the weight of the armor pulling him down like lead. Peller didn't seem in the slightest tired. It was now or never.

It seemed to happen in slow motion. Peller's arm was still outstretched from the thrust. Trenson thrusted his blade forward, but it was not aimed for Peller. Instead, he thrusted a little above the hilt, to where the two hilt guards overlapped. Then, with a quick flick and twist of the wrist, he twisted his hilt guard around Peller's and yanked the sword to the side.

All this happened in a matter of seconds. Before Peller realized what had happened, he felt the sword being twisted from his grip, and felt a turn in his stomach as the blade was yanked out of his hands. The clever disarming trick had worked, and Peller's sword flew away to the side, out of reach and landing softly on the grass.

The crowd was instantly silent. No one spoke as they waited to see what would happen.

Peller turned to look at Trenson, and was faced with a blade, glimmering orange in the torchlight, pointing inches from his face. Behind the blade was Trenson, a knowing smile cresting his face. Peller returned the look with a frown and gritted teeth. He couldn't believe he had lost.

Deloys was the one to finally break the silence. Walking forward from the crowd, he approached Trenson and, grabbing Trenson's sword arm, held it high in the air. "We have a champion!"

A deafening roar erupted from the crowd. The orderly circle dispersed as knights ran up and patted Trenson on the shoulders, congratulating him. It was a riot of armor and smiled faces and cheering and soldiers said, "Good job!", "That was a clever move!", and "It's about time Peller lost! He never loses!" All Trenson could do was stand, dumbfounded and panting hard, as the crowd surged around him.

Peller stood alone as the knights surrounded Trenson with applause and praise. He felt anger at losing the match, and even angrier that no one was coming to console *him*. But he knew that it would be better to save face and keep at least a little reputation with him, so he put on a smiling face and approached Trenson, pushing aside knights to reach him.

"Congratulations, Trenson," he said. "That was a smart technique. I've never seen anyone do it before. You'll have to teach it to me sometime."

Although he had no intention of being within a mile of Trenson at the moment, he said it to be polite. He figured it would at least give him the appearance of a fair loser and keep some of his reputation intact. And Trenson knew this as well.

Trenson nodded, knowing with certainty that Peller didn't really mean it. He search the crowd for a face, and eventually found it: Agrond, standing a little distance from the crowd, his arms across his chest, a giant smile across his face. *You deserve it*, he mouthed to Trenson.

***

"Wot do we have here, Bill?"

Jayfor awoke suddenly to the words. He felt a throbbing pain on the left side of his head and was conscious that he was lying facedown in the dark. He groaned softly. He didn't remember what happened, except the sensation of falling, and then feeling pain explode from the side of his head.

"Well, would ya look at that!" He heard voices above of him, faint and hazy like they were being said inside of a cave. "Looks like more than a hart wandered into our traps this time!" there was a chorus of laughter.

"He fell right in, I bet. One second, he's daintily walking 'round, and the next, bam! Right in."

"Wot's he lying like that for? Ay you!" one of the voices cried out from above, "Are ye dead?"

Jayfor didn't respond. He lay as still as a rock. He was barely conscious, and pain swirled around him and taunted him, threatening to knock him unconscious once again. He didn't know who the men were above him, but he guessed by their speech that they were ruffians and dishonest men. Better for them to think him dead than alive, or who knows what they might do to him. He wished he could see them. He was facedown in the dirt, and all he could see was blackness. It hurt to even open his eyes.

"Notin'," the voice said. "I guess we 'ave our answer."

"Nah, Bill! I wager he's still alive. Just senseless, is all."

"Aye! Senseless to walk into our trap in the first place!"

Another chorus of laughter followed.

"Well, wot are we going to do with him?"

There was a period of silence. "I say we bring 'im back to camp and to the boss. He'll want to know about this little pest that wandered into our traps. Who knows, it may be someone important!"

"I doubt that. But I agree. We need ta take him back 'fore he wakes up, *if* he wakes up."

"I got a rope, then. I'll lower one of ya down while..."

The voices faded away as Jayfor drifted back into unconscious. The ringing in his ears grew louder, and the pain from his head seemed to radiate throughout his entire body. He wanted to stay awake, to find out what these men intended to do with him, but the will to fall asleep was too strong. Once again, he was out cold, oblivious to the men lowering the rope and raising him out of the pit.

Trenson leaned against the bark of a familiar tree, the one he had been leaning against earlier when he first found out about his duel. He smiled as he recounted that moment, how he had been so certain that he would lose. Now, he had a hard time escaping the praise of the knights, and he had already heard his victory being retold at least a dozen times that evening.

While the praise was nice, Trenson was hopeful that things would return to normal soon. He knew that Jayfor was probably feeling left out, and he was a solitary person anyway, so he preferred to be left alone and for everything to go back to the way it was.

"See?" Agrond said, also leaning across the tree that he had sat against earlier. "I did you a favor."

Trenson snorted. "It's all well now that I've won, but that could have turned out much worse." He locked eyes with Agrond, and there was a hint of a threat in his tone as he said, "Don't do that to me again."

Agrond laughed the threat away. "Aw, come on, Trenson! Where's your sense of victory? You won! Don't be so gloomy about it."

Trenson shot Agrond another look. "I am *not* gloomy."

Agrond shrugged. "If you say so."

Trenson reclined farther against the bark of the trunk. Truth be told, he was a little glad that Agrond had roped him into fighting the duel. He didn't know that he possessed enough skill to beat a real knight, and it allowed him to do more than just the practice jousts that he was doing with Jayfor. Agrond was unbearable at times, but Trenson was a little grateful that he had fought the duel.

"I tell you," Agrond said, "Va'ar must have a sense of humor. Peller always wins in sparring duels! To be beaten by someone who just picked up a sword a few weeks ago — Well, I bet his pride is damaged, to say the least."

"You never told me Peller always won," Trenson said with a little anger.

Agrond shrugged. "What does it matter? Peller doesn't always win now!"

Trenson sighed. There was no use in trying to make the battle commander feel bad about anything. He was, as the old saying had it, about as serious as a horse with a sugar cube.

"I just got lucky," Trenson said.

But Agrond shook his head. "I know as a fact that there's no such thing as luck. Va'ar wanted you to win, and so you won. That's all there is to it."

Trenson was a little doubtful. Va'ar seemed like someone from a bard's tale, not someone real and actual. "I doubt that Va'ar cares about my sword fights," he said.

"Oh, He cares about your sword fights, all right." Agrond said convincingly. "There's not a single thing that He doesn't notice. He even watches over the birds of the field. And don't you think that you're of more worth than a bird?"

There was sense in that, Trenson realized. "But how do you know if He really exists? If no one has seen Him, then how do they know that He is real?"

Agrond smiled. "Can you see the wind?"

"No."

"But you've felt the wind before. You see it move the tallest and mightiest trees; you feel it cool you off when you are hot. But have you ever seen it?"

Trenson knew what Agrond was getting at. "No."

"So how do you know it exists?"

Agrond had him backed into a corner now. "I... well, at least you see the wind doing things, like moving the trees and stuff. That's how you know it's real."

"Right," Agrond said. "You see the evidence that it is there. That's how you know it is real."

"But where is the evidence for Va'ar?" Trenson thought that the question might finally baffle Agrond and put an end to the arguing that he was losing. But he should have known better, for Agrond smiled.

"Look around you, Trenson. Do you think the world formed itself?"

"Well, I -- No," Trenson said reluctantly.

Agrond nodded. "Exactly."

Trenson didn't respond. Every question or point that he had made, Agrond had countered and refuted, and he was sure that if he raised more points, then Agrond would refute those, too, so he kept silent.

The more he thought about it, though, the more he realized that Agrond was right. What else had created the world? Some uncreated, all-powerful being must have formed it. And the story of the three kingdoms, and of how the king rebelled and opened the gate at the Mountain of Power, and how the power spread across Elara. That did make sense. The dark beings who controlled Elara and plotted for Faldon's downfall…

Trenson suddenly realized that he may have encountered one of those being while on the road. The dark knight, Gornar. He had almost killed him. He certainly seemed to fit the criteria of an evil warrior. Trenson didn't know who the mysterious person who had rolled the boulder down was, though. He hoped to find out one day. In any case, Trenson had only just survived it.

But even with all of these facts, it still didn't mean that it was true that Va'ar actually exists. It could be something entirely different for all he knew. He decided to put off deciding to some other time.

"What does Jayfor think?" Trenson asked. "I mean, about Va'ar."

Agrond's good humor diminished slightly. "I honestly don't know. He doesn't talk about it much, but I can tell he thinks it a little foolish. He may believe it, but he believes *that* Va'ar, not *in* Va'ar. There's a difference. You can believe that Va'ar exists, in the same way you believe the wind exists, or that the sun will rise in the morning. But to believe *in* Va'ar means to put your trust fully into Him, to follow Him where there are no roads." He shook his head sadly. "No one in Faldon believes in Va'ar anymore. And if they do, they believe *that* Va'ar. That is why we are losing this war, because we have abandoned the One who determines that fate of all battles."

Trenson was silent. He couldn't think of anything else to say. If what Agrond had said was just a made up-story, written by the whim of a minstrel on the night of a feast, then there was really no point in life. Everything would be useless, because in the end, everything that you worked hard for would come crumbling to the ground, and you would eventually be forgotten by everyone who knew you. There was really no point in life. But if it was true…

Then, with a jolt, Trenson suddenly realized something. "Where's Jayfor?"

Agrond's eyes became wide, and the smile disappeared from his face. "Jayfor!" He scrambled to his feet. "By lands, I almost forgot! He's still hunting, isn't he? And it's late! It's been dark for hours!" His voice was frantic. "We need to go find him!"

Trenson started to his feet as well, an expression of fear on his face matching that of Agrond. "I'll grab the knights."

"Hurry!" Agrond called after Trenson as he sped off to the camp. "He could be in danger!"

***

Jayfor didn't know how long he slept, but when he woke up, he was conscious that he was sitting upright, not lying down on the ground. He groaned as the pain in the side of his head returned, and he moved his hand to cradle it. That's when he felt the pull of ropes on his arms and torso.

He opened his eyes and looked down. What he had hoped was just a hallucination turned out to be real, because he wasn't in the hunting trap anymore. He was tied against a tree, his feet bounded together, and his entire body bound by thick ropes to the trunk. The ropes were tight, preventing Jayfor from moving in even the slightest.

He sighed and looked around him. He was in a camp of some sort. Large tents were set up in a random order in a small clearing, about have a dozen in all. A small fire stood in the center of the clearing, a pot dangling in the flames from the rope of a makeshift camp stove. The fire was dying out now, and embers floated lazily in the sky, sharply contrasted in the black sky.

And there were people, too. They sat around the fire, about five of them, although there were more of them walking around the tents and talking and laughing with each other. They monitored the pot on the fire and occasionally threw meat or something else in it. They were decked in tarnished and threadbare attire, and bore scars across their arms and faces.

No one seemed to notice Jayfor or offer him any food. Jayfor was starving. The last time he had eaten had been when he grabbed a light snack that morning. Now his stomach growled with hunger, and he probably would have taken the chance and eaten from the pot of unknown food in an instant. Unfortunately —— or perhaps fortunately—he was unable to do so.

He turned his attention to the men sitting around the fire. Straining his hearing, he was able to catch parts of the conversation.

"I didn't like that one very much," another one of the men commented.

Another man, who the comment was directed, scowled. "Well, it ain't my fault! You men practically need a story every night before you go to sleep, just like children! You've gone through all my stories faster than a dog on fire! Make your own stories!"

The other man grunted a reply. There was a period of silence. Jayfor heard crickets calling loudly in the woods, dozens, probably hundreds, of them. While nothing was happening, Jayfor looked around for his bow and arrows. He didn't see them. Of course, they had searched him for weapons, he thought glumly. He had nothing sharp on him to cut the ropes.

A man sitting beside the fire spoke lazily. "Where's Mc'Nell gone to?"

"He's telling the boss what we found in our trap," another man replied, jerking a thumb to Jayfor. They must have thought that he was out of earshot. Jayfor, deciding to use the assumption to his advantage, pretended not to be listening. "You know the boss, though. It takes him forever to do anything."

"Aye, that be true." Another man pipped in. "I wish we had our old leader, Dimitri. He was a leader and a fighter. Farrell is a decent leader when the time comes, but he's got nothing on Dimitri."

There was a murmur of agreement across the group.

"It's too bad, what happened to him." Another man said as he threw something else into the pot. "He was the best leader we ever had. Now he's gone."

The men nodded. "You're right," one said. "I guess that's the way it goes. If only that traitor didn't leave our group, or else he might still be alive."

The men muttered in agreement.

"What do you think Farrell's gonna do about him?" another man said, referring to Jayfor. It was hard for Jayfor to not look at the group when they were talking, especially when the matter concerned him.

Another man shrugged. He opened the pot and stirred the contents with a long wooden ladle, steam rising from the cauldron. "I dunno. Farrell doesn't like to waste his time. Maybe we can hold him for ransom. But, like I said, it'll likely be too much trouble, and we got enough loot as is. I doubt Farrell would want to kill him, but it would save time." He shrugged as if it was no big deal. "I doesn't matter. If this man is a worthy fighter, then maybe Farrell will give him the chance to join us."

"Aye," one of the men piped, grinning. "Because nothing says 'worthy fighter' more than stumbling into a hunting trap!"

A peal of laughter erupted from the group. Jayfor felt cold sweat began to run down the back of his neck as he contemplated what exactly these men might do to him. He hoped that Trenson and Agrond would come looking for him. He realized now how foolish he had been, trying to prove himself to his soldiers. He was the prince of Faldon; he had plenty of prestige as it was. And what gain did fame bring? Nothing. And now he would pay for his carelessness.

Suddenly, the laughter in the camp stopped. Jayfor, feeling like it was safe to look towards the camp, quickly saw the reason.

A large, barrel-chested man strode into the group. He was bald, with an ugly ridge running from his forehead to his left cheek, a battle scar from a past battle. He was tall; very tall, Jayfor noticed. His brow was furrowed in a permanent scowl, and he scanned the faces of the camp like a hawk. "Where's this boy?' he demanded.

Jayfor guessed that this was the leader, Farrell. His stomach churned in fear. He was hoping for a sympathetic, somewhat normal-sized man. So much for that idea.

One of the men pointed at Jayfor, tied to a tree a little out of the way. "Over there."

Farrell, without any acknowledgement or thanks, turned his head and locked eyes with Jayfor. The prince's heart turned to ice as he withheld the man's cold stare. Farrell starting walking towards him in a long, uneven gait, never turning his eyes away from him. Jayfor forced himself to avert his eyes as Farrell approached him.

"So, you're the one who fell into that trap of ours," Farrell grunted. His voice was flat and low.

Jayfor didn't reply, feeling like it was better that the obvious was left unsaid.

"Stupid of you to do that," Farrell continued. "Of course, I don't give a beggar's scraps to what you do. Now you got a gash the size of my hand on your head."

If it was as big as this man's hand, Jayfor thought, then it must be bad. He looked up at Farrell, determined not to show weakness. He was met by a steely gaze, and his courage started to waver. This man looked like he could snap him in half, and not think twice about it.

"What's your name, boy?" There was a slight tone of mockery laid on *boy*.

Jayfor kept his voice steady and firm. "Fillan," he said. It was a somewhat common name in the area. He decided not to give out his real name. If they found out that he was a prince, then they would hold him for ransom, and Xavson would find out about him, which would leave no hope for the cause.

"Fillan." Farrell repeated. "Well now, it falls on me to decide what to do with you." He crossed his arms, toying with Jayfor's courage. "I could let you go. It would be the fastest and least messy way. But then you might rat on us, and that wouldn't be good, would it?"

Jayfor kept silent.

"Or I could kill you. That would be messy, to be sure, and some work, hiding the body and all. But it would guarantee our safety. The work wouldn't be too bad if it kept our whereabouts unknown."

Jayfor felt more sweat run down the back of his neck, but kept a straight face. "Who are you?" He asked. There was no harm in asking a question if he was to die anyway.

Farrell laughed. "Who am I? I suppose I am many things. A lover of freedom, for one. A man who sees that there are many who have things they don't deserve, and so I take them and give them a use. A hater of control, and the way that those in power try to control us. A stout supporter of free will, who does what he wants, how he wants, where he wants." He glared down at Jayfor. "Are you any of these things?"

Jayfor shook his head. It was true that he did believe in some of these things, but the way Farrell believed in them... it was twisted from what it really was.

Farrell's scowl deepened. "I see. That's a shame. For a second, I was considering giving you the chance to join us. You seem a strong lad and could be whipped into fighting shape in no time." He nodded over to the men at the fire, who were still waiting and stirring the pot. "These men believe in freedom, too. They recognize that no one has the authority to tell them what to do. They follow their own path and do as they please." He slowly returned his gaze to Jayfor. "Do you not think the same?"

Jayfor swallowed. "No." he said. His voice had not a trace of fear in it, or at least, he hoped it didn't.

"I see," Farrell said coldly. "You're not much for words, are you?"

Jayfor didn't reply.

"Guess that answers my question. I'll let you think on it for a while before I make you decide. Just remember, if you decide not to join us, well, you may not live to see dawn."

And with that, he turned away and started to walk back to the camp. Jayfor breathed a silent sigh of relief. He was glad that Farrell didn't recognize him, or else all hope of being released was gone. Then he realized that his chances of being released were slim anyway, and his sigh of relief change to a sigh of hopelessness. He couldn't join these brigands. His fate was sealed.

Please, Trenson and Agrond. Please come quickly.

Suddenly, Farrell stopped in mid step. His body froze. Slowly, he turned around to face Jayfor, his brow furrowed. He stared at Jayfor, as if searching for something. Then he walked back to Jayfor briskly and grabbed him by the chin, holding his head up. Jayfor's heart quickened with fear, and he avoided eye contact with Farrell, afraid that his courage might give way. Farrell continued to search Jayfor's face, and Jayfor was fearful that he may have been discovered.

Finally, after what seemed like an eternity, Farrell smiled and let go of Jayfor's face. He stepped back a little from Jayfor, his face smug. "Well, well. I knew I had seen your before. I had a feeling that you were something special, but royalty! I must say, Prince Jayfor, that your presence is welcome. Very welcome."

XXV

TRENSON CALLED OUT JAYFOR'S name for what seemed like the millionth time that night.

They were still looking for Jayfor, and so far, no one had any luck. They decided to split up into groups to better improve their chance of finding the prince. Trenson had taken five knights with him, while Agrond took another five, and five more went by themselves to search for Jayfor. The rest of the knights remained at the camp to stand guard.

"Jayfor!" Trenson called out, cupping his hands around his mouth to make his voice reach maximum distance. "Jayfor! Where are you?" The knights following Trenson repeated the same cry. The entire forest probably knew that there was a missing person named Jayfor that they were looking for.

Trenson patted his sword at his side to reassure himself. He had the feeling that something bad had happened to Jayfor. Maybe he was captured, Trenson mused. But who would he be captured by? He didn't know. Or maybe he had fallen asleep by accident. That would be the simplest reason he hadn't returned, but Trenson doubted it. Jayfor was smarter than that.

In any case, the prince of Faldon, the one who was leading the resistance to Xavson, was missing, and without him, the entire plan would fall apart. They needed a good leader.

They had a torch, but it was being held by one of the knights behind him, and they were loosely following the light spreading out into a large area. Trenson felt his the wrist sheaths make sure he had all his throwing knives. He counted ten hilts on the knives and was a little comforted that if there was conflict, he was prepared.

He was just about to call out Jayfor's name again when he suddenly saw a faint light far away in the woods. Curious, he started to walk towards it and leave behind the light of the torch. Perhaps it was Agrond or another company of knights. After all, they had torches as well. There was something different about this light, though, that drew Trenson in.

He stayed low and tried to keep as concealed as possible in the underbrush as he approached the light. As he got closer, he began to see that it was a campfire. He also saw that there were people sitting around it, and he felt relief that maybe he had found the group that may have captured Jayfor, and anxiety that Jayfor was possibly being held by this group.

Trenson stopped just outside the circle of light that the fire created and blended in with the vegetation. He scanned the camp. None of these men looked to be very honest people, in ragtag outfits and bearing what looked to be very used swords. He counted about ten men at all in the camp, and there were probably more in the tents that were scattered about. Brigands, probably; raiders looking for money or some form of payment. If anyone would have captured Jayfor, it would be these men.

His suspicion turned out to be right, for on the other side of the camp, sitting down against a tree and bound by thick ropes, was Jayfor.

Trenson was relieved that he had found the prince. But now he needed to find a way to set him free. He blamed himself for not calling for the knights in the group to come help him, or they might have been able to create a distraction while he cut Jayfor's ropes.

He felt a hand tap on his shoulder, and nearly cried out in fear, but restrained himself and whipped his head around. He met Agrond's face, and even though there were no torches, the moon was bright overhead, and he saw that, for once, Agrond was in a serious mood. "It's OK, it's just me," the commander whispered. "I brought my men, along with yours, with me. We have about twelve men with us in all, and I know that Jayfor is over there." Seeing Trenson's look of confusion, Agrond explained. "I found this place, too, a few minutes ago, and then I saw that you were a little way away from where I was. And now here we are."

Trenson wanted to reprimand Agrond for scaring him but realized that it would be to no use. Instead, he sighed. "I was thinking, maybe you could create a distraction with the men while I go around and cut Jayfor's ropes." Jayfor was too close to the group around the fire to not be noticed. If he snuck around to Jayfor, then he would be seen for sure.

Agrond nodded. "I was thinking the same thing. Just give us the word, and we'll start the distraction." Trenson now saw the other knights crouching behind Agrond, ready to spring forward at a moment's notice.

Just then, one of the brigands, who was walking near where the group was hiding, stopped and peered through the underbrush. He couldn't see very well, but he caught the glint of armor in the moonlight and could make out several men hiding in the bushes. "Hey!" he said, loudly. "What are you doing there?"

There was no point in continuing to hide. "Now!" Trenson yelled, starting to his feet.

With a cry of determination, Agrond and the knights rose to their feet and, brandishing their weapons, charged at the group of men around the fire. The man who had discovered them screamed in fear and ran back to join his comrades. The brigands were startled, to say the least, and hastily rose to their feet. They fumbled with their weapons, some of them even dropping them before they quickly picked them back up. As soon as they were prepared, Agrond and his knights were on them, fighting with swords and spears and axes. The once quiet forest was now a riot of battle cries and clashing metal.

Trenson stayed behind when the group rushed forward. His goal was to free Jayfor. Agrond and the men were simply a distraction. He waited a few moments after the battle began for the chaos to reach its peak, then he ran forward and towards Jayfor.

But he wasn't the only one. Another man, very large and brutal looking, also ran for Jayfor. He was closer than Trenson, and in seconds reached him. With a knife, he quickly cut the binds on Jayfor. After cutting the ropes, the man hauled Jayfor to his feet and, holding onto him and pointing a knife into his back, made Jayfor run away from the camp and into the darkness. The man gripped Jayfor's arm as they ran.

No! Trenson thought. Drawing his sword, Trenson dashed through the camp, dodging blows and weaving in between knights and brigands. Once he was through the initial fray, he ran headlong into the woods where he last saw the man run with Jayfor.

He didn't have to run long, as he was faster than the man who was holding Jayfor. The moon gave ample light to see, and in its white glow, Trenson saw the man was pushing Jayfor forward while running with all of this might. He wasn't faster than Trenson, though, and was aware of this fact.

Then the man unexpectedly stopped. His arm still holding Jayfor in an iron grip, he whirled around and faced Trenson. One arm held Jayfor close to him, and the other held the knife close to the prince's throat. "Stop where you are!" the man cried.

Trenson skidded to a stop. Placing a ready hand on his sword, he was prepared to draw it out at a moment's notice. He stared at the man, who was glaring at him with loathing eyes, and Jayfor, whose eyes were wide with fear as the knife was pressed against his throat. He looked at Trenson pleadingly.

Trenson looked again at the man holding Jayfor, then recognition, ugly recognition, hit him. "Farrell," he said in a disgusted tone.

Farrell peered closer at Trenson's face, not understanding. Then he, too, recognized who he was talking to. "Well, look at this!" Farrell said with dark humor. "Isn't this a day for familiar faces?"

Before he could stop himself, Jayfor cried out, "Trenson!" while in desperation tried to move the arm that was pinning him to Farrell. In reply, Farrell pressed the knife further into Jayfor's throat, until Jayfor felt the warm trickle of blood running down his neck. He immediately stopped, his heart beating out of his chest.

Farrell laughed, then said with scorn, "Is that what you call yourself these days? 'Trenson'?"

Trenson gritted his teeth and gripped the hilt of his sword tighter. "Let him go," he said, in a low and dangerous voice.

"Ha!" Farrell spat in reply. "As naïve as ever. You haven't changed at all since you left us, since your betrayal."

Trenson's face was steady and solid as a stone while he continued to glare back at Farrell.

"Oh yes, don't think we've forgiven you for that. You left us behind." Farrell pronounced each word distinctly, his words echoing inside Trenson's head and burning in his mind like fire, as they arose the memories of his dark past. "Dimitri's dead. Don't look so surprised! I bet you planned on it all along. It was the night you left us. You agreed to help him and protect him. He didn't want anyone to come with him except you, because you were like a brother to him." Farrell's scowl lessened and was replaced by a look of sadness. "For years, you helped us. You killed without a thought. And then we trusted you..." Farrell shook his head, the scowl returned. "That was a mistake."

Trenson took a deep breath, repelling the urge to rush at Farrell right now. "Let. Him. Go."

Farrell ignored Trenson's words. "Imagine how Dimitri would feel if he could see you now. Serving those who threaten to abolish our freedom!" In anger, Farrell pressed the knife harder into Jayfor's throat. The prince gasped as pain burned from his throat. "He trusted you as well. Like a brother, he trusted you. But you turned your back on us. He's dead now, and it's because of you." Farrell paused, anger boiling inside him uncontrollably. In a cry that told Trenson of all the enmity there was between them, he screamed, "Traitor!"

That was it. It only took a matter of seconds. Trenson held up his left arm, pulled a knife from it with his right hand, and threw the blade at Farrell. It was in slow motion. The knife, with incredible speed, spun around as it darted for Farrell and Jayfor. Farrell didn't move. He knew that Trenson was skilled with throwing knives, but thought he had no need to fear them. He had Jayfor as a human shield. The only thing exposed was the arm holding the knife across Jayfor's throat. He doubted that Trenson would even get close to hitting it.

Big mistake.

Jayfor watched with wide eyes as the blade came whirling towards him. He was certain that the blade was going to hit him. But, in a split second, it changed course. He could only watch as the blade spun around and landed, with perfect precision, into Farrell's knife arm, almost at the elbow.

Farrell screamed with pain. His once iron hold on Jayfor became limp. Farrell was unconcerned with Jayfor as he tried to get the knife out of his arm. Jayfor recognized the opportunity and quickly unwound himself from the man's arms. Then, before Farrell had time to think, he jerked the knife from Farrell's hands and plunged it into him, right below the chest.

Farrell gasped in pain. He stopped flailing and, eyes wide, slowly looked down. Seeing the knife, he then looked up at Trenson. His face turned white. He clenched his teeth, both in pain and in anger.

He gathered his strength for his final words. "This—is all ——your... fault."

Then he sighed and fell to the ground, lifeless.

Trenson and Jayfor were left standing there, staring down at Farrell. *What just happened?* Jayfor wondered. It had happened so quickly that he hadn't even thought about it as he was doing it. Now it was all over.

Jayfor didn't realize how heavy his breathing was until now. He swallowed hard, trying to calm his nerves. Turning towards Trenson, he saw that he was also standing still, lost in thought. He was staring at Farrell.

There had to be some kind of connection between the two men, Jayfor thought. No wonder Trenson never wanted to reveal his past.

Although now Jayfor was even more curious about what Trenson was hiding, he didn't think about it too hard. He was exhausted and eager to return to camp. He walked over to Trenson and reached out his hand.

"Thank you," he said.

Trenson, jerked from his trance, at first stared dumbly at Jayfor's outstretched hand. Then, with a faraway look, he gripped it and shook it. His grip was limp, though, and it was clear that his mind was elsewhere. When they met eyes, Jayfor could see pain in his expression, a deep pain that reached to his soul. Jayfor felt sorry for his friend, even though he had no idea why he was so downhearted.

Then, without another word, they turned and went back to where Agrond was waiting.

XXVI

"FOR THE HUNDREDTH TIME, Agrond!" Jayfor held his hands up in a gesture of surrender the day after the hunting incident. "I promise not to go out alone like that again. You have my word. Is that enough?"

Jayfor was getting tired of telling and retelling and retelling the story of how he was captured and his experience with the brigands. It was interesting the first few times, because looking back on it now, he did see that it was almost a sort of adventure. Except, after every knight came up and asked him what had happened, along with Agrond's constant fussing over him, it was starting to get a little tedious.

He always left out the part out about Trenson's talk with Farrell. Of course, he told everyone about Trenson's incredible knife throw, along with him grabbing the knife from Farrell's hands and using it against him. But he always left it at that. Jayfor felt that what he had witnessed was very personal with Trenson, and something that he shouldn't pry into, so he never mentioned the scene, not even with Trenson. In turn, Trenson never explained or talked about it either.

"I just can't believe that you would leave us and wander off to go hunt in the middle of the night! You could have been killed!"

Agrond wasn't letting up. He was almost furious that Jayfor would endanger himself and almost get killed. Agrond viewed himself as Jayfor's protector. To lose Jayfor would be a devastating blow to the group, and Agrond would view himself as responsible. "I never would have forgiven myself if you had died."

Jayfor met eyes with Agrond and gave him a reassuring look. "I know. And I'm sorry, Agrond. It was foolish of me to go out in the first place. It won't happen again." Jayfor felt like a disobedient child talking to his father. "I promise."

Agrond sighed. "Alright, if you say so. If anything like that ever does happen—"

"It won't," Jayfor cut him off. Agrond had been going on about *if anything like that does happen again* for a while now.

Agrond opened his mouth to say something else, then apparently thought better of it and closed it again. He simply nodded and then turned and began to head towards where the other knights were gathered.

Yesterday, Agrond and his band of knights were able to subdue the brigands rather easily. The criminals were outnumbered, and most of them threw down their weapons and begged for forgiveness. When Jayfor and Trenson returned to the ruffian's camp, Agrond was debating what to do with the ruffians. He seemed to be in favor of holding them all as prisoners, but Jayfor did away with that, explaining that it would take too much time and effort. In the end, they decided to let all the brigands free and leave them in their camp, with stern warnings if they were caught raiding or causing harm. By the look of fear on their faces, Jayfor felt sure that they would have no more trouble with them.

Trenson, who had been watching the whole scene from a distance, now approached Jayfor. "Is he finally done?" he asked knowingly, a rare smile cresting his face.

Jayfor nodded, a look of relief cresting his face. "I was beginning to think that Loronis might re-conquer itself before Agrond would stop. It's worse than my father being here!"

"I'm sure he means no harm. He simply cares about you and doesn't want anything to happen to you."

"I know that," Jayfor replied. "Still, what's done is done. I promised him that I wouldn't do it again, and he still goes on about it like I will."

"He'll stop, eventually. He just letting out some steam. And with someone as big as Agrond, he can hold a lot of steam."

Jayfor couldn't help but laugh. "I guess that's true."

Inwardly, Jayfor wanted to ask Trenson why Farrell and he seemed to know each other. He was dying to know why Farrell had called him a traitor, and what had happened in his past, because, obviously, there was a lot he was hiding. Yesterday, Jayfor and Trenson had left Farrell as he was. They figured that the brigands would find him, as he was close to camp, and give him a proper burial.

Out of respect, though, he restrained himself. Jayfor was starting to see the reason why Trenson kept his past a secret, and if *he*, Jayfor, had a dark past, then he wouldn't want anyone to know about it. So he kept silent.

There was a pause, then Trenson asked, "Is your head alright?"

Jayfor shrugged. "It should be fine. It doesn't hurt as much as it used to, and it will hopefully go away before long." There was an ugly red scar on the side of Jayfor's head. It was only half visible through his sand-colored hair, but the contrast between his hair and the gash made it even more visible.

"It looks pretty bad," Trenson remarked.

"I wouldn't know. Besides, men have survived from worse."

"Men have also died from less," Trenson pointed out.

"Maybe the weak men," Jayfor replied, then put his hands on his hips and looked away in the distance in a mock-heroic stance. "But I am no weak man."

Trenson smiled and said nothing. Jayfor looked at him as if waiting for confirmation that he was indeed a strong man. Trenson simply shrugged. Then Jayfor burst into laughter. Even Trenson smiled.

After they caught their breath and stopped laughed, Trenson asked, "So, do you want to spar some?"

Jayfor knew it was coming. Trenson asked him this all the time. "Sure," he said. He wanted to wear off some of the stiffness from last night, anyway. They walked over to the area where the weapons were kept.

"I heard that you beat Peller." Jayfor commented, grinning at Trenson.

Trenson quickly looked down, but Jayfor could see there was a faint look of pride in his features. "I did. He probably went easy on me."

Jayfor shook his head. "I doubt it. Peller doesn't go easy on anyone." They were almost to the weapon tents now. "Was he tough?"

"Yeah, pretty tough. I almost lost to him. He got reckless, though, and tried to end the fight quickly with a wild thrust."

Jayfor smiled. "I know that was a big mistake." He grabbed his sword, resting in its sheath, from the pile that they put their weapons on. Jayfor's was by far the grandest looking. He reached for Trenson's sword and tossed it over to him. Trenson had long since abandoned his peacekeeper sword and was using a standard broadsword that the knights had, courtesy of Norman's supplies.

"Now," Jayfor said good humoredly, pulling his sword clear of its sheath with a *shing*. "Let's see how well you do against a strong man."

XXVII

X AVSON STOOD STRAIGHT BEHIND the wooden lectern on the raised podium and waited patiently for the crowd below him to settle down.

Gathered before him in one large crowd, churning and moving like an ocean in a tempest, were hundreds of people. They swarmed the street below, held back from the podium by a line of guards standing before it. They came from all occupations: Cobblers, bakers, merchants, minstrels, smiths, carpenters, innkeepers, apothecaries, millers... But one thing was common among them. They came to hear Xavson speak.

King Xavson assessed the crowd below. Many of the people were dissenters, individuals who didn't know better than to stand against the king. These people had been the cause of great trouble the past month: refusing to pay taxes, abusing any knight that passed by, and the most annoying, rioting in the street day and night.

It was this last one that angered him the most. He had set a strict curfew for when people could and couldn't be on the streets. He even enforced this law by having guards marching in the street at night and arresting any that he caught out of doors. But still, the people did not listen.

Recently, one of Xavson's advisors asked him why he chose to enforce something as trivial as a curfew so harshly. The answer was simple: make the people conform to one thing, no matter its importance, and soon they will obey anything you tell them.

But there were many out in the crowd who were growing sympathetic to Xavson's laws. *Sympathetic* is a strong word: it was more accurate that they simply knew better. They knew they had businesses to run, families to feed, and a reputation to keep, so they didn't say or do anything. They would rather compromise on practically whatever Xavson would say.

It was this group that Xavson wanted. He didn't expect loyal supports. He wanted a populace that didn't care, that would blindly follow him and keep their ideas to themselves.

At the moment, the number of rebels to conformists was hard to say, but it was likely around a two-to-one one ratio. Rebels were put in prison, and so their numbers were diminishing rapidly.

That's why he was giving this speech now: to further lullaby the people with promises of stability and prosperity. This would increase the amount of people who didn't care, while rebels would be viewed as extremists.

King Xavson cleared his throat. Everyone had the sense that Xavson was about to speak, and so they quieted until there was silence.

"Good people of Loronis," Xavson began, looking at the hundreds of faces staring up at him. "I thank you for gathering here today to listen to my plea. I know you have things to do, places to be, and businesses to run. But you stopped it all to listen to my words. I am grateful to you for this."

Flattery, Xavson had learned, was the best path of control. If the people thought that he was "nice" and "cared for them," then they would feel sympathy for him. And sympathy was one of the greatest weaknesses.

"For many years, hundreds, even, Faldon has been a powerful and prosperous kingdom. In the days of old, we prevailed against even the largest of armies. We were insurmountable, the greatest kingdom in Ralladin. No one could match our trade, our strength, our wealth. When other nations were engulfed in civil war or turmoil, we stood strong. There was nothing that could bring us down, not even the powers that created the world!

"But as time wore on, eventually we became weaker. More exposed. Less protected. Our once undefeated armies were crushed by our enemies, men of renown and bravery were struck down by the hundreds. The war that our enemies declared on us, that we had easily been winning, was now uncertain. We became afraid, so we sent more men out, more leaders, and raised more troops than ever before. But nay."

He paused to let the words sink in. Gazing upon the upturned faces before him, he saw some with anger, some with approval, but many with nonchalant apathy. Good.

"But you already know this. It is a well-known fact that we have been losing this war for a long time. Even now, there are those who are clawing at our throat, waiting for the right moment to take our precious Faldon away from us, the one whom your fathers, brothers, husbands, and sons have died for.

"Are we, then, to let our proud kingdom fall? Is this to be the end? Do we have no other option than to do nothing as the kingdom of our ancestors is destroyed?

"I know not what you decide, but I made a promise long ago that I would save our kingdom. My father, who was sadly brought down with poison from an evildoer many weeks ago, could do nothing to save our kingdom. I loved him dearly, but in the end, his plans never worked. We continued losing the war. Before I could talk to him more about the fate of the empire, he was killed.

"Annor, my brother, was no different. I tried, I promise you, I tried, but he was stubborn. I told him that we needed to do something different, that what we were doing was only costing us more troops. But he wouldn't listen. In fact, he threatened me whenever I tried to talk with him.

"On the day of his coronation, I tried one last time. I plead with him, begged him to see that the way that we were going would lead to nothing to ruin. He wouldn't listen. He called me a traitor and even, to my horror, tried to kill me. He told me if I was so committed to what I believe, he couldn't have me in his way. I only struck back in self-defense, for had I not, he would have killed me."

Lies, all lies. Xavson knew this. He wasn't telling the people the truth; he was telling the people what they wanted to hear. He had learned a long time ago that people don't really want to know the truth; they just want to be told what they want.

Some of the people began to look angry, though. It was clear that *they* didn't believe him. No matter. As long as most of the people remained neutral, then he would have no worries. The people that opposed him would eventually be arrested, and then there would be even fewer rebels in the city.

"And so, I began to see just how unwilling my kin were to make changes, even if these changes meant that we could save our homeland. Even my younger brother Jayfor, when I told him of my dream, fled the castle. Everyone close to me had abandoned me. I was alone." He paused and sighed, as if truly sad about what had happened.

"But I knew that I couldn't leave behind you, the people of Ralladin. I promised to make things better, and so I will. Even though everyone that I loved left me, I will still fulfill my oath.

"So why? Why do you stand against me when I strive to make Ralladin a better place? I have already lost so much in pursuit of a better land, and should the very people I was seeking to protect stand against me as well? I know some of you do support me and are aware that I have nothing but goodwill towards you. But my words are for those who disagree. Why do you stand against me when all I strive for is peace?"

He paused, as if waiting for an answer, and to let the message sink in. He drew in the breath to speak again, but, surprisingly, one of the people in the crowd spoke out. "And how do you plan to make Ralladin better?"

Some others in the crowd, emboldened by one person speaking up, echoed the same question. The people began to change from apathetic to uncertain, and the tension began to escalate.

Xavson held up his hand to silence the crowd. Then he said, "It is simple, really. I will enforce more protective laws, that shall keep crime away and further protect you, the people. I shall also strengthen the military force to make sure that the laws are enforced. In addition, all business shall be watched over by the monarchy and will be encouraged appropriately."

Xavson waited for a rebuttal, but there was none. Xavson couldn't have been more pleased. With his sly and double-meaning words, he had convinced the people that all he would do was keep them safe. He smiled. How wrong they were.

"And what about the war?" Another member of the crowd spoke up.

"The war, I believe, is almost already a lost cause," Xavson replied. "We have lost so many men and gained nothing to show for it. Should we let more brave soldiers die for nothing? I think not. I wish to end this war diplomatically; perhaps a peace treaty... " he paused, "or an alliance."

And, like a rope stretched too far, the tension snapped. Xavson knew as the last syllable rolled off his tongue that he had said too much. The crowd immediately began to churn and protest. "An alliance!?" "After everything we've gone through?" "Elara wants us all dead!" "An alliance would be a surrender!"

Now the dissenters were beginning to surge against the podium, shaking their fists at Xavson. The knights held their spears forward to keep them back, but the crowd continued to push towards the stadium, like water rising against a dam.

"Your majesty!" One of Xavson's personal guards hollered from beside the podium. "We need to get you back to the palace!"

Xavson agreed. He looked back over the crowd and felt his anger rise. The entire speech was out the window. The people were harder to manipulate than he had hoped.

He descended the stadium from the right, and instantly the direction of the crowd was surging changed in his direction. More knights arrived, forming a large defensive wall behind Xavson. They began to strike blows against the citizens who were coming too close, and this only added to the uproar.

Xavson, however, felt no pity for those struck down.

"It is a miracle that you returned safely, your majesty!" Xavson's chief secretary said when Xavson returned to the palace and the knights dispersed.

Xavson ignored his secretary's concern. "They wouldn't listen," he said angrily. "After how much trouble I go through to change them, and they still won't listen!" he slammed an angry fist into the table. Xavson had returned to his office where he now sat, forced to do some work that was required of him. The wooden table shuddered, and the papers shifted positions from the blow.

His secretary, who had seen other secretaries disposed of, knew how to deal with the ever-changing temperament of the king. For example, he knew now that it was better for him to remain quiet and let Xavson blow off steam.

"After weeks of telling them what to believe, after *weeks* of this, they still won't obey!" Xavson shouted. His face was starting to turn red.

The secretary said, in a quiet voice, "It will take time. You have already come far and made many changes. Naturally, they don't agree with some of them."

"I don't care if they agree with them or not!" Xavson shouted. "*I* am the king! The people do not listen to anyone else besides the king! I *am* the people!"

Xavson exhaled loudly. The secretary didn't reply.

Eventually, Xavson calmed down. "Well, no matter. Those who disagree will face the consequences." He sat straight in at his chair. "Now, to business. What concerns me today?"

The secretary had it memorized down to every detail. "To begin with, the prisons are becoming full."

Xavson huffed impatiently. "Then build more."

"It's not that simple, your majesty. See, the prisons are literally overflowing. We have already begun the work to build more, but under your orders to arrest anyone that is caught disagreeing in any way, we can't keep up with the demand."

Xavson realized the problem and thought about it for a few moments. Then he came to a conclusion, and said, in the same tone he would have used in remarking about the weather, "Then execute the prisoners."

The secretary, usually used to Xavson's harsh mindset, was shocked. "My lord?"

"You heard me!" Xavson seemed completely oblivious to why the secretary was surprised. "Execute them! Tell the lawmakers to add the death penalty to... actually, add the death penalty to every crime." He smiled, as if it were something to be happy about. "Why didn't I think of it before? Now the people will surely obey or die! The number of rebels will diminish quickly now."

The secretary opened his mouth to say something, then shut it, knowing that, by definition, if he disagreed with Xavson, he would suffer the same penalty. "Yes, my lord. It shall be done."

Xavson reclined in his chair smugly. "With this, the people will think twice about disobeying me."

The secretary nodded in acknowledgement and decided to move on, making a mental note to visit the prison master sometime. "Yes, they shall. We have also received our taxes from Ronar fief."

Xavson huffed. "Finally. Norman has a reputation for being stingy. Does he support what we plan to do?"

"As far as I am aware, my lord. The ambassador that we sent their returned with a good report, so I believe it's safe to say he gives us his support."

"Excellent." Before the secretary could say anything, Xavson said, "Has there been any word from Elara?"

The secretary shook his head. "The last thing that we received from them was a month ago, and it acknowledged that the insurrection was successful, and they would send ambassadors to Loronis as soon as possible."

Xavson grunted. "Inform me immediately when you receive word from them."

"Yes, my lord."

Irritated, Xavson sighed. Elara was supposed to send a message concerning when they would arrive. So far, it had been a month, and no message was obtained. Xavson couldn't guess why they hadn't said anything, but it better be good. He was the one going through all the trouble to form this alliance.

"Well, go on!" Xavson snapped impatiently, startling his secretary. "Don't just stand there! What is the last thing that you came to tell me?"

The secretary knew that he was on dangerous ground now. When Xavson was angry or even the slightest ill-tempered, all bets were off. "Well, the last thing is that Fort Lyson, on the southern side of the Ashdin woods, has declared that it won't support our cause."

Xavson glared at the secretary, as if the reason for the Fort's rebellion had been his fault. "Oh, really?"

"Yes, my lord. Randolph, the baron of the fief, says he will not join with the enemies that we have so long fought against. He said he would rather lose his life than to lose his honor, and that he would rather stand alone against the armies of both Faldon and Elara before serving either. He has called up all the levies in his dominion, and it appears he intends armed resistance."

"Ha!" Xavson laughed. "The fool. He'll learn. He won't be able to stop what we have already almost completed." He glared up at his secretary. "Has anything been done about him?"

The secretary almost said, *we can't do anything without your command*, but held himself in check. "No, sir."

Xavson huffed. "I always do everything myself. Send a division of three hundred men to lay siege to the fief—the mercenaries that we hired; they will work well for mission. Tell them to execute anyone under Randolph's banner. Do not stop the siege until Randolph surrenders or is killed. How many men does he have?"

"Estimates vary, sir, but it appears no more than two hundred."

"Then it should be easy. Order the men to march at once. Send five onagers for the siege. That should be plenty, and I don't imagine that Randolph will be so bold when he realizes that the chances will be against him. Most likely he'll surrender."

The secretary, exceedingly glad to be finished with Xavson, bowed respectfully. "Your will be done, your majesty."

Xavson waved him away as if shooing a fly. "You may leave now."

The secretary needed not to be told twice. In seconds, the secretary was out of the office and closing the door behind him, and Xavson was alone.

The king was glad to finally be rid of the secretary. He wasn't a big fan of people. He relaxed in his chair and was looking forward to the prospect of being alone until he caught sight of the mountain of paperwork that he had pushed to the side.

He sighed. Why was being a king sometimes so boring?

XXVIII

"I HAVE GOOD NEWS and bad news." Jayfor strode into the camp and sat down opposite of Trenson and Agrond, who were leaning against nearby trees. The prince did the same and found a smooth-barked tree to rest on. "Which do you want to hear first?"

Trenson glanced at Agrond, who returned the glance. Then they both looked at Jayfor and, simultaneously, Agrond said, "Bad news," and Trenson said, "Good news."

Jayfor grinned. The two men looked at each other, a conflicting look in their eyes. "I suppose I'll choose Trenson's first," Jayfor said.

Agrond gave a look of rejection, while Trenson beamed with pleasure.

Jayfor continued. "Well, the good news is that we just receive a message from Norman." In his hand was a rolled-up parchment, which he showed to the two men. The seal, bearing the star of Faldon, was broken.

Interested, Trenson nodded. "I see. What does it say?"

Jayfor, who had already read the message, set the parchment beside him and leaned back, placing his hands behind his head and enjoying the refreshing breeze. "He said that he will continue to send rations as he has been. But that's not the point of the letter. He also gives us information on how it is in Loronis."

Now both Agrond and Trenson perked up, and they leaned forward, ready to listen.

"He says that communications with Loronis have been going well for him. Beside the messenger that came while we were there, no one else has shown up or questioned Norman's loyalty. Loronis thinks that Norman is loyal to their cause, and so he has no issue with them.

"But even more interesting is what he says about Loronis. The capital is engulfed in civil war. About half of the people support Xavson, and half would rather drown than pledge their loyalty to him. Xavson captures and... executes, any who resist. Even children."

Jayfor's voice was thick with emotion. Trenson and Agrond sensed that they shouldn't press Jayfor to continue. It was sad for them to think what would happen if they had a brother who wanted to kill him and had already slain dozens of innocent lives for nothing but personal gain. They had faced their share of trouble, but what Jayfor was going through was internal, something that was much harder to fight than any foe.

Jayfor regained his composure quickly and went on. "Norman says that Xavson has a lot more to be concerned about than us. Right now, he is busy trying to finalize agreements with Elara to ally each other, but it appears that the armies on the borders are unwilling to stop fighting. He delivered a speech a few days ago, and when he mentioned the word, 'Alliance,' the crowd immediately started to riot and forced Xavson to retreat to the palace."

Agrond stared at the ground, thinking over what Jayfor was saying. "That's good to hear. With the people on our side, it should make things easier."

Jayfor and Trenson agreed. There was a pause, after which Jayfor said, "That's all the good news. Now we can move on to the bad news that Agrond is dying to hear."

Jayfor turned a baleful eye on Agrond, who grinned and said nothing.

"The letter also said that Norman has received word that the baron of Fort Lyson, Randolph, has openly declared his hostility towards Xavson and refuses to join him. Xavson is enraged by Randolph's blunt opposition and has sent a troop of about three hundred men to put the opposition down." He swatted at a fly that had landed on his arm. The warmer weather was nice, but it brought its own share of inconveniences as well. "This all happened a few days ago."

Agrond and Trenson were both silent, waiting for Jayfor to go on.

"Well, Randolph got wind of it and amassed troops as well. The two armies met outside Fort Lyson, and a fierce battle ensued. My guess is that Randolph thought they would have a better chance of beating the army if they were on the offense, so they left the protection of the castle. Either way, it didn't work. Although both sides lost men, Randolph lost more. He retreated and is now stuck in his castle.

"That was yesterday. Now, the army is laying siege to the Fief with onagers, which, as you know, Agrond, are not very formidable siege devices. But the defenses of fiefs are small, regardless. If they keep at it, the walls of Lyson will be reduced to rubble in a few days."

Jayfor finished. He had told them everything that was in the letter.

Agrond and Trenson both came out of their trance of listening. "I can see why this is bad news," Agrond said. "That army is close. Too close. Lyson is about a day, maybe even a half-day, from here, and not only that, but Randolph would make a good ally." He sighed. "It's too bad we didn't get there first."

Trenson, who looked like he was thinking hard on something, suddenly piped in, "What if this is an opportunity in disguise?"

Jayfor could already guess what this plan was. In fact, he had come up with a gambit that could save Randolph and get rid of the army, possibly. He decided to let Trenson have the moment, though, and said, "Go on."

Trenson, for once, seemed excited to share something. "It's simple. I don't know much about sieges and armies, but they must stop beseiging when it's night, right? So, I think we should sneak over there in the cover of the night, burn their siege stuff and take their equipment. At least we can be a thorn in their side."

"That's a great idea, Trenson!" Agrond exclaimed.

"It is," Jayfor said, smiled. He had been right. Trenson's plan was exactly the same as his own. He thought about pointing it out, but decided against it, preferring to let Trenson get the credit for once. "We will be able to help and not get killed ourselves. I like it."

Trenson looked elated that his plan had been approved. He grinned and savored the moment. He usually couldn't provide much help to anything, as Agrond and Jayfor always beat him to a plan. Now the tables were turned, though. He had even outsmarted Jayfor!

The attention didn't last long, as Agrond changed the subject. "I like Randolph. Now that's a fighter we could use!"

"Is he a skilled warrior?" Trenson asked.

"Who, Randolph? Oh yeah, one of the best! He could easily knock Xavson clean out of Faldon with that claymore of his! He's a lot more of a man than Norman, that's for sure."

No wonder you think highly of him, Trenson thought.

"He is a deft commander, and having him would be a great asset," Jayfor said. "He is also a baron, which would give us more troops and supplies. The hard part will be getting rid of that army. We can't have Randolph's help unless Xavson's army is gone."

Trenson and Agrond pondered what Jayfor said and realized that it was true. The army was the only problem. They only had thirty men. Assuming that Xavson's army had lost fifty men in the battle, that still left them with two-hundred and fifty men to deal with. It would be a massacre to meet them openly.

"We could do a full-scale attack and draw the enemy out, allowing Randolph to attack from the rear," suggested Agrond.

Jayfor assessed the commander's words. "Interesting. You know, that might just work. After we burn their siege devices and take their supplies, they will be on guard, that's for sure, but also downhearted. Knowing that they will have to send for more onagers from the palace, morale will probably drop in the army."

Agrond smiled. "Then the army will be weak, and then we can call on Randolph's army to attack and pin them between two fronts!" Agrond's voice was charged with excitement.

Jayfor looked doubtful, though. "I don't think we'll get that far. We only have thirty men, remember, so even if we did lower their morale greatly, that still pits us against two-hundred and fifty men. No matter how you put it, I don't like those odds."

Agrond shook his head. "I wasn't thinking about meeting them by ourselves. Randolph has around two-hundred men, most likely. Once we reduce the morale of Xavson's army, we can draw the army away, try to make them follow us. Then Randolph can use the opportunity to rush them from the back." Agrond was grinning wildly from talking about his favorite thing: tactics. And surprise raids, drawing the enemy out, and attacking from two fronts was just up his alley.

Jayfor scratched his chin thoughtfully. "It's a gamble, to be sure. We are *assuming* that Randolph will leave the fief and attack from the rear. If he doesn't, then we're done. There is no way that we can stand against a force almost eight times as great as ours."

"Randolph will come," Agrond replied confidently. "I know it. Who would pass up an ambush?"

Jayfor thought about the plan, scrutinizing for any loopholes or flaws. He had become a master at doing this at the palace; he was taught to always do it before making any decisions. But now he saw that there *were* some flaws in the plan: they could get caught in the night while they tried to burn the siege weapons, they could attempt a surprise raid but not accomplish anything, they could try to lure the army and the army doesn't follow, they could flank the enemy just as planned and still lose...

But then again, this was war, he told himself. And in war, you take risks. He saw Agrond and Trenson looking at him expectantly, and eventually decided that the loopholes would have to remain.

"Alright, it sounds like a plan to me. We burn the siege weapons, then we draw the army away while Randolph attacks — or is supposed to attack — from the rear."

Agrond clapped his hands and rubbed them together jubilantly. "I like it! Short, simple, and easy to remember."

XXIX

I T WAS BLACK. PITCH black. It was so dark that, other than the torches glowing faintly in the distance, Trenson couldn't see anything. The moonless and starless sky make it feel that they had stepped into a void, where there was no light.

Trenson crouched behind hedgerow, situated at the top of a low rise. To improve their visibility without torches (which Jayfor said would reveal their location), they chose to climb higher. Apparently, Trenson thought with satire, he likes to stumble around in the dark, because so far that was exactly what they were doing.

Now, though, they saw torches in the distance. "Is that them?" Trenson whispered softly. He could barely hear Jayfor's and Agrond's breathing beside him, which assured him that he was not alone. Jayfor's was lighter and even, while Agrond's huskier and deeper.

It was Jayfor's voice that answered. Even though he whispered as well, it sounded like a shout in the heavy darkness. "Yes. At least, probably. Most likely there will be an encampment around the fief so that the defenders can't try to escape."

Trenson didn't reply. It wasn't because he disagreed with Jayfor. The real reason was because he didn't feel like breaking the silence once again. The woods were deathly silent, silent to the point where the silence seemed loud. Any time Trenson stepped on leaves or whispered something, it felt as though he were disturbing the silence, like the woods itself resented his noise.

He heard shuffling beside him, and then Jayfor's voice whispered, "Come on."

Trenson heard another shuffling, this one much louder, and concluded that it was Agrond. Or a bear. Either one would have made the same amount of noise.

The light shuffling and leave rustling — Jayfor — started to get fainter, as did the loud rustling and leaf shuffling — Agrond — so Trenson guessed that they were moving forward. He hurriedly scrambled to his feet and started walking after them. The problem was he couldn't *see* them, so he followed the sound, hoping that he didn't run into them, something that had happened an embarrassing number of times.

This time, though, it was easier to guess where Jayfor and Agrond were walking, the faint torchlight ahead acting as a guide. All he had to do was follow it and he would be fine. That didn't prevent him from running into Agrond three times, unfortunately.

The light increased in brightness the closer they crept towards it. What was once one light turned into multiple, individual lights that spread out in a line. Judging by the way the lights flickered and their color, Trenson guessed that they were torches.

His hunch proved right. Before long, the underbrush began to thin out, and the trees were not so close together. Jayfor softly called for a halt, and the light was now close enough that Trenson could make out a faint silhouette of Jayfor. The prince stayed low to the ground as he slowly walked forward. Trenson did the same, and so did Agrond, although Agrond wasn't the best at bending over, so he didn't get very low to the ground.

After moving in that way for a while, Jayfor held up his hand in a halt. Before them was a wall of shrubs and bushes, creating the perfect cover for them. Agrond and Trenson took their place beside Jayfor and peered over the vegetation.

"Well, this isn't going to be as hard as I thought," Jayfor whispered. He sounded relieved.

Trenson replied, sounding far from relieved, "'Easier'? There are so many of them!" Trenson swept his gaze across the hundreds of tents scattered around the fief castle, a torch at each tent. The castle looked very similar to Norman's, Trenson noted.

There was a smack that broke the silence, the result of Agrond slapping a bug that had landed on his arm. "It's not so bad," he said, in a voice that was a little too loud for Trenson's liking. "Look. The siege weapons are far from the tents. That'll make it easier to light them on fire."

The plan on how to get rid of the weapons had been discussed earlier. The three of them would scout and light the siege devices on fire. Then they would return to camp. The next day, they would launch what they called their "bait attack," which would draw the army out while Randolph attacked from the rear. Or at least, was supposed to attack from the rear.

First, they needed to initiate step one: burn the siege devices and stir up a hornet's nest.

"That's right. The onagers are separated from the camp, and therefore farther away from the torchlight. And the farther away it is from the torchlight, the better chance we have of staying hidden." Jayfor nodded towards a mass of dark objects a distance from the army camp, which Trenson guessed were the 'onagers' or whatever they called them. "It looks like they're close together, too. This ought to be simple."

Trenson didn't see how this was going to be even remotely simple. Jayfor and Agrond both seemed relaxed and calm, but not Trenson. Ever since they entered the woods, Trenson had the feeling that at any second, someone would see them. He felt shivers of adrenaline running through him, and the hairs on the back of his neck stood upright. Nervous would be an understatement.

"I don't see any guards," Trenson commented. He said it out loud, but he was really talking to himself to keep calm.

There was a pause, then Agrond's unmistakable voice drifted through the darkness. "You're right. I don't see any either." Another pause. Then Agrond spoke again. "What do you think, Jayfor?"

Trenson saw Jayfor's head slowly turn from left to right, and he guessed that the prince was once again sweeping the camp. "I'm not sure. Perhaps they're hiding, maybe trying not to be seen, that way they can catch anyone that trespasses."

"Or maybe they're lazy and didn't post any guards," Trenson piped in.

"Maybe," Jayfor said, sounding unconvinced. "Let's hope so. In any case, we'll need a closer look."

Trenson heard the rustle of leaves and saw the silhouette of Jayfor start to move again. He also heard a much louder rustling and guessed that it was Agrond, or the bear that was following them. He hurried to catch up with them.

Torches illuminated the camp with dozens of individual pools of light, the tents casting large shadows in their wake. Trenson noticed that the tents were arranged so that one was not too far from the other, and they were stretched out in a chain that surrounded the castle like a noose, preventing anyone from escaping the castle without it being noticed. The tents were a little farther than a bowshot away from the castle walls, no doubt so Xavson's army would be out of the range of Randolph's archers.

Before long, they were out in the open, concealed from sight by cloaks of darkness. They stayed low and walked slowly to the tents until Jayfor gestured for them to stop while they were behind one of the shelters. Trenson felt his heart beating out of his chest and felt sure that the entire army could hear it thumping right now.

Surprisingly, as they stood still behind the tent and stretched their hearing to as far as it would go, they hear no sound. Well, the snoring coming from inside the pavilion was quite loud, but there were no sounds of movement, no talking or noises. It was silent.

Trenson had no idea why Jayfor made them come so close to the camp. After all, the siege devices were over *there*, far away from the tents. Why weren't they going over there? They would get caught, Trenson felt sure, if they lingered so close to the tents.

Jayfor caught a glance from Trenson and saw the impatience in his eyes. He held up one finger in a gesture of silence, then leaned over and grabbed a fist-sized rock from the ground.

Before Trenson could do anything, Jayfor jumped to the side to where he was no longer concealed by the tent, cocked his arm back, and threw his arm forward. The stone flew forward, sailing in the air, and landed hard on the ground, rolling and bouncing while making a distinct puttering noise. The noise broke the silence abruptly and seemed louder since there was no sound in the camp.

The noise stopped as the stone halted its rolling, and silence once more pervaded the air. Much to Trenson's astonishment, Jayfor didn't return to the cover of the tent. He stood out in the open, his eyes scanning the area in front of him. Trenson motioned violently for him to return, but Jayfor ignored him.

Trenson waited for the sound of shouting, the clamor of weapons and armor, the calls of "Someone's here!" to burst from the tents and for them to get captured by Jayfor's foolish move. But there was no sound. The silence was just as still as it had been earlier.

Jayfor nodded with satisfaction, then returned to the behind the tent with Agrond and Trenson. "You were right, Trenson. No guards."

Trenson was tempted to lash out about how big of a risk Jayfor had just taken, but he held it in check. Yelling at Jayfor wouldn't be the quietest thing to do, either.

"This should be easy. The siege devices are a fair distance away, so we should have no problems setting them on fire and getting away. Xavson's getting lazy," Jayfor commented.

"And he'll pay for it," finished Agrond.

***

The general of the army sent by Xavson to quell the rebellion at Fort Lyson was a hard man. Bearing a permanent scowl from years of hard work, and with scars and a massive frame, it was no surprise that this general was a mercenary commander before being hired — along with other bands of mercenaries — to serve in the Faldon army.

He had a short temper and an even shorter tolerance. He preferred things to run smoothly, without interruptions or people constantly bombarding him with news or reports. He also preferred being left alone, and once almost beat a man to death when he had questioned his orders.

So, when the head sergeant, uninvited, suddenly walked into his tent while he was in the middle of breakfast, he was a little miffed, to say the least.

"General," the nervousness was clear in the sergeant's voice, "There's been a problem." He paused, glancing around the tent as if looking for something other than the general to focus on.

The general was in no mood to be patient, especially this early in the morning. He shoveled another handful of bacon, eggs, and potatoes into his mouth with his hand, then said around the half-chewed food, "Well, get on with it!"

The sergeant nodded quickly. "Yes, sir! My apologies, sir!" He remembered what happened to the last man that angered the general.

In most cases, a man as violent as the general would never be appointed to such a position in Faldon. Commanders in Faldon were chosen not just by their skill, but also for their leadership qualities and respect.

The general had neither of these. Brash and brazen, he was nearly the opposite of the model for a good leader. In the old days, such a man would never be given such a position. But the new king of Faldon was a different sort of king, one who preferred victory to virtue, and expected his army to have the same mindset.

Which is why this general quickly replaced the former one, who, as Xavson said, "Cared nothing about victory. All that mattered was his troops."

The sergeant cleared his throat and continued. "It seems that... we will not be using our onagers anymore."

The general was growing even angrier with the sergeant's delaying. "And why is that?"

The sergeant swallowed, sweat building on his forehead. "Well ... best if you saw yourself."

The general swore under his breath before rising from his table. He pushed the sergeant aside on his way out and strode out of the tent. The sergeant hurried to follow. He soon wished he hadn't.

Upon sight of the charred remains of the siege devices, the general first said nothing, in shock. What had once been five large onagers, ready for use and to throw large stones into the walls, was now five piles of black and gray ashes. An explosion of loathsome curses and oaths erupted from the general.

He had been looking forward to using the weapons. In fact, he had requested that there be more than five onagers, maybe a trebuchet and mangonel as well. His request had been declined, however. The general like to see destruction and was optimistic about using the devices.

Now, with the army of mercenaries gathered around the piles of ashes and looking on with astonishment, it seemed that they wouldn't be used after all.

"What in blazes happened here?!" the general shouted.

The sergeant was at a loss for words. "It seems that someone has burned all the onagers," he said, exasperated.

"Fool! Do I like blind to you?" The general grabbed the sergeant by the neck with one hand and almost completely lifting him off the ground, shaking him like a rag. "Do I?!"

Gasping for breath, the sergeant grabbed at the hand circled around his neck, mustering the strength to whisper, "No... sir."

With hardly an effort, the general flung the sergeant to the side as if he weighed nothing. The sergeant flew through the air and tumbled to the ground, lying in a heap. He gulped for air and rubbed his bruised neck. The general turned back to look at the ashes of the siege weapons.

Without turning his head to face the sergeant, the general said, slow and cold, "Find whoever did this. Find them and kill them. I don't care what you do with them, as long as they're dead by the end of it. Search the woods, and if you find anyone, kill them. I want them dead." Now he turned to face his sergeant. "Either they're dead, or you are. Understand? Now go!"

XXX

"How do you wear this stuff?" Trenson asked, pulling his chain mail coif over his head over the rest of his armor.

Agrond shrugged. "I don't know. In fact, I've worn it so long, I think it's comfy."

"Comfy" is not a word that Trenson would use to describe the armor.

They were getting ready for the raid that would lure Xavson's army away from Lyson fief. The men were ready for the battle, as it had been months since they engaged in any battle or conflict. Armor clanged as it was donned, swords and spear glinted from the sunlight, and everyone's face bore a look of enthusiasm, but also of knowing resolve. They knew the numbers they were going up against. Prudence would be needed to win this battle.

Jayfor smiled a knowing smile. "I remember the first time I had on chain armor. It was... uncomfortable."

"Well, this isn't my first time wearing it," Trenson replied, repeatedly adjusting the coif around his neck. "I wore some when I was fighting against Peller. I just didn't have to wear this steel plate thing on top of it." Trenson referenced the steel plates that Jayfor insisted that he wear.

Jayfor's smile turned into a grin. "Ah, yes, that's a whole new level. But you'll get used to it. Look, everyone else here has on chain and plate armor!"

Trenson grunted. "I still don't think that I'm ready for a real battle. I've been training for what — a month or two? I would be an easy target for anyone."

"Not necessarily," Jayfor replied. "On the contrary, anyone that faced you in battle would be very unlucky. It takes some soldiers years to get to where you are now."

"Yeah, like how you beat Peller!" Agrond chorused. "He's been at it for years. And you come in with a few weeks of experience and beat him with ease!"

Trenson replied dryly, "I wouldn't say 'with ease.' He almost got me. I just got lucky."

"I told you earlier, Trenson, there's no such thing as luck. Va'ar wanted you to win, and so you did." Agrond said confidently.

With a look of irritation, Jayfor sighed. In his opinion, Agrond believed too much of all this Va'ar stuff. "In any case, you have nothing to worry about. Just keep your head."

"Both figuratively and literally!" Agrond joked with a grin.

Trenson grunted, unamused. There was a period of silence, save for Trenson's mumblings as he adjusted the strap on his waist scabbard. He was still using the standard sword that he used when he fought Peller, discarding the peacekeeper sword.

Agrond brought up a new topic. "Maybe today will be as easy as yesterday."

Looking doubtful, Jayfor replied, "I don't know about that. There are many ways that we can mess this up. Everything needs to be perfect."

"I still don't see," Trenson interjected, fidgeting with the plate on his forearm to scratch his arm, "how we even have a chance. I mean, they have, what, more than two hundred men? And combined, us and Randolph have less than two hundred."

Jayfor glanced at Agrond, knowing what was about to happen. A grin spread across the battle commander's face. He rubbed his hands together. Then he said in an eccentric voice, "It all come down to my favorite thing... *tactics*."

Jayfor rolled his eyes. Here we go, he thought.

"Basically," Agrond began, "the entire reason Randolph and his army lost was because they had the disadvantage. Usually, the attackers have an advantage on an open field, like they were on. And it was likely that the types of troops that Xavson's army had were different than Randolph's, which can affect the outcome of the battle in numerous ways. There are countless other factors why he lost, but in the end, he was forced to retreat, as you know. So now he is stuck inside of his castle. You know how we saw last night that most of the tents were up near the gate? Well, that's so Randolph would have a tough time getting through the gate. He'll be met with spear point and be confined to fight in a small area. Worse, if Randolph retreats again, Xavson's army will pour into the gate and conquer the fief. So, he's stuck now. He can do pretty much nothing.

"But, when we burned the siege weapons, we lowered one of the most important things in battle: morale. Now Xavson's army will have a low morale, and when we lure them out, they will be exposed from the rear, unaware of another attack from behind, unprepared from an attack from behind, on the defense... With the same number of men that Randolph lost with, he'll be able to beat Xavson's army easily with the use of these tactics."

Agrond was red in the face and panting from going on for so long. But he looked like he would talk more if Jayfor didn't cut him off.

"Thank you, Agrond. I'm sure Trenson understood everything you just said." He glance at Trenson, who looked like he understood none of it. "Yes, we're all so glad that you enlightened us with your tactic's speech. Very interesting."

"He asked!" Agrond countered, still trying to catch his breath. "What was I supposed to do?" He looked at Trenson. "You understood what I was saying, right?"

Trenson shook his head, a sorry look cresting his face. "I lost you at 'basically.'"

Jayfor burst into laughter.

***

Randolph was mad.

The baron of Lyson fief paced across the wall of the castle, impatient. From his vantage point, he could see the mercenary army below. Tents dotted the area around the fort. Hundreds of tents. They were all identical, arranged haphazardly, with fires every so among them.

Randolph could see people, undoubtably the mercenary scum that had trapped him within his own walls, sauntering around their camp. They looked totally defenseless, he pondered, walking around in the open without a care in the world.

As Randolph was walking and thinking, he came near one of the guards, who was leaning against the crenellations, spear in hand, looking much too casual for Randolph's liking. "Good afternoon, sir," the guard said respectfully.

Randolph was in no mood for pleasantries. "Good afternoon?! What's so good about it, may I ask?"

The guard was startled by Randolph's sudden fury. "Umm... well..."

"Nothing! That's what's good about it. 'Good afternoon!' Hah! Look around you, man! We are surrounded by enemies! We are confined to a cage of stone, with a clear disadvantage! In another few days, we will all be dead! And you think that this is a 'good afternoon'?!"

The guard was so taken aback that he lost his grip on his spear. It timbered to the ground and landed with a clatter, just a few inches from Randolph's boots. The soldier hurried to pick it up, but Randolph lost no time in taking advantage of it.

"Pick that up!" the baron roared. "By the sun, what type of soldier are you! Pick it up, now! In some places, you get flogged for that!"

The guard was absolutely bewildered now, so much that the first time he grabbed for the spear, it fell out of his hand with another resounding clatter. He cringed as Randolph exploded into another outburst. Luckily, he managed to retain his grip the second time he seized the weapon, and he stood upright once more, at full attention.

"That's better!" Randolph commended in a not-very-commendable voice. "Be more careful with your weapon next time, soldier. The last thing that we need in this fief are more butter-fingered warriors."

The guard quickly replied, "Yes, sir!" He made every effort to act respectful and knightly.

Thankfully, Randolph didn't go into another speech. He simply shook his head in exasperation and continued walking across the battlements.

Randolph couldn't believe how lackadaisical the soldiers had become. He chastised himself for letting them get this way. That guard had been leaning casually against the battlements, not even guarding the wall! He made a mental note to drill the soldiers more. He would have a word with the fief's drill master.

"My lord!" From behind him, the voice of the guard he had scolded shouted. "Something's happening!"

Randolph whipped around to look at the guard and saw him pointing fervently across the wall in the direction of the besieging army. Shifting his gaze, Randolph quickly saw what was going on.

From the mercenary camp, the usual tranquil atmosphere of the site was now gone, replaced with men rushing back and forth, like a disturbed anthill. Even from here, Randolph could hear the shouting and clamor of the mercenaries, as light flashed from the armor and weapons the mercenaries' donned as the sun reflected it.

But that wasn't what caught Randolph's attention. What did was the fact that, emerging from the woods, arrayed in shining armor and running forward with a courageous battle cry, was a band of knights, charging towards the mercenary camp with weapons raised high in the air.

Randolph watched as, without stopping their rush, the knights dashed into the camp. The mercenaries still scrambled for their weapons, and the few that were prepared attempted to resist the onslaught to no avail, the raiders swiftly cutting them down with barely an effort. In all, Randolph counted around twenty men in the raiding party, all in glimmering armor. They formed a loose group as they ran headlong through the tents and campfires, cutting down foes left and right.

"It seems that we are not alone!" the soldier said, his voice brimming with hope.

"Maybe," Randolph said, a little less hopeful. "It could just be a party of bandits. In war, bandits sack an armies' supplies all the time."

The soldier shook his head. "They have on armor! And weapons!"

"So do bandits," Randolph dryly replied.

"Well — Look!" The guards suddenly exclaimed, pointing once more at the raiders.

Glancing again in the direction of the camp, Randolph spotted one of the raiders, amid the fray, holding a banner proud in the air. It was the crest of Faldon.

"There, see! It must be others that resisted! We're saved!" The guard was practically jumping up and down from excitement. He looked like an ecstatic child on a sugar rush.

Randolph's face was a stone. "'Saved' is a rather hopeful term."

The guard stopped. "My lord?"

Randolph sighed. "How much worse can it get? Did you learn anything from your training here, soldier? It's thirty against almost three hundred! It would be a miracle if the resistance fighters survived, let alone defeat a force almost ten times as great as them."

The guard realized what the baron said was true, and his hopeful demeanor diminished slightly. He watched as the mercenaries began to regroup and prepare themselves. The advance of the band of soldiers came to a halt as they engaged in multiple fights from the army, the ring of crashing steel and battle cries reaching the fief. It was clear that, before long, the small group would be overwhelmed.

Randolph squinted, both in response to the blazing sun overhead, and to assess the group. "I wonder what they have planned," he said to himself. "Surely, they know that they will be obliterated by the army. There must be some other reason for their attack."

Now he saw something else: the small band of rebels was retreating. It was slow at first, almost unnoticeable. Then it became more evident, the group forming a closely knit circle as they backed away from the sea of mercenaries swarming towards them.

Then, all at once, the group disbanded, turning around and fleeing. They ran the opposite direction of the castle.

The hope welling inside the guard deflated. He said in a flat voice, "They're fleeing."

Randolph was tempted to scold the guard for pointing out the obvious, but then he saw something else that absorbed his attention.

The guard noticed it as well, and, to no surprise, pointed it out. "Hey — The army is chasing them!"

It was true. As the band of resistance fighters fled, the mercenaries, in no order at all, pursued them. The siege army seemed to have forgotten about the castle that they were laying siege to. Mercenaries chased after the band, in small numbers to begin with, but before long the entire three hundred mercenaries were running out of the camp, pursuing the knights, who were now far in the distance.

Soon, the siege camp was almost completely deserted. All that remained were the men who had been struck down.

Randolph scratched his chin thoughtfully, looking at the empty tents and campfires, watching the men fade into the distance. He pursed his lips as he tried to make sense of the situation.

The guard didn't seem too perplexed. "They left! We're free now!"

"Free?" Randolph replied, "On the contrary, we're far from free! I have no idea why the mercenaries chased that small group, or why, when they did, every single one of the soldiers chased them, but we are not free. As soon as the army returns, we'll be stuck again."

The baron sighed and started to walk away, feeling pity for the resistance fighter, knowing that they would be crushed by the larger army, and confused on why the army decided to chase them.

Suddenly, he stopped. He turned and stared at the deserted camp for a few moments. Then he slapped his forehead with his

"Of course! Why didn't I see it? It's a feign attack! They drew the besiegers out so that we could attack from behind!" He started to run across the wall to reach to the ladder that led down from it faster. He mumbled to himself. "For once, that guard could be right. Freedom may yet be in sight."

XXXI

IT TOOK MAYBE TEN minutes for the knights in the castle to prepare themselves once Randolph had given the word, and, after that, another five minutes to explain the plan.

"The knights have given us an opportunity to attack from behind." Randolph's voice was crisp and loud. He paced before the front line of the gathered before him. "The mercenaries have fallen for the trap, and are now disorganized, unequipped, and most importantly, unprepared. If we attack from the rear, we will have all the advantages on our side, and may yet secure our freedom."

He reached the end of the row of knights, so he turned around and began pacing the other way. "Our fate is determined by this battle. If we lose, then we all die. So don't lose."

Some of the soldiers laughed, thinking that Randolph had made a joke. They should have known better, as Randolph's scowl remained, and he showed no sign of mirth.

"The plan is simple: I want archers to remain in the back, foot soldiers in the center, and mounted units in the front. We will approach from the mercenaries' rear, as silent as possible. No battle cries or loud noises. Then, once we get close, I will give the signal, and the archers in the back will fire a volley as the horsemen charge.

Then we'll blast the horn and start with our battle cries. After that, it's just a matter of who gets lucky."

He stopped his pacing and gazed steadily into the faces of the knights, which were concealed by the iron helmets they wore. "All I ask is you fight with everything you've got. I will be most displeased if you don't!" Once again, a few knights chuckled at Randolph's unintended joke. "Let us take this opportunity to regain the freedom that Xavson wrenched from us! Let us strike back at his tyranny! Let us fight for freedom!"

An arouse cry of courage erupted from the knights. They raised their spears, swords, and axes high in the air as a symbol of their support.

Randolph, himself in armor and bearing a large claymore sword, turned around towards the barred gate of the castle. "Open the gate!"

Almost immediately, there was the rhythmic clanging of metal, and slowly the large iron gate of the fief, which had before closed to keep the tide of mercenaries at bay, now open to release a wave of knights, weapons gleaming in anticipation.

"For freedom!" Randolph yelled as he ran through the gate.

The same cry was repeated by every knight that followed him out of the gate.

***

Trenson's sword darted from left to right like a death adder, striking viciously at foes from every direction. His ears were filled with the sounds of battle, the crashing of metal on metal, the rushing noise of hundreds of men swarming around him, the cries of men, both in encouragement and in pain.

His vision was blurry. He had discarded his helmet; it hindering his perception too much. Dirt and blood stained his face and hair. His armor was no different. His body shook, not from exhaustion, but from adrenaline. He was far from tired. He felt like he could do anything. He had a newfound strength that only those in battle can relate to.

A sea of gray armor surrounded him, churned around him. The mercenaries' armor was different from the knights; instead of silver chain mail and plate armor, it was a dull gray, and they only wore chain mail, and no helmets. It was the only way to tell a friend from foe.

Another mercenary entered Trenson's area and, brandishing a two-handed axe with a curved blade and yelling a brutal war cry, locked eyes with Trenson. Like a wheel turning, he swung the axe in both hands behind his back, over his head, and down, aimed at Trenson's exposed head, the head of the axe barreling through the air with incredible speed.

Before the axe even began its descent on Trenson, he knew what was going to happen. Right before the blade contacted his head, he sidestepped the swinging axe, letting it crash and embed itself in the ground. The welder of the weapon let out a cry of anger, which soon turned to a cry of pain, as, before the mercenary could free his axe, Trenson jumped forward, rotating his shoulder the same direction to double the speed of the blade, and thrust his sword deep into the midsection of the mercenary. In another second, he retracted his sword, and the mercenary fell dead on the ground.

"Trenson!" He heard Jayfor call his name. Turning around, he saw the prince coming near him, his visor up, revealing his sweat-soaked face. "We can't last much longer! We're being forced back!" Jayfor's voice was frantic.

Just then, another mercenary, welding a sword, jumped into Trenson and Jayfor's ring. With a grotesque cry, he swung his sword in an overhead arc towards Jayfor. The prince held his sword up and blocked the slice perfectly, stopping it in midair. Without wasting a second, Trenson aimed a thrust into this opponent's torso. The blade hit home, and another mercenary fell dead to the ground.

"I thought Randolph was supposed to follow us and give us aid!" Trenson yelled over the sounds of battle.

"He will!" Although Jayfor's voice was firm, a faint note of uncertainty was noticeable. "I know he will!"

Trenson was starting to have doubts. They had been at battle by themselves for far longer than Trenson thought possible. Their small group of thirty men was getting pulverized by the large army. Every soldier stood firm, but it was only a matter of time before they were overwhelmed and destroyed.

Trenson felt a rocket of pain shoot up his arm as the cudgel of an unnoticed mercenary behind him slammed into his shoulder plate. He involuntarily fell to his knees from the weight of the blow. Although relatively unharmed, he was now something worse—exposed. He didn't even have to turn around and look to see if the club was bearing down on him; he instinctively knew it was.

Gathering his wits, he rolled over to the side, just in time to hear the deep thud as the club struck the ground where he had been. He regained his footing and stood up, facing down his burly opponent.

The man gave a cry of anger at missing his target and now swung his club in a semicircle arc around himself. Trenson ducked under the swing, and in response, brought his fist crunching into his foe's jaw. For an instant, the mercenary was dazed, and Trenson used the opportunity to grab the club from his hands and slam it into his head. The mercenary spun around from the sheer force of the blow and fell to the ground.

Trenson grabbed his throbbing shoulder. His breath was hot and heavy. Where was Randolph? He was starting to doubt Jayfor's assurance that the baron would come. It wouldn't be long now. All around him, his comrades were falling, the mercenaries swarming in, their hope fading...

Then the crisp, clear note of a trumpet shattered the air.

The fighting immediately ceased, the crashing of metal and battle cries coming to a halt. Everyone looked around in wonder to see what was going on.

Then Trenson spotted what looked like a giant flock of birds rising in the distance. Small, black birds. They rose high in the air, then leveled out, then started to fall back down to the ground.

That's when he realized: it was arrows. A massive cloud of arrows.

Like a hailstorm, the arrows plunged to the ground, far away from Trenson and his group, but close enough to see the arrows as they fell. The mercenaries wore little to no armor, preferring the increased agility of padded and leather armor. Leather had nothing against the force of these arrows. Every mark it hit was deadly.

Screams and cries of panic rose from the mercenaries. Many fell, pierced by sometimes multiple arrows.

"It's Randolph!" Jayfor cried. "We're saved! Attack!"

With a mighty battle cry, both Randolph's army and Jayfor's group charged into the mercenaries ranks, like the tide against the shore.

And likewise, the tide of battle had also turned. The mercenaries were shaken by the fact that Randolph had escaped the castle and had amassed such a force to oppose them. They turned their attention to Randolph's army, which allowed Jayfor as his troops to cut down foes from behind with ease.

With passion and zeal, potency and tenacity, honor and commitment, the two forces fought on. Their courage was undaunted, their resolve unquestioned. Randolph's claymore crashed through the ranks of the mercenaries easily. Trenson's sword sliced and thrusted into every weakness in his enemy's defense. Jayfor's blade found its mark almost every time.

They had a disadvantage in size, that was to be sure. The mercenaries outnumbered them in a three to two ratio. In most cases, on an even field, the size difference would have played a bigger role. But this was not an even field. The knights had something that the mercenaries didn't: hope.

The mercenaries were fighting because they were told to do so, and to earn money. They couldn't care less about the fate of Faldon. All they looked forward to was the time of the month when their fair share of earnings came in.

On the other hand, the knights cared nothing about riches or glory. They fought for the homeland that had been taken from them, to free their kingdom from the oppression of tyranny, for the ones who had lost their lives standing against evil as they were. For every one resistance soldier that was stuck down, another five mercenary troops were defeated in response by his comrade. They had the confidence and the resolve, and that was of greater importance than any number of soldiers.

Trenson felt his resolve reborn at Randolph's aid. His sword suddenly grew lighter and struck at opponents faster than before. At the beginning of the battle, he had tried to count every enemy that he brought down — not just as an encouragement, but also so later he could try to bring down more. He stopped, though, because the extra thoughts distracted him. His last count was twenty-five.

To the mercenary general's dismay, he found his men bolting into the woods, apparently deciding that it wasn't worth it to fight any longer. He swore at the sight of his men abandoning him, then swore three more times at the resistance soldiers. *Curse these filthy rebels! Why won't they just lose?* His wishes were in vain.

The general tried to rally his troops together amid the unstoppable onslaught of the rebels. "Pull yourselves together, men!" He cried in fury. "We are better than this! They can't win against—"

It was the last words he ever said. Another withering volley of arrows sailed through the air and rained down on where the general was. An arrow caught him through the throat, ending his speech and life at the same time.

It was the breaking point of the mercenary army. Cries of dismay erupted from the besiegers as they found out their captain was dead. Now, in bigger and bigger groups, did the mercenaries flee. The resistance soldiers only became more emboldened at the sight of their enemy fleeing.

Finally, after another destructive hail of arrows rained from the sky, the entire army broke rank and fled. Wildly, they ran from the two small groups that had obliterated their forces. They made for the forest. They didn't look back. They left their fallen comrades behind as they dashed into the underbrush, and before long, the few mercenaries that remained disappeared into the forest.

And for a few seconds, all was silent.

Then one knight shouted, "We won!"

And then an air-splitting roar of victory rose from the two groups, standing across from each other and raising their visors to reveal jubilant faces. Trenson, still tasting the tang of sweat from battle, raised his weary sword arm in the air to join with his companions. He smiled. The victory was hard earned, but it was it was worth it. So worth it.

XXXII

T HAT EVENING, RANDOLPH'S DINING hall was filled with loud laughter and noise. Long tables stretched across the room, dozens of them filled with food and drink. Overhead, candleholders dowsed the room with amber light and revealed the cheerful chaos below.

Knights sat around the tables on long benches and talked and laughed and ate. Fresh mutton, brown and steaming and set on a large plate in the center of the tables, was demolished as the men mercilessly cut chunks of meat off the bone and added it to the mountain of food already on their plates. Mutton wasn't the only food on the tables. There were steaming mashed potatoes drooling with butter, slabs of bread still hot from being in the oven, ropes of sausage coiled in large bundles, and, a specialty, strawberry pastries that had a light sprinkle of one of the rarest and most sought-after ingredients: sugar.

The soldiers laughed and joked about the battle as they dined. Mead was passed around by servants and tankards were filled and quickly emptied. The entire scene was very messy: no silverware besides knives were used, and no clothes to wipe the mouth were in sight either. As a result, everyone inside the hall had grease stains all over their mouth and tunics, and the amount of food on everyone's face and clothes rivaled the amount on the table.

Seated around a separate, smaller table, Trenson, Agrond, Jayfor, and their host, Randolph, sat and relished the food prepared for them.

"This is good!" Agrond exclaimed around a mouthful of sausage.

Jayfor and Trenson both nodded, their mouths equally full of food. Well, almost equally. Agrond could fit more food in his mouth than Trenson thought possible.

Randolph nodded in appreciation. "Last year was a plentiful harvest. We had no famines or droughts or fires. Our storehouses are practically overflowing."

Jayfor reached for another roll of bread from the bowl in the center of the table and stuffed it into his mouth. He had decided to abandon the strict etiquette that he had been taught at the palace and shoved food into his mouth just as much as the other men did. He felt slightly rebellious in doing so, but he didn't care. "I was wondering why you decided to throw such a feast for so many men."

"I can see why you would," Randolph said in a casual tone. "I needed to get rid of some older crops and provisions before they went bad. Plus, this is a good way to celebrate an unlikely victory."

Agrond grabbed a roll of bread and slathered butter on it until there was more butter than bread. "That was a comeback victory, if I ever saw one," he said before stuffing the bread into his mouth.

Randolph nodded. "I agree. I am surprised that we were able to win. We had an extreme disadvantage in size, but it seems that we managed to push through."

He gingerly cut a small sliver of meat from the mutton and placed it in his mouth, chewing it formally. Randolph was more proper in his manners than anyone here. Trenson could not spot a single crumb or stain on the baron's face or clothes, and he never saw him talk with mouth with food in his mouth. For a second, Trenson wondered if maybe he should be a little more proper as well. After all, they were here to ask Randolph for aid against Xavson, and looking like a pig probably wouldn't help. But the food was so warm, so fresh, so good... He inwardly shrugged and teared off meat from the bone in his hands. Looking like a pig wasn't a vice in Trenson's mind, and if Randolph wanted to judge him for it, so be it.

Randolph continued after swallowing. "I did not expect for anyone to come to my aid, let alone that person be prince Jayfor." He glanced at the prince skeptically. "I thought you were dead. Everyone does."

Jayfor smiled. "There are many who wish I was. But as far as I know, I'm still well and alive."

Randolph let out a single laugh. "I know how you feel. Xavson wants my head, and he wants it separate from my body, mind you. That's why he sent that giant force of mercenaries to deal with me."

"Mercenaries?" Jayfor asked.

"That's what I said. Most of the army has deserted after Xavson came to power, and rightly so. Xavson's not what you'd call a good king. He's having to hire mercenaries to replace the soldiers that left. The entire army that we fought was mercenaries." Jayfor nodded. "I see. I knew that there was something different about them."

Randolph took a long swig of mead from his flagon and returned it to the table, whipping his mouth. He stared at Jayfor. "I can already guess why you're here."

"You can?" Jayfor responded.

"It's obvious. A few weeks ago, one of Xavson's fops came here and told me everything: How Annor had 'attempted to kill innocent Xavson, how Xavson had struck back and 'accidentally' killed his brother, and how you ran away in fear thinking he would kill you." Randolph's expression was hard. "Lies, I knew. All of it. And you're proof of it. The lackey asked me if I was going to support Xavson in his reign." He chuckled. "I sent him packing."

Jayfor noted that Randolph had also received a messenger from Xavson, just like Norman had.

Randolph continued. "I openly declared that I wouldn't fight for someone that would murder his own family for political advantage. That made the messenger mad, and it apparently made Xavson mad as well. That army came, we fought, I was driven back behind my walls, and then you showed up." The baron glared at each member sitting at the table. "You want me to help you bring down Xavson, don't you?"

Trenson glanced at Jayfor and saw that the prince was on the edge of his seat as well. "Yes," Jayfor responded simply.

Randolph didn't reply for a few seconds. Trenson, Agrond and Jayfor both waited intently for the baron's decision.

Then Randolph leaned back in his chair, crossed his arms, and let a rare smile crest his face. "That sounds like something I might enjoy. Count me in."

It didn't take long to explain what they had gone through and whose support they had already acquired. Randolph nodded when Jayfor told him that they had secured Norman's help, but that Xavson didn't know it.

"That was probably a good idea, to not let Xavson know that you are against him. Why didn't I think of that?"

Jayfor also told of his escape from the palace with Trenson's help, how they had fled to the woods and decided to fight back against Xavson, their meeting with Norman, and how they came to aid Randolph in hope that they could join forces. Jayfor left out their meeting with the bandits, as it was somewhat embarrassing and, he decided, unimportant.

Randolph listened with interest, although he seldom showed it. He made a few remarks and asked a few questions, but other than that, he was silent.

When Jayfor had finished, Randolph held his chin thoughtfully. "You three have been through a lot, haven't you? It must be the will of Va'ar that you have made it so far."

Agrond nodded. "Indeed," the commander said, "we never could have made it so far without His protection."

Trenson noticed how uncomfortable Jayfor became when the subject of Va'ar was brought up. Usually, the prince was quick to change the subject, so it came as no surprise to Trenson when he did so now. "Yes, we have been very fortunate. And with your aid, we now have the help of two barons on our side, along with a handful of knights already with us. We have formed a force to reckon with."

Randolph nodded. "That's true. Lyson and Ronar fief are two particularly large fiefs, with many towns. It should be easy for each of us to call upon the levies in the area to form a considerable force." He emptied the last of his mead and set the tankard to the side. "Who else do you plan on securing help from?"

Jayfor considered the question, then shrugged. "I don't know. Perhaps there are others out there who would join us. I know for certain that we'll need more help before our assault on Loronis. Maybe a few other barons would join us?" He cast a questioned glance in Randolph's direction.

The baron understood. "There's no one that I know. I've never been particularly close to any of the other barons. I know as a fact that the baron of Dakdom fief has joined forces with Xavson, but aside from that, I know not about any other fiefs."

Jayfor sighed. "I figured that Dakdom fief would join Xavson. Well, that rules out the last of the close fiefs. Any other fiefs are at least a week's journey from our camp. Still, it is likely that we can find others who would join us."

"For sure!" Agrond interjected, his mouth filled with food. Crumbs sprayed across the table. "There's got to be others out there that would bear arms to see Xavson brough down."

Randolph politely ignored Agrond's somewhat improper manners. "I have no doubt. In the meantime, what do you want me to do?" He directed the question towards Jayfor.

"For now, just be on guard. You've already raised the alarm for Xavson, so keep calling up all the men in the area willing to fight.

Our camp is a few hours away, located deep in the woods. Keep us updated on any information that you find. When the time is right, we'll call upon you to send your men, and then we'll begin our assault on Loronis."

Randolph let a rare smile touch his lips. "Gladly."

XXXIII

"THAT WAS, WITHOUT A doubt, the best meal I've had in months!" Agrond exclaimed the morning after they returned to their camp, referring to yesterday's feast.

Trenson had to agree. The food that he had eaten yesterday while at Randolph's feast was better than anything he had eaten from the provisions Norman sent. The churning in his stomach suggested that maybe he had eaten a little too many of the strawberry pastries, though.

But he certainly hadn't eaten as much as Agrond. Trenson had counted six plates, with food piled high, that Agrond had wolfed down as if they were nothing. In fact, Trenson was sure that he saw a considerable bulge in Agrond's stomach.

"It was very good," Jayfor agreed. "I think I may have eaten too much, though." He stretched his arms above his head and let out a sigh of contentment.

It was still early in the morning. They had just finished breakfast and were puttering around the camp, not doing anything in particular. Jayfor was trying to think of their next plan of action, and who to acquire help from, although so far no one came to mind. They had acquired the help of the two closest fiefs, Ronar and Lyson; and Dakdom fief, according to Randolph, had given their allegiance to Xavson, so that ruled out all the close fiefs. Jayfor considered that maybe Dakdom was pretending to ally with Xavson, just like Norman had, but it would be too risky to find out.

There weren't any other fiefs close enough to aid them tangibly, so they would need to secure help from elsewhere. But where else was there to secure help from? Jayfor didn't know.

"So, what are we going to do today?" Trenson asked.

Jayfor shrugged. "I don't know. To be honest, I don't know who else to seek help from." He glanced at both Trenson and Agrond. "Any ideas?"

Agrond held his hands out in a helpless gesture. "Nope. Norman and Randolph were the only two barons I really knew much about. Other than them, there's no one else I can think of."

Trenson shook his head. "I wouldn't know. I still barely know the lay of the land, much less anyone in it."

That makes sense, Jayfor thought. The prince sighed. "Well, I'm sure we'll think of something. In the meantime, I need to sharpen my sword. Any of you have a sharpening stone?"

Agrond and Trenson both shook their head.

"I'll just find one in the woods," Jayfor mumbled. With that, he started walking out of the clearing and into the deeper woods. His sword was already on his hip; he preferred to carry it with him wherever he went.

"Watch out for those hunting traps!" Agrond called with a grin on his face.

"You're hilarious, Agrond," the prince curtly called back, without turning his head, as he disappeared into the underbrush. In a few seconds, he was gone.

Agrond put his hand on his back and arched backwards, grunting as he did so. A staccato of cracks and pops followed, so much that Trenson couldn't help but raising his eyebrows. If he hadn't seen Agrond's lethality in action, he would have presumed that the burly man would be nothing more than a large target in battle.

"Well, I guess I should go sharpen my axe, too. It's suffered a few dents too many," Agrond said, then started walking towards the tent where everyone's weapons were kept.

Trenson now realized that he was alone and, rather dumbly, standing still, like an old fencepost, doing nothing. "I should probably sharpen my sword, too," he said aloud, even though no one was listening.

In a few minutes, Trenson retrieved his sword and throwing knives — deciding that he might as well sharpen them while he had time — a well-shaped stone, and a comfortable sitting spot, and began running the stone along the edge of the sword's blade, enjoying the ringing sound as the stone scraped against the steel. His blade had more knicks in it than he originally thought. The closer he looked, the more dents there seemed to be. That usually was the way it worked, he mused. Most of the time, the smallest problem had more consequence than it seemed at first when you looked closer.

As he sat there, calmly running the stone across the blade's edge, he couldn't help but marvel at how far he had come. In fact, he was still having a hard time accepting the fact that he was even here, with people he never thought he would be with, in a place he never thought he would be in, fighting for a cause that was radically different from the one he had started fighting for.

He smiled. He had learned that life had a habit of doing that, of bringing you places you never thought you would be. It was dangerous letting the current of life sweep you away. If you weren't careful, you never know where you might end up.

After a few minutes of sharpening both edges of the blade, along with the triangular tip, Trenson decided that the blade was good enough. His knives were still razor sharp, and besides a few knicks, hardly needed any attention, so he breezed through them quickly. He slid the sword back into its sheath and returned it to the weapon's tent. He spotted Agrond working on his weapon. The captain was taking extreme care with the axe, leaning over to examine it closely, running the stone very finely over the blade, as if afraid he was going to shatter the weapon if he wasn't careful. Trenson couldn't help but smile.

Trenson suddenly wondered where Jayfor was. His eyes scanned the camp, but he didn't see his friend. The prince should have finished sharpening his sword a long time ago. Maybe he was still looking for a good stone to use, he thought. The stone had to have a certain texture and shape to work effectively. But then again, Trenson had found a good stone within a few moments, and had already finished his work.

He remarked on the fact to Agrond. "Oh, I wouldn't worry," Agrond said, not looking up. "He likes to take his sweet time with his weapons. He'll be back, you'll see."

"That's what you said right before Jayfor got caught by the bandits," Trenson retorted.

"Eh, maybe so. But I'm rarely wrong twice," Agrond replied. It was clear that he had no intent of keeping this conversation going.

Trenson decided that Agrond was probably right. Not about being wrong twice, but about Jayfor being fine. It was probably just Déjà vu from the last time Jayfor had wandered into the woods.

He didn't have to wait long. A few minutes later, Trenson saw Jayfor emerge from the woods. The prince was walking very slowly, and after he had taken a few steps inside of the clearing, he stopped.

Trenson had a strange feeling that something wasn't right. Trenson approached Jayfor. Not used to starting a conversation, he fumbled for something to say. "Did you finish sharpening your sword?"

Jayfor didn't answer. Something *was* wrong. Jayfor's face was ashen, and his eyes were wide. His lips were pursed, and he had a look about him that Trenson had never seen before. He didn't answer. In fact, he didn't even look at Trenson. He just stared off into the distance, a faraway look in his eyes.

"Jayfor?" Trenson said, concerned.

Again, Jayfor didn't answer, or act as if he had heard. Instead, slowly, he started walking farther into the encampment, never once glancing at Trenson or without that strange look in his eyes.

Trenson feel into walking beside him. "Jayfor!" he said. No reply.

Fear ran through Trenson's mind. What had happened to his friend? Never had he been like this. Something must be wrong.

Trenson looked closer at Jayfor's face to discern what was going on. Surprisingly, he didn't see any signs of trauma or fear. Instead, it was... peace? And awe. Peace and awe. It looked like Jayfor had witnessed something so amazing, so terrifying, so grand, that he was speechless.

They were getting close to Agrond now, and once they were a few paces from him, Jayfor stopped. The captain still didn't look up from his work, oblivious to their presence. Trenson cleared his throat impatiently. Agrond jerked his head up, saw Jayfor and Trenson, and smiled.

"Ah, you see, Trenson, I told you he'd be fine!" he said, then he caught sight of Jayfor's dazed face, and the smile slowly faded. "Jayfor? What's wrong?"

Jayfor took a deep breath and seemed to gather himself. He looked first Agrond, then Trenson in the eye, with eyes that seemed to have a spark in them. Then he said, in a soft but firm voice, a voice that told of the wonder and amazement that he felt, a voice that sounded more confident and resolute than anything Trenson had heard before, "Va'ar spoke to me."

XXXIV

"WHAT?!" Trenson and Agrond both cried in disbelief.

Jayfor simply nodded.

Trenson and Agrond exchanged a glance. "What did you say?" Trenson asked slowly, thinking he must have misheard.

Jayfor, who seemed to be regaining himself a little more with each passing second, said unmistakably, "Va'ar spoke to me."

There was a pause. There was no doubt that Trenson had heard right, but... it was unbelievable.

"Are you sure?" Trenson asked.

Jayfor looked him in the eye. "Yes." The fire in Jayfor's eyes seemed to burn from his soul, like it had been ignited by something beyond comprehension.

"What did he say?" Agrond said, a ring of awe in his voice. It seemed that Agrond decided to believe Jayfor, even it did sound impossible. But then again, Agrond believed in Va'ar, so that was no surprise.

Jayfor began, looking off into the distance as he spoke, "I went into the woods to sharpen my sword, looking for a good rock to use. I couldn't find any. So, I went deeper into the woods. Finally,

I found a good stone, so I turned around to come back. Then I heard someone calling my name.

"I wish you could have been there to hear it. It was amazing. It came from everywhere at once, and all the other sounds faded away, making that one voice so much louder. The voice was calm, but powerful, like it had the power to create anything in the universe. He *does* have the power to do anything in the universe. The voice seemed to pierce into me, searching, seeing everything, my thoughts, my dreams, my doubts…

"I know, now, how wrong I've been. In my heart, I doubted Va'ar. I used to think that it didn't matter what I thought of Him. Even if he was there, it didn't concern me. But then I realized that I was wrong. So wrong."

A faint smile touched his lips. "I told Va'ar that I wasn't worthy to talk with Him, that I had doubted him. I was afraid that he might kill me for all the wrong that I've done. But then he said that He has called me for a purpose, to fulfill a role in his plan." He looked at both Agrond and Trenson. "And he said that both of you have parts to play in that plan, as well."

Jayfor paused, gathering himself, then continued. "He said that it was time. That now was the time to attack Loronis. He said to order the barons to call up their levies, and for every man to be ready, and to march for the capital in two weeks, even if all the men have not yet been called up. He said that he will deliver Loronis and Xavson into our hands, and that we will not fail."

Jayfor took a deep breath. "Then it was over, and He left. All the sounds returned, and I came back to here."

There was silence. Jayfor seemed to be lost in recollection of the event, and Agrond was doing the same thing as Trenson: thinking hard on what Jayfor had said.

Trenson still couldn't believe it. It was unbelievable. It was farfetched. It was, well, very unlikely. How could it be possible? It couldn't be. It just couldn't. But what if it was? No, It was impossible.

He looked Jayfor in the eye and saw the fire burning in them. Had he ever known Jayfor to lie? No, he had to admit. What reason would Jayfor have to lie? There was none. So why should he doubt the prince?

For the first time, he realized that he could be wrong, that Va'ar might exist. He had always thought of Va'ar as *probably not existing,* or *maybe existing,* or *it isn't important if what I think of Him.* But what if, instead, it was Va'ar *definitely existed?* That He was real? The idea startled him. He had not really considered the alternative. But what if it was true?

"That is truly amazing, Jayfor," Agrond said, breaking the silence. "Va'ar hasn't spoken to anyone in hundreds of years. Consider it an honor."

Jayfor smiled. "Yes, it was pretty amazing." Jayfor's smile faded. "Agrond, I'm sorry I doubted Va'ar. I should have... Well, I shouldn't have doubted. You were right about everything."

Agrond held his hands up. "Don't apologize, Jayfor. The important thing is that you believe now."

Jayfor nodded, then he turned to Trenson, who had been silent on his thoughts.

And with good reason, for Trenson still wasn't exactly sure what he *did* think. He was still debating whether he could accept Jayfor's word as true. He had every reason to; there was no reason why he shouldn't trust the prince. For months, he had survived and fought alongside Jayfor, never regretting a second of it, and not once had Jayfor deceived him. And yet, there seemed to be an invisible force pushing against him, trying to make him doubt what Jayfor said.

Eventually, Trenson returned to his old thinking: does it really matter? And do I really need to decide right now what I believe in? I can put it off, he thought. I can pretend to believe in Jayfor, just for everyone's sake, and decide what I think of this whole "Va'ar" stuff later.

Deciding that was what he would do, he finally spoke, "It is incredible that Va'ar spoke to you, Jayfor, and even more that he is aiding our fight against Xavson. With him on our side, we will not fail."

Trenson said these words convincingly, or at least he hoped he did, but Jayfor saw through them. The prince didn't say anything, but it was clear by his expression that he knew what Trenson was doing. *I know that you don't believe,* it said, *but you will. I know you will.*

Trenson looked away.

Agrond, once again, broke the uncomfortable silence that settled in the air. "Well, I guess we know our next plan of action now." He paused, looking at Jayfor, letting the prince finish for him.

And Jayfor did. "Yes. Va'ar has spoken; our future is clear. Today, we will send word to Lyson and Ronar fief to call up their levies, giving them two weeks to prepare themselves for an assault on the capital."

Agrond scratched his chin. "Fourteen days isn't very long. I can't say how many levies will be able to answer the call to arms in that short of a time, but I can guess it won't be many."

Jayfor shrugged and smiled. "It'll be enough."

Trenson said, "I sure hope so. After all, this is the largest capital in Ralladin that we're talking about."

Jayfor put his hands up in a gesture of surrender. "Hey, it wasn't my idea to attack the capital now! If you want to know the details, ask Va'ar."

Trenson didn't know how to respond to that.

"I'll gather the men and tell them the plan," Agrond said. He cast a questioning glance at Jayfor. "Should I tell them about yo ur... meeting, with Va'ar?"

Jayfor considered the question for a few seconds, then replied, "Sure. There's no harm in letting the men know that the creator of the universe is on our side, is there?"

Agrond smiled a wry smile. "There's truth to that!" He set his axe to the side, which was still in the process of sharpening, and stretched his arms out, which resulted in another staccato of pops and cracks. "I'll pick a few men to send out to Lyson and Ronar, but I'll send them to you first. I don't know exactly what you want to say."

Jayfor nodded. "Sounds good with me."

As Agrond started to walk away, he said over his shoulder, "Some day this has turned out to be!"

Jayfor grinned. "Just another day in the woods!"

XXXV

As he walked towards the study where king Xavson was, the secretary contemplated what exactly he was going to say.

He knew that this was a bad time. The king had been even more irritable than usual. The secretary guessed that it was because the number of rebels in the capital had increased, rather than diminished. Despite attempts to suppress any uprisings, there were more riots, more fires, more chaos... more things for the king to deal with. The addition of the death penalty for any crime against the crown had only made the people mad.

And that, in turn, made Xavson mad.

The secretary knew that he had to be careful. Xavson was known to fly off the handle when he heard news he didn't like, and more than one of his men had paid the price for it with their lives. The most recent of these was during yesterday's dinner, when one of the king's servants had dropped a potato on Xavson's shirt while replenishing his plate. The potato had hardly been removed, leaving no mark, before the servant was taken away and executed.

The secretary swallowed. This was more important than mishandled potatoes. He was beginning to consider why he had taken this job in the first place.

In a few moments — much too short for the secretaries liking — he reached the oak door. Pausing for a few seconds, he then tapped four times on the door, the standard knock that secretaries and news bearers were required to use.

"What?" The king's voice was brusque.

"My lord, I bear news."

Silence.

For a second, the secretary hoped that maybe Xavson would turn him away or say that he didn't want to hear it. That hope quickly vanished.

"Come in, then. Make it short."

With great trepidation, the secretary eased open the door, careful not to be too loud. Xavson had his back towards the secretary and was leaning over, mulling over something on his desk. The secretary was a little relieved. There was something dark about the king's eyes that he preferred to avoid.

Leaving the door open behind him, in case he needed to make a quick escape, the secretary stepped a few paces into the room and placed his hands behind his back in usual habit. He wrung his hands nervously as he thought about how he should begin.

He realized that he had said nothing for too long when Xavson spoke. "Do you find it amusing, staring at my back while I am busy?" The tone was dark and dangerous.

The secretary open his mouth to speak, then found that his lips were dry. He quickly moistened them. "No, sir," he replied, his tone in a much higher pitch than he would have liked.

"Then get on with it!" Xavson suddenly yelled. He whirled around in his chair and stared at his servant with fury. "You've ruined my train of thought already. Now you're making me wait! Spit it out!"

"Y-yes sir! My apologize, sir!" Now he had made the king even more mad. Sweat ran down the secretary's neck. He tried to look into Xavson's steely eyes of fire, but it burned too much. He dropped his head and found his voice.

"I have received word on the siege of Fort Lyson."

Xavson didn't move. "And?"

"And it appears that... the siege was unsuccessful."

Xavson's scowl hardened. "What?!"

"Well, a few moments ago, the remnant of the army that we sent to Lyson returned. They said that an unknown group appeared out of the woods and burned their onagers, and destroyed most of the army. The men claim that there must have some wizardry or magic involved."

"More like stupidity!" Xavson roared. "I spent half the treasury funding those useless fops of soldiers. And this is how they repay me?"

The secretary swallowed and was silent. He continued to wring his hands uncontrollably.

Xavson sighed. "Guess that's what happens when I hire dimwits for soldiers. At least most of them are dead now." He locked eyes with the secretary. "And what of Randolph? Is he dead?"

"No, my lord. He survived, along with most of his men. We don't have too much information, but it seems that the mysterious group burned the weapons and lured the troops out while Randolph attacked from behind. The baron is free."

Xavson cursed and slammed his hand onto the table. Some of the papers laying on the desk flew into the air. "Every day it's something worse. I have enough rebels inside of my walls to deal with. Now there are groups of them outside messing with my plans!" He turned his attention back to the edgy secretary. "Find this so-called 'mysterious group' and have them all killed."

Xavson, thinking that was the end of it, briskly turned back to his desk and began to look down on his papers once again.

The secretary didn't move. More sweat ran down the back of his neck. He continued to wring his hands, trying to find the best way to continue. He had aroused the monster now, he thought. He made sure that he was out of the king's reach and cleared his throat.

Xavson turned around and faced the secretary once more, his patience gone. "There's more, isn't there?"

The secretary nodded. "Yes, my lord. Both Lyson fief and Ronar fief are... calling up their levies."

The secretary wait for another outburst of rage from the king, but, strangely, there was none. Instead, Xavson remained unmoving, waiting for more. "What do you mean?"

Gathering courage, the secretary continued. "I received word of it today. Almost immediately after Fort Lyson defeated the siege army, both that fief and Ronar fief sent word to all men in the area, calling upon all men that are against you to rally to arms."

"A rebellion is what you mean," Xavson concluded coldly.

The secretary nodded. "Yes, my lord."

Xavson was silent. He had figured that there would be some fiefs against him. Lyson fief was a prime example of it. "Didn't Fort Ronar declare its allegiance to us?" Xavson said.

"Yes, my lord. It seems that they betrayed their word."

Xavson huffed. "Evidently." He went back to thinking. Both of those fiefs were large and owned lots of land, not to mention that they were also close to the capital. Together, both of those fiefs could amass a large number of men; no doubt they were in league together.

If those fiefs were amassing men in rebellion, it was clear what they intended: an assault on Loronis. Maybe not immediately, but at one point or another, they would attempt an attack on the capital. Xavson felt sure of it. The 'mysterious group' that had assailed the siege army had no doubt been another renegade band of dissenters.

But maybe this was an opportunity in disguise. Loronis was virtually impregnable. Any army that attempted to lay siege to it or attack it would be at an extreme disadvantage, and Xavson doubted that, even if the army was three times the size of his own, once the alarm had been sounded, there was no chance that anyone could ever take the capital.

The secretary waited patiently for a reply, or, better yet, a dismissal. The reply soon came. "I think it would be best to let them be for a while."

The secretary was shocked. "My lord?" he said involuntarily. The king had executed a servant who had dropped a potato on him, but wasn't going to punish rebels who killed his men?

"Yes, I said let them be. Think about it. The rebels are going to try to retake Loronis, right? If they are brash and brazen like I expect they'll be, I guess it will not be long before they attempt a direct assault. But there is no chance that they could ever take the capital. With all the escape routes and traps, it'll be a miracle if they get past the drawbridge. When they come here, they will all die."

He chuckled sadistically. "So, in essence, we'll let them gather all the troops they want. Then, when they attempt a move, we'll crush them all at once."

Now the secretary understood. He should have known that Xavson had some scheme for getting rid of the rebels. He clarified. "So don't do anything about the rebels? Just let them be?"

"Yes, that's what I said. It'll be easier to crush them all at once when they get here."

The secretary nodded.

Xavson glared at him. "Is there anything else that you want to pester me with?"

The secretary shook his head quickly. "No, sir."

"Then get out and leave me alone!"

The secretary couldn't have been happier to comply.

XXXVI

L ATER IN LIFE, TRENSON would look back on the two weeks before their assault on the capital as a blur. He would not be able to recount many specific details about those days, only that there was a lot that was going on.

For example, there was training to be done. Even though the men had occasionally sparred and practiced with each other during their months in hiding, it was nothing compared to what they were doing now. Agrond started them on a strict training routine that had Trenson thinking about battle and tactics in ways he never had before, and at the end of every long day, Trenson would fall asleep to the sound of his muscles screaming in protest of the day's training.

And there was also packing to be done. The tents and everything that they had set up had to be packed up and put away, ready to be returned to Norman when he arrived, along with all the food and everything they weren't going to take with them in battle. Easier said than done. Everyone had become a little lazy, spreading out everything in a not-so-neat fashion. Now they were regretting it.

But, more than anything, there was lots and lots of planning. The three men were always busy deciding if they should take this thing with them, if that thing was needed, when they should move that other thing, who should carry what, where they should move that thing, how should they deal with this problem… it was exhausting. Trenson was glad that he wasn't in the process of planning much, Jayfor and Agrond taking most of the burden, but he still had to deal with it a little, mainly helping the two men carry out the plan, such as putting up tents and dealing out armor and weapons. Trenson considered it a small price to pay, as long as he didn't have to deal with preparations. He was more of a doer than a thinker.

But at last, after two weeks of training, preparing and packing, the fourteen days were over. Every soldier was ready. There was a road in the woods; a wide one that ran straight through the trees. At one point, this road split into two different paths as it ran away from the capital. One of these ways went to Ronar, the other to Lyson. Jayfor had informed the barons that they were to bring every soldier they could with them and to meet early in the morning at the intersection.

And so, Agrond brutally jarring Trenson out of his peaceful sleep far before the sun was up, everyone was ready that morning. There would be no stopping after the three forces started for the capital, Jayfor reminded them. Once they met, they would organize their men and start marching. So everyone needed to have armor on, weapons on hand, food in their stomach, before they started out, or you'd have to be defenseless or hungry. The thought of being in the middle of battle without weapons or armor or food horrified everyone, so there was nobody not ready.

Trenson, despite Agrond's warnings, had strapped both throwing knife sheaths on each wrist over his armor. Agrond had said that throwing knifes would be useless, given that he would be so weighed down in armor and in close quarters while fighting. Trenson had ignored him and strapped the sheaths on, making sure that each knife was snug in its home. If there was anything that he had learned in his life, it was to be prepared.

Trenson was also faced with another dilemma: his horse. He had almost forgotten about it. It had become so tame that it stayed in camp, letting the men pet it and feed it, never wandering off or causing trouble... Trenson had grown fond of it, even though it still didn't have a name, and every time he looked at it he was reminded that it wasn't really his. He asked Jayfor about it.

"Are you sure you don't want to let it go?" Jayfor asked. "You could let it go free in the woods and not worry about it."

Trenson had shaken his head. "I'd rather not."

Jayfor thought about it for a few seconds. "Well, if you wanted, you could tether him to a tree just on the edge of the woods close to the capital where the battle will be. He'll be out of harm's way, and if... *when* we win the battle, you can go get him."

Trenson nodded. "That's sounds good to me. That is, if I'm alive by the battle's end, I'll get him."

"Va'ar said we will win the battle," Jayfor reminded.

"I know that. But did he say if any of us were going to die in the process?"

Jayfor opened his mouth to say something, then shut it.

So Trenson rode his horse in the front of the troops as they made their way to the meeting point. The animal was obviously glad to be ridden and to walk farther than the small area that was the campsite, and it shook its mane and neighed happily as it pranced forward.

Trenson wondered what Jayfor had in store for them. He had asked the prince earlier what their plan of attack was.

Jayfor didn't look Trenson in the eye, but Trenson caught sight of a mischievous grin on the prince's face. "What do you mean?" Jayfor had asked.

Trenson knew that Jayfor was toying with him, but decided that it was the only way to get the answer to his question. "I mean, are we simply going to march up to the front gate, knock until they lower the drawbridge, then bang on as many heads as possible until we reach the palace?"

"No, of course not!" Jayfor had said. Then he was silent for a long time. He tried to hide it, but there were traces of a grin still on his face. He was, once again, messing with Trenson.

But Trenson was in no mood to be messed with. "Well," he had said, somewhat in an ill temper, "What do you plan to do?"

Jayfor cast a sideways look at Trenson. "I plan to retake Loronis. What do you plan to do?"

"Don't banter with me, Jayfor!" Trenson said angrily. "You know right well what I'm talking about. Now what is it?"

Jayfor couldn't hold it in any longer. He burst into laughter. "You know me all too well, Trenson!"

Trenson didn't say anything. He was genuinely mad now, and he stood still, staring at Jayfor, waiting for him to stop laughing so that he could have his question answered. He didn't crack a smile as he waited.

Finally, Jayfor ceased his laughter, and, finally, answered his question. "Well, my friend, you'll just have to wait and see. You're right, I do have a plan. But I would rather share it with Randolph and Norman and Agrond all at once, just to save me some breath. But you'll hear it eventually."

Trenson huffed. "You just enjoy driving me insane, is why."

Jayfor grinned but said nothing.

Now, as he was riding to meet with the other two forces, Trenson tried to guess what this plan was that Jayfor was intent on not telling him. It probably had something to do with distraction, he thought — those seemed to be Jayfor's specialty, and they had freed Lyson using its concept — but he could never come up with an idea that would work.

The last time he had been in Loronis, he had seen the massive stone walls, the giant drawbridge and the moat that stretched far across the ground. He had seen small glimpses of the city inside, not many, but enough to know that they had some serious work to do if they wanted to reclaim it. What he had noticed above all, though, was the giant palace that stood in the city's center, a mountain of stone and craftsmanship, visible from far, far away.

That's where Xavson is, Trenson reminded himself, *in that palace.* It would take a miracle to take something that big and defended. The more Trenson thought about it, the more he was starting to think that this may not work.

But then again, Trenson told himself, almost sarcastically, Va'ar said to do it. So here we are.

***

It didn't take the small group long to reach the intersection in the woods. Trenson remembered it; he had gone through this intersection on his way to Loronis so long ago. He smiled, remembering how far he had come since then. How different his goals had been then than they were now, and how different he was now because of it. Once again, Trenson marveled at how far he had come. He wondered if he would ever look back on the assault on Loronis in such a way.

Possibly. If he was still alive.

The small group stopped at the agreed upon branch in the road and waited patiently. There was a square sign at the intersection, in between where the roads split. A few words were written, then an arrow pointed left. The words said, RONAR FIEF. There was another arrow, this time pointing right, and some more words, LYSON FIEF. There was also an arrow pointing down, indicating the road that went straight back and to the capital, with its own words: LORONIS.

It was by this sign that Trenson, Jayfor and Agrond waited. The rest of the men stood in the road, standing and kicking at the dirt, adjusting the uncomfortable armor they had to wear, talking with each other. They waited for the barons to arrive.

After a long period of time, Agrond whispered to Jayfor, although it was loud enough for Trenson to hear, "Do you think that Randolph and Norman will show up? I mean, we agreed to meet in the morning before sunrise." He looked at the orange-fingered sky that started to show in the distance through the trees. "It's almost sunrise, now."

"I'm sure they will." Jayfor said simply, although there was a note of worry in his voice.

Another period of silence passed, during which the sun continued to show glimmers of itself over the horizon. Trenson started to become worried. What if no one came? Then they would have to use only thirty men against the largest and most fortified capitals in Ralladin. Now matter what Va'ar said, Trenson thought, they would be crushed.

Finally, one of the knights called out, "I see them!"

Trenson whipped around and looked down the roads. Sure enough, much to everyone's relief, it was the barons. Both barons could be seen in the distance, Norman coming down the Ronar fief road, Randolph on the Fort Lyson road, each baron leading a assembly of men decked in armor and weapon behind him, dusting clouds rising in the air from the large groups. They came steadily towards them.

Everyone in Jayfor's group cheered at the sight of the barons. Their spirits soared now that they had help, and, from the looks of it, lots of it. The baron's had been true to their word. Jayfor would not have to stand alone.

XXXVII

"There it is." Jayfor's voice was filled with awe. He looked down from the ridge he and the men were standing on and gazed at the capital a few miles away, which looked huge even from a distance. Beside him were Trenson and Agrond, along with Norman and Randolph, who were mounted on horses.

"I never thought I'd return here," Jayfor continued. He was in a dreamlike state. "I mean, I know we worked so hard to get here, and now... It's about to happen."

Everyone else was silent, thinking it better to say nothing. They knew that Jayfor had to be going through inner turmoil right now, going to war against his brother, the same one that was out to kill him and had destroyed everything he loved. Nobody else here could relate to that, and so, wisely, they didn't try to lighten the mood or say anything.

Trenson also had some thinking to do. A few months ago, he had been on this very same hill, looking down on the same capital, on the same horse. It felt like that was ages ago. Loronis seemed to have regained order since the last time he was here: there were no burning buildings or screaming, no signs of an insurrection. It looked the same as it had for years, with tall proud walls, a wide moat, orderly streets and houses, and a massive palace in its center. Everything looked quiet and peaceful.

But looks can be deceiving.

Randolph, his claymore strapped to his back, gazed across the plain at the capital below. "I never thought I would be attacking this place."

Agrond grunted. "Me neither. Yet here we are!"

"How did I get dragged into this?" Norman moaned. He held a spear in his right hand, though it looked like he did so reluctantly. His horse sensed that his rider was nervous, and so it in turn was nervous, pawing at the ground and twitching at the reins, which Norman fingered anxiously.

Randolph cast a glance at Norman. "You signed up for it, that's how."

"I never imagined that I would be in *battle*, though!" Norman replied. "I thought I would simply supply the means to retake our kingdom and be done with it. I had no idea I would be *fighting*! What if I die?" he said, as if he were the only person who had thought of the possibility.

Randolph replied in a level voice. "Then we'll speak fondly at your funeral."

For some reason, this didn't make Norman feel any better.

Jayfor apparently didn't hear any of the exchange, and he said softly to himself, still lost in thought, "Maybe there is a way we can end this without bloodshed. Perhaps we can settle our differences, to leave behind everything that has happened to walk the same paths." Jayfor was silent for a few moments.

Then he spoke again. "No, it would be impossible. We serve two different lords, one of the Light, the other of the Shadow. This is the only way. Va'ar has commanded us to retake Loronis. And so that is what we will do."

Agrond stepped forward. "I will fight with you, my prince."

"So will I," Trenson said.

"And I," Randolph joined.

"Me too, seeing as I have no choice," Norman said dolefully.

Jayfor looked at his companions. He also looked behind him at the army of knights that Norman and Randolph had gathered. There were hundreds of them, men from all walks of life, coming together to fight for a common cause. All these men had sacrificed to fight for him. The weight of the realization hit him hard. He was leading them. They would follow him anywhere.

"Thank you," was all Jayfor could say.

Then Trenson spoke up. "Well, I guess should find a tree to tether my horse to."

***

There was a small wooded area close to the front gate of the capital, the last hidden area before it opened into plains. Jayfor led the army there. "It will be better to stay hidden as long as possible," he said. "Surprise is not essential to my plan. However, it may help."

The plan. Trenson had heard Jayfor refer to his 'plan' countless times during the last two weeks. It had driven Trenson insane, how

Jayfor would weasel his way out of revealing this plan every time he asked. Trenson had spent every second trying to guess this plan.

So when Jayfor called for a halt in the woods and took Trenson, Agrond and the barons to the side to discuss 'the plan,' Trenson was ecstatic.

"Well," Trenson started when they had gathered together, "tell us about this plan of yours! You've kept us waiting long enough."

Jayfor couldn't help but smile. "That I have."

Everyone stared intently at Jayfor, waiting for his plan. Clearing his throat, the prince took unfurled the map of Loronis across his arm, holding it up for everyone to see. It showed the city and its walls, along with some of the area outside the walls.

"As you all know," Jayfor began, "Loronis keeps roughly five to ten thousand soldiers in its reserves."

Trenson let out a low whistle. That was a lot. Randolph, however, looked surprised. "I thought they kept more."

"They would," Jayfor replied, "and they usually do have more men. But the war has forced them to send more men to the front, and a lot of soldiers have decided to quit in the last few years. So, in an average circumstance, they would have about five to ten thousand men on hand."

Agrond scratched his chin. "This isn't a normal circumstance, though."

"Exactly. Xavson has some new policies now that he's king, and from what you told me, Randolph, Xavson is having to hire mercenaries to replace all the knights that are leaving his ranks. This will help us greatly, not just because most mercenaries are lousy fighters, but because it means that there will be fewer men for us to fight. I would say about five thousand at a maximum will be defending the capital."

Everyone nodded. That made sense.

Then Norman piped in. "So, are we doing a frontal assault?"

Agrond quickly responded before Jayfor could. "We can't. First there's the moat. Then there are the walls and drawbridge. On top of that, we don't have enough men to starve them out, or any siege weapons to knock over the walls. A frontal assault is out of the question."

"Actually," Jayfor corrected, "We will be doing a frontal assault, to some degree."

There was a stunned silence. Everyone stared at Jayfor. A frontal assault? With how little men they had? Jayfor calmy returned their looks with confidence.

"But... how?" Agrond stammered. "First there's the moat. Then there are the walls and drawbridge. On top of that—"

"We don't need to get through their defenses," Jayfor said. "They will come out to us."

Once again, everyone stared blankly at Jayfor. Everyone knew that Jayfor was letting the silence drag on for his personal enjoyment, but they were starting to get tired of it. Jayfor let the silence continue for a few more seconds before the withering stares forced him to comply.

"Alright, alright," Jayfor said with a smile, "I'll told you the plan. But first, let me tell you a story.

"A long time ago, when I was around nine or ten, I went out of the palace to do some 'treasure hunting.' Recently, I had read a story of a man who found a map that led lead him a to buried treasure, and he became rich. Well, I thought, I might as well try to dig up some treasure myself, even though I don't have a map.

"So I went outside the castle walls and into the woods, digging at many places, but I didn't find anything. I decided to try to dig at one last spot, and that's when I found something."

Jayfor pointed at the woods they were in on the map, to a spot a little distance away. "It was a trapdoor. It led underground, under the streets of Loronis, and into the palace, where it opened up into the palace gardens.

"I kept what I found to myself, thinking I might get in trouble for finding something that was supposed to be kept a secret. As time went on, I was showed all the escape routes, hidden entrances and exits, and other things about the palace. But this trapdoor was never mentioned. I asked many times if they were sure that they knew all the hidden passages, and the reply was always yes. I am confident that this is the only entrance that Xavson doesn't know about."

Faces lit up in realization. They started to see where Jayfor was going with this.

Jayfor continued. "My plan is this: Me, Randolph and Norman will lead the bulk of the force to the front gate of the capital. We have about five hundred or so men with us, so that will allow us to pose enough of a threat that Xavson will have to send a force to deal with us. In the meantime, while the bulk of the guards are distracted with us, Agrond and Trenson will lead a group of about fifty men through the secret passage and into the palace. Once there, your goal is to get rid of Xavson. After Xavson is defeated,

I have no doubt that the army will either lay down their arms or flee."

Jayfor took a deep breath. "After that, Faldon will be free."

There was silence. Each person let the final words soak in, knowing what they were about to do. After months of hoping, that hope would finally be a reality.

At least, they hoped it would.

XXXVIII

Xavson looked up from his study when a series of sharp raps drummed on the door. "My king?" said a voice hesitantly, "I bear important news."

Letting out an ill-tempered sigh, the king set the book that he was reading to the side. He was currently studying political power and advancement from a book that he had requested, since it was usually banned from the palace. The book was written by a king from Kallary a long time ago, and it details steps to ensure a successful and powerful reign. With its narcistic methods, it was considered a work of tyranny by most, but Xavson didn't care. Already his reign was more powerful and stronger from doing what the book said.

Xavson muttered a curse under his breath. "Come in," he said, in a voice that clearly said *this better be important.*

The door slowly opened, and a frail, small servant poked his head through the door. His face masked in fear, though he tried not to show it, as he edged the door open carefully and stepped tentatively into the room.

As usual, the king's study was a mess. Books and papers littered the desk and floor, some stacked in neat piles, others strewn haphazardly everywhere. It seemed that the kingdom wasn't the only thing thrown into chaos; Xavson's study had suffered the same effect.

"Well," Xavson snapped, "Don't just stand there! Open your dumb mouth and get on with it!"

The servant's face turned even whiter. He swallowed hard. "M-my lord," he stammered, "there is... an army at the front gate."

Xavson, who was expecting an unimportant report, snapped to attention. "What did you say?"

Distraught, the servant nodded, sweat building on his forehead. "There are... well, to put it plainly, there is... there is an army waiting at the front gate of the capital."

Realizing that he wasn't going to get anything more from his servant, Xavson growled and stood up from his desk. The servant stepped back, cowering, thinking that the king was coming for him. Instead, thankfully, Xavson walked briskly to the small circular window at the right wall of the room and looked out, scowling deeper as the sun shone in his eyes. He could see a large part of the city from here, including the main drawbridge. Although it was so far away, it was hard to see.

Sure enough, on the other side of the wall, looking like a smidge of gray in the distance, Xavson saw what had to be hundreds of soldiers standing before the drawbridge. It was hard to tell, but even from this far, Xavson could tell that this force was relatively small.

Ridiculously small, in fact, compared to the might of Loronis.

Xavson huffed. "Fools. This is the uprising I heard about, the one I have waited for. They have even fewer men than I thought they would." He turned to the servant, who was waiting nervously for an answer, and said, as calmy as if he had been asked about the time, "Send out the army from the palace barracks. Kill them all. Spare no one."

The servant, used to orders like this, nodded, but he didn't leave the room. Instead, more sweat built on his forehead. Xavson knew this meant there was more to come, and he turned and gazed scornfully at the servant. The servant stuttered, "There is more, my lord. The one leading the army is Jayfor, your brother."

Startled, Xavson took a step back in surprise. He looked out the window, as if trying to see Jayfor far away in that smidge of gray in the distance. Then he looked back at the servant, his eyes like burning coals. "Jayfor?"

The servant nodded and edged closer to the door, ready to make a quick escape.

For the first time, the king seemed at a loss for words. He sank back into his chair. He was silent, thinking about what he had heard. The servant remained quiet, the silence inwardly killing him, wanting more than ever to run from the king's presence. The servant wondered if maybe the king would pity his brother. After all, it was his own flesh and blood, and perhaps Xavson would show some mercy to him.

At last, Xavson smiled a terrible smile. "Of course," he said softly to himself, "Of course it's Jayfor. Who else would raise such an army against me? I should have known that it would be him. Now I can make sure of his death." He turned on the servant again with his eyes of burning coals. "Your orders remain the same. None of them shall live to see the light of day."

Then, in one quick motion, the king stepped forward, grabbed the servant by the neck, and pulled him close. The servant let out a gasped in fright, which was quickly cut off as the king's grip tightened around his neck. The servant felt Xavson's hot breath and felt the burning sensation he always felt whenever he looked into the king's eyes, now close to his own. "Above all," Xavson said softly, "I want Jayfor dead." Then he shook the servant and suddenly screamed in his face, "Dead! Do you hear me? *Dead*!"

All the servant could do was grab at the hand encircling his neck and nod as much of a nod as he could manage.

With barely any effort, Xavson hurled the servant down to the ground, hard. The servant lay crumpled on the ground, eyes wide, gasping for air.

"You may leave now," Xavson said, in a completely normal voice, like nothing had happened.

The servant needed no further prompting. The second the last words were out of the king's mouth, the servant scrambled for the door, half crawling, half running. He quickly made it through the door and shut it behind him. Xavson was once again left alone.

Xavson chuckled. He enjoyed inspiring fear in his subjects. It made them obey, no matter what order he gave them, without question. He walked over to the window and looked once again at the gray stain in the distance, and he chuckled again. "How nice of you to come to me on a silver platter. It makes it so much easier than to hunt you down. Now I can crush you along with the other rebels! Thank you, Jayfor, for making this so easy."

XXXIX

THE SILENCE WAS UNNERVING.

Jayfor's horse pawed nervously at the dirt, as did almost every other calvary horse in the army. The animals could sense the suspense and urgency in their riders, and so they, in turn, felt the same. The experienced horse knew to stay calm. They had years of training instilled into them, and had fought many battles. The newer horses pulled at the reins, eyes wide and alert. It took all their riders had to keep them under control.

It was similar for the soldiers. The veterans held their weapons ready with eager anticipation. They shouted encouragement to everyone, encouragement that the levies — most of which had hardly held a weapon in their life — needed.

After all, they were facing down an enemy that was impossible for them to defeat. It depended on Agrond and Trenson. If they failed, then they were all dead.

Randolph paced his horse across the front lines of the army to where Jayfor was mounted on his horse. The prince wore his royal sword strapped to a back sheath, since he didn't plan to use it in battle. The sword was too small and not heavy enough to be used effectively on horseback. Instead, he brandished a steel-tipped spear, heavy enough to pierce through armor when it built momentum. His royal sword was to be used only when needed.

"We've been out here for a while," Randolph said bluntly, breaking the silence.

Jayfor turned to the baron. Both of them were decked in full chain and steel armor and had their visors up. "It hasn't been as long as you think, Randolph. Be patient."

Randolph grunted and continued to stare at the drawbridge across the moat, just like everyone else was doing.

Silence.

Seeing the drawbridge brought back memories for Jayfor. A few months ago, he had fled from this drawbridge with Trenson's help, the only survivor of his group. Barely had they managed to escape.

Turning around and gazing at the company under his command, he couldn't help but feel proud. Now they were the ones coming for their enemies.

Silence.

Norman, who was on horseback beside Jayfor, was doing something Jayfor had instructed him *not* to do before the battle: eating candies.

Jayfor scowled at him. "Norman! I told you not to do that!"

Norman, just finishing shoving another handful into his mouth, looked timidly at the prince. "I am sorry, my prince!" he mumbled through the mouthful, "I just can't help it! It's my poor nerves." He held in his hand the same box of candy that Jayfor had seen while they were in Ronar fief. His spear was resting in a cup by the stirrup, not in the baron's hands.

Norman's horse was also angsty. It whined and strained at the bit, clear signs that Norman didn't ride or train his horse very often. In an attempt to calm the animal, Norman grabbed some candies from the box and leaned forward in the saddle, about to feed the horse some of the candies.

"Norman!" Jayfor said, scornfully, "Don't feed your horse those things! That'll only make it worse."

Norman retracted his hand and put the sweets he would have given to his horse into his mouth. "It makes me feel better! Why shouldn't it make him?"

Jayfor sighed. "Just put those things up soon, please."

Norman, looking relieved that he didn't have to give up his precious box, nodded. Then, while the silence was broken, he said, "I have never before fought a battle so large, or... so hopeless."

Jayfor scowled at him. "It's not hopeless. We're simply the distraction. If... *when* Trenson and Agrond make it to the throne room and kill Xavson, we will have won."

Norman was skeptical. "What if the army decides to keep fighting even after they lose their king?"

Jayfor was about to reply, then stopped. He hadn't thought of that. It was unlikely. But what if it *did* happen? "I—"

Sudden, there was a clang from the drawbridge. Then the sound of gears turning mechanically. Every soldier snapped to attention. The drawbridge started to lower.

"Steady!" Jayfor called, "Steady!" He gripped his spear tight. Randolph held his claymore ready. Norman hastily put his box back into his saddlebag and grabbed his spear.

The clanging continued. The drawbridge continued to lower. It was about halfway down now.

"Be strong, everyone!" Jayfor cried out. "Remember, we fight not for ourselves, but for Va'ar! We will not lose!"

The soldiers replied with a roar of courage. The drawbridge hit the stone bridge that spanned a little way across the moat with a thud. The sound of gear turning stopped…

As did the cries of Jayfor and his army.

For, on the other side of the drawbridge, was the largest army Jayfor had ever seen.

In columns, the soldiers across the drawbridge stood, their spears pointed toward the sky, visors all lowered. The calvary stood at the front lines. Not a single horse was not armored, not a single horse pawed or was nervous. Standing behind the calvary were knights, hundreds of them, *thousands* of them.

Gasps of surprise ran along Jayfor's army. Jayfor felt the cold hand of fear grip his heart. He couldn't even see the end of this massive wall of troops. How did they even stand a chance?

Then he remembered Va'ar and His promise that victory would be theirs. His courage returned. He gripped his spear tighter.

Slowly, he raised his right arm in the air. Then he threw it down, pointing it forward, and yelled one word, "CHARGE!"

With a chorus of battle cries, the resistance army rushed forward, weapons ready, into the front lines of the enemy. Seeing their foe attack, Xavson's army responded with an ear-splitting roar and charge forward, a sea of gray armor.

Trenson, Jayfor thought, *don't fail us now.*

***

"We're getting close," Agrond said, excitement building in his voice.

Trenson peered at the map from beside the battle commander. Although no expert on map reading, Trenson could tell they were getting close. The X that Jayfor marked on the map was getting closer and closer.

Although he knew it was just an immature fantasy, Trenson couldn't wait to see the secret passage. He had never seen one before. He wondered what it was like. He imagined it as a sort of corridor, with stone walls and stairs that led underground. He had also never seen the inside of a palace before, which was something else he was looking forward to.

Stop being so excited. You're on a mission to reclaim Loronis, not a sightseeing trip.

They had been walking for some time, always staying in the woods to avoid being seen. By the look of the map, they were about one-tenth of the way around the capital. By how long it had taken them to get here, Trenson felt like they should be halfway around the city by now. He was once again reminded of just how big the city really was.

Behind them followed the fifty knights that had been assigned to them, and they were following the commander as he looked at the map. Trenson hoped that fifty men would be enough. It wasn't a full-blown assault; the only reason they brought that many men was in case they met with some resistance while in the palace.

"Stop!" Agrond suddenly shouted.

Everyone stopped short. The knights in the back of the company ran into the ones in front, leading to a short period of confusion. They soon reorganized, and the confusion quickly turned into excitement.

Agrond held the map close to his face, his brows furrowed. "A large gnarly tree," he muttered. He looked up. Sure enough, twisting around itself and gray with age, with barren branches, was a large gnarly tree.

Agrond walked up to it and felt the smooth outside of the tree. It was so old it didn't have any bark; it was just smooth. Trenson felt his heartbeat quicken. Agrond sudden exclaimed, "Aha!" and grinned at Trenson, motioning for him to come over. Trenson did and saw what Agrond was excited about: there was scrawny X crossed into the tree. The mark was deep and distinct, clearly made a long time ago.

Agrond turned around and set his back to the mark. Then, counting out loud, he took eight steps away from the tree. His steps were carefully placed and were an equal distance from each other. Everyone watched intently.

After taking the eighth step, Agrond stopped. Agrond kicked the ground a few times where his eighth step landed, leaving an indention in the ground. He looked up and met the eyes staring at him with a smile. "Here! Dig here!"

The soldiers had brought three shovels with them, courtesy of Norman's fief. Jayfor told them that the trapdoor wasn't buried deep, maybe a few feet or so down. The knights who carried the shovels stepped out from the regiment and gathered around the mark that Agrond made on the ground. Then they started to dig, scooping up clods of dirt and moving them to the side, creating dust clouds that hovered in the air.

They had dug for less than a few minutes before they were rewarded by a loud, hollow *thud*. The digging stopped, and the soldiers, along with Trenson and Agrond, ran forward to see if they hit home.

Throwing aside their shovels, the soldiers now eagerly scraped dirt away from the hole with their hands. They felt something hard and smooth on the bottom, and were positive that they had finally hit what they had been digging for. Even Trenson and Agrond leaned over the hole and scooped out dirt.

Before long, a small wooden hatch was revealed, with a handle on one side. They finished clearing off the dirt from the top of it and stood back. The wood was reinforced and had been in good condition at one point, but now it was half rotten and gray, and waterlogged from being in the ground.

Still, they weren't very picky about its appearance.

"There it is!" Agrond grinned. The knights chuckled in agreement.

Trenson walked forward, grabbed the handle on the hatch, and pulled. It didn't budge. He pulled again, this time harder. It still didn't move. He grabbed it with both hands and pulled up as hard as he could. Finally, there was a groan of wood, and the trapdoor reluctantly opened.

Immediately, noxious fumes rose from the opening, so foul that Trenson let go of the handle and stumbled backwards, gagging. The trapdoor lid fell backwards and stayed open.

"Phew!" Agrond said, waving the air in front of his nose, "That stinks!"

Trenson, holding his nose, nodded in agreement. Already the appeal of the secret passage was wearing away.

Agrond cast a mischievous glance at Trenson. "Well, you opened it, so I think you should have the honor of going in there first."

Trenson returned the glance with a withering look, but Agrond ignored it. Trenson sighed, realizing he wasn't getting out of this. He approached the hole. The smell seemed to get worse by the second. Turning around, he let his leg dangle until he found the ladder rung. Then he lowered himself down into the darkness.

"SHIELD WALL! FORM A shield wall!" Jayfor shouted.

Immediately, the shield-bearers rushed to the front lines and set their shields forward, halting Jayfor's army advance halfway across the drawbridge and creating a formidable wall as the defending army rushed towards them.

"Spearmen, form a wall!" Jayfor shouted.

The spearmen came forward and set their spears into the gaps between shields, keeping them level, pointing them at the oncoming foe with a look of determination under their helmets, ready for anything. Now an iron spiked wall had been formed. When the shield wall held, it could defeat hundreds of soldiers before it dissolved into individual fighting.

But that was the hard part: making sure the shield wall held.

Jayfor's army was hallway across the drawbridge. Although the bridge was large, it could only hold about thirty men standing towards each other with its width. This was an advantage for Jayfor's army. It took away the ability for the larger force to surround them or to use their numbers effectively.

The calvary of Xavson's army continued to charge, the hoofbeats of the horses making the wooden drawbridge shudder.

"Steady, men, steady!" Randolph called out.

The calvary came closer, their spears leveled at the gaps in the wall, the horses plowing forward with flaring nostrils, the armor glinting the sun, the thundering hoofbeats becoming louder and louder—

Until, like a tidal wave on the shore, the calvary slammed into the shield wall with tremendous force.

A shock wave ran through the line of shields. Horse impaled themselves on spear shafts and tumbled over, screaming and taking their rider down with them. Shieldmen struggle to hold the line. Spears thrust out from gaps in the wall, sometimes banging against armor, other times striking home.

And still, the onslaught continued. More calvary ran forward to replace those that had fallen, pummeling the shield wall with everything they had. But the wall, although already battered, held firm. The momentum of capital's army had stopped.

Knowing that this was an opportunity to turn the tide, Jayfor held his spear high. "Attack! Hold nothing back! For Va'ar!"

The momentum of the battle changed. The shield wall dissolved, and the calvary and foot soldiers poured through the opening, slashing and hacking with spears and swords and axes. Jayfor rushed forward and through the wall, his spear darting to each opponent like a death adder. Rare was the time when Jayfor's thrusts didn't fell his foe.

Xavson's army was surprised at the sudden charge, and began to falter back. The resistance army took full advantage of this, and pressed forward, striking down foes left and right, holding back nothing, fighting for a cause greater than themselves.

***

"Someone light a torch," Agrond said through the murky darkness. The small light which came from the open trapdoor above made the outline of Trenson and Agrond visible, along with the few other knights who had made it down as well.

It was clammy, dark, and even more foul-smelling inside the cave than Trenson had imagined. Wooden beams stretched in intervals across the dirt roof, held up by posts along the walls. The wood holding up the roof and walls looked extremely deteriorated, waterlogged and rotten. The floor of the cave was wet; enough that Trenson's boots sunk just enough to allow water to seep through the material.

More men descended from the ladder from above. Only about half of the knights had made it down so far. As Agrond instruct, torches were taken out, sparks flew, then, before long, they had lit all dozen of the torches that they brought, and the cave that had been dark for ages was finally illuminated.

"It's not as cramped in here as I thought it would be," Agrond commented.

Trenson looked around at the passage. "I actually think it's way too tight in here." The roof was tall — about a few feet over Trenson's head — but it wasn't very wide, only allowing for about three men to walk side by side at a time.

Agrond shook his head. "I've been in worse." Without explaining, he took a torch that one of the knights was handing out and held it out in front of him, trying to pierce as much of the darkness as possible. Everyone saw that the cave sloped down steadily into the unknown, the light of the torch only revealing so much until its reach was cut off by darkness.

"Looks like we're going down!" Agrond said, almost as if he was glad that there would be more dirt hanging over their head later. No one responded.

Trenson shifted his feet, which were becoming wetter and muddier by the second. "This is... different, then I imagined," he said in a downcast voice.

Agrond nodded. "As far as secret passages go, this one is terrible. It's like a mining shaft, not an escape route. Most of them are better than this, I think."

Finally, the last man climbed down the ladder, and the entire group of infiltrators were successfully cramped into a dark and humid cave. The men muttered about the overcrowded and stench of the cave, but the small space amplified the voices enough for them to be heard by all.

Agrond clapped his hands together. The clap echoed many times until it rippled away in the darkness. "Well, if this isn't exciting, I don't know what is! Let's hurry and get out of this stink hole before we miss out on the action."

***

"Lord Xavson." The military commander walked up to the king, who was leaning against the railing on the balcony, watching the vivid battle below. "The battle has begun."

For perhaps the hundredth time that day, Xavson silently cursed his dim-witted servants. Of course, he knew the battle had started. He was literally watching the battle right now, as he had been for the past ten minutes. Without averting his eyes from the battle, he said evenly, "Are you implying that I am blind?"

Fear immediately overtook the military commandment. What had he said wrong? "Uh... no sir, I never—"

"Then what do you think I'm doing? Cloud watching?" Xavson's voice rose. "I know the battle has started! I can see it right there! If you have nothing better to say, then leave!"

The military commander realized his error and made a hasty bow. "Yes, my lord." He left the balcony as fast as he could.

Xavson shook his head in disgust. Why was it so difficult finding people that held his same ideals along with common sense?

The pesky servant gone, Xavson turned his attention back to the battle. He couldn't tell which side was which. It was all a surging sea of gray armor from this far away. The sounds of battle still carried over to the palace. Cries and shouts mingled with clanging armor to create an indistinct hum.

Xavson scratched his chin thoughtfully. *Jayfor knows better than this. Why forfeit his life in a hopeless attempt?* Sure, it was convenient for Xavson; it saved him the trouble of hunting down the resistance fighters. But Jayfor was a crafty one. He was smarter than this.

Xavson voiced his thought out loud. "What do you have in mind, Jayfor?"

"JAYFOR!" RANDOLPH SHOUTED ABOVE the turmoil. He swung his heavy broadsword down in an arc that dispatched a soldier to his left. Then he swung the sword around to his left, using the unstoppable momentum to slam the blade into the helmet of another soldier, which sent him flying.

Jayfor paused fighting to see the baron racing towards him, his long sword stained red with the blood of his enemies. His horse was also covered in blood and sweat. Randolph reined his horse to a stop beside Jayfor. "The vanguard is failing!" he shouted. "Their calvary is too strong!" He paused to strike down another foe. "We need a new plan!"

Jayfor knew this was true. They needed to hold off the enemy until the palace was taken. The sounds and stench of battle made it hard to think clearly. "Move the remaining spearmen to the front and call the archers to fire from the back! Continue to press the calvary forward!" He thrust his spear into the nearest enemy soldier and quickly withdrew it. The foe crumpled to the ground. "We must hold fast!"

****

"We have to be getting close," Trenson said desperately. "We have to be."

He couldn't bear this passage much longer. The stench, the darkness, the closeness of the roof and walls... At first, he thought the secret passage would be exciting and interesting, the kind of thing only heroes would use. And it was exciting and interesting at first. Not anymore.

"We've been walking for a while," Agrond said, his face illuminated in the flickering torchlight, "so we should be reaching the end before long. Then again, this is the largest capital in Ralladin. Naturally, it's pretty big. Not too much longer, by my reckoning."

That would be a relief, Trenson thought.

Which each step forward, the mud squished under Trenson's feet, the cavern only becoming more wet the deeper they went. It wasn't just Trenson's boots, though; the sound of fifty pairs of boots squelching away at the same time was maddening.

The passage had no turns. It continued to wind steadily downwards, on and on. The damp air and small space suffocated Trenson.

"What are we going to do when we get out of here?" Trenson asked Agrond. It was something that weigh heavily on his mind.

"Well," began Agrond, "according to Jayfor, this passage exits somewhere in the palace gardens. I've personally never been in the gardens before, but I know it's layout. Once we're outside this hole, I'll lead the way out of the garden and through the palace, all the way into the sanctum, where Xavson, hopefully, will be. Most of the guards should be in battle. Of course, there will still be some at the palace, but hopefully we can avoid them or keep moving until we reach the throne room, or sanctum, and deal with Xavson."

Trenson nodded. That made sense.

The palace gardens... Trenson had never seen a palace garden before. He imagined it was probably giant, with exotic plants and fruits everywhere. Of course, he had been optimistic about the secret passage, and that turned out to be a flop. He hoped that the gardens wouldn't be equally disappointing.

Thankfully, the cavern began to slope upwards. Everyone breathed a sigh of relief. Nobody was having a good time in the passage, and everyone was eager for when they could finally be out in the open again. They had lost track of how long they had been in the cavern.

"Everyone, stop!" Agrond suddenly called out.

The soldiers in the back crashed into the ones up front and it took a few moments to reorganize, but when they saw the reason they had stopped, everyone let out a chorus of joy.

It was a ladder, identical to the one they had used to climb down into the passage. The corridor ended a few feet after the ladder, a solid wall of black dirt. The ladder reached to the roof, where a trapdoor was.

"There it is!" Agrond said jubilantly. He walked over to the ladder and put one foot on it, testing its strength. After deciding it would hold him, he quickly ascended the small distance from the floor to the roof and pushed on the trapdoor. It wouldn't move. He put both hands on it and grunted as he pushed hard, but it remained still.

"It feels like it's buried under a few layers of dirt," Agrond said. "That makes sense, though. The other trapdoor was buried too. Well, I guess we'll have to break the trapdoor. Someone hand me a spear."

One of the knights walked forward and offered Agrond, who climbed down the ladder and took it from him. The commander looked back at the group staring at him. "Everyone stand back. A load of dirt will fall in once this breaks."

Everyone acknowledged the warning and took a few steps back.

"Well, here it goes!" With that, Agrond began to thrust violently at the wooden trapdoor.

***

Directly above where Agrond was, an overseer was ordering the servants in the garden. He, as always, shouted his commands angrily.

"Move that potted plant over there! And fix its branches. They don't need to droop like that!"

Wearily, the servants complied and heaved the pot up, staggering under the weight of the large tree as they moved it to where the overseer directed.

"That's better. Actually... no, move it over there! Hurry up!"

The servants all groaned. The new overseer was harsh and demanding, unlike the kind master they had before. This overseer knew nothing of gardening or flora, but he always managed to blame the problems on his workers.

The overseer shouted when he saw the servants hesitate. "Come all!" he yelled. To emphasize his point, he stamped his foot down hard on the ground.

The pot never did get moved, for at that moment, something happened.

The ground below the overseer suddenly opened up and fell in on itself. With a cry of surprise, the overseer fell straight down into the square hole at his feet and disappeared.

The servants stopped and stared, awestruck. A cloud of dust rose from the small square hole that the overseer fell into. Voices came from below.

Then, a large, muscled knight, covered in dirt, poked his head out of the hole. He grinned. "We made it!" he said.

***

Time was running out.

It was as clear as day. Jayfor tried to ignore it, but it was something that could not be ignored, and every second that passed it become harder and harder to avoid.

They were losing.

Jayfor's spear darted at foes in swift, lethal strikes. He felt his strength waning, like the sun setting, every blow a little weaker than the last. He felt it, and it angered him that he was tired, so he tried to fight harder and urge his horse on farther, but it only made him weaker.

Everyone else felt the same. The resistance fighters felt their strength slowly drain like the hope they had when they started the battle. Xavson's army had lost hundreds of men, more men than the resistances army had at the start of the battle. Their losses were heavy, embarrassingly heavy, considering how small their enemy was. But with every soldier the defenders lost, three more took their place. The water of the moat was red, red from the blood of the soldiers who had fallen off the drawbridge, both dead and alive.

"We're losing!" cried Norman in fear. His horse shied and tried to bolt, while Norman did his best to keep the animal under control. The fact that his horse was crazed with fear had actually turned into a benefit, though, as every enemy soldier that got close to it went flying from the animal's flailing. It wouldn't surprise Jayfor if the horse had killed more men than the baron, although, to be fair, Norman did fell a few soldiers in self-defense.

"I know!" Jayfor shouted. "But we're not supposed to be winning! Our goal is to hold them off until Agrond and Trenson reach Xavson!"

A soldier with a spear ran at Norman and thrust the steel tip at the baron. Norman ducked and let the shaft pass harmlessly overhead. Then he returned the thrust with his own, and the mercenary fell to the ground. "What if Agrond and Trenson don't make it?" he asked.

Jayfor's reply was emotionless. "Then we will all die."

"Jayfor!" Randolph's voice rang over the battle sounds. "Look! In the streets of the city!"

From being mounted, Jayfor had a sweeping view of the battle. He turned his eyes over the hundreds of helmets of the mercenaries and felt a surge of hope at what he saw.

Countless people, bearing makeshift weapons and indomitable resolve, clashed with Loronis' army from behind. The citizens were rebelling.

For too long had Xavson oppressed the people under his foot, and now the effects of his tyranny were starting to show. Tailors, blacksmiths, cobblers, scribes, merchants, carpenters... from all walks of life, people banded together for a common cause. The hornet's nest had been aroused.

Now they came, weapons in hand, and assailed the mercenaries from behind with fury. The defenders were surprised at the sudden ambush, and now had to face two forces at once. They mercilessly cut down every citizen that was in their way, but that did nothing to stop the people's resolve.

Thank you, Va'ar, Jayfor thought. *There is still hope.*

***

Trenson ran up the flight of stairs as fast as his legs would carry him, which wasn't fast enough.

"Come on!" Agrond shouted as he sprinted upward. "Not much farther!"

Thank goodness, Trenson thought. The palace seemed to go on forever.

After hoisting the bewildered overseer out of the hole and leaving the garden, Agrond led Trenson and the force of men through the palace. Although it had been some time since he had been at the palace, Agrond knew the interior like the back of his hand, and he led the group with through the winding halls and stairs with ease.

Luckily, they had not encountered one guard so far. Trenson was surprised. For the largest capital in Ralladin, he expected hundreds of guards to be patrolling every hallway, but that wasn't the case, and he remarked on the fact to Agrond.

"This is the whole reason we let Jayfor distract them!" Agrond replied with a grin. "Most of the guards in this palace are also part of Loronis' defense army — because they're so low on troops. So, most of the guards are out fighting Jayfor. And besides, the few guards that remain are guarding the front gates and openings of the palace, never considering that someone may have gotten in under their watch."

Trenson was glad. The day had already been tiring enough; he didn't need to fight off more guards to top it off.

Up the winding stairway they ran, their muddy boots leaving a trail of stains on the carpet. Trenson was surprised that they hadn't been heard yet. Fifty men in full armor charging around a spacious palace was not a very quiet sound, but thankfully, no one seemed to notice. Agrond explained earlier that the gardens were relatively close to the throne room, which would allow them to reach their destination faster and with less fear of being caught.

At last, they mounted the last stair.

"There it is!" Agrond panted. "Behind those doors is the throne room, and hopefully, Xavson!"

The huge oaken doors, embedded with intricate designs, stood only fifty yards away. They were so close. Everyone cheered and gave one last push. They were almost there...

When a large company of soldiers, larger than they were, turned around the corner in front of them and blocked them.

***

"Jayfor, look out!"

The warning, called out by Norman, came all too late. Jayfor turned backwards in the saddle just in time to see a large warrior, wielding a heavy battle-axe, swing his weapon down towards Jayfor's horse, the blow aimed right behind where Jayfor was sitting. There was nothing he could do to stop it. The second he spurred his horse forward to avoid it, the blow landed a few inches behind Jayfor.

The horse screamed in pain and reared high into the air. Jayfor felt his feet slide out of the stirrups and desperately tried to retain his grip with the reins, but it was no use. He fell backwards off the horse and landed with a crash on the ground, still holding his spear, his landing cushioned somewhat by his armor. The horse convulsed, still in the air, fell sideways and on the ground, dead, joining the hundreds of other deaths that had happened that day.

Jayfor hardly had time to process what had happened before the same warrior who had down his horse stood over him. With a savage cry, the muscled warrior hurled his axe down in a deathblow on Jayfor.

The prince rolled to the side just as the axe came down and slammed into the wood of the drawbridge where Jayfor would have been. Jayfor regained his feet, threw aside his spear, and pulled his sword with a *shing* out of its sheath, holding it ready.

The warrior was trying frantically to remove his axe from the wooden ground of the drawbridge. His blow had been so hard that the axe embedded itself into the wood and refused to move. Jayfor took advantage of the opportunity, ran forward, and thrust his sword into the warrior. The warrior cried in pain, then was silent when Jayfor pulled his sword out and kicked his opponent to the ground.

Jayfor's breath was hot and heavy inside his helmet, his arms and soldiers aching from constant fighting. All around him, the battle raged on, soldiers falling on both sides. He turned his eyes to the faraway tower of the palace. *Please, Trenson. Hurry!*

***

"What are you doing here?" The leader of the guards said.

Agrond, Trenson and the infiltrators came to a halt. Dread gripped them.

The captain of the guards squinted. "Wait a minute, that's Agrond! He's with Jayfor!" Realization came over him and his comrades. He drew his sword. "They're after the king! Kill them!"

The guards drew their weapons and started stalking towards the rebels, their intent clear. Trenson drew his sword, Agrond brandished his axe, and the knights behind them readied their weapons.

"This is bad," Agrond said. There was no grin or good humor in his voice. "We can't get to Xavson until we clear a way past those guards!"

Trenson didn't reply. He held his sword before him, ready, prepared to fight.

The guards ran towards them and engaged them with brutal force. The silence of the palace was shattered as the clanging of steel echoed throughout the great halls. Trenson quickly found an opponent, and a few slashes were exchanged before Trenson downed his foe. Then he moved on to the next one.

The guards held their ground firmly, determined not to let the rebels get to the doors of the sanctum. They didn't advance forward often or give up ground. They knew that others would hear the sounds of battle and come to their aid. All they had to do was wait.

And the wait paid off. The fight had not happened for long before another group of guards emerged from the stairs behind Trenson, took inventory and figured out what was going on, and quickly joined the fray. Now the infiltrators were trapped on both sides, outnumbered, with nowhere to go.

Agrond's axe was a whirlwind, sending any guard that came close flying, taking down multiple enemies with one swing and yelling battle cries as he fought. Trenson's sword was fast, faster than his opponents. He engaged, parried, thrust, then the fight was over, and he found another opponent to engage, parry, thrust, then move on.

But there were too many of them. More guards came from the hallways and stairways, the sound of boots making the ground shake. Before long, they would be overwhelmed. They *were* already overwhelmed.

This is getting nowhere, Trenson thought. With unmatched vigor, his sword darted left and right, dodging blows at him, then countering them. The number of knights in their group was diminishing. The circle was becoming tighter. It wouldn't be long…

Trenson cast his eyes to the large oak doors of the sanctum, the doors they were fighting to reach. There were too many of them to reach the doors. Agrond and the entire group would have to defeat all the guards before they could focus on Xavson. But one person might be able to dodge through the guards and reach the doors undetected.

But should he abandon his comrades and risk running through enemy lines, and probably get killed in the end by the king of Faldon, who was — very likely — a much better swordsman than him?

Trenson looked at his fellow knights. If something wasn't done soon, then they would all die, anyway. More guards were sure to come, as if their chances weren't already slim. This could be the only way to save them. To save everyone.

Trenson hardly made up his mind what to do before a guard swung his sword in an overhead slash down on Trenson. In the nick of time, Trenson held his sword up and halted the arcing blade dead in the air. Then he kicked with his foot at his opponent's midsection. The guard stumbled back, then tripped on another guard's foot and fell backwards.

Without wasting another second, Trenson broke into a dash for the oaken doors of the sanctum, ducking and weaving, dodging friends and foes, avoiding spears and swords and axes, his eyes locked on the doors of the sanctum. So occupied were his comrades in keeping the guards at bay that they didn't notice Trenson sprint through the guards, and the guards hardly noticed him weave through their ranks as they fought.

Finally, Trenson emerged through the ranks of guards. He didn't stop there, though. He kept running until he stood before the massive doors of the throne room, then he stopped. *I guess they just push open.*

His hunch proved to be right. Although heavy, Trenson pushed on the doors until they slowly opened without a sound. The moment the doors were open enough, Trenson dashed through the gap and let the door close behind him...

And stood before the king of the insurrection.

XXXXII

Xavson saw the sanctum doors open and close out of the corner of his eye, but paid no attention. He assumed it was another bothersome servant coming to ruin his peace and quiet. His head was down as he read the scroll in his lap. "What do you want?" he demanded without moving. "Whatever it is, it can wait. Leave, now." His tone was threatened.

He had no interest in another interruption. The scroll that he was reading was a reply from the armies at Faldon's eastern border. It wasn't a favorable reply. He had instructed the border to cease fighting with Elara in preparation for their alliance.

Instead, the generals of the border said that they would not stop fighting the dark forces, that they would, in their words, "not surrender to the evil that we have so long fought to keep at bay, even though it costs us our lives, to protect the innocent people at home."

Xavson was infuriated. He was king! He and only he told the people what to do! This was intolerable. His own army was defying his orders. He thought about ways to punish the army. Perhaps he could go after their families still at home...

Xavson suddenly realized that he didn't hear the sanctum doors open and close. Impatiently, he turned his eyes towards the doors.

He was surprised to see a lone knight, dressed in full armor except for a helmet, standing silently in front of the doors. His brown eyes stared back at Xavson with a defiant look that immediately miffed the king. What caught the king's eye the most was the sword that the knight gripped firmly in one hand.

At first, Xavson thought this must be one of the palace guards. "What are you doing here?" he demanded. "I said leave!"

The soldier made no move to leave. He simply continued to stare at Xavson and said, ominously, "It is you who leaves today, Xavson."

There was a stunned silence. The two guards that stood ready beside Xavson's chair gripped their weapons tighter, ready to fight this young rascal who insulted the king, but secretly, they were also on edge, waiting to see how the king would respond.

Xavson's face turned red with anger. "I know who you are!" he said, pointing accusingly at the soldier. "You're one of those rogue firebrands that defies my authority, that Jayfor's leading! How did you get here?"

"That's none of your concern," the soldier calmy replied.

One of the guards on Xavson's side took a step forward. "Watch your tongue, rebel! The king –"

"Be quiet!" Xavson snapped. "I will deal with this myself!"

The guard cowered and stepped back into his place. Xavson turned his seething gaze to the knight.

Before the king could speak, the soldier spoke, "Your days of being a king are over, Xavson. Today your tyranny ends."

"Ha!" Xavson snorted. He rose from his throne. His long black cape flowed around his tall, broad figure. A large sword hung on his hip.

"You certainly are a bold one," he said smoothly. "To come all this way, fighting through all the guards of my palace, abandon your company, and to make your way here, to face me alone," he chuckled, "I must say, I am impressed." His boots thudded on the ground with every step as he walked towards the knight. He expected the knight to cower, but instead, he held his ground and didn't move.

Xavson continued. "No doubt you attempt to recreate a scene from the old stories." He smiled darkly. "The lone hero, woefully undermined and inexperienced, defeats the evil lord and reclaims the throne, all by himself!"

Xavson intended to say more, but the soldier cut him off. "Your arrogance will be your undoing, Xavson. I know what you did, how you murdered your brother and father, all in a monomaniacal quest for power." The soldier's eyes burned with fury. "Did you really think that you would get away with that?"

Xavson smiled again. This rogue was certainly amusing. "Arrogance, you say? Monomaniacal, you say? Take a look around you, boy. Who has achieved more? Who has reached their goals? Who now is the king of the most powerful kingdoms in Ralladin? Is it someone perfect that adheres to what the weak call virtues? No. It is someone who realizes that virtues are a trap. Nothing can be achieved through them, because they only slow you down, make you weak. A fool invented them, because he feared that others would surpass him, so he made virtues that everyone would stay at his level, that no one would reach their goals too fast and leave the rest behind."

Xavson stopped a few yards away from Trenson and locked eyes with the soldier. "You no doubt have spent your life trying to do 'good.' Now look at yourself, then look at me, and tell me who has accomplished more."

"I won't play your mind games, Xavson!" the soldier said angrily, but there was a hint of doubt in his voice. "I have come to end your oppression." He pointed his sword at Xavson in challenge. "And to end it now."

Xavson chuckled. This soldier had made his day with his child-like hero mindset. It would be enjoyable to end his foolish hopes. "The only thing ending today, boy, is the beating of your heart."

Slowly, allowing the ring of steel to intimidate his foe, Xavson drew his large, menacing sword from its black sheath. He gripped the ridged handle firmly with one hand, then undid the strap of his cape with the other, letting the black cape fall to the ground. The twisted insignia with a mountain at its center lay in the hilt guard's center. The tint of the blade, sharp and lethal, had a dark luster to it. A shadow seemed to wrap itself around the blade.

"Now," said Xavson, pointing the tip at the soldier, "Let's get started. Try to make things interesting, will you?"

The first blow came with tremendous force, a sideway slash aimed straight for Trenson's midsection. There was no cautious footwork, no plan, no hint of hesitation from Trenson's foe. The attack was designed to be the first and the last. Clearly, Xavson didn't expect Trenson to be able to block or counter the blow.

Which was a mistake. Instinct taking over, not even knowing exactly what was happening, Trenson held his sword to the side and perfectly blocked the blow, stopping the sword dead in midair with a shower of sparks. Xavson looked confused. To stop such a blow took not only strength, but skill. He hesitated too long. Trenson pushed the blade to the side and in one fluid motion made an upward slash at Xavson. The king jumped back just in time as the blade passed up in front of his face, sending a breeze of air across his face as it missed its mark.

Xavson was surprised. In a few seconds, this knight had shown himself to be a skilled warrior. Now he realized that this duel might prove to be more enjoyable than he had anticipated. And that pleased him.

Trenson felt adrenaline rush through him as he spread his feet apart and held his sword ready. He felt in control, but at the same time, not in control at all. He could will his sword to do things, and from there on, it just seemed to happen automatically. This was what he had trained for.

Trenson didn't wait for Xavson to attack. With a courageous cry, he rushed at the king and began to attack, his sword effortlessly slashing from left to right. Xavson was temporarily off balance, but soon he regained his footing and met each blow with skill and power. His easygoing attitude was replaced with grim resolve as he realized that there was a chance, however unlikely, that this soldier may beat him.

They exchanged blows with ease. Both men knew that the other was skilled, skilled enough that if they attempted to end the fight quickly, it could end disastrously. If they wanted to win this fight, they would need to know their opponents' strengths and weaknesses, then exploit them when the time was right. The only way to know the other's weakness, though, was to deliver easy blows, which would be just as easily countered, to the opponent.

As a result, neither man was trying very hard to end the other, but to see where the other's weak points were. Trenson would thrust, and note regrettably that Xavson's footwork allowed him to sidestep thrusts and counter with intensity. Xavson would deliver an overhead blow, then note with satisfaction that Trenson stumbled slightly while blocking. It was a game of cat and mouse, each one waiting for the other to decide that he had learned enough about his opponent's skill to strike.

Xavson was the first to strike. Trenson aimed a diagonal crosscut at Xavson, which the king intercepted and pushed to the side. Then Xavson stepped forward and thrust his blade at Trenson's chest, rotating his shoulders for maximum force. Trenson turned to the side just in time for the tip of the blade to rush past his chest.

Trenson, seeing that Xavson was slightly off balance from the thrust, sidestepped to give himself more room. Then he brought his sword over his head and swung down in a descending arc, aimed right at Xavson.

Xavson foresaw the move just in time. Leaping backward, he tried to avoid the blade, but it was too fast. It skimmed his face, from above his left eyebrow down almost to his lip. A bright red cut appeared.

The king stumbled backwards, shocked. He raised his hand to the slash mark on his face, then looked at his hand, red blood smeared on it. His burning eyes locked on Trenson. "You will die for that!" he screamed.

Trenson held his sword firmly before him, then he gasped. It was Xavson's sword. The blade suddenly turned a darker color, a visible shadow wrapping itself around the blade in wisps. Xavson's rage seemed to fuel the blade. It seemed to pulse with darkness and radiate power. Trenson felt like he recognized the sight from somewhere.

Then it hit him: Gornar. At the Idonia Mountains. The dark warrior had pitch black swords, ones that seemed to spread fear, like they reached into his heart and made it cold. Xavson's sword wasn't quite as black, and Trenson didn't feel the same chilling dread that he felt while on the mountains, but it was still there. Trenson felt his resolve waver.

It was true, then. Xavson had allied with the Dark Order and had received some sort of power in the process. The thought of it chilled Trenson.

With newfound wrath, Xavson rushed at Trenson and let fly a torrent of wild blows. Trenson's control vanished as he tried to meet every blow with his own. The dark blade darted left to right, each blow reverberating through Trenson's arm and tearing away at his resolve. The king held nothing back.

Trenson found himself retreating. The power and boldness he had possessed earlier was gone. His courage faltered as he struggled to deflect every blow. It took everything he had to keep his grip on his sword. With each blow, Xavson coupled it with a ferocious war cry. Blood ran down his face from the gash.

Trenson retreated backwards a few steps. Xavson saw that he was gaining the upper hand. With even more force, he hacked away at Trenson's sword. Trenson felt a shock wave of pain from every slam of the blades.

Xavson drew his sword around to deliver a powerful sideways cut. In anticipation, Trenson held his weapon up to deflect the cut.

But it was futile. Xavson's sword, shrouded in darkness, whirled around and, with uncanny ease, sliced clean through Trenson's sword like hot butter.

The top half of Trenson's blade fell to the ground with a clang. Before Trenson could react, Xavson brought a crushing fist into Trenson's abdomen. Trenson flew backwards and landed helplessly on the ground. His useless sword flew out of his grip.

Gasping for air, Trenson attempted to rise, but Xavson's dark sword soon pointed inches from Trenson's neck. The king smiled with sadistic glee. Blood mixed with sweat poured down the king's face. "Now you die, 'hero,'" he spat.

Pain radiated from Trenson's entire body. He was helpless. There was nothing he could do. He had failed. His courage was replaced with fear.

Xavson lifted his sword in the air to deliver the final deathblow. "I am the only king of Faldon!"

The deadly blade began its descent down, the black blade rushing towards Trenson's heart. Hope vanished in Trenson. *So this is truly the end.* He closed his eyes and waited for the final stroke to come.

That's when something happened.

XXXXIII

A BLINDING WHITE LIGHT suddenly filled the room, so bright that nothing else could be seen. Even Trenson, whose eyes were closed, could see the light and was momentarily dazed.

What is happening? The light gradually dimmed, enough for Trenson to open his eyes. He was shocked at what he saw.

Xavson, instead of going for the piercing downward stab, had decided to decided to use a downward arc to finish Trenson. There was nothing better about the arc; in fact, a stab would be quicker and easier. Xavson wasn't one for quick and easy, though, and for whatever reason chose the dramatic vertical cut as a dramatic finish to his foe.

Now, Xavson's dark blade was halted halfway in the air, inches from Trenson's face. The razor edge taunted Trenson, but he was still alive. It was what was stopping the dark sword that left Trenson speechless.

A white sword, glowing with white light, was the only stopping the lethal blade from descending. The blade glowed radiantly, sharply contrasting Xavson's blade. The light of the white blade almost blinded Trenson by itself.

Turning his head, Trenson's eyes grew wide as he beheld a white knight, shining even brighter than the sword, standing beside him.

The knight was dressed in full armor, save for a helmet, but instead of it being gray, it was pure white. The warrior stood tall and majestic, his arm outstretched with his sword as he stopped the dark blade. But it was the face. The shining knight's face looked exactly like...

Agrond?

But it was impossible. Agrond was still fighting with the knights on the other side of the door. How was he here? And why was he... like this?

Xavson withdrew his sword and backed away. His face showed the deep level of surprise and fear he felt. "What?!" he gasped. His sword was limp in his hands. The weapon seemed to lose its dark tint slightly.

Agrond, eyes locked with the king, brandished his shining sword and held it before him, no longer bearing his axe. His stance and posture testified to true mastery and otherworldly power. The light that radiated from him filled the room.

Trenson, still lying prone on the ground, stared in wonder at the former battle commander. "Agrond?!"

Agrond looked down at Trenson with a smile that he had seen countless times over the last few months. "Trenson," Agrond said, with the same voice that Trenson had always known. "You have done well. You have nothing to fear. Va'ar is with you."

Va'ar? Trenson thought. It struck him hard, like a hammer. He had been wrong. Va'ar *was* real.

Agrond turned his piercing gaze upon Xavson. "You, however, have much to fear."

Xavson's mouth hung open slightly. He was at a loss for words. Then, recovering himself, he held his sword ready. Although he scowled, a deep fear lay in his eyes. "I... I know who you are! They told me about your kind. You are a Senver!"

Agrond chuckled and spun his sword around in his hand. "I am."

The king hopelessly tried to assume a bold face. "You will not win!" he said wildly. "You will die! All of your kind will die! My lord is the only true master of the world!" With a fiendish cry, Xavson charged at Agrond, sword poised to strike.

The blow never landed. Before Xavson was even close to the shining knight, Agrond swung his sword. Power exploded from the blade, white light radiating everywhere. The power of the blast caused Xavson to fly backwards. The king screamed as he flew through the air, then was silent as he hit the ground hard and rolled, finally coming to a stop a few feet away from his throne. The guards standing beside the throne were hiding behind the chair in fear of this great warrior and made no move to help their king.

Trenson slowly rose to his feet. He gaped in wonder at Agrond, the brilliant warrior, his companion. Agrond stared at the crumpled king, determination in his eyes, the shining sword in his hands.

Xavson managed to rise, staggering and wobbling. He hunched over, clutching his side in pain. He looked at Agrond, a loathing hatred hardened in his face.

Agrond spoke. "Your days are numbered, Xavson. Did you really think you could defy the High Lord and get away with it? Your master shudders at the name of Va'ar, as you should too, for his anger burns against both of you."

He pointed his white sword at the large doors leading out of the sanctum. "But your day of judgement is not today. Leave now, and never return."

Xavson gazed at Agrond incredulously. He looked at the doors. Then at Agrond. Then, holding his sword in one hand and his side with the other, the ruined king of Faldon limped to the doors. The two guards followed him, but made no effort to help the king walk, as they were too busy staring in wonder at the shining warrior that had reduced their king to nothing. Agrond watched him, as did Trenson. Xavson looked at Trenson one last time, eyes like vipers, a vow of revenge in his countenance.

He reached the large doors of the throne room and looked over his shoulder one last time at Agrond. The Senver stared back at him. Xavson didn't linger for long. He pushed open the doors with his side, grunting with the pain it caused him. He still held his sword in one hand, but the black hue that once surrounded the blade had vanished.

After the door had opened enough, Xavson quickly slipped through the closing gap and was gone. His guards followed him, and the door closed. And Trenson and Agrond were left alone.

***

"The king has fled!"

The cry was repeated by the generals and soldiers along the front lines of Xavson's army. The generals and soldiers in Xavson's army listened with disbelief. The king fled? But they were winning! What reason did he have to flee?

Jayfor, drenched in sweat and blood, heard the news with hope. It was hope that immediately dispelled all of his weariness, all his doubts, all his uncertainties, and replaced it with hope, strength, and courage.

"He has ordered the remaining forces to pull out from the city by the northern exit!" The generals of Xavson's army cried, although it was clear that the last thing they wanted to do was to flee. "The city is to be abandoned! Cease fighting! Cease fighting!"

Slowly, the fighting between the armies fizzled out. The people who had engaged the mercenaries from behind also stopped fighting, not knowing exactly what was going on. The mercenaries, not without a great deal of complaining, organized into one group on the other side of the drawbridge. Jayfor's group did the same, but with an awed silence, mumbling running across the group whether this was actually true.

"Move out!" The mercenary general yelled. "We'll take the way through the city. Move out!"

And with that, the hundreds of mercenaries began to turn around and march away from Jayfor's group.

Randolph and Norman, both still mounted, both weary and tired from fighting, stood beside Jayfor. Jayfor sheathed his sword and removed his helmet. A cool breeze instantly hit his face. He, along with every other soldier in his group, watched silently as the army marched away slowly.

Did he dare hope it to be true? Was it really over? He glanced at Randolph and Norman, and the two barons looked silently back at him.

Then Jayfor shouted, "Victory!"

A roar of joy exploded from the company. Soldiers raised their weapons and shouted as loud as they could. The noise was deafening.

But nobody shouted louder than Jayfor, who raised his stained sword high in the air, joy, relief, and happiness flooding over him all at once. For so long, he had toiled for this moment. For so long, he had striven to take back Faldon.

And now it had happened. After so much toil and bloodshed, Faldon was free.

And he couldn't be happier.

***

"Agrond... is that really you?" Trenson's voice was shaky.

Agrond sheathed his sword, the white blade sliding easily into the sheath on his back. He stared at the door for a few moments before turning his warm eyes towards Trenson. "Yes," he said, "Same Agrond you always knew."

Trenson fumbled for words. He had a hundred questions to ask, but didn't know where to start. "What... How... Why...?" He cleared his throat, then finally found his voice. "I thought you were fighting with the other knights behind the door?"

Agrond chuckled. "I was. But I knew where you had gone and knew what was happening in here. I disappeared from the fight just in time to save your life." He smiled. "You're welcome."

Trenson opened his mouth, then shut it, then looked Agrond up and down, taking in his glowing figure, donned in white armor and holding a shining sword. He looked different, but at the same time similar, to the Agrond Trenson always knew.

Agrond sensed Trenson's confusion and spoke for him. "A long time ago, when I was at home, I was assigned a special mission by Va'ar."

He had a faraway look in his eyes as he spoke. He still glowed vibrantly, almost as if he was made of light itself. "My task was to take on the guise of a mortal and apply for the role of supreme general of Faldon's army. I was then to aid the third son of King Hailar in escaping the capital when his brother usurped the throne. It was also I who pushed the boulder down at the Idonia mountains and saved you from certain death." He crossed his arms. "You can guess the rest."

Trenson still didn't know what to make of it all. His entire world was shaken. "So... you were a Senver all along? One of the knights of Va'ar?"

Agrond nodded. "That's right."

Trenson looked down at the floor. "I doubted Va'ar's existence. I didn't believe." He looked into Agrond's eyes. "I'm sorry."

Agrond returned the look with a compassionate smile. "What you used to believe or think does not matter anymore. You believe now, and that's all that matters."

Trenson sighed gratefully. "Thank you."

Agrond nodded. "I have fulfilled my role now. You and Jayfor are safe, and the kingdom of Faldon is secure, at least for now. I must return to my King, and await my new orders."

"Wait. You have to leave, now?" With this newfound knowledge, Trenson couldn't believe that Agrond was just going to leave.

Agrond nodded. "Unfortunately, yes. I had direct orders that only you were to see me. I can see you're confused, don't ask me why, that's just what Va'ar said. So I best leave as soon as possible."

Trenson spoke quickly, trying to use his time with Agrond as wisely as possible. "What about Jayfor? And the army?"

"Oh, they'll be fine. Once they hear news of what's happened with Xavson, they'll pull out and leave the city. You can consider Loronis reconquered, Trenson, and no small thanks to you. See? You didn't fail in the end, after all."

The light around Agrond grew brighter. Trenson backed away a few steps and shielded his eyes.

"There is, however, one thing you should know." Agrond's voice came again. "When I was told of my mission, I was told that protect not only Jayfor, but you as well. At first, I didn't understand. From what I had been told, you were a secretive man with a dark past that found out about the insurrection and, on top of that, weren't going to get here in time to stop it."

Trenson felt a slight stab of regret at the memory.

"And yet, as time went on, I knew there was more to you. Externally, there was nothing special about you. But I could tell that something was different. It wasn't until later that I figured out just how much you would do for Ralladin."

Trenson, his eyes adjusted to the light, let his hand drop as he watched Agrond with awe-filled expectation.

"I'm not allowed to tell you about what you will do — although I sorely wish I could, if only you knew — but I will tell you this: your role is more important than you realize. Through you, many things will be accomplished, things that will lead to the reclamation of the world. Jayfor bears a role in this as well. You both have been chosen to accomplish Va'ar's will."

The light around Agrond grew even brighter. Trenson couldn't make out Agrond in the light anymore.

"I'm leaving now. Tell Jayfor that I'm personally proud of him. He's got a good head on his shoulders. And don't worry, Trenson. Nothing shall be impossible for you."

Trenson quickly asked, "Will I ever see you again?"

But it was too late. As quickly as it had appeared, the light disappeared. Agrond, revealed as a Senver of Va'ar, was gone. Trenson was alone.

No, he reminded himself; he wasn't alone. Va'ar was always with him, always watching over him. As long as he trusted in Him, he was never alone.

EPILOGUE

"I DON'T REMEMBER MUCH about my home, where I was born," Trenson began, a faraway look in his eyes.

Jayfor looked out over the city from the balcony of the palace, but listened intently as Trenson started the story of his past. It had been a week since the capital had been reconquered, and this was one of the few moments of quiet they had in the hustle and bustle of restoring order to the city.

"Go on," Jayfor said. He was looking forward to hearing the story that Trenson had so long kept from him.

"I do remember a few things about my home, though, like the small cabin that we lived in. It was cramped — but in a good way. We never had much, so we didn't need a big house. I also remember the farm. It was huge, with long rows of barely and crops that I could run through for hours and never reach the end of. My brother and I used to play hide-and-seek in those fields.

"But it wasn't like that for long. When I was... eight? Nine? I don't know, but sometime around there, a band of criminals came to the house. In Marindale, robberies and theft were common, I found out later. A group of about ten of them came to the house. I was off playing in the woods, but I watched from the bushes as it all happened."

Trenson's voice was heavy with emotion, and he paused. Jayfor didn't press him. He could guess where this story was going.

"After they stole everything of value from the house, they burned it, all of it, to the ground, making my father, mother and brother watch as they destroyed everything. They held them and beat them. I... remember my father. He fought back, and killed one of them, but then they stabbed him through with a spear.

"I remember they took my brother and mother away, after they had taken everything they wanted. They bound them with ropes and led them away as they disappeared into the woods. My mother and brother cried, but there was nothing they could do.

"I ran away, into town, and went to the peacekeepers, trying to get them to help, but they wouldn't. They ignored me and chased me away. I found no help. I knew that I couldn't return to my home; there was nothing there, and I couldn't bear to see the still figure of my father. So, for a few years, I was a beggar, gnawing on apple cores that people threw out their door and surviving on a few coins a month.

"Then, one day, a man came to me and asked me if I wanted a better life, to learn how to defend myself and eat three times a day. I said yes, and he led me to an abandoned building where a band of thieves dwelled. And that started me down a life of crime and thievery, where I was taught that nothing is true and everything is permitted. I stole and took what I wanted. I did what I wanted. I learned how to use a quarterstaff and throwing knives. And I was praised for this all."

Trenson took a deep breath. He had spent years burying his past, locking it away out of memory and never thinking about it. Now he felt regret and pain as he reached into the chasm he had thrown the memory into and relived the moments.

"Dimitri was the name of the man who invited me to join them, and he was our leader. Farrell was second in command." He cast a glance at Jayfor. "The man who held you prisoner when you fell into that trap, the one who you killed with the knife, that was him."

Realization dawned on Jayfor's face. So *that's* why Farrell and Trenson knew each other. The pieces were coming together.

Trenson continued. "I wasn't called 'Trenson' in the thieves' guild. Dimitri explained that, to keep as much secret as possible, everyone had a different name that they used. Mine was Judas. I knew my original name, the name I was given at birth, but I kept it a secret except from the other thieves.

"I served them for many years. Apparently, the Dark Order was hiring criminals to send orders and information to Loronis about the insurrection, so we all knew about the uprising months before it happened. I was never sent on these missions, but others in our group were. I was glad not to be sent on these missions; I would rather stay in Marindale than leave on a long journey.

"Then, one night, we decided to raid a merchant caravan and steal the goods. I was sent with Dimitri to the back of the caravan to steal supplies while the rest of our group distracted the guards in the front. When night came, me and Dimitri snuck around the back and started to loot the supplies. But there were people in the wagon: a family.

"I think they were the merchants that owned the caravan. There were four of them: two young boys, a father, and a mother. Their faces resembled those of my own family. I was struck with realization, realization that I was doing the same thing that the ruffians that had killed my family were doing, that I was no better than those criminals. The father stood up against Dimitri and called for the guards to come. Then Dimitri... he killed him, Dimitri did.

"It was too much. Me and Dimitri had killed countless people without a second thought, but now as I saw my family's massacre relived before my eyes, I couldn't take it. I ran away, into the woods, ignoring the cries and shouts behind me. I ran until the sounds of battle faded away, and my lungs were about to explode. Then I feel to the ground, exhausted. I didn't know what to do. I know knew that what I was doing was wrong, and that I needed to redeem myself of my past.

"I remembered the revolt that my comrades had talked about, and how it was about a month from happening. I decided that I could do something to help. I had my satchel and a few coins, my quarterstaff, no throwing knives, but I decided that I had enough. That night, I started off on my journey." He stopped looking into the distance, his eyes focusing as he was brought back into the present, and looked at Jayfor. "You can guess what happened after that."

Jayfor nodded. "I can," he said. Then he frowned. "I had no idea that it was so... sad. I'm sorry that I pressed you to tell."

Trenson shook his head. "No, you're fine. In fact, it feels better to finally tell someone this, after harboring it for so long. It feels like a weight has been lifted."

There was a pause. Neither Trenson nor Jayfor knew what to say next, so they kept silent, looking over the city wistfully, thinking about how far they had come, and wondering what lay in store for them in the future.

Trenson broke the silence. "Is my horse in the stables?"

Jayfor nodded. "Yes, last I checked it was. Going somewhere?"

"Yes. I'll be gone for a few weeks."

"A few weeks?! Where in the world are you going?"

Trenson turned towards the doors that led into the palace. "I have some things to do. By the way, do you mind if I borrow some money from the treasury?"

Now Jayfor was more confused than ever. "I... guess not?"

Trenson nodded, as if everything was normal. "Thank you." Then he started to walk into the palace.

"Wait!" Jayfor called. "What are you doing that makes you leave for weeks?"

Trenson looked back over his shoulder. "Let's just say that I have an inn that I need to pay for and a horse that needs to be returned."

"What?" Jayfor asked, bewildered.

Trenson simply kept walking. "Never mind!" he called.

Did you like this book?

That's great, thank you! If you really want to help me, please leave a review for my book on Amazon or Goodreads. Those reviews really make a difference.

I also love to hear from readers and hear what they thought of my book! Reach out to me through my email, contact@gunnerl ong.com, and let me know what you thought!

If you want to stay updated on my books and learn more about my life as an author, follow me on Facebook or Instagram @Author Gunner Long.

OR: Subscribe to the email list for updates delivered straight to your inbox!

Also by Gunner Long

1. Insurrection

2. Endeavor

3. Destiny (*Coming Soon*)

About the author

Gunner Long always read the works of C.S. Lewis and J.R.R. Tolkien, and was moved by the stories and messages they conveyed. Dedicated to the Lord, he was always searching for age-appropriate books that offered the same thrilling tales and adventures, but without the immorality that seemed to plague modern action books. So he decided to change that. He created the world of Ralladin and started his first book, *Insurrection,* when he was just thirteen, driven to create something that not only kids, but people of all ages could enjoy. He hopes that people read his books and leave with not only a story, but a message. He lives with his family near Brunswick, Georgia.